GOD DON'T MAKE
NO MISTAKES

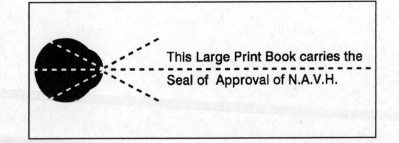

GOD DON'T MAKE NO MISTAKES

MARY MONROE

THORNDIKE PRESS
A part of Gale, Cengage Learning

Detroit • New York • San Francisco • New Haven, Conn • Waterville, Maine • London

GALE
CENGAGE Learning®

LIBRARY OF CONGRESS CATALOGING-IN-PUBLICATION DATA

Monroe, Mary.
  God don't make no mistakes / by Mary Monroe. — Large print ed.
    p. cm. — (Thorndike Press large print African-American)
  ISBN 978-1-4104-4806-4 (hardcover) — ISBN 1-4104-4806-1 (hardcover)
  1. African American women—Fiction. 2. Female friendship—Fiction.
3. African American families—Fiction. 4. Ohio—Fiction. 5. Large type
books. I. Title.
PS3563.O528G614 2012
813'.54—dc23   2012012125

Published in 2012 by arrangement with Dafina Books, an imprint of
Kensington Publishing Corp.

This book is dedicated to my fans.

ACKNOWLEDGMENTS

To my readers, old and new, I sincerely appreciate your support.

I especially thank all of my readers in the various branches of the military, not just for reading my books, but for protecting our country and trying to make the world a better place for everyone.

To the book clubs, libraries, and bookstores throughout the world, thank you for promoting my books and for blessing me with so many new fans through the first social network: word of mouth.

The folks at Kensington Publishing have made it possible for me to live the dream life of a best-selling author. To my editor, Selena James; my publicists, Adeola Saul and Karen Auerbach; the folks in the sales department; Steven Zacharius, Laurie Parkin, and everyone else involved, I thank you all from the bottom of my heart.

With sympathy and eternal respect, a

belated thanks to the late great Walter Zacharius. He was one of a kind and I will miss him dearly.

To my agent, Andrew Stuart, I can't thank you enough for representing me with so much vigor.

Thanks to Lauretta Pierce for maintaining my Web site and for being such a good friend.

To all of my new fans reading my work for the first time with this book, *brace yourselves!*

Please continue to send your comments and suggestions by e-mailing me at Authorauthor5409@aol.com or by visiting my Web site, www.MaryMonroe.org. You can also communicate with me on Facebook and Twitter.

All the best,
Mary Monroe
June 2012

PROLOGUE

March 1998
Excerpt from *The Richland, Ohio Review* newspaper:

LOCAL WOMAN ARRESTED IN WORLDWIDE CHILD PORNO RING

Federal investigators dismantled an international network of pedophiles and pornographers who exchanged sexually explicit videos and photographs of children on a regular basis. At the center of the investigation is a Richland child-care provider and Sunday-school teacher; a single mother of three daughters all under the age of thirteen.

Harrietta Jameson, 46, was arrested in her home last night following a brief investigation. Evidence indicates that Jameson was the mastermind of a network that specialized in graphic images of the sexual abuse of children under the age of ten, including infants.

More than fifty people have been charged so far, including thirty arrested in the United States, Canada, Germany, Sweden, Nigeria, Italy, and France. The organization used a server in Cleveland, Ohio, that Jameson maintained to upload material, solicit new members, and collect "membership" dues. Authorities estimate that about five hundred people were members of the organization and more than one hundred were "pending." Some of the victims have been identified as the investigation continues . . .

"I don't believe my eyes!" Annette hollered. She was so horrified she held the newspaper away from her face like it was contaminated. She could not believe that what she had just read about one of her friends — one that she had trusted to look after her child — was true. But it was . . .

CHAPTER 1

Eight months earlier

My mother had told me years ago that if I ever got married, I'd better keep a parachute nearby, because I was probably going to have to jump out of the relationship sooner or later. A parachute wouldn't have done me much good. A trampoline was what I needed. I did a lot of bouncing back and forth with Pee Wee, my estranged husband. Despite our bitter breakup several months ago, he still spent a lot of time in bed with me.

"I guess I still got it, huh?" Pee Wee asked with an anxious look on his dark, still-handsome face. Except for his receding hairline and that spare tire around his waist, he was still attractive for a man of forty-eight.

"Still got what?" I asked, with my eyes on the five crisp $100 bills that he had dropped onto the nightstand next to my bed, just before he dropped his pants. Even though I had a high-paying job and we didn't have a financial arrangement, he gave me a couple thousand dollars a month for me to spend on myself and our daughter, Charlotte.

Pee Wee's eyes got wide. "Don't mess with me, woman. You know what I'm talkin' about. Judging from the way you was whoopin' and hollerin' in that damn bed a few minutes ago, I *know* I'm still handlin' my manly job well for a man my age," he teased.

I rolled my eyes and gave him an exasperated look. "So it's a job to you now," I pouted. The last thing I wanted to hear was the implication that sex with me was a "job," because that's exactly what it had been to me at one time. I had made my money working as a prostitute during my teens. When my husband pulled out the $500 a few minutes ago, it brought back some painful memories. "You make me feel like a prostitute. . . ."

Pee Wee shook his head, rolled his eyes, and glanced at his watch. "Look, I got to get to my shop and open up. I got a lot of hair to cut today. So if you are tryin' to tell me somethin', hurry up and tell me."

"I did tell you something."

"So what if I do make you feel like a

prostitute? Whores need love too."

I threw up my hands. "If I were you, I'd stop while I was ahead," I warned. I rubbed the back of my neck and sucked in some air. We had had conversations similar to this one so many times that I felt like I was rehearsing for a play. "Look, I think we can still work things out and not do . . . *this*," I told him, patting the bed and hoping that he wouldn't agree with my last statement. "Every time you come over here now, we end up in bed. You don't have to sleep with me, and you don't have to pay me to do it. That's why I suggested we still date other people, until we can decide if we want to reconcile or not."

Pee Wee gave me a confused look. "Don't you enjoy these little get-togethers as much as I do?"

"I do, but I don't want you to think that we have to do it."

He gave me another confused look, this time blinking so hard and fast I thought something had got caught in his eye. "Why? Do you not want to make love with me? You don't find me attractive anymore?" he asked.

"Don't be so sensitive," I scolded. "You know I enjoy making love with you. I always have."

"Then why we talkin' all this crap, baby?

You know that the money I give to you is for my daughter. I ain't payin' you to make love with me. I ain't never paid for no pussy before in my life, and I never will. Not even with you."

I didn't see any reason to remind Pee Wee about the times he'd told me that when he was in the army, he and every other member of his platoon had paid Vietnamese prostitutes for sex.

"You don't need to make our situation no messier than it already is," he reminded.

"I know, I know. It's just that every time you come over here, we . . . uh . . . we end up in bed and you hand me some money. Just like I was still a . . ." Pee Wee knew that I had once worked as a prostitute. Even though that dark episode had occurred more than thirty years ago, I knew that he probably still thought about it as much as I did.

"Let's not bring up the past. We already have enough to deal with in the present. My mechanic is comin' by the house next week to take a look under the hood of your car to see why you keep hearin' that buzzin' noise. Do you need any yard work or anything else done around the house, baby?"

"No, I don't need anything like that," I told him.

"Well," he yawned as he rubbed his chest and licked his lips. "I'm feelin' real good. Even better than the last time I was here. Thank you very much!" he exclaimed with a wink. "Is there anything else we need to discuss before I leave?"

"Since you asked, there is just this one other thing." I locked eyes with Pee Wee. Then the words rolled out of my mouth like marbles. "Will you tell your whore to stop calling my house?"

His jaw dropped so fast I was surprised it didn't lock in place. "What? I — I ain't got no whore! You know you are the only woman that I'm involved with these days!" he yelled.

I gasped. "Is that right?" I asked, patting the side of my head. I usually wore my medium-length hair in braids, but lately I'd been getting by with a mild perm and a French twist. It had come undone during my ten-minute romp with Pee Wee. I could feel clumps of my hair standing up on my head, pointing in all directions. I must have looked like Don King.

"But . . . but . . . I . . . I," Pee Wee stuttered.

"Well, the woman I'm talking about is a straight-up whore! *Your* whore!"

I could see that my outburst had surprised Pee Wee. It had been a while since I had mentioned the woman whom he left me for last March. He folded his arms and a frightened look appeared on his face. He knew that he had to be careful about what he said to me, unless he wanted to deal with my wrath. The day that he had brought his mistress to my house to tell me that he was leaving me and moving in with her, I'd knocked out one of his teeth. And I had given his mistress a thorough, well-deserved ass whupping with my rolling pin.

"Are you talkin' about Lizzie Stovall?" he asked dumbly, shifting his weight from one foot to the other.

"Who else would I be talking about?" I hollered, giving him an incredulous look. "Lizzie is the only one that I am aware of! Was there another one?"

"No! No, there was no other woman other than Lizzie. You know better. You know I don't lie to you."

My eyes got as big as saucers and I gasped. "You're lying *now*."

"Aw, Annette, you know what I mean."

"Do I?" I barked, giving him a critical look. "Whether I do or not, it doesn't matter. The thing is, that woman called here last week — several times — and she called again yesterday."

"She did? Uh, what did she want?"

"She was trying to catch up with you, fool! She claims she's been trying to reach you for days."

"Oh. Well, it's over between me and her, and has been since she left me and moved in with Peabo Boykin. If she calls here again, just hang up on her. That ought to stop her."

"Don't you think I've already tried that?" I snapped. "But until you talk to her, she's going to keep calling here."

"I . . . I . . . I'll look into it," Pee Wee stammered, waving his hands in the air. I could see that he was nervous and anxious to get away from me now. His hands were shaking so hard that when he squatted down to put his shoes back on, he put them on the wrong feet.

CHAPTER 2

Pee Wee gave me a dry look and shook his head. Then with a jerk, he turned and scurried across the floor like a frightened rat. He tripped on the area rug on the floor at the foot of my bed. He didn't like it when I brought up Lizzie's name.

"You don't have anything else to say to me?" I wanted to know, looking at him from the corner of my eye as he was about to flee.

Pee Wee's hand was on the doorknob, clutching it like it was trying to escape. He didn't even bother to turn around and look at me. He shook his head again. "I'll call you," he yelled over his shoulder, literally running out of my upstairs bedroom. He clip-clopped down the hardwood stairs so fast and hard, you would have thought that the cops were chasing him. This was the first time that he had left without kissing me good-bye.

As soon as I heard Pee Wee shut my front

door, I got up and went to the window with the sheet wrapped around me. I raked my fingers through my hair, holding several strands away from my eyes so I could see him better. I watched him scramble into his red Firebird.

It was only seven-thirty. It had rained a few hours earlier, so it was a chilly day for July. Because of the low, dark gray clouds hovering in the sky, it felt and looked like it was much later.

I released a loud breath and eased back down on the bed. I didn't need to be at work until nine, but I usually went in earlier just so I could be prepared for any unexpected issues. You could expect just about anything to happen at Mizelle's Collection Agency. A couple of weeks ago, I got caught up in a ruckus between two of the women who reported to me as bill collectors. The night before, Rita Lockett had discovered that Beverly Hawkins was dating her fiancé. Rita had come to work early to confront Beverly. It didn't take long for things to escalate into a violent physical altercation between the two angry women. They had hurled staplers, paperweights, and other desktop items at one another. I got scared when Beverly picked up a letter opener, but I quickly wrestled it from her hand. Had I not been present at the time, there was no telling how much damage they might have done. I had no choice but to fire both employees. I had been going in an hour early all this week, but two days ago, the temp agency that we worked with sent me a young Asian man. Not only was he extremely personable, he was so efficient that he got us all caught up before noon on his first day. It was because of Daniel Hong that I didn't think it would be a problem if I took my time going in today.

I was even thinking about taking the day off. I needed to get my nails done, I needed a facial, and I wanted to run a few errands that I had been putting off. I also wanted to treat myself to a nice lunch and a movie. Afterward, I could come back home, put on my robe, and kick back on my couch with a large margarita. I couldn't get that comfortable at home on the weekend or in the evening because that was when most people dropped in on me unannounced. Another inducement for me to take the day off was that I would not have to rush home to cook dinner today like I usually did. I still had some of the barbecue in the freezer left over from the Fourth of July cookout that I had hosted a couple of weeks ago.

I already regretted the harsh way that I

had jumped on Pee Wee about Lizzie calling my house. It wasn't his fault that she was such a bold-ass bitch. As a matter of fact, I was even thinking about calling him up and offering to take him out to dinner as my way of apologizing. In spite of our separation, we still had one of the strongest relationships in town. I knew people who had never been separated who didn't have a relationship as strong and hopeful as ours. I couldn't deny the fact that Pee Wee was the best thing that had ever happened to me, as far as men were concerned. One reason I thought it was in my best interest to get back with him was because despite his cheating, he was still a good man. He was dependable, successful, generous, hardworking, smart, and family oriented. I was all of those same things myself, so I felt that I was just as good of a catch as he was.

I decided that it would be smart for me to wait a couple of hours before I called him. I didn't want to seem too eager. And I wanted him to cool off a little so that when he heard my voice, he wouldn't get defensive. In the meantime, I planned to relax in my bed for a few more minutes.

Before I could get comfortable and finish reading the latest edition of *Jet* magazine, the telephone on the nightstand rang. I

21

looked at the clock next to the telephone. "Now who in the world is calling my house this time of morning?" I asked myself out loud. Unless it was my mother or my best friend Rhoda, the only time my phone rang this early was when somebody dialed my number by mistake.

The telephone in my bedroom didn't have caller ID, so I had no idea who was calling me at this ungodly hour. It was none of the above. To my everlasting horror, it was Lizzie Stovall again, the woman who had broken up my home.

I was so taken aback, there was only one thing I could think to say. "Well, speak of the devil!" I shrieked.

"Whatever!" Lizzie hissed. She sucked on her teeth before continuing. I didn't know if that was because she was tuning up her mouth to say something I didn't want to hear, which would be anything that slid out of her mouth, or because she was nervous. "Annette, I advise you not to hang up on me like you did the last time I called." This woman had no shame whatsoever!

"What the hell —" I almost choked on my words just as she cut me off.

"Let me speak to Pee Wee. And don't fix your lips to lie to me like you usually do and tell me he's not there. I just passed your house a little while ago and I saw his car parked out front," Lizzie snarled, her words striking my ears like rocks. "Like I told you the last time I called, I've been trying to get a hold of him for several days! I am not going to stop until I reach him. You can tell him that. The sooner he talks to me, the sooner I can stop bothering you."

"Bothering me? Woman, as long as you live in this town you will be bothering me. You didn't care about bothering me when you were fucking my husband! Well, I've got news for you. Just hearing your name bothers me these days!"

Something that I didn't know and didn't want to know was the details of Lizzie's affair with my husband — like exactly when it started or which one of them initiated the affair. But the one thing that I really didn't want to know was *where* they'd slept together the first time. The thought of her sleazy ass stretched out in my bed was unbearable. If I ever found out that they had been tacky enough to fuck in *my* bed, I would not be responsible for my actions. There was just no telling what I would do to Lizzie — and Pee Wee — even though their relationship was over.

Or was it?

"Are you still fucking my husband?" Even

if she was, I didn't expect her to admit it. But I had to ask anyway.

"Annette, you've got some nerve asking me that. How dare you!" Lizzie erupted.

I could not believe how calm I managed to sound. "Well, are you?"

"No, I am not still fucking your husband! I wouldn't let that man touch me again even if he had healing hands!"

My pulse was racing and my eyes were burning. I had balled my free hand into a fist. "Why did you call my house again? Why do you keep calling here? Don't you have anything better to do with your time these days? Can't you find another innocent woman to torture?" I jeered.

"You innocent? That's a joke! You've got a lot of nerve to even think of yourself as in-nocent —"

"Get your ass off this phone, bitch!" I hollered. "You're about to make my bowels move!"

"I will hang up when I am good and ready. Look, I know you're still jealous of me, but I can't help that. It is what it is. I gave your man something that you weren't giving him, and probably never did. That was some good loving. The very first time he was with me, he realized what he'd been missing."

These were the last words that a scorned

24

woman — especially a scorned black woman — wanted to hear. If Lizzie had been standing in my room saying that shit to my face, she would be stretched out on the floor by now with my fist mauling the side of her head. I couldn't imagine what Pee Wee had said to her for her to think that I didn't give him what he needed in the bedroom before she slid into our lives. I didn't believe what she had just said for one minute — at least not her version.

"Hmmm. Then tell me, why is he not still with you? Why is he coming over here to be with me whenever I let him? And I can assure you that we do a lot more than just talk when he's here. Does that sound like I don't know how to give him what he needs?" I taunted.

"What*ever*, Annette. I just need to talk to Pee Wee."

"Pee Wee is not here, goddammit!" I roared. "And let me tell you again —"

"You're a damn liar! He is there! Now, you look, girl! I am not in the mood for any of your shit this early in the morning!"

I hated profanity. It was crude. I didn't like it when people cussed in my presence, and I didn't like to cuss myself. But under the present circumstances, there was no reason for me to act like a "lady" with Lizzie.

"Now, you look, bitch! If you don't want to deal with my shit this early in the morning, don't call my fucking house this early in the morning!"

There was a long moment of silence. I wasn't even sure that Lizzie was still on the line. I was just about to hang up when I heard her spit out a few sobs. Then she started to wheeze and cough like she was choking on some air. I had heard enough. I slammed the telephone back in its cradle. I felt like I was on fire now, so I needed to get out of the house as soon as possible. I no longer considered playing hooky from work. I couldn't wait to get to my office.

Just as I was about to go to my closet and pick out what I was going to wear to work, Lizzie called back. "You can't get rid of me that easily, Annette."

"Look, bitch, I'm going to hang up again. This time I'm going to leave the phone off the hook, so don't waste any more of your time calling here again," I told her.

"Don't you hang up on me! I advise you to put Pee Wee on this telephone, Annette," she ordered in a voice that was dripping with a combination of anger and desperation.

"I advise you to go straight to hell."

"Let me ask you again. May I speak to Pee Wee? I don't want to keep calling your house any more than you want me to, but I don't have any other choices." She had toned down her voice, but that made no difference to me. "This is really important. If it wasn't, I wouldn't be trying to get in touch with Pee Wee this hard."

"Why don't you tell me exactly what it is you need to talk to my husband about? I can tell him, and if he wants to talk to you about it, he'll call you."

"You'll find out soon enough," Lizzie mumbled in an ominous tone. It sounded like she had a mouthful of food, or that her hand was covering part of her mouth. "And believe me, *you won't like it.*"

CHAPTER 3

Lizzie's last words had piqued my interest. And because of the snooty way she had spoken those words, I felt that I needed to know right now what it was that she wanted to talk to my husband about.

"Look, Lizzie, if you want to tell me what it is that you need to talk to my husband about, that's fine with me. I will track him down and make him call you back. That is, if he wants to talk to you. I'm willing to do just about anything if it'll make you stop calling here."

"That's fine with me. The only reason I keep calling your house is because Pee Wee changed his cell phone number and the number at the apartment. When I try to reach him at his barbershop, they always tell me that he just left or he's too busy to come to the telephone," Lizzie whined. "I even tried to go talk to him at the old apartment last week, but he had the locks changed. He wouldn't even answer the door when I knocked. I left him a note in his mailbox. I even sent him another note by registered mail and he signed for it — so I know he received it. I still have not heard a word from him! What else can I do but call your house and hope to catch him there?"

It dawned on me that whatever it was that Lizzie needed to talk to Pee Wee about, it might affect me in some way. That being the case, now I was even more interested in hearing whatever that was before I hung up. Knowing her, there was just no telling what it was. I knew that she was living with another man now, and that she was working for his nephew. I seriously doubted that she wanted to move back in with Pee Wee. I had heard that she was not too happy with her new job, so it was fairly reasonable for me to assume that she wanted to beg Pee Wee to rehire her. What else could be so urgent for her to be trying so hard to get in touch with him?

There was no way in hell that I was going to let my husband rehire this woman. I'd do everything in my power, except burn his barbershop to the ground, to prevent that from happening.

I was the one who had practically forced Pee Wee to hire this backstabbing home wrecker in the first place. If he was crazy enough to put her back on his payroll, his relationship with me would be dead in the water immediately this time.

I was really curious now. "Why don't you go ahead and tell me what it is you need to talk to my husband about? That is, if you don't mind."

Lizzie hesitated for a few seconds. "I think you should hear it from him. You just tell Pee Wee that if he doesn't call me back by the end of today, he will be hearing from my attorney." There was a threatening tone in her voice that chilled me to the bone.

Attorney?

I was no longer just curious. Now I was also frightened. A sharp pain shot through my stomach like a ball of fire. Why would Lizzie need an attorney? And why in the world would she use that word in the same sentence with my husband's name?

"Did you just say that my husband can talk to your attorney?"

"That's exactly what I just said! If he won't talk to me, he'll be hearing from my attorney. And after today, that's the way it's going to be. I won't waste any more of my time trying to reach him."

"What do you need an attorney for?" That was one thing that I needed to know before

I got off the telephone. Had something happened while Lizzie was doing manicures at Pee Wee's barbershop that constituted legal action? Money! This ruckus that this no-good heifer was causing *had* to be about money! What else could it be? "Why, you greedy bitch," I snarled in a loud voice, hoping I sounded as menacing as I felt. "You don't know when to quit, do you? I know for a fact that my husband gave you a generous severance package when you left. If you think you're going to get paid again, you're wrong."

Lizzie let out a dry laugh. "As usual, you are too stupid to figure out what is really going on. No wonder it was so easy for me to take your man."

"Good-bye, slut —"

"Don't you hang up yet!"

I didn't care what it was Lizzie had to say now. I was not going to let her verbally assault me any longer. I was going to hang up on her again, but when she cut me off, I decided to continue listening. I didn't think our conversation could get any worse.

But it did.

"This is not about money, Annette. Well, not directly." She paused and cleared her throat. "It will eventually involve money . . ."

"I can't imagine how." As far as I knew,

when Lizzie quit working for Pee Wee, she got everything that she had coming and then some. Not just two weeks' severance pay; he had also paid her for vacation time that she had not even earned. What more could this miserable beast want?

"When you see your husband, you tell him that I said we need to discuss my future."

Her attorney and now her future? Something told me that this was a lot more serious than I thought.

"Your *what?*" I guffawed. "What in the hell does my husband have to do with your future, woman? You've got some goddamn nerve! First you con me into helping you get a job at my husband's barbershop and you wasted no time hopping into bed with him. Then you went behind his back and screwed his rival's uncle, and moved in with that man! I've known some skanks in my life, but you give the ordinary skanks a bad name!"

"Are you finished?"

"Hell yeah, I'm finished. Are you?"

"All right, bitch. I didn't want to drop this bombshell on you before I told Pee Wee, but now I'll be happy to tell you *why* I need to talk to your husband. I just wish I could see your face when you hear it."

"You've got exactly one minute to tell me

and then I'm hanging up this telephone whether you've said it all or not," I warned.

"I don't need a minute." Lizzie sniffed. Then she immediately announced in a mocking tone that made my blood boil: *"I'm pregnant and your husband is the father of my child."*

She hung up before I could respond, but the telephone suddenly got so hot in my hand I dropped it to the floor.

CHAPTER 4

My house was located on Reed Street in one of the most exclusive neighborhoods in town. It was the only place in the world where I could get as comfortable as I wanted — most of the time. The mortgage had been paid off years ago, so it was mine free and clear. I was in complete control. I could even lounge around naked like I was doing now. I had come a long way from the shabby, one-room shacks with no plumbing that I'd lived in as a child in Miami, Florida.

Next to my living room, my bedroom was the biggest room in the house, and it was in the best location. I could see most of the houses on my block from the large front window facing my king-sized bed. From the same window, I could reach out and pluck fruit from the apple tree and the cherry tree in my front yard when it was in season. The apple tree was bigger than the cherry tree. The apple tree provided a lot of shade in the summertime, and it was one of my favorite spots to relax in a lawn chair and enjoy a glass of iced tea. This residence had been my home since I was thirteen. Judge Lawson, who had employed my mother as a housekeeper for several years, had left the property to her when he died.

I had moved from the smaller bedroom at the end of the hall to this one after my mother remarried and moved out. I didn't even like to go into my old room anymore. It held so many painful memories — everything from loneliness to rape. Even though there was not a single spot in my house where I allowed anybody to abuse or disrespect me now, my bedroom was especially sacred. I was not about to let a woman like Lizzie upset me too much on my turf. But that was exactly what she had done.

Friday was the least favorite day in the week for me. Just about everything unpleasant that had ever happened to me had happened on a Friday.

When I was just three years old, out of nowhere my father deserted my mother and me for another woman on a Friday. And it had been Friday the thirteenth at that. My life had gone downhill from there.

Before I even started elementary school, I had experienced everything from hurricanes and tornadoes to persistent bill collectors, and being harassed by the supremely dangerous Ku Klux Klan, all on Fridays.

Not long after Daddy had run off, my mother and I moved from Florida to Ohio on a Friday. I was sick with grief, and cried off and on during the whole two-day ride on that segregated train.

Mr. Boatwright, one of my mother's Bible-thumping male acquaintances who had rented a room in our house, raped me for the first time when I was seven, on a Friday.

When I was sixteen, I discovered that I was pregnant with Mr. Boatwright's baby on a Friday. That gloomy day also happened to be a Friday the thirteenth. My list of black Fridays seemed endless. Last year, my husband left me for Lizzie on a Friday.

Now here I was today, on another Friday, with more crap being rubbed in my face.

"Lizzie is pregnant!" I yelled into the telephone as soon as Rhoda O'Toole, my best friend of more than thirty years, answered on her end.

"By who?" she asked, sounding as stunned and disgusted as I was.

"By my husband, that's who!" I screamed. I was glad that I was home alone. My twelve-year-old daughter, Charlotte, was at my parents' house, but she could barge in at any time. The last thing I needed at the moment was for her to hear my end of the conversation. "What in the hell do I do now?" I was talking so loud and fast, I almost bit my tongue several times before I paused.

"Holy shit! How did you find out? Did Pee Wee tell you?"

"No, he didn't tell me. That heifer had the nerve to call my house a few minutes ago to tell me herself!"

"Damn! This is the last thing I expected to hear," Rhoda said, suddenly sounding too relaxed for me. I wanted her to be as upset as I was. "How do you know she's tellin' the truth?"

"Why would she make up something like that?"

"Well, I can't answer that question. But sister-girl is our age. And the last time I checked, forty-seven was a little long in the tooth for a woman to be gettin' pregnant."

"Are you forgetting that Sims woman from church? She was forty-nine when she had her last baby a few months ago," I reminded Rhoda.

"Oh yeah," Rhoda snorted. "Well, if Lizzie is pregnant, how do you know Pee Wee is the daddy? That sister has been gettin' around in the bedroom these past few months. She dumped Pee Wee and moved in with Peabo Boykin. Do you know *when* she got pregnant? When was her last period?"

"Girl, I wasn't taking notes when she called."

"What does Pee Wee have to say about this mess?"

"He doesn't know yet! At least that's what she claims. She's been trying to catch up with him all week so she could tell him. He changed the phone number to his apartment and his cell phone," I reported.

"So she calls your house and tells you before she tells him?"

"Yeah."

"And I thought I had some monster problems," Rhoda lamented.

"I can tell you one thing right now; this new development between Pee Wee and that wench is not going to be my problem! I do not want that woman in my life again! If Pee Wee and I do get back together, I'd have to deal with Lizzie and their child from now on! I don't think — I know — I couldn't handle that, Rhoda. I'd go crazy!"

"Annette, calm down —"

"Calm down? I can't calm down knowing my husband got some other woman pregnant! I can't wait to call up my attorney again so I can resume my divorce proceedings!"

"I wouldn't do that yet if I were you," Rhoda told me. "Divorce is a very serious situation."

"So is another woman having my husband's baby! As far as I am concerned now, divorce is probably the only solution to this!"

Rhoda was taking too long to respond, and it didn't take me long to figure out why. She didn't believe in divorce. When her husband, Otis, cheated on her more than twenty-five years ago, divorcing him didn't even enter her mind, even though she had a lover at the time herself (and *still* had that same lover . . .).

There was another reason that divorce was such a sensitive issue to Rhoda. Her twenty-one-year-old daughter, Jade, had gone through a very nasty divorce this year, and it had practically destroyed her. Rhoda had taken it very hard, too, because Jade still lived with her. That girl was, and had always been, a very difficult person to deal with. Living with Jade, having to support her financially and tolerate her bad attitude, had to be hellish for Rhoda. Jade was a nasty piece of work in every sense of the word.

She was spoiled, hostile, self-centered, vindictive, and more; the list was endless. Right now she was so depressed and upset about her divorce that she couldn't go out and get a job, or even clean up after herself. But being depressed didn't stop her from shopping up a storm several times a week with her parents' credit cards and partying with her friends at the bars, almost every night. I knew that Rhoda had her hands full already, so I wasn't too thrilled about bothering her with my problems. But this was something that I couldn't deal with on my own.

"Don't jump the gun, Annette. Get all of the facts first. Find out for sure if this baby really is Pee Wee's. And if it is, it's his problem, not yours."

CHAPTER 5

"Rhoda, are you listening to me or not? If Pee Wee and I do get back together, he'll be bringing Lizzie's baby around! She might even be coming to my house herself — with that baby! And you know how I went off on her the last time she was brazen enough to bring her skanky self up in here!"

"No matter what happens, I'm goin' to be here for you. You know —"

"Hold on," I said, cutting Rhoda off. "There is another call coming in. Let me call you back. We are going to have to get together for drinks. I'll call you when I get to work!" I clicked over to the call that was waiting for me. It was Pee Wee. He was the last man on the planet that I wanted to talk to at the moment.

"Hello, baby," he began, doing a fairly good impression of Barry White. He could be real sexy when he tried, but his timing was way off. "I didn't mean to run off the way I did this mornin', but I promise I'll make it up to you." I was just waiting for him to stop talking long enough so I could jump in and say what I had to say. "Listen, I'm goin' to get in touch with Lizzie today. I'm goin' to tell her to stop callin' your house."

"You do that," I said in a stiff voice.

"I don't like to see you as upset as you were when I was there — and that's the only reason I left so abruptly. I just wish you had said somethin' sooner. Like when I first got to the house. I felt like a fool runnin' off the way I did right after we'd made love. But I had to be by myself so I could clear my head."

"I hope your head is clear enough now," I said, my voice still stiff.

"Oh yes, baby! Everything is real clear now, and I hope it stays this way. I can tell you one thing: after I talk to Lizzie, you won't have to worry about her pesterin' you no more. I am goin' to make sure she gets out of our lives for good. If she don't, I am goin' to file a harassment charge against her, hear?"

"Uh-huh," I muttered. I decided to let Pee Wee say all of the sweet things that he wanted to say to me now while he still wanted to. I knew that after I told him what

Lizzie had told me, things would never be the same between us again. "See, baby, I just wanted to let you know how wonderful you made me feel this mornin'," he continued, making kissing noises with his lips. "Oomph! I am so glad that things are workin' out so well between us. I know we agreed to take things real slow, but . . ."

"But what?" I barked.

Pee Wee was so caught up in a state of rapture that he didn't even notice the anger and coldness in my voice. "Well, we've both made some mistakes, but nothin' we can't overcome. We can put the past behind us. I know we can move forward and resume our marriage. It'll be like neither one of us ever messed up at all."

"We could probably forget that I ever had that affair with Louis Baines last year. He's long gone and — and he didn't leave me a souvenir like Lizzie did you!"

"Annette, you ain't makin' no sense. Lizzie didn't leave me no souvenir. The important thing is, she will never be part of our lives again. I am goin' to make sure she realizes that when I talk to her. And I hope I can catch up with her today."

"I've got news for you. That slut will always be part of our lives now! Yours at least!"

"Say what? Part of my life? Uh-uh. Once Lizzie left me and moved in with Peabo, she was no longer part of my life. You should know that by now. I don't see, or talk to her. The last time I saw her walkin' down the street, I made a U-turn on a one-way street just so I could avoid her." Pee Wee sounded exasperated, but he was not half as exasperated as I was.

"Pee Wee, you will be connected to that woman forever now," I informed him, almost choking on each syllable. The words left a bitter taste in my mouth.

"Whoa now! You just hold on right there! Annette, I got a feelin' you are tryin' to tell me somethin', but I have no idea what it is. Do you think I still have feelings for Lizzie? If you do, you are wrong. My relationship with that woman is over and done with. She wasn't even clean! You know how I am about that subject. That woman used to wear the same underwear for three days in a row!"

"You didn't know she was nasty before you screwed her?" I demanded.

"No! She kept herself clean until she took advantage of me!"

If I had not been as pissed off as I was, I would have laughed about what Pee Wee had just said. It was just as ridiculous as a rapist claiming his victim wanted to have sex as much as he did. I decided that it was better for me to pretend like I didn't even hear his last comment.

"Annette, I swear to God, even if that woman had not left me and moved in with Peabo, I would have kicked her to the curb anyway. Don't you trust me?"

"Brother, I wouldn't trust you as far as I could throw you," I wailed.

The silence that followed for the next few moments was chilling. You would have thought that Pee Wee and I both had suddenly turned into mutes. I cleared my throat and was about to speak again, but he beat me to it.

"Wait a minute now. You sound more upset now than you were when I was there! You wasn't talkin' this crazy then. What the hell happened since I left you less than half an hour ago? I know you was mad about Lizzie callin', but you couldn't have been that mad if you waited until after we'd made love to mention it. Does your sudden mood change have anything to do with that comment you made about me makin' you feel like a prostitute? You was the one who brought that up. You know I don't ever go there because I know it's somethin' personal in your past that you don't like to discuss.

45

Not even with me. Now, is that why you suddenly got such a big bee in your bonnet?"

"No, it's not. But I'm telling you now that you couldn't pay me enough to crawl back into bed again with your ashy black self."

There was more silence. This time it was even more disturbing. I coughed to clear my throat some more. "If you are still on the line, say something," I ordered.

"Maybe I should hang up and call again. Let's start all over. I don't know why in the hell you are talkin' so crazy. And the way you keep beatin' around the bush, I'll be on this phone all day tryin' to find out why. Now, if I did or said somethin' to upset you before I left you, I'm sorry. But I would like to know what it is that I did or said, so I'll know not to say or do it again. I ain't no mind reader."

I could still hear Lizzie's shrill voice ringing in my ears. It was as painful as somebody batting my head with a baseball bat. I was so glad that she had called me up and not come to my house again — for her sake as well as mine. If she ever came to my house again, she'd probably be carried out on a stretcher. I had seen her on the streets and walking through the mall a few times since the day she stuck a knife in my back. Each

46

time I saw her, I had to leave the premises as fast as I could. Otherwise, I don't know what I would have done to her, whether she provoked me or not. But come to think of it, she didn't have to do or say anything to provoke me now. She'd already done that by befriending me and then stealing my husband.

"Lizzie drove by here this morning. She saw your car parked out front. She called me up again a few minutes after you left."

"Oh. Well, now . . . uh . . . now I can understand why you seem so much more upset," he sputtered, releasing a sigh of relief. "Uh, I'll try to reach her right now. The sooner I straighten her out, the sooner you can stop worryin' about her callin' you again."

"You do that, Pee Wee. And when you talk to her, ask her what she's going to name *your* baby."

He let out a gasp that was so profound, it sounded like it had come out of a geyser. I hung up before he could say another word.

CHAPTER 6

I called up Rhoda again around ten during my first coffee break. "I'm glad I found out about this baby before I let Pee Wee move back home," I told her, speaking into the telephone on my desk in my office. "God is good."

"That is so true," she agreed. "Look what the good Lord's done for me." I knew exactly what Rhoda was talking about. She often gave God credit for allowing her to survive breast cancer and a stroke. "And He's done a lot for you too."

"I know He has, but where do I go from here?" I wondered out loud.

I clutched a large cup of coffee that I had picked up in our employee break room, wishing it was something a lot stronger. I needed something a lot more potent than coffee to dull my senses. Like a shot of tequila. But I was glad that my mind was sharp and alert. I didn't want alcohol or anything else to alter my mind until I had digested this latest uproar.

"Does this mean that there is no chance that you and my boy will get back together now?" Rhoda asked. From the tone of her voice, I could tell that she was worried about her boy Pee Wee. But I knew she was even more worried about me.

I took another sip from my coffee cup before I answered her question. The coffee was too hot for my taste, but the sudden discomfort on my bottom lip didn't even faze me. I continued to drink anyway.

"What would you do?" I muttered, sliding my tongue across my irritated lip. "What if it was your husband who got another woman pregnant? Can you imagine the hurt you'd have to deal with for the rest of your life? Would you welcome that child into your home with open arms? I don't think I can do that, Rhoda. Pee Wee having an affair is one thing; him making a baby with another woman is another. Do you think he would want to get back with me if I was pregnant with another man's child?"

Rhoda's silence spoke volumes. Early in her marriage, during her affair with Ian "Bully" Bullard, her husband's best friend, she had become pregnant with Bully's child. Unfortunately, the little boy died when he

49

was a toddler. To this day, as far as I knew, I was the only person, other than Rhoda, who knew about her indiscretion.

"You know what I mean, I hope. I didn't mean to bring up bad memories for you. I'm sorry," I apologized.

"You don't have to apologize for anything," Rhoda told me. I could tell by the way her voice suddenly dropped that she was getting emotional. "What I did happened a long time ago. I was very young and very foolish. And there was no excuse for me bein' so careless that I would get pregnant by another man. I've learned to live with what I did, and I still think of that child as a blessin' from God. With that in mind, I can only imagine how that baby boy would have enriched my life if he had lived." Rhoda stopped talking long enough to exhale. "Now, I know you don't want to hear this, but you might one day look at Lizzie's child by Pee Wee as a blessin'."

The next thought that entered my mind was that Rhoda had lost her mind. She knew how badly I'd been hurt by Pee Wee's affair. Why would she think I would ever look at his love child as a blessing? "A blessing? Woman, have you lost your damn mind?"

"No, I have not lost my mind," Rhoda said calmly.

"You must have! What makes you — of all people — think that I'd ever look at my husband having a baby with another woman as a blessing?" I was sorry that Rhoda was not in the same room with me. If she could have seen the look of disgust on my face because of what she'd just said, she would have taken back every single word. Despite how I was feeling right now, one of the many things that I loved about Rhoda was that when I approached her with a problem, she approached it with caution. But she was being a little too cautious for me right now. "I know how close you and Pee Wee are. But whose side are you on?"

"Annette, honey, I'm on your side. You know I'm always on your side when you have a crisis. Pee Wee will always be my boy, but my first allegiance is to you. You *know* I've got your back no matter what."

"Then act like it. Don't say any more stupid shit like what you just said!"

"Annette, please be quiet and let me finish. First of all, I am sorry to hear that that woman is pregnant with Pee Wee's child. But let's not jump the gun."

"Meaning what?"

"Well, first of all, we don't know for sure

51

if Lizzie is tellin' the truth," Rhoda pointed out.

"All right. We don't know if Lizzie is telling the truth about being pregnant, or telling the truth about Pee Wee being the daddy?"

"Both."

"I will find out for sure soon enough!" I boomed. "Just when I thought things were going so well between Pee Wee and me, now this." Lizzie's announcement had hit me like an atomic bomb. "Rhoda, I don't know if I can get through this in one piece," I admitted.

"You can and you will," she assured me. "Because I am goin' to make sure that you do."

"I really appreciate your saying that," I managed, feeling slightly better.

"Annette, I really am truly sorry about what's been goin' on between you and Pee Wee. And it's normal for you to be upset right now, but let's look at the whole picture."

"I think we are already looking at the whole picture. If a baby doesn't complete a relationship, nothing does."

"Just listen and let me talk. You told me that your half sister Lillimae was one of the best things that ever happened to you. You

52

didn't let it bother you that another woman had her by your daddy. . . ."

That was true. I loved my half sister, who happened to have a white mother. My relationship with Lillimae was very important to me. Other than Rhoda, she was the only female in my age group whom I could turn to in a time of crisis. Lillimae's mother was the woman whom Daddy had left my mother and me for. Lillimae had her mother's blond hair and blue eyes, but she also had features similar to mine. Every time I looked at her, it was like looking at the photo negative version of myself. I loved my half sister to death.

"Lillimae is . . . an exception."

"And why is that?"

"Oh, I don't know. I just know she is. I don't know what I'd do without her in my life."

"Uh-huh. Exactly. That's what I'm talkin' about."

"How can you compare Lillimae with —"

"Now, you shut up and listen to me!" Rhoda ordered, her voice so shrill it made me flinch. I was glad she had cut me off, because some of the words coming out of my mouth were contradicting my feelings about Lizzie's baby. It didn't make any sense to me that I could accept my daddy's

53

love child, but not my husband's. I was concerned because I couldn't help the way I felt. A sharp pain shot through my head, right behind the thought that I might some day accept Lizzie's baby. "I know your mother was hurtin' real bad when your daddy took off. Her findin' out that he had kids by the other woman must have ripped her heart in two."

"That happened a real long time ago. My mother eventually got over it or she would not have taken my daddy back after a thirty-year separation."

"Exactly," Rhoda said again, louder and with more conviction this time.

"Exactly what?"

"I am not condonin' what Pee Wee did, but don't let it destroy you today, because you don't know how you will feel about it next year, or in a few years. Do you understand what I'm tryin' to say?"

"Hell no! And I don't know why you're saying what you're saying. This is not the time to be telling me that something good might come out of this. I am too mad to even think that far ahead! When you walk in my shoes, maybe you'll know what I'm feeling like right now."

"I haven't worn the same shoes you have on now, but I've had my feet in shoes that

54

didn't feel too comfortable. Had my son lived, I know my husband would have accepted him and raised him as his own."

"But Otis didn't know that your son wasn't his, did he?"

"No, but I was goin' to tell him the truth one day."

"Rhoda, your situation was not nearly as traumatic as the one I'm going through right now — or the one that my mother went through with my daddy. You could have kept your son's father's true identity hidden until the day you died. Otis and Bully look enough alike that they could pass for brothers. If your son had lived and grown up to look like his biological father, nobody would have guessed the truth. You know how bitter my mother is when it comes to Lillimae and her siblings. I don't want to be like her."

"Yes, I do know and I don't blame your mother. But she's not as bitter as she was when it first happened. A few years ago, she told me that she wouldn't change anything that had happened to her because it eventually made her the woman that she is today."

Rhoda was right. It was because of what my daddy did that my long-suffering mother had gone from living in poverty to living in the lap of luxury. She was now one of the happiest women I knew.

My mother was an uneducated woman with very little family to fall back on. After Daddy left us, she had endured some hellish jobs working as a maid and a nanny for rich white women — most of them pit bulls in heels. One of her last employers had beaten her with a mop handle and promptly fired her because she had caught her husband trying to fondle my mother's breasts. Well, those days were over. My mother owned and operated The Buttercup, the most successful black restaurant in Richland. She had sold it twice. But each time she had gotten bored and restless, and purchased it back. Next to me and Daddy, the restaurant was her most important possession. All of that had come about because of Daddy's betrayal. Albert King, my mother's deceased second husband, had left The Buttercup to her in his will. I could understand what Rhoda was trying to tell me, but it didn't make me feel any better.

"Think about your daughter," Rhoda advised. "Charlotte has always wanted a siblin'. She and . . . uh . . . Lizzie's child might bond the same way you and Lillimae did."

That was true too. My daughter had been telling me for years that "an only child is a lonely child." She used to beg me to give her a baby brother or a baby sister so she'd have somebody to boss around. And I had tried to do just that. I had stopped taking birth control pills, I had done all kinds of things to make myself more fertile (including Jell-O douches), and none of it had worked. I had accepted the fact that I'd never have another child to raise. At least not one from my body.

It seemed so unfair that Lizzie was the one pregnant by Pee Wee instead of me!

"My head is spinning. Let's change the subject," I suggested.

"We can change the subject, but this baby thing is not goin' to go away. You need to face it head-on. The best way to do that is for you and me to talk about it some more. No matter what I say, I'm on your side. Just to let you know way in advance, no matter how involved Pee Wee gets in Lizzie's child's life, I will not tolerate him bringin' it around me. And that's somethin' I want to do for your sake because I know how much it would hurt you."

"I hope you mean that," I bleated.

"I mean it, and you know I do. It's the least I can do."

We remained silent for a few moments. My mind went back to what Rhoda told me my mother had confessed to her. My mother

57

had never been so candid with her feelings to me! This was one revelation that I was going to spend a lot of time thinking about, now that I knew about it. I had a notion to throw it up in Muh'Dear's face the next time she complained to me about Lillimae. But no matter what I thought or felt, this news about Pee Wee and Lizzie having a baby together angered me to the bone. I really needed to talk more about it, but I didn't want to do it over the telephone.

"Annette, can you meet me at the Red Rose for drinks when you get off work this evenin'? But you need to do some coolin' off first. I really want you to spend the next few hours alone so that you'll have some time to think about everything I've just said. I don't like knowin' you're in so much pain. But, like I always do, I will do everything I can to help you get through this."

I heard everything that Rhoda had just said, but my mind was on something else. "Rhoda, what would you have done if that woman your husband had the affair with had gotten pregnant with his baby?"

CHAPTER 7

Rhoda was taking too long to answer my question, so I asked it again, "What would you have done if your husband's mistress had gotten pregnant with his baby?"

"I can honestly say that I don't know how I would have handled my husband havin' a baby with another woman. Anyway, the situation with my husband and his outside woman was a lot different than what you're goin' through with that Lizzie heifer. In my case, the other woman lives in Miami. Even if she had had a baby by my husband, she's down there; I'm up here in Ohio. I wouldn't have to worry about runnin' into her on the street. This town is small; you will have to see Lizzie and her baby everywhere you go. This is somethin' that you are goin' to have to deal with head-on."

"I wish I knew what to do," I lamented. "I never thought that I would have to deal with something like this at my age. I need to talk to you about this some more."

"For sure. Like I suggested, let's hook up at the Red Rose after you leave your office this evenin'. Drinks are on me."

"This evening? Oh no. I don't think I can wait that long." I looked up at the big clock on the wall facing my desk. "I need to get up out of here a lot sooner than this evening. I am so agitated right now that I can't sit still. A liquid lunch might calm me down," I admitted. "Can you meet me around eleven-thirty at that deli on the corner from my office? They've got some great French wine."

"Oh, I can't do it that soon," Rhoda groaned. "Jade's still not feelin' well, so I'd better stay close to home for the next few hours. I picked up a prescription for her last night, and now she's complainin' about its side effects; one bein' diarrhea."

Rhoda's daughter had not been feeling well for several days. Last Monday, after she'd indulged herself with one of her hour-long bubble baths, she'd developed a severe urinary tract infection. I felt somewhat responsible for Jade's condition. A ninety-nine-cent bottle of bubble bath, which my daughter had given to Jade as a gift on her last birthday, was the cause of her discomfort. The reason I felt responsible was because Jade, who was about as high maintenance as a female could be, didn't know that the bubble bath had come from a discount store. That was because Charlotte had poured it into a bottle from Victoria's Secret. She had purposely left the very expensive tag stuck to the front of the bottle. I didn't know what my daughter had done until she confessed her prank to me after she'd already given it to Jade. I scolded Charlotte and made her promise me that she would never do something that deceitful and tacky again.

"Poor Jade," I said dryly, feeling slightly sympathetic. I had had my share of female-related discomforts over the years, including the one Jade had now. It was no picnic. Mine had also been caused by my bathing in cheap bubble bath. However, if somebody had to have it, I couldn't think of a more deserving woman than Jade.

"Well, poor Jade is beside herself havin' to deal with all that itchin' and burnin' between her thighs; not to mention all that pressure on her bladder. She didn't even make it to the bathroom in time a few times yesterday. I've stepped in so many puddles on the floor between her bedroom and the bathroom, you'd think I had half a dozen un-housebroken puppies runnin' around," Rhoda groaned, grinding her teeth. "She hasn't wet her bed this much since she was in diapers. Her silk thong panties and those white, six-hundred-thread-count sheets on her bed will never be the same again. We had to leave the grocery store yesterday before the clerk even rang up our purchases so Jade could get to a toilet. Lord! She didn't make it. She had to squat down and relieve herself between two parked cars in the grocery store parking lot!" Rhoda snickered for a few seconds. "Maybe now she won't be so quick to sit in a bathtub for an hour with bubbles up to her neck."

"I hope not." I had to hold my breath to keep from guffawing like a hyena. But I couldn't stop myself from saying what I was thinking. "They have those Depends in her size, you know." I was glad that I could shift my mind off Lizzie's pregnancy for a few precious moments. I almost laughed, but I was glad I didn't.

"Depends? Annette, that's so gruesome!" Rhoda almost choked on her words. "Those damn adult *diapers?* That girl is so vain she won't even wear cotton panties! Look, this conversation has drifted in the wrong direction. I want to talk more about this new development with Lizzie. You know I don't want to spend my time on this telephone talkin' to you about Jade's bladder condition. Instead of us goin' to the bar, what if I come by your house later tonight after Jade goes to bed?"

"That's fine. What time do you think that'll be?"

"Well, you know Jade. She's my baby and I love her to death, but that child behaves like she came out of Pandora's box instead of my womb," Rhoda said in an apologetic manner. She mumbled some gibberish under her breath that included a few cuss words. She took a deep breath before continuing, "Nothin' she does surprises me anymore, so I have to work around her annoyin' antics. If she comes home from the clubs before eleven, I can come over around midnight in time for the *Cheers* reruns on Channel Four."

I was not surprised to hear that Jade didn't even let a severe urinary tract infection keep her from going out to party. As far as she was concerned, life was all about having a good time, no matter the cost. She had trotted off to a bar to participate in a "hot body" contest the night that a processor server tracked her down and slapped divorce papers in her hands right in front of her friends.

"But don't count on Jade comin' home in time. You know how much that girl likes to have a good time," Rhoda added.

Unfortunately, I did know how much Jade liked to have a good time. She had wanted to "have a good time" with my husband while she was still in her teens. Her sinister plan was to break up my marriage and take over my role in Pee Wee's life. Even though she and I had been more like family, she had attempted to destroy me by driving me crazy with anonymous hate mail, vicious telephone calls, and vile packages. When her plan fell apart, so did she. She now treated me like I had leprosy, but Rhoda and I maintained the friendship that we had developed when we were still teenagers by "working around" Jade, so to speak. Rhoda and I usually got together at my place or some place in public. I only went to her house when I knew Jade was out, or when I really needed to see Rhoda in person and didn't mind having to endure Jade's hostility. This was one of those times.

"I can leave work and come over," I suggested, looking at my wall clock again. "Right now, if you don't mind."

It was only a few minutes past ten. I had not even finished my first cup of coffee. I had a lot of work on my desk and a staff meeting to attend at ten-thirty. I could delegate most of my work, but attending a staff meeting was the last thing that I wanted to do. I was in no shape to spend two hours with my staff trying to come up with ways to get people to pay their delinquent bills. Some people thought my job was easy. But when people's unpaid bills ended up with a collection agency, it was obvious that these individuals were irresponsible. When they received calls from us, they were usually so hostile and angry, they only made the situation worse. I could recall only one case that didn't fit into that unpleasant category. Last year an elderly woman from my church had a stroke and lapsed into a coma. She had previously given her daughter authorization to handle her finances. Well, the daughter handled the finances all right, but only the ones in her favor. She spent a fortune of her mother's life savings in Atlantic City in the casinos and didn't pay a single one of her mother's bills. When the poor old woman surprised everybody and recovered, her life was in shambles. Her house was in foreclosure, her utilities had been cut off, and her car had been repossessed. The district attorney, the old woman's former employer, was fit to be tied. The daughter was charged with elder abuse and grand theft. She was put on probation and had to pay a huge fine. Part of her punishment was that she had to catch up the payments on the bills that she had ignored. However, it was too late to salvage her mother's previously excellent credit rating. The old woman begged me not to sue her. She didn't want to lose what little money she had left, because she had no other family to turn to. I had no problem arranging a payment plan that the daughter could afford. After she made two payments, both late, she stopped paying on her mother's accounts, quit her job, and went on welfare. It amazed me how often friends and family members betrayed one another.

Lizzie used to be one of my closest friends. . . .

"Annette, are you still with me?"

"Oh. I was just thinking about something," I sniffed, wiping a huge tear from the corner of my eye. "Uh, do you want me to come over to your place right now?"

"Oh, I wish you could, but this is not a good time for me. My houseguest is on his way from the airport. You know how helpless men are about things like unpacking and whatnot. I need to be here when he arrives so I can get him settled in. Besides, he'll be all turned around and exhausted because of the time difference between Ohio and England. Between him and Jade, I'll have my hands full for the next few hours. Like I said, I will come to your house later tonight if Jade gets home before too late. I want to be here to make sure she takes her medication before she goes to bed."

"Yeah, I — oh shit! Don't worry about us getting together at all tonight. I just remembered that I have a date with Roscoe Grinter."

"Roscoe? Girl, do you mean to tell me that after what you found out today, you're still goin' out on a date? Don't you think that's a little odd?"

"No more so than your daughter going to the clubs tonight in her condition," I smirked. "At least Roscoe will be a distraction, and that's what I need until I get my bearings back."

Rhoda chuckled. "We'll get together tomorrow for sure. We can talk then. I'll come over first thing in the mornin'."

After Rhoda hung up, I sat at my desk and stared at the wall. When it began to look like it was moving, I shifted my attention to some of the items on my desk. I glared at the large silver-framed photo of Pee Wee sitting next to my telephone. There was a foolish grin on his face as he stood over the barbecue grill in my backyard. This picture had been taken two years ago, so he looked like he didn't have a care in the world. And at that time, he didn't. I couldn't believe all of the things that had happened since he'd posed for that picture. "You dog," I snarled, almost barking at the picture. "You low-down, funky black dog!"

CHAPTER 8

I liked to keep up with the news, local and worldwide. I watched CNN, *Dateline,* and most of the other news programs on a regular basis. It was amazing how the media could give a detailed report within a matter of hours on something that had occurred in some remote part of the world. They had satellites and all kinds of technology to work with, though. But some of the people I knew had all of those reporters beat when it came to spreading news. On any given day, news shot through Richland faster than a speeding bullet.

I knew that before the day was over, the local grapevine would be buzzing like wasps about Lizzie's pregnancy.

Lizel Hunter, one of the two young women who helped Rhoda manage the child-care business that she operated out of her home, called me up five minutes after I ended my conversation with Rhoda.

"Annette! I am so glad I caught you! I wanted to make sure you were all right!" Lizel exploded, talking in a voice so loud my eardrum throbbed. "I was so worried about you."

"Hello, Lizel," I replied in a tired voice. "You don't have to worry about me."

"I'm going to pray for you anyway. Lord knows you're going to need it more than ever now. You poor thing, you. As if Pee Wee and Lizzie haven't hurt you enough. Now this baby thing! I wish to God that I was there with you now so I could give you a hug and rub up and down your back 'til you feel better. People have been telling me all my life that I got healing hands."

"I appreciate your concern, Lizel," I murmured. "I appreciate your taking the time to call me, but I'm doing just fine, thank you. I know you're busy with the kids, so I'll let you get back to work. My inbox is overflowing with things that I need to address."

Lizel kept talking like she had not heard a word I'd just said. "Annette, you know I'm in the church, so I won't say anything too harsh. But if I was you, I would skin Lizzie's pale ass alive for what she did!" Lizel thundered. "Bless your soul." There was so much emotion and pity in her voice, you would have thought that somebody close to me had died and she was calling to offer her condolences. I couldn't have felt any worse if someone close to me really had died. "Why that hussy wasn't using protection is beyond me! She is going to look like a fool walking around pregnant at her age — and by a married man."

Before I could respond again, Lizel's cousin Wyrita Hayes, the other woman who worked for Rhoda, came on the line. "I've been through the same thing you're going through myself. Remember my ex, Vincent Proctor? That real cute cabdriver with that cone-shaped head? He got my cousin's best friend pregnant while he was still living with me. The boy is nine now, and even though Vincent denied Jeffrey was his son, I know he's that boy's daddy because they got that same long-ass head. But you know what, he's a real sweet little boy. Me and my whole family just love him to death. Don't you worry none. In time, Lizzie's child will become a joy to have in your life because of a daddy like Pee Wee."

I was listening to Wyrita, but I couldn't stop thinking about what Rhoda had said. She and Wyrita seemed to be on the same page. I wondered if they both truly believed that something pleasant was going to come

71

from Lizzie having a child by my husband. Would Lizzie's child become a "joy" in my life? Would my daughter having a sibling benefit her and enrich her life the way that Lillimae did mine? I wondered.

Despite those thoughts, and what Wyrita had just said, just thinking about my husband's baby growing in Lizzie's belly left a bitter taste in my mouth and a headache that felt like my brain was on fire.

"Annette, I know you are mad as hell right now, and you should be, but you can get over this. Just like you got over Lizzie stealing Pee Wee. And you know me and Lizel always got your back."

I couldn't figure out what made anybody think that I'd gotten over Lizzie stealing my husband. Especially Wyrita. I was surprised that she would even say something like that. She was still angry about losing her first boyfriend to another girl when she was still in high school, more than ten years ago. I knew that I would eventually get over losing Pee Wee to a woman who I had thought was a friend. But it was one thing that I would never forget. And busybodies like Lizel and Wyrita would make sure of that.

I didn't even want to know how Lizel and Wyrita had found out about Lizzie's condition so fast. When it came to gossip, rumors, or any type of juicy news, these two must have had some type of radar. It was a good guess that Rhoda had told them, but it didn't matter to me how they found out. It wouldn't be long before everybody else knew too.

This was a situation that I never expected to face. I didn't even know what to say to Wyrita, a woman who had already experienced something similar. I said the next thing that came to my mind. "So you really got to know your ex's child, Wyrita?"

"Uh-huh," she replied in a dry voice.

"I know that must have been hard for you to do."

"Honey, you don't know the half of it. I cussed and fussed up a storm until I got tired. But then after a while, it didn't even faze me. Look on the bright side; Lizzie's child might bring more joy into your life — just because it'll be part of Pee Wee."

Lizel and Wyrita were two of the most meddlesome women I knew. They were good workers and they had lots of friends, but they could be pretty vicious. If they could come around and embrace Wyrita's man's illegitimate child, anybody could embrace an illegitimate child.

Anybody but me . . .

"Wyrita, that child will be a constant

73

reminder of your man's infidelity. That doesn't bother you?" I asked.

"It bothered the hell out of me for a long time. But I had other things going on in my life, so I couldn't spend too much of my time being pissed off about something that I couldn't change. Well, the boy and his mama lived in Sandusky the first few years. Four years ago, when she came down here for her family reunion, she brought the boy with her. He was such a sweetie; so once I got to know him, I was all right. Me and Vincent ended up getting back together. I got attached to his son, and before I knew it, that boy was like the child I always wanted. I see him all the time now, even though me and Vincent are no longer together. But while we were trying to work things out, he dated other women, I dated other men. Just like you and Pee Wee, huh?"

I didn't respond to Wyrita's last comment. I had just found out about Lizzie's baby a few hours ago, so there was no way I could "look on the bright side" this soon. If there was going to be a bright side, it was going to take either divine intervention or a pair of 3-D glasses for me to see it.

After I got Wyrita off the phone, I called up my mother to tell her to keep my daughter, Charlotte, with her until Saturday morning. She wasted no time getting on my case about Lizzie's baby. "It was bad enough that you let a *white* woman take your man! Now you are gwine to have to deal with your husband draggin' his half-breed child around town and up in your face. Lord have mercy on you, girl."

I didn't even bother to remind my mother again that Lizzie Stovall was only half white, and I didn't bother to ask her how she had already found out about the baby that Lizzie claimed she was carrying.

My mother answered one of the questions that was on my mind. "Everybody in Claudette's beauty shop was talkin' about that baby when I went to get my hair done this mornin'. Them women were clickin' their thick tongues like pigs lappin' from a dipper. I thought I would fall out in the middle of the floor and ball up and die. Listenin' to all that gibberish about my only child was the hardest thing I ever had to do! If you had treated Pee Wee right and not let that white woman get too close to y'all, you wouldn't be in this mess." For a woman who lived in a "glass house," she sure tossed a lot of stones.

"Muh'Dear, Lizzie is only half as white as the woman who stole Daddy from you," I reminded. "And from what I remember, you

75

treated him right, and he still left us."

My mother's prolonged silence told me that I had struck a nerve in her. "Well, that was a real long time ago. I was a fool in love back then. I always prayed that you wouldn't make the same mistakes I made with men. And anyway, Frank eventually came to his senses, gal."

"He sure did. And it only took him thirty-something years to do it," I said with a sneer. I heard my mother sigh with disgust, but I kept talking anyway. "Thirtysomething years and three half-white kids later. I'll bet that if that woman hadn't left him, he'd still be with her."

"Don't you try to change the subject! You are the one with the mess on your hands now! This ain't about me and Frank and his white woman. This is about you and Pee Wee and his white woman. Lord have mercy! Jesus would weep! My poor grandbaby Charlotte! She's lucky I'm still around to keep her life halfway normal, praise the Lord."

I groaned. Then I had to rub my forehead to ease the sudden new headache that I had developed. "Muh'Dear, I have to hang up now. There is a huge pile of work on my desk, and I have a staff meeting to attend in a little while. I'll call you back later. We'll talk about this some more then."

"We sure will," my mother assured me. I could hear her grinding her teeth. "Is your spare house key still under that flower pot in the corner on the front porch?" My mother didn't wait for me to respond. "I'll be at the house waitin' on you when you get home from work this evenin'."

"Muh'Dear, please don't come over this evening. I have a date —"

"A date? What in the — do I have to keep remindin' you that you got a husband? How in the world do you expect to get your marriage back on track with you slippin' and slidin' around town with other men? Poor Pee Wee. What's wrong with you, girl? You want to grow old and die alone?"

"Muh'Dear, please make up your mind. You go on and on about how 'poor' Pee Wee betrayed me, and then you turn around and jump to his defense. Do you even know what you think I should do?"

"What you do is your business. I just like to let you know what I think, but you ain't got to listen to me if you don't want to." My mother's voice dropped from a near roar to a whimper. "I . . . I'm just tryin' to keep you from makin' more mistakes with men. I . . . don't want to see you keep on settin' yourself up to get hurt." She ended with a sniff.

"Muh'Dear, Pee Wee and I decided to take things very slowly before we make a decision about our marriage. I've told you that at least a dozen times. In the meantime, he's datin' other women, I'm datin' other men. I've told you that a dozen times too."

In a flash, the harshness returned to my mother's voice. "Humph!" she snorted. "Only God knows what's gwine to become of your generation, girl. If you take Pee Wee back, I don't want that heifer's baby in that house. The dearly departed Judge Lawson originally left that house to me. When I married the dearly departed Albert King, I put your name on the deed. I made you promise me that you would never put no man's name on that deed, not even Pee Wee's. If you do and somethin' was to happen to you, Lizzie might be sashayin' around that house like Queen of Sheba, raisin' her young'un in it. I paid too high a price to get that house to let that happen. Judge Lawson was one hard old white man to please. Buh'lieve you me, it took a whole lot of blood, sweat, and tears out of me to keep him happy enough to remember me in his last will and testament. But I done it for me and you, and your children, and nobody else. That's why I ain't never gwine to leave nothin' to

78

your daddy Frank, because I will never accept his other young'uns. *Never.*"

CHAPTER 9

I had no idea that my mother's words about my father's other children would come back to haunt her a few hours later. Around seven P.M., as I was running around the house trying to get ready for my date, somebody knocked on my front door. Roscoe wasn't due for another hour, so I knew it wasn't him. Bracing myself, fearing that it might be Pee Wee or that bitch Lizzie, I padded across the floor to the front window and pulled the curtains back just far enough for me to see who was standing on my porch.

I could not believe my eyes! It was my half-white, half sister Lillimae from Miami, clutching a large suitcase in each hand. She wore an off-white shawl over her flowered muumuu and a pair of sandals with straps wrapped and knotted around her ankles like nooscs.

"Speak of the devil!" I exclaimed as I snatched open the door. "Your name came up earlier today."

Lillimae set her largest suitcase down by her feet. "Associated with somethin' tolerable, I hope." She stood in the doorway, fanning her face with her hand and moaning like she was in pain. "No wonder my ears were burnin' ever since I got on that airplane." She paused and moaned some more. "Lord, I feel like I've been run over by a bus. Travelin' ain't what it used to be. All that rippin' and runnin' up and down those airport corridors and standin' in those mile-long lines just about wore me out! Not to mention babies squallin' like pandas all the way. And that damn turbulence once you get on the damn plane is enough to make a person want to get a lifetime ticket with Greyhound." She offered me an ear-to-ear smile. "And don't let me forget those weak drinks they serve."

"Well, what strong wind blew you up this way?" I asked.

"I've left Freddie for good. He's drinkin' like a fish again and throwin' away our money with both hands. I need to stay with you for a while," Lillimae told me. "I hope you don't mind. . . ."

"Well, come on in the house and have a seat," I muttered, waving her into my living room.

Lillimae picked up her other suitcase and stumbled across the threshold like a drunkard with a club foot. I thought she was going to drop to the floor, but she steadied herself as she set her suitcases on the floor by the couch and gave me a one-armed hug. I had to hold my breath to keep from gagging because there was the strong smell of alcohol on her breath.

"I . . . I wish you had called to let me know you were on your way. I could have picked you up at the airport." The door was still open. I looked over Lillimae's shoulder. The dusty yellow cab that she'd just piled out of backed out of my driveway, turned around, and zoomed back down the street. "You're lucky I happened to be home right now," I said with a broad smile as I kicked the door shut.

I was glad to see my sister. However, I was slightly aggravated because she had not been courteous enough to check with me beforehand to make sure it was all right for her to visit. I rarely dropped in on folks uninvited or unannounced. And this was the worst time for me to have a houseguest — especially Lillimae — while my mother was presently on one of her rants about the evils of "white women."

"You know me. When I get a notion, I

usually do things ass-backward," Lillimae said with a sheepish grin, looking around. "I see you got some new furniture since my last visit."

"I did," I replied, sticking my chest out. "I hope you like it."

"I love anything in plaid," she told me, admiring my brown and gold couch and love seat with nods of approval.

I glanced at my watch. "Uh, I'm expecting company in a little while. I'm going out to dinner, so I hope you don't mind spending a few hours alone."

Despite my initial annoyance, I was so happy that my sister had come to spend some time with me. Had I known in time that she was on her way, I would have postponed my date with Roscoe. But I didn't know. And since I didn't want to disappoint him and risk the possibility of running him off while I still needed him, I decided that it was better for me to keep my date with him and deal with Lillimae later.

"Pshaw!" Lillimae responded, waving her hand. "You know me. As long as I can find my way to the refrigerator and the liquor, I can be happy as pie."

"The refrigerator is full of food, and the liquor cabinet is full of all the goodies you like. Knock yourself out," I chirped.

"Sugar, you go on your date." Lillimae leaned forward and gave me a conspiratorial look, then added in a low voice, "And you knock yourself out too . . . if you know what I mean." I was glad that she didn't encourage me to change my plans.

I was not worried about Roscoe coming to the house and meeting Lillimae when he did not know about her in advance. He got along with everybody. Therefore, I knew that the two of them would hit it off. My main concern was my mother and her reaction when she found out that I'd let one of Daddy's other children move into the house that meant so much to her.

Lillimae reared back on her thick legs, slapped her hands on her spacious hips, and frowned as she looked me up and down. Her lips barely moved as she let out a loud yelp. "My God! Your hips have practically disappeared! You done lost almost half of yourself, ain't you?"

"Almost. I've lost a little over a hundred pounds since the last time I saw you," I replied, sucking in my stomach and patting my almost-slender hip.

Lillimae gently slapped the side of her head. "You poor thing, you. It's that bad, huh? Somethin' kept tellin' me that your life had become as raggedy as a hillbilly's teeth. I'm sorry to see that I was right." My sister and I called one another up on a regular basis. She knew that Pee Wee and I were separated, and why. "It's a cryin' shame that you've been neglectin' your health and not even eatin' right all on account of a man. Well, don't you worry none, sugar pie. I'm here to help you get your life back together."

This was a strange comment coming from a woman who had just left her own husband.

"We can still be happy, husbands or no husbands. I know for a fact that they are makin' sex toys these days that are twice as good as the real things," Lillimae chortled with an exaggerated wink and a loud sniff as she looked toward the kitchen. "Mmmm. Somethin' sure smells good. Greens, I suspect."

I had cooked some cabbage greens two days ago. Only a dog with a keen sense of smell, or somebody like my sister, could still smell those greens. "You're right," I laughed. "And there's plenty left in the refrigerator."

"Good!" she hollered, clapping her hands like a trained seal. "Girl, you wouldn't believe the pooh-butt snacks they gave us on the plane! It would make Mickey Mouse weep! One pack of peanuts an hour after the plane left Miami, and after that, all we got was an itty-bitty pack of pretzels! And if that wasn't stingy enough, those airline scrooges made us *pay* four dollars for an itty-bitty plastic cup of wine! *Four dollars, girl!* I don't know what this world is comin' to! I'd better hurry up and eat a little somethin' before I pass out." Lillimae fanned her face some more and swayed a little, an indication that she was gearing up for a feast.

I motioned for her to sit down. She plopped down on the couch so hard its legs squeaked like mice. I eased down on the love seat facing her.

"Well, like I said, there is plenty of food and alcohol in the house."

"Praise the Lord for that," Lillimae swooned. "After I fortify myself with a few plates of food, then I'll get settled in. Is that first bedroom at the top of the steps still empty? The one closest to the toilet?"

"No, that's where my daughter sleeps. She's spending the night with Muh'Dear and Daddy. You can put your things in the room next to hers. How long do you plan to visit us?"

"Honey chile, I just might stay up here 'til the cows come home. I want to teach

Freddie a real good lesson this time. Maybe Pee Wee can introduce me to one of his men friends. My coochie could sure use some fresh meat, and a mighty big piece, I declare." Lillimae giggled like a horny schoolgirl. "Freddie is the only man I've been with in twenty years. Ain't that a damn shame?"

I didn't think that it was a bad thing for my sister to have been faithful to her husband for twenty years. As a matter of fact, I admired her for doing so. "I took my marriage vows real serious."

"I wish that I could say the same thing about myself," I admitted, looking at the floor. I looked up in time to see the embarrassed look on Lillimae's face.

"Uh, I only slipped up a few times durin' the last twenty years," she confessed. "But I didn't get caught like you did. As far as Freddie and everybody else knows, my record as a virtuous woman is spotless. Speakin' of Pee Wee, did he move back home with you yet?" Lillimae looked around the living room, then back to me with both of her eyebrows raised. "Last time me and you talked, things were goin' real good between you and him." She wobbled up from the couch and waddled over to me. She leaned down and hugged me with both arms and patted my back.

"Things are not going too well between Pee Wee and me right now," I told her, my voice cracking. "That woman he left me for, she claims she's pregnant by him."

Lillimae's mouth dropped open and her eyes got big. She shuffled back to the couch with a groan. "Why, that heifer! Oh, good gracious alive! You poor thing, you! Sugar, are you all right? That's a mighty nasty piece of news to swallow."

"I'm doing as well as can be expected," I mouthed. Somehow I managed a weak smile. "Bad news is nothing new to me."

"Wait a minute." Lillimae held up her hand and gave me a curious look. "I thought that wench was the same age as you? Isn't she too old to be havin' a baby?"

I shook my head. "I guess she wasn't."

"Well, it looks like I got back up here just in time. Like I said, don't you worry none, sugar. I am goin' to help you get through this mess."

"I'm glad to hear that." I looked toward the front door. "And we'll have a nice long talk once you get unpacked and settled. Are you sure you don't mind spending the evening alone? My date is probably on his way, so it's too late for me to call him up and cancel our plans," I said, looking at my watch again. "Feel free to make yourself

88

right at home," I added. "You know where the bathrooms and kitchen are."

"After the way they neglected us on that airplane, I'm goin' to eat and drink myself into a spasm," Lillimae assured me, looking toward the kitchen again. "As you can see, I haven't let a bad marriage or anything else interfere with my appetite." She laughed as she lifted one of her massive thighs and gave it a mighty slap.

"Everything is where I always keep it," I chuckled. "There are extras in the freezer in the basement and in the pantry."

I knew that I had to talk to Pee Wee again soon. He hadn't called since I hung up on him earlier, but I knew that it was just a matter of time before I heard from him again. Lizzie's pregnancy had already become a major thorn in my side, and it had not even been twenty-four hours since she'd dropped her bombshell.

I was tempted to call Pee Wee up, but I wasn't sure yet what I wanted to say to him next. In the meantime, I was looking forward to getting out of the house for a few hours — and with another man. I knew that if I kept myself busy and distracted, I would spend less time sitting around fuming about Lizzie.

In spite of Lillimae's unexpected appearance, this felt like one of my blackest Fridays ever. But it was just the beginning of one of the most destructive, multilayered catastrophes in my life.

CHAPTER 10

"Your sister Lillimae sure seems like a real nice lady. Her Southern accent is almost as cute as your girl Rhoda's is. Now, your sister is *way* on the heavy side, but a lot of men like a woman with a set of nice healthy ham hocks below her waist. I didn't know you had folks still down in Florida," Roscoe said with a curious look on his face. "She got out of that dangerous state just in time, huh? Down there the folks are getting shot up on the street in broad daylight, and by people that they don't even know."

The world-famous fashion designer Gianni Versace had been gunned down a week ago. Each day since then, the TV and radio reported every new development. Today's news had announced that Versace's alleged assassin had taken the coward's way out and committed suicide by shooting himself in the head on somebody's unoccupied houseboat. Lillimae had enjoyed a cup of coffee in the News Café where Versace had read his last newspaper and consumed his last cup of cappuccino. Tears formed in her eyes when she told me how he had eagerly autographed a napkin for her just as she was about to begin her mail delivery responsibilities on that fateful morning.

"Yes, my sister got out of that dangerous state in time," I agreed. "It's a shame about Versace getting shot down like that in front of his own house," I lamented.

"Well, that just goes to show you that death does not discriminate between the rich and the poor. That dago designer had more money than God, and it still didn't keep him from getting shot down in the street like a brother in the 'hood."

Roscoe had arrived right on time, like he always did. His punctuality was one of the things that I liked about him. Within five minutes after I had introduced him to Lilli-mae, they started drinking wine and chatting like they'd known each other for years. "We could have brought your sister along with us," Roscoe said as he backed his shiny black Camry out of my driveway. "I wouldn't have minded her company at all. But I didn't know you had white kinfolk."

"She and I have the same father," I explained. I was not in the mood to elaborate, but Roscoe was one of the nosiest men I knew, so he didn't let up until I had told him the whole story. When I told him that my parents had resumed their relationship after a thirty-year separation, he almost drove into a streetlight.

"Damn! Your mama must be one understanding woman to take back a man who left her for another woman, married her, and had kids with her."

"I don't know if my mother is what most people would call 'understanding,' " I said with a chuckle.

"Shit! She must be. I know how you sisters can be — especially sisters you and your mama's age. Y'all don't take no mess like a man making babies with another woman too lightly. I mean, take you for instance."

"For instance what?" The conversation was making me uncomfortable, but I knew that the only way to get it out of the way was to ride it out.

"For instance, you didn't waste any time kicking Pee Wee to the curb when he shit all over you to be with that Lizzie woman. In the first place, I can't imagine what was going through that brother's head for him to choose a woman with a defect like Lizzie got, that shriveled-up leg. I bet she can't even walk a straight line! Why a man like Pee Wee would leave a normal-legged woman like you for one with legs two different sizes is beyond my scope."

"Lizzie had polio when she was a child. She can't help having a leg that's slightly thinner than the other," I said.

"Oh well. That just goes to show you that to some men, tail is tail," Roscoe chortled. "But you are still a woman with a lot to offer a man. You kept your head up high and kept on stepping. You didn't have a breakdown or slash the tires on Pee Wee's car like my boy Ernest Porter's wife did to him. You've got real good self-control for a black woman. That kind of discipline is hard for a woman to maintain. Especially one that must be as lonesome as you must get on some of these long nights when I'm not with you! That's what I like about you. You didn't drop down like a dying horse and wallow in self-pity. You didn't roll over and take Pee Wee back like your mama did with your daddy — and I hope you don't. Continue to be like your mama, girl. Strong! Women like y'all can put up with any and everything, and still land on your feet."

My being like my mother was a scary thought.

I didn't feel like telling Roscoe again that it had taken my mother over thirty years to forgive my father enough to allow him back into her life. But I had to remind him that I was not my mother. "I refuse to put up with any and everything. I'm not like my mother."

"Ha! Yes, you are! You might not realize it, but I do! A woman like your mama is the kind of woman a man like me can appreciate." Roscoe glanced at me. The way his jaw started twitching, I thought he was gearing up to say something else that I really didn't want to hear. I was right. "Uh, I . . . I have to ask you something," he stammered.

I looked at the side of his head as he maneuvered his car down the street at such a cautious crawl that you would have thought he was leading a funeral procession. He was holding on to the steering wheel with both hands. He glanced at me again, but promptly returned his attention to the road.

"What do you want to ask me, Roscoe?"

"Seriously, is there a chance that you and Pee Wee might get back together? Not that I got anything against him, but I was hoping I'd have a future with you, Annette. I've been looking for a woman like you all my life." Roscoe had begun to sound like a lovesick schoolboy.

"I don't know what's going to happen between Pee Wee and me. And if you don't mind, he's one subject that I'd rather not discuss tonight."

"No problem. I'm cool with that." Roscoe didn't seem too cool with that to me. He sounded like a disappointed child. The pout on his face confirmed my opinion. "That's fine with me. I understand," he replied, lifting one hand off the steering wheel. "I was just hoping that I could find out exactly where I stand with you now, that's all."

"I enjoy your company, Roscoe. You know I do. But I don't want to get too serious too soon." I gave him a big smile as I squeezed the side of his arm. That seemed to please him for the time being.

"I see." He caressed the side of my face. A few seconds later when he stopped for a red light, he leaned over and kissed me on the cheek. Then he added, "I guess I can live with that for the time being."

We rode in silence for the next five minutes. Suddenly, he began to yip yap like a magpie about things of no importance to me — sports, his job, the grout in his bathroom, and his mama's health.

Roscoe sometimes seemed like he had a mild split personality disorder. There were times when I correctly predicted what he was going to say or do, and there were times when he surprised me and did something that I didn't expect. Tonight was one of the nights that he surprised me.

Without a word, he cruised past the restaurant where he had reserved a booth with a candlelit table for us to have a quiet dinner. I promptly brought that to his attention. He promptly told me that he had decided to take me to his house instead. "I didn't think you'd mind if I canceled our reservation."

"No, not really. But it would have been nice for you to let me know before now," I mouthed.

Roscoe lived alone on the outskirts of town, across the street from the city park and two blocks from the steel mill where Rhoda's husband, Otis, worked. "I'm kind of in the mood for a quiet evening at home," he grinned, not even bothering to ask if the change of plans was all right with me.

Since I liked the big white house that Roscoe had recently remodeled and because it was in such a nice scenic location, I didn't protest. "That's fine with me." I smiled.

"Good! I figured you'd say that," he gushed. "See, that's what I'm talking about. You are the kind of low-maintenance woman that a real man can appreciate, on account of you are so easy to please."

I was somewhat disappointed that he'd changed our plans without consulting me, but I decided that I'd get something out of it anyway. I didn't want to admit to him that I was glad we were not going to be around a mob of people in a busy restaurant. After the day that I had endured, I needed to be somewhere with some peace and quiet. That was one thing. Another thing was that Roscoe had a large garden in his backyard. It contained a variety of fruit and vegetables that he often sold at the farmers' market on weekends during the summer and fall. I could load up on strawberries, potatoes, tomatoes, yams, or cucumbers; maybe all of them. And if I got a little sex, too, that would be an additional bonus. That made me smile, but not for long. Sex with Roscoe was rare to say the least. Very rare. In the three months that we had been together, we had made love only three times. Actually, it was two-and-a-half times. During the middle of the second time, we had to stop so I could go use the bathroom. When I returned to his bedroom five minutes later, he had put his pajamas back on and was snoring like a moose.

"I hate to bring this subject up, but my

lumbago's been bothering me all week. I can't get too romantic tonight," he told me, casting a few nervous glances my way. "I hope that's all right with you." I couldn't figure out why Roscoe even bothered to be apologetic anymore. Now that I knew what I knew about him, the one thing that I didn't expect to do with him when we got together was have sex. "Sex is not all that it's cracked up to be anyway, huh?"

"No, it's not," I agreed, my smile fading. It was moments like this that I missed Pee Wee the most.

CHAPTER 11

I assumed that Roscoe was going to have some takeout items delivered. He surprised me again when we entered his house. As soon as he clicked on the living room light, he led me straight to the kitchen.

"I hope you like smothered chops and gravy over garlic mashed potatoes," he told me with excitement in his voice. Roscoe was a good cook for a man, and surprisingly fit for one who liked to indulge himself with all of the foods that liked to stick to a person's body. "I thought that a home-cooked meal would be more enjoyable than us going to a restaurant. I just plucked those red skin potatoes out of my garden this evening," he told me, removing his brown corduroy jacket, which was too heavy for the warm summer night. It had been some-what chilly most of the day, but now the temperature had risen to the mid-eighties.

"Tell me what I can do to help," I suggested, squinting at a pile of dirty dishes in the sink. "I should probably wash those dishes."

"I'm glad you brought that up on your own! I was just about to tell you to do just that! And after you finish washing the dishes, go out in the garden and pick us a bowl of strawberries for our dessert."

I had to keep reminding myself that Roscoe was a harmless distraction. And right now I needed a distraction more than I needed a lover. Especially one whose bedroom skills were still at the level of a teenage boy anyway.

Other than my estranged husband, Pee Wee, whose real name was Jerry Davis, Roscoe was one of the other two men that I was currently dating. He had lost his wife, Joyce, to breast cancer a year ago. They'd been married for thirty years, so he was having a hard time adjusting to single life again. When it came to looks, Roscoe was no Denzel Washington, but he was no creature from the black lagoon either. He had thick, silky black and gray hair, and smooth, cinnamon-colored skin. Except for a nose that looked something like a boomerang, his facial features were fairly pleasant to look at. He had been doing heavy construction work for more than twenty years, so he had a fairly nice body for a man in his early fifties.

One of the first things that Roscoe had told me at the beginning of our relationship was that sex was not, and had never been, that high on his list of priorities for years. Then he told me one of the strangest stories that I had ever heard. According to him, when he was sixteen and still a virgin, his stepfather took him to a prostitute to "break him in." The insensitive hooker had made fun of his clumsy performance, and it had depressed him for months. His next few times with other females had been just as traumatic. At that point, he put sex on the back burner. He didn't attempt to do it again until his wedding night, several years later. By then, his sex drive had practically disappeared.

Since Pee Wee's sex drive had once slowed down because of a medical condition, I felt a lot of sympathy for Roscoe. I told myself that if I could survive without sex from Pee Wee for a whole year, I could survive without it from Roscoe for as long as necessary.

During the drought that I had suffered through with Pee Wee, I'd turned to another man for intimate comfort, but I had done it behind closed doors. But now with Pee Wee and me being separated, I didn't have to sneak around with other men. And just so I wouldn't get myself into any embarrassing situations, I always made sure each man in my life knew that I was dating others.

Even without much sex, I liked Roscoe enough to stay in the relationship anyway.

After we'd devoured our dinner and settled onto the crushed velvet couch in his neat living room with a bottle of wine on the coffee table and Miles Davis on the cassette player, he turned to me and gave me a pitiful look.

"Annette, please don't get mad, but I need to discuss something important with you," he said in a shy voice. "I can't put it off any longer."

I blinked a few times and shook my head. I was glad that I had already filled up a bowl with some strawberries to take home, in case Roscoe said something that might make me mad enough to leave in a huff. "I won't get mad," I told him.

First, he cleared his throat, scratched the side of his head, rotated his neck, and moved a few inches away from me. He also took a long drink from his wineglass. These were not good signs.

Roscoe began to speak like he was reading from a cue card. "I know that you have a lot of feelings for me, but . . ." he paused and scratched his chin.

"If you are trying to tell me that you want to date other women, that's fine with me," I assured him. "I told you from the beginning that I was going to continue to see other men."

"Yeah, you sure did, but I don't want to see any woman but you. I've been looking for a woman like you all my life."

"I see. Well, if you are trying to tell me that you want me to date only you —"

"Oh no! I am not going to ask you to stop seeing other men! Not yet anyway." Roscoe paused and poured himself another drink. He took a long swallow before he returned his attention to me. "Oh shit! I . . . I'm having a hard time saying what I want to say."

"Maybe this is something we should discuss at another time," I suggested. "We don't want to ruin our evening."

Roscoe shook his head. "Now is as good a time as any, I guess. Look, baby. I didn't want to tell you this, but I was happy to hear from Carl Hopper who works at the gas station on Morgan Street that Pee Wee got Lizzie Stovall pregnant. If you do divorce him now, I'd be happy to marry you. You are a good cook and you do real good household chores. Even better than that trifling cleaning woman I just fired —

and I was paying her."

I didn't know whether to laugh or cry. For one thing, I had no desire to jump into another marriage, especially since I was still in one that seemed to be flying out the window at breakneck speed. And as much as I liked Roscoe, being married to him didn't sound too appealing.

He needed a housekeeper more than he needed a wife. A couple of hours ago, while he was still cooking our dinner, he had asked me to run the Dirt Devil over his new carpet. One reason that I did domestic favors for Roscoe was because he usually spent a lot of money on me when we did go out for a night on the town. Since our sex life was practically nonexistent, I figured that a few housekeeping chores for him was the least I could do.

"You already know that I am no sex maniac like a lot of these men around here. If you were my wife, I wouldn't pester you every night in the bedroom like I know Pee Wee probably did."

I looked at Roscoe and blinked some more.

"I am flattered that you care enough about me to want me to be your wife. But there is too much going on in my life right now for me to even think about a long-term relationship with another man," I said, my voice cracking.

He gave me a blank look. I couldn't decide if he was desperate, confused, or what. And that made me feel sorry for him. I was fond of him, but he was probably the last man in the world that I wanted to be married to.

"Annette, I'll say it again; I've been looking for a woman like you all my life."

"If you don't mind, let's discuss this subject at another time," I suggested, glancing at my watch. "And I think I should be getting back home."

Roscoe drove me home a few minutes later.

As soon as his car stopped in front of my house, my porch light came on. Muh'Dear's face immediately appeared in the living room window. She didn't even try to hide behind the curtains and peep out like a normal nosy person was supposed to. She stood there in plain sight with her hand shading her eyes, looking at me like I was something good to eat.

CHAPTER 12

Muh'Dear snatched open my front door and stood in the doorway with her arms folded and a severe scowl on her face. "Who was that?" she demanded as soon as I walked up on the porch. She had on the drab, dark green smock that she wore to work. That, and her demeanor, made her look like a prison warden.

"Don't you remember Roscoe? I met him at the Easter church picnic," I responded, gently waving my mother out of the doorway so I could enter the house. "You've been buying vegetables and fruit from his garden all summer."

"What about that Ronald Hawthorne? I thought you was foolin' around with him."

"Uh . . . I'm still dating him too." I gave my mother a guarded look and braced myself for her response. "I'm not serious about either one of them," I quickly added. "Roscoe is a fun guy, and I like spending time with him."

"What in the world do you think you doin', girl?" Muh'Dear asked, following me across the floor.

"Do you mean me dating two men at the same time?" I asked dumbly, moving toward the couch with her so close behind she was stepping on my heels.

"That ain't what I'm talkin' about!" I could smell the BENGAY that Muh'Dear had slathered over various parts of her body, a nightly ritual of hers for years.

"Then what are you talking about?" I asked as I set the large Tupperware bowl that I had filled with strawberries from Roscoe's garden on the coffee table. I removed the blue knitted shawl that I'd worn over my matching blue dress and placed it across the back of the wing chair in front of my big-screen TV.

"You know damn well what I'm talkin' about, gal!" Muh'Dear hissed. "You ain't got no shame. What I want to know is what you got to say for yourself this time?"

"This time? What do you mean by that?" I asked as I plopped down on the couch, breathing through my mouth. I kicked off my shoes, crossed my legs, and began to massage my left foot. "I don't know what I should be ashamed of, Muh'Dear. It's no secret that I have a social life. I told you earlier today when we were talking that I had a date tonight."

Muh'Dear narrowed her eyes and gave me an impatient look. "Didn't you just hear what I said? I ain't talkin' about them men you foolin' around with," she snapped, pointing toward the steps leading to the rooms upstairs. "You know what I'm talkin' about."

"Oh, I guess you're talking about Lillimae being here," I muttered, rolling my eyes.

"Yes, I'm talkin' about that Lillimae bein' here. After all I done said to you today, you got your daddy's white child up in this house *again* anyway? Didn't you hear all what I said to you about Frank's other kids? Why didn't you tell me then what you was cookin' up?"

I was tired, and not remotely interested in doing battle with my mother. I had things a lot more critical on my mind that I needed to be concerned about. The news about Lizzie's pregnancy had not really sunk in yet, but I knew that when it did, I was probably not going to be the most pleasant company for anybody to be around. I could already feel the knots forming in my stomach and the bile rising in my throat.

I did not enjoy having this conversation

with Muh'Dear. What I really wanted to do was run upstairs, dive into my bed, and pull the covers up over my head.

"What's Lillimae doin' up here, Annette? You know how I feel about that woman in this house."

"Muh'Dear, I didn't even know that she was coming up here until she showed up this evening. She has left her husband again and needed a place to stay until she decides what to do next," I explained. "She had no place else to go."

"Well, this ain't the place for her to go! You know better! Ain't you in enough of a mess with your own husband?"

"Muh'Dear, keep your voice down. She'll hear you," I whispered. The only light on downstairs was the one in the living room, so I assumed Lillimae was upstairs. "We don't want her to hear us," I said with the hint of a smile on my face. "She's company."

"Company? Company my foot. She's the result of your daddy's shame, and she's come to rub herself in our faces again. I don't care if she hears me! I tried to call you before I came over here, but the cab that I called showed up quicker than I expected." Even though my mother owned an Altima that was only a few months old and my father owned a truck, she often rode around in cabs. She didn't like to drive at night, and she didn't like the way Daddy drove. Besides, he was so grumpy and nervous now, that riding in a vehicle with him behind the wheel was like riding on a roller coaster. And his mind was not as sharp as it used to be. A trip that normally took everybody else a few minutes to drive usually took him up to an hour.

"Muh'Dear, don't get mad, but I am kind of glad Lillimae came up here. She really needs my support, and with this latest mess with Pee Wee and Lizzie that I'm going through, I need some emotional support too. Lillimae has always offered her shoulder for me to cry on."

"Oh? Since when was my shoulder not good enough for you to cry on?"

"I didn't say that —"

"You don't need her as long as you got me."

"Muh'Dear, you are not being reasonable," I protested.

"Reasonable, my foot. I am bein' a mother. I can give you all of the emotional support you need. When you can't catch up with me, you can always find your god-mother Scary Mary and get some emotional assistance from her."

After all of these years, I still didn't have

the heart to tell my mother that she and my godmother were often the reasons I needed to cry on somebody's shoulder. Between the two of them, I got badgered and harassed enough for three people.

"Muh'Dear, I am sorry that you feel the way you do, but I can't please everybody. Now, Lillimae is here, so let's make the best of it," I bleated.

I was already tired of defending Lillimae, and she had only been in the house for a few hours! But as long as Muh'Dear or anybody else trashed her, I would defend her. As far as I knew, Lillimae had done nothing to deserve even the slightest bit of hostility. "Muh'Dear, Lillimae is a really nice person once you get to know her," I declared. "She's one of the nicest women I know."

"Only in a pig's eye. I know she's after somethin'," Muh'Dear insisted.

"I can't imagine what that something could be. I don't have anything that Lillimae doesn't already have," I shot back. "I wish I could be more like her."

Despite Lillimae's estranged husband's multiple flaws, she had supported him and their two sons on her own for years at a time. She had even helped support half of her in-laws. Before I'd left to go out with

Roscoe, she told me the main reason that she had left her husband: He'd slapped her because she sassed his mama. That didn't sound like a good enough reason for a woman to quit her job and run away from home, but I didn't get in my sister's business, unless she invited me to do so. I knew that there was more to her story than her face getting slapped, but it didn't take a genius to figure out that that slap was the straw that broke the camel's back. I was just happy that we had each other's shoulders to cry on. Besides, I knew that Lillimae would eventually tell me all she wanted me to know about her breakup.

I couldn't stop myself from recalling what Rhoda had said to me about Lillimae and how important she was to me. Since I'd met Lillimae and gotten to know her, not once did I ever wish that my daddy had never slept with her mother. But that still didn't stop me from wishing that Pee Wee had never slept with Lizzie.

I didn't like having to listen to or respond to Muh'Dear's less than pleasant comments about my beloved sister. I loved my mother in spite of the many flaws in her personality. She was still my most important role model. She had raised me to be strong and independent. Unfortunately, when it came to dealing with her, those qualities usually worked against me. Despite the fact that she'd overcome poverty and so many other obstacles, and was now one of the wealthiest black women in Richland, Muh'Dear was also my biggest critic. As far as she was concerned, her opinion of me was the only one that really mattered. And even though I was approaching fifty, she still took it upon herself to tell me how to live my life.

"Muh'Dear, I'm tired. It's been a long day for me, and all I really want to do now is get some rest."

My mother gave me a weary look. "I bet you are tired. That Roscoe looks like a bull. I was raised on a farm, so I know how frisky bulls can be. . . ."

"Oh, come on now! Let's not go *there*," I retorted with my hand in the air and my eyes rolling from side to side like marbles. My mother and I had some tense conversations from time to time. But there was one subject that I absolutely did not feel comfortable discussing with her: my sex life.

I just shook my head. Rhoda was the only person I'd told about Roscoe's lack of interest in sex. That was not the kind of information an opinionated blabbermouth like my mother needed to know. I decided to divert the subject back to Lillimae. It was the less painful of the two. "I hope you didn't hurt my sister's feelings, Muh'Dear."

"No, I didn't hurt your sister's feelin's. I was real nice to her, but she ain't as stupid as she looks. She got real good sense for a white woman. She knows I don't care too much for her."

My mother said a lot of things that could have easily been construed as racist, but that was hardly the case. She had a lot of white friends. I knew that she would have been just as bitter if a black woman had stolen my daddy.

"What is that white woman gwine to do for money while she's stayin' with you? A woman her size must spend a fortune on food every week." Muh'Dear glanced toward the kitchen with a pinched look on her face.

"That's for sure. I used to be a woman that same size, and I spent more on groceries than I spent on all of my other bills put together," I admitted.

From the way Muh'Dear's lips were quivering, it looked like she wanted to laugh. Instead, she clamped her lips together and shook her head. But the amused look remained on her face anyway. "This ain't about you. It's about that woman and how she is goin' to support herself while she's in this house."

"You don't have to worry about that. She brought enough money and credit cards with her to last a few months," I replied. That was true. Lillimae had emptied out the joint savings account that she shared with her estranged husband, and she had cashed in some bonds. She had also sold most of her jewelry. She informed me that she would split the cost of the utility bills and pay for half of our groceries for as long as she stayed.

Muh'Dear gasped so hard that her top dentures shifted and almost popped out of her mouth. She clamped them back into place and continued her rant, but speaking more slowly. "A few months? She plans on stayin' in this house for a few months? Lord help me! Girl, you have truly lost your mind, ain't you?"

I knew that no matter how I answered my mother's last question, she wouldn't be satisfied, so I ignored it. I looked around the living room. "Did you bring Charlotte home?" I asked.

"She was asleep when I left the house. Curled up on my couch like a snail. I came over here so I could be here to soothe you when you got home from your date. I know firsthand how painful it is for a woman to hear that her husband done shoved a bun into another woman's oven." Muh'Dear gave me a look that made me feel like the most mistreated woman in history. I was surprised that I was still conscious. She sucked on her teeth before she allowed herself to release a hearty, open-mouth cackle; one that could have easily dislodged her dentures again if she did it for too long. She stopped abruptly, as if she knew what I was thinking. "I about dropped to the floor when I stepped into your livin' room and seen Lillimae on that couch, lappin' up wine like a seal. And drinkin' out of one of them monogrammed wineglasses that I gave you for your birthday last year that you told me you'd only use for special occasions."

I was glad when the telephone rang on the end table. Other than my mother, it was the last person in the world I wanted to speak to at the moment: Pee Wee.

"Annette, I talked to Lizzie after I talked to you this mornin'," he began. "Uh, yeah, she is pregnant. I met up with her and . . . I . . . I saw the doctor's report. I'm comin' over tomorrow to talk to you about it."

CHAPTER 13

"Oh." That was all I could say at the moment. Pee Wee had confirmed Lizzie's pregnancy, and it had almost left me speechless. Hearing the shocking news had been painful enough coming from her, but hearing it from Pee Wee made it sound like a death sentence. If this didn't kill our marriage, nothing could.

"Annette, are you all right? It sounds like you're cryin'," Pee Wee said. Yes, I was crying, and it sounded like he was about to do the same thing.

"I'm fine. I just choked on some air," I lied. The inside of my throat felt like somebody had just scraped it with sandpaper. I had sobs forming in me that were so massive I couldn't even squeeze them out. I just stood there sucking hot, stale air into my lungs. I sounded like a drowning man. I was having such a difficult time breathing, I had to open my mouth and lift my chin up so high that I almost slid off the couch. Some-how, after only a few seconds, I managed to get some more words out. "Uh, we can talk about this when you come over here."

My mind was reeling. I could not believe what Pee Wee had just told me.

PREGNANT! Right now that word sounded like the most obscene term in the English language. It stung my eardrum like a wasp! Hearing that Pee Wee had actually seen the proof in a doctor's report was almost more than I could stand. Now I could easily see how people snapped and lost all control of their senses. I felt like go-ing outside and running up and down the sidewalk screaming like a banshee. But what good would that do? Lizzie would still be pregnant *by my husband!*

For a moment, I forgot that my mother was still in the room. "Who was that?" she asked, looking at the telephone in my hand.

"Uh, nobody," I mumbled.

"Now, you know you can talk to me about anything. But if you don't want me to know your business, just say so," Muh'Dear told me. My mother could pout better than a two-year-old. Her bottom lip was sticking out so far, it extended beyond the tip of her nose. "But if you do want me to know, tell me quick so I can give you some good advice."

"I said it was nobody," I repeated, giving her a dismissive wave. "Nobody important."

There was a lot that I wanted to say to Pee Wee about this turn of events. And I would do just that when I saw him again, but only if he and I were alone. My mother was going to be all over my case again soon enough. There was no doubt in my mind about that. And so would everybody else I knew. This was the kind of scandal that the people I knew reveled in.

"Nobody? Your telephone rang, you picked it up. Somebody was callin'. And they must have said somethin' mighty bad for you to have such a sour look on your face now."

"It was just somebody from work," I lied. "There's been a small emergency at the office."

"This time of night?"

"Uh, it was something that happened earlier. Right after I left to come home."

"Oh. You need to be more like me, you know. I told my people not to call me after work hours unless the restaurant was on fire. Whatever your coworker just said, it must not have been too nice for you to be screwin' your face up like you just bit into a rotten lemon."

"It's nothing, Muh'Dear," I insisted.

Muh'Dear gave me a suspicious look, but at least she dropped the subject. "So what are you gwine to do about Pee Wee? Especially now."

"What do you mean by that?"

"Girl, you know what I mean by that. Everybody is talkin' about Lizzie bein' pregnant with Pee Wee's baby. And I do mean everybody."

"News sure travels fast around this town! I wish those women at Claudette's beauty shop would mind their own business. This is something that you should have heard first from me, not those gossips," I boomed.

"I didn't hear it at the beauty shop first. I heard it first from my butcher when I went to get some neck bones this mornin', before I even got to the beauty shop. He plays checkers with Lizzie's stepdaddy. Wouldn't it be a shame if Lizzie gives Pee Wee the son he always wanted?"

I couldn't stand another minute of Muh'Dear's comments. I knew that she thought she was being supportive, and she was. But her kind of support was usually just as destructive as the source of my pain. "Muh'Dear, I hate to be rude," I groaned, wobbling up off the couch. "But if you are not going to spend the night, please go on back home so I can get some sleep. There are a lot of things that I need to sort out in my mind."

Muh'Dear looked at me with a tortured look on her face. "Uh-huh. I guess you better get some sleep because you look like a mud puppy. We'll deal with this Lillimae problem later. But I hope you agree with me that the main thing you need to figure out now is what you are gwine to do about that Lizzie baby-mama drama."

"What do you mean? Exactly what am I supposed to do about Lizzie's baby? I have no say-so about that subject whatsoever."

Muh'Dear gasped so loud and hard, her eyes rolled back in her head. "What are you gwine to do when you see *it?*" The way she practically spat out the last word made "it" sound like a cuss word. It was an innocent baby that she was talking about. And from the looks of things, the father was my husband.

DAMN!

In spite of my anger, I knew that it was in my best interest for me to keep things in perspective. A baby was a baby, and there had not been a single one yet who had asked to be born.

"Muh'Dear, Lizzie is carrying an innocent child, not the anti-Christ. I hope it's healthy,

122

and that she raises it right."

For a brief moment, my mother looked disappointed, as if she had not expected me to show any compassion on this subject. But I did. That baby did not ask to be conceived, and I could not allow myself to harbor any resentment toward him or her.

I knew that I could not change what had already happened. I decided that it would be easier for me to be somewhat sympathetic than for me to let my anger consume me. At the end of the day, Lizzie would still be carrying my husband's child, or so she claimed. . . .

Muh'Dear gave me a pitiful look as she shook her head. "Oh, it'll be raised right as long as Pee Wee is involved. And he will be if that wench stays in this town. With Pee Wee bein' such a do-right man, he'll do the right thing, like he always does. Well, not always. If he did always do the right thing, we wouldn't be talkin' about him and this woman havin' his baby in the first place." Muh'Dear paused as if to give me time to process what she'd just said. I guess I didn't react fast enough to suit her. She snorted and gave me one of her meanest looks. Then she continued, "Pee Wee's daddy, may he rest in peace 'til the rest of us join him up yonder in heaven, he raised Pee Wee up right. Pee Wee'll take care of that child the way that a man is supposed to. I know 'cause I seen him do it with Charlotte. The pope couldn't have done a better job of raisin' a child."

"I'm going to bed," I reminded her, glancing at my watch. "I'm so tired I can barely keep my eyes open." My stomach had begun to churn. It took all of my strength for me to keep down the pork-chop dinner that Roscoe had prepared.

"I let my cab go," my mother whined. "And you know that I ain't about to call your daddy and make him come pick me up this time of night. If you ain't too tired, you can drive me home."

"I'll call you another cab," I said quickly, already dialing the cab station number. My fingers felt and looked like grilled hot links. I knew it was just my imagination, so I didn't let that bother me, especially since my body was letting me down in so many other ways. For one thing, my throat felt like thorns were growing in it on all sides. My stomach felt like it contained more gas than anything else. And my eyes felt like somebody had rubbed them with raw onions.

I was glad that Muh'Dear didn't mention my situation with Pee Wee any more during the ten minutes that it took for her cab to arrive. But she spent the whole time talking about Lillimae like a dog. By the time she left, I had a headache on both sides of my head.

I don't know how I managed to get to sleep that night. I woke up around four in the morning in my bed under the covers, but I was still in my street clothes. As hard as I tried, I could not get back to sleep. Even listening to some soft jazz on the radio and trying to watch a religious program on the portable TV on my dresser didn't do me any good. I could not concentrate on either one, and I couldn't fall asleep.

Around five-thirty, I wobbled up out of bed. I went downstairs to the kitchen and warmed up a glass of milk. It soothed my aching throat. But my head was still throbbing, and so was most of the rest of my body, even my ears. Each time I recalled Pee Wee telling me that Lizzie's pregnancy had been confirmed, my ears suffered, even more so than my weary brain.

Rhoda had told me that she would come over before noon, but I had no idea what time Pee Wee was planning to visit. Somehow I managed to doze off again.

Around seven, the birds started to chirp outside my window. I was still drowsy and disoriented, wondering if everything that had happened the day before had been a dream. When a bird pecked on my window, I perked up real quick. That was the moment that I knew for sure that what was happening to me now was no dream.

CHAPTER 14

I remained in bed listening to a jazz program on the radio until eight-thirty. Knowing that everything that happened the day before had not been a dream made it hard for me to get up and face the day.

After I got tired of listening to the radio, I spent the next hour reading yesterday's edition of our local newspaper.

I didn't want to face Pee Wee or Muh'Dear again anytime soon, or at least not until I'd spent some time with Rhoda. But I couldn't remain in my room too long. I knew that if I did, somebody would barge in on me.

I could smell the sweet aroma of honey-cured bacon floating from the kitchen up to my bedroom. The scent of roses could not have pleased my nose more. My stomach was empty and beginning to growl. But from past experience, I knew that it was going to be a difficult day for me. I knew that I would not be able to eat much, if at all. I took a long shower. After that I spent twenty minutes trying to decide what to wear. I slid into my favorite warm-up suit. Not only was it comfortable, but because it was black, it made me look like I was ten pounds slimmer.

Even though I had on Nike's, my feet felt as heavy as lead as I made my way downstairs to the kitchen.

"Hello, sleepyhead!" Daddy greeted as soon as I entered the kitchen doorway. He occupied a chair across the table from Lillimae. My daughter, Charlotte, looking more like her daddy than ever, stood behind Daddy with her hands on the back of his chair. "I got over here as soon as I heard Lillimae was back in town." There was a huge smile on my father's scraggly face. I knew that he loved me as much as he loved Lillimae, but I had a feeling that she was his favorite of all his children. That didn't bother me. She was the one who had taken him in and cared for him when her mother left.

"Get in here, girl! There's a mess of grits, bacon, eggs, biscuits, and home fries just waitin' on you to dive in," Lillimae yelled, as she made a sweeping gesture around the table with her plump hand. There was enough food on that table to feed ten people. "Me and Daddy, and this child here, we can't eat another bite. Pee Wee and Rhoda called. They are both on their way over here, and told me to save them a plate."

This was much worse than I thought. A "party" atmosphere was the last thing that I needed right now. Especially when it was going to include Pee Wee.

"I don't have much of an appetite," I mumbled, pouring myself a cup of coffee. "As a matter of fact, I don't feel too good, so I'm going to go back to my room and lie down for a while."

"What's wrong with you, Mama?" Charlotte asked, giving me a concerned look. "You don't sound too good either."

"She don't look too good neither," Daddy noticed. "Annette, child, if you looked any worse, they'd be embalmin' you."

Before I could respond, Charlotte ran up to me and wrapped her arms around my waist, hugging me so tight I could barely breathe. "I know what's wrong with you, Mama, and I know you can't help it," she said, her nose twitching like a nervous rabbit. "You're just a miserable old woman. But don't you worry too much. Daddy'll be here in a little while."

My poor brain felt like it was sizzling on a grill. I knew that things had to be bad if a twelve-year-old was analyzing me. She was right, I was "a miserable old woman." Even though a lot of people loved me, my life seemed somewhat empty and sometimes adrift. There were times when I didn't know which way was up. I couldn't stop thinking that I'd failed as a wife. I didn't have the heart to tell my daughter that her daddy's upcoming visit was one of the reasons I was feeling so down in the dumps.

"I'm all right," I managed. I disguised my unhappy face with a smile that was so tight it made my jaw muscles ache. "I must have eaten something that didn't agree with me." I rubbed my stomach and scrunched up my face like I was in pain. "Somebody holler at me when Pee Wee and Rhoda get here." I left the kitchen as fast as I could. Not because I was being antisocial, but because I didn't want anybody to see the tears forming in my eyes. I lumbered back upstairs, moving my feet like a woman twice my age.

As soon as I reached my room, I looked in the mirror. I did look a bit scary. Dark circles surrounded my eyes like moats. I looked like a brown panda bear. I couldn't stand to look at myself too long without feeling sorry. I dabbed on some liquid makeup and just enough face powder to blend it in. Once I was satisfied with my appearance, I called Rhoda.

"Things aren't going too well over here. If you don't mind, I'd rather come talk to you at your house, instead of you coming over here," I told her, my voice wobbling like a pair of clubbed feet.

"I'm glad you caught me. I was just about to leave the house and head over to your place," Rhoda informed me. "What you just suggested is even better. I need to take a recess from what's goin' on around here, if you know what I mean. . . ."

I did know what Rhoda meant. Her long-time lover Ian "Bully" Bullard, or her "houseguest" as she usually referred to him, had kept her up into the night making love. And with Rhoda's husband, Otis, in the room right next door to the guest room!

"I understand," I croaked. "Tell Bully I said hello."

"You can tell him yourself when you get here," Rhoda gushed. Then she let out a long sigh that was followed by what sounded like a moan of ecstasy. Bully must have really laid her out this time, I thought. She sounded as giddy as a prom queen. "When do you think you'll make it over here?"

Even though I was used to Rhoda acting a fool over Bully, I was still somewhat taken aback. It took me a few moments to respond. "That all depends. I don't know what time Pee Wee is coming over, or how long he's going to stay. By the way, Lizzie *is* pregnant. He called me up last night. He told me that he saw her doctor's report. That's what he's coming to talk to me about."

"Damn. Are you all right?"

"I'm still breathing, but I've had better days. Muh'Dear is not happy about Lilli-mae coming up here, but I'm glad my sister is here. At least her presence will keep me from spending all of my time thinking about this mess with Pee Wee and Lizzie."

"You know that I will do anything I can to help you through this," Rhoda assured me, and I knew she would. She had proved her allegiance to me by killing the man who had raped me throughout my childhood. And she'd gotten away with it!

"All I need is for you to be available for me to talk to when I need you," I said. "Nothing more than that."

Rhoda read me like a book. She knew exactly what I meant by my last comment. I did not want her to do anything foolish to Lizzie, like causing her to have a fatal "accident." Especially now that Lizzie was pregnant.

After I finished my conversation with

Rhoda, I called up Pee Wee. "Can we meet someplace other than my house?" I asked him. "I don't want to talk to you with an audience." I wasn't really asking him to meet me at a different location, I was telling him. "I can meet you at Jonnie Mae's coffee shop across the street from the hospital this afternoon around two."

"Hmm. I already made plans to go to the pool hall around that same time," he grumbled.

"Well, if you really want to talk to me today, you can do it before or after you go to the pool hall."

Pee Wee hesitated for a few seconds. "What time?" he asked.

"In an hour," I suggested. "I'd like to get this over with as soon as possible. It shouldn't take more than a few minutes."

"A few minutes? Annette, this ain't somethin' that we can chitchat about for just a few minutes and be done with. I want to get with you today so I can let you know how I feel about this new development. I was hopin' to spend at least a few hours with you."

"A few hours? Ha! I do not have a few hours to spare to talk about Lizzie today — or any other day. What all is there to say?"

"There is a lot that needs to be said —"

"I can't imagine what. I don't know about you, but what I have to say to you on the subject of another woman having your baby won't take me but a few minutes."

"Look, let's try to get through this with as little pain as possible. I don't know what the hell you want me to do or say now. I can't change what's already happened. But I don't see why we can't continue to move forward with our plans to repair our marriage. I still love you, and I always will. Ain't no woman in the world ever goin' to take your place."

"Don't make me laugh!" I guffawed, long and loud. "Hello? Another woman has already taken my place," I snapped. I thought about the comment that Muh'Dear had made about Lizzie possibly giving Pee Wee the son he'd always wanted. It made me want to scream my lungs out. "I don't know why you keep acting like it's business as usual between us. After what you did, things are never going to be the same between us again."

"Say what? Now, you hold on there, woman! After what *I* did? In the first place, I didn't bust up our marriage by myself. Don't put all of the blame on me. Don't forget that you are the one who started messin' us up first!"

"Listen, *Romeo,* as far as I'm concerned, this conversation is over."

"We can finish it at the café." Pee Wee sounded like a man twice his age. It suddenly dawned on me that he would be close to his late sixties by the time Lizzie's baby finished high school. And so would I. That thought turned my stomach.

"We are finished. There is nothing else to say. Don't bother going to the café, because I won't be meeting you there this time — or any other time. Now that I know Lizzie is pregnant, I know what I have to do. You'll be hearing from my attorney."

"What? I — I — what do you mean by that? Annette, all I know is that the woman is pregnant. I don't even know if that baby really is mine! I won't know until Lizzie has it, and I can get a blood test done. That's supposed to be pretty accurate."

"What if you find out the baby is yours? Then what?"

Pee Wee hesitated; then he said: "I'll love that baby and treat it as good as I treat Charlotte."

Pee Wee was the most successful black barber in Richland. And he had inherited a few properties from his late grandparents in Erie, Pennsylvania. We had both invested wisely over the years, so our estate was quite

135

impressive. Since it looked like Charlotte was going to be our only child — well, *my* only child — there was going to be quite a lot left behind after Pee Wee and I passed on. The thought of Lizzie's child taking half of my daughter's inheritance made my flesh crawl!

"If Lizzie's baby is mine, I will adjust my will, and set up child-support payments through the court," he declared.

"I have to go," I choked, struggling to hold back my tears. "You do what you have to do, Pee Wee. From now on, you don't have to bring over the money for Charlotte. You can send mine through the court, too. . . ."

"Annette, I will still be comin' to that house to see my child. I can bring the money with me then. Don't make this no harder than it already is!" he boomed.

I hung up before he could get another word in edgewise. I was so angry, I was about to explode.

CHAPTER 15

Somehow, I made it through that Saturday without falling apart. But I experienced a lot of anxiety and apprehension throughout the day. Around three that afternoon, I called Rhoda again and told her that I would visit her at another time. I was glad that Pee Wee didn't call back, and I had no desire to call him again anytime soon.

Now I had to deal with the situation downstairs. My daddy loved to reminisce about any and everything. That alone was bad enough. He liked to repeat everything several times. I lost track of the number of times he regaled me and Lillimae with stories about his civil rights activities during the 60s, and all of the times that he had locked horns with the Ku Klux Klan. I noticed how Daddy avoided the subject of him leaving Muh'Dear and me for Lillimae's mother. By the time he left, I was feeling like a hostage in my own home.

Lillimae got up early Sunday morning to fix breakfast, and to fill me in on what she'd been up to since our last telephone conversation. Like Daddy, she repeated herself a lot. She must have told me ten times about how she'd met Versace just before his assassination, and how he had signed a napkin for her. "He had just wiped some cappuccino off his whiskers with the same napkin," she sniffed.

After we'd cleaned up the kitchen, Lillimae borrowed my car. She took Charlotte to the mall for some shopping and a movie. I was glad to be alone so I could sort through my thoughts, which was something I did a lot of these days.

Muh'Dear and Daddy came to the house after they attended church service. As usual, they spent several hours in my living room roasting first one person and then another. They bombarded me with detailed comments that included Sister Ledbetter coming to church in a blond wig, and Brother Crutchfield coming to church with alcohol on his breath. The yip yapping went on for two hours before they got to the finale. Unfortunately, that was Pee Wee and me and our latest problem: Lizzie's pregnancy.

"Maybe you ought to pay that woman off to relocate," Daddy suggested. "As long as she's out of sight, she'll be out of mind. I seen somethin' like that in a movie one time."

Muh'Dear rolled her eyes and looked at Daddy like he had suddenly sprouted horns. "Only a man would believe some hogwash like that!" she snapped. "Even if Lizzie moved to the moon, Pee Wee is gwine to be very active in that baby's life. Especially if it turns out to be the son he always wanted. . . ."

I knew that my parents meant well. But their "support" was like a double-edged sword. No matter what they said, it either made me feel better or it made me feel worse. Unfortunately, their comments generally made me feel worse.

"I know you both care about Pee Wee and me, and I know y'all want what's best for us. That's what I'm praying for too," I said when they finally let me get a word in.

That seemed to satisfy them, because not long after that they left.

I was happy to get back to work on Monday morning. And I was happy now more than ever that Lillimae was in the house. She was more than eager to baby-sit, so Charlotte didn't have to spend time at my parents' house until I got home from work like she usually did.

It was a slow week. Pee Wee left several voice-mail messages that I had not returned by that weekend.

The following Saturday morning, I woke up a few minutes before ten. With three pillows supporting my throbbing head, I remained in bed until I had finished reading the latest edition of the *National Enquirer*. By the time I made my way downstairs, after I'd taken a long shower and read a few pages in last month's *Ebony* magazine, my parents had returned. It was a few minutes past noon. This time Muh'Dear had brought along Scary Mary, her best friend. Scary Mary was one of the most beloved and generous people I knew. But this grumpy, fish-eyed old hag was also the most meddlesome senior citizen in Richland. As the madam of the oldest and most popular brothel in this part of the state, she was also the most brazen woman I knew. She paid more attention to other people's business than her own. Especially mine.

"Annette, I heard the bad news. Tsk, tsk, tsk," Scary Mary began, sucking on her false teeth so hard I was surprised that they didn't slide out of her mouth the way Muh'Dear's often did. A hot iron couldn't smooth out the deep lines and wrinkles on her mulish, nut-brown face. She wore a plaid smock and a pair of black pants. As usual, she had on a pair of men's backless house shoes. She sat on the arm of my couch with her legs crossed. One of her many canes, one with a dragon's head and a brass handle, lay across her lap. A shot glass, with a few drops of what was left of a high ball, was in her hands. "What a mess. When my second husband pulled the same baby-makin' trick on me — with a Chinese hussy — I cooked his goose to a crisp. My divorce settlement took him for everything he had, and then some. I got everything except the gold crowns off his teeth, but when that sorry old sucker died, I got them teeth too! The undertaker was one of my best clients, a coochie-eatin' old goat with a tongue as long as a serpent's. He was a favorite with my girls. Anyway, you need to clean Pee Wee out like you guttin' a hog. If I was you, I would take that barber shop right out from under that nasty buzzard's ass. Pour me another dose of that vodka," Scary Mary told me, waving her shot glass in the air. Distress must have been contagious. Scary Mary was as upset as Muh'Dear.

"Pour me a double of the same stuff," Muh'Dear requested, fanning her face with a rolled-up copy of *Black Enterprise* magazine. "Annette, whatever you do, don't you dare let no man get his paws on the deed to this house so it'll end up in some white woman's hands. . . ."

I just nodded and smiled as I poured more vodka for Muh'Dear and Scary Mary.

"Gussie Mae, ain't you gettin' ahead of things?" Daddy protested with his hand in the air. He shared the couch with Muh'Dear. I was glad he wasn't drinking. Alcohol made him even more talkative.

"I ain't gettin' ahead of nothin' fast enough!" Muh'Dear hissed, looking at Daddy like she wanted to slap him. "You was the first and last man that I'm gwine to let make a fool out of me! If I was to die and you ended up gettin' my house and my restaurant, you'd have another white woman enjoyin' it all before they put me in the ground." Muh'Dear kept glancing at Lillimae, giving her looks so hot I was surprised that Lillimae's face hadn't melted off. My mother was a bitter woman. I prayed that I would not end up like her. But I had already begun to head in the same direction. That was why I wanted to keep things in perspective, and not let my problems consume me.

"Let's not get too carried away," Lillimae suggested, slumped in that old La-Z-Boy recliner that Pee Wee had left behind. I was surprised that it could accommodate her humongous frame. Her thighs and legs were squeezed together so tightly, the bottom half of her body looked fused together, like a mermaid. Despite Lillimae's black blood, she was as white as a person could be. All of the flesh that was not covered by the Bermuda shorts that she had the nerve to wear looked like raw pork. "We are all family." As soon as Lillimae said that, Muh'Dear shot her another hot look. I didn't encourage anybody to drink early in the day. But I was glad to see that Lillimae had a double shot of Jack Daniels in her hand. Under the circumstances, she needed it.

"My mama didn't raise no fool, and I didn't neither!" Muh'Dear shrieked as she took a quick sip. There was a glassy look in her eyes. She was slurring her words and she kept releasing single hiccups every few seconds. It was obvious to me that she already had an adequate buzz. She chuckled and looked around the room. "Frank is a good man, but he ain't good enough to end up with everything I done worked for." Muh'Dear sniffed and gave my father a hopeful look. "But I will leave you a little bit of somethin'," she said with her head cocked to the side.

"Harrumph! You ain't got to leave me

nothin', old woman," Daddy whined, blinking so hard his sad, hooded eyes dilated. "I got along real good before I came back to you, and if I have to, I can get along again without you. I left home when I was thirteen, so I know how to make it in the world."

"You ain't gwine no place, fool," Muh'Dear snickered, giving Daddy a dismissive wave. "Ain't a woman alive would have what's left of you now. Me, I just keep you in my bed so you can keep my back warm." Everybody in the room laughed, even Daddy.

But there was a sad, vacant look in Daddy's eyes as he gave Muh'Dear a dismissive wave back. "I can always go back to live with Lillimae," Daddy pouted, looking to Lillimae for confirmation.

"You sure enough can," Lillimae confirmed with a weak nod. She knew that my mother disliked her. I appreciated how well she handled the situation. So far she had shown nothing but the utmost respect to my mother. But it seemed like no matter what Lillimae said or did, it offended Muh'Dear anyway.

"Harumph!" Muh'Dear boomed, her face twisted with disgust. Even though she had growled just that one word of gibberish, it was very effective because of the harsh way she said it.

Lillimae glanced at me and winked. I gave her a conspiratorial nod. I was glad to know that Muh'Dear's nasty reaction to what Daddy had said didn't faze Lillimae.

One thing I knew for sure was that my mother was not a mean woman. She seemed harsh, not just toward Daddy and me, but other people as well. She had had such a hard life, and so many people had taken advantage of her kindness, that she was afraid to let her guard down now. Underneath her gruff exterior, she was as sensitive as a lamb. I was especially glad that Lillimae knew that my mother's bark was way worse than her bite. And everybody else knew that too.

I graciously announced how happy I was about everybody's desire to spend more time with me. I delivered the obligatory comments like how nice they all looked and how glad I was to see them again so soon. "I've got some calls to make." I apologized before I promptly made a U-turn and went back upstairs to my bedroom where I immediately dialed Rhoda's number.

"Rhoda, I'm going crazy. I know you're probably busy with Jade and Bully, but I don't care. My place suddenly feels and looks like a zoo. I have to come talk to you. I can't wait another day. I'll be there in a few minutes," I told her.

Rhoda laughed. "Get on over here, girl. I'll be waitin', and don't you worry about Bully. He's well trained. And Jade, well . . . let me worry about her."

I took several deep breaths before I went back downstairs. I shuffled across the living room floor with my purse in my hand, ignoring the surprised looks that I received. "I have to go out for a little while," I announced as I grabbed my car keys off the hook on the wall by the door.

"I thought you had some phone calls to make," Scary Mary said, giving me a suspicious look. She looked at me that way a lot. Ever since she'd caught me out in public with the man I'd had my affair with last year.

"I'm going to make them when I get back," I stated in as firm a voice as I could manage under such a high level of stress. "I'll be with Rhoda for a while." I volunteered that last piece of information so that everybody wouldn't speculate on where I was going and whom I was going to be with (they were probably going to do that anyway).

"Can I go with you, Mama?" my daughter

146

asked, already moving toward me with an anxious look on her face. "Sitting around here ain't no fun."

"I'm going to meet Rhoda so we can discuss something that you don't need to hear," I said quickly, holding up my hand in her disappointed face.

Poor Daddy looked absolutely miserable. His face looked like a Halloween mask. It looked like his eyes had sunk even more deeply into their sockets. I felt sorry for him.

Lillimae was the only person in the room who didn't look like she was constipated. "I'll have the kitchen cleaned up before you get back, Annette," she offered. "And I'll save you a plate in the oven so your food'll keep warm."

"Lillimae, don't worry about me," I replied, snapping my fingers and forcing a smile. "I'll get something to nibble on while I'm out."

"Lillimae, I hope you do clean up that big mess in the kitchen, since you the one that made it," Muh'Dear said with a smirk, not even bothering to look at Lillimae.

I knew that Lillimae was tough enough to take care of herself, so I didn't feel bad about leaving her with the pack of "wolves" in my living room.

CHAPTER 16

Rhoda met me at the front door of her lovely ranch-style house. She gave me a brief hug and led me in by my hand. She had two double shot glasses of Jack Daniels with Coke already on a tray on her living room coffee table. I was glad because a strong drink was certainly what I needed after the mob scene that I'd just fled. I snatched a glass off the tray and immediately took a long swallow.

"I was goin' to fix us some iced tea, but I had a feelin' you'd want, *need,* somethin' a lot stronger," Rhoda said, giving me a pitiful look. "You've got a crisis goin' on, but a drink will make you feel better, or so damn bad you won't care."

I took another sip from my glass so fast I hiccupped before I even swallowed. "You got that right. Boy, do I wish we could go back to the days when a 'strong' drink for us meant a Pepsi or a cup of black coffee."

A great sadness consumed me. There was a time when a "crisis" to Rhoda and me meant a broken fingernail.

"We were teenagers then. But even though life had already bitten us in the ass, we were smart enough not to use alcohol as a crutch like some of our classmates did," Rhoda pointed out, taking a long drink.

"Those were the good old days," I sighed, nodding in agreement.

Rhoda shook her head. "But the only reason we weren't guzzlin' wine and the serious shit like vodka and rum back then was because we weren't old enough to buy it."

I laughed. "Yeah, that is so true." I gave Rhoda a pensive look. "How come the house is so quiet?" I asked, looking around. Rhoda had hired an interior decorator to make her home the showpiece that it was. She'd recently replaced her white shag carpets with a dazzling maroon and black print. The living room was filled with luxurious period mahogany. Framed pictures of her loved ones, my family and me included, dominated every wall in the large room, even the space above her fireplace. There was also a beautiful Japanese vase on the mantel above the fireplace. My living room looked like the one on *Roseanne.* It was plain, inexpensively furnished, and even gaudy. But it was neat, clean, and comfortable.

"Bully is in the backyard fiddlin' around with that jalopy Otis bought for Jade. It doesn't matter if he gets it to run or not — she says it's not 'cool' enough for her to be ridin' around in. That girl," Rhoda mouthed with a look of exasperation on her face.

I gave her a mournful look. "Where's Otis?"

"He had to rush over to the plant this mornin' again. Somethin' about more union problems. If I didn't know any better, I'd think he was havin' another affair. You know how the men their age do us . . ."

I looked away because I didn't want Rhoda to see the pain in my eyes.

"Not that we women are any better. I don't know what I'd do if I had to give up Bully after all these years," Rhoda confessed. "Just like you, he's been like a lifeline to me all this time. Especially when that daughter of mine is actin' up."

"And where is that daughter of yours?" I asked, bracing myself as I shot a quick glance toward the door leading to the hallway.

Rhoda glanced at her watch and shook her head. "It's only half past noon. She's still in bed, of course. She gets up about every fifteen minutes to run to the bathroom. I keep tellin' her that that urinary infection is not goin' to clear up as long as she keeps drinkin' and runnin' out to a damn bar every other night. That girl is so damn hardheaded!"

"I'm sorry to hear that she's still sick and not behaving herself," I muttered. "She's going to find out one day that a hard head makes a soft ass."

"Tell me about it." Rhoda chuckled and made a dismissive wave with her freshly manicured hand.

"So?" I said, looking around some more. Despite the fact that I was like family to Rhoda, I never took it upon myself to make myself at home until I was told to do so.

"So." Rhoda blinked and snapped her fingers. We were still standing in the middle of her living room. "Don't just stand here! Make yourself at home, girl." She waved me to the couch. It felt like I had just plopped down on a cloud. She sat down in the matching wing chair facing me. "Have you given much thought to what you're goin' to do about Pee Wee now?"

Before I answered, I took another drink from my glass; then I nodded. "I've given it a lot of thought, but I am not sure yet what

I'm going to do. I do know that if Lizzie's baby is Pee Wee's child, he's going to be in its life as much as he is in Charlotte's. But I can't have that child in *my* life. And I am so sorry that I feel this way about an innocent child."

"Annette, you don't have to apologize for the way you feel. I am sure that almost every other woman on this planet would probably feel the same way. But for your sake, I hope you don't make any decisions without thinkin' it through very carefully. Pee Wee has been my best male friend since he and I were in elementary school. And you and I have been friends for almost as long. Our lives wouldn't be the same if you divorced him."

My mouth dropped open so suddenly and so wide that the jawbones on both sides of my face felt like they had been forced open with a pair of prongs. "Nothing is going to be the same whether I divorce Pee Wee or not," I announced.

"I know that, but what do you want now? Do you want to spend the rest of your life being bitter and miserable and lonely? Or do you want to forgive and forget, and repair what was once a great relationship with a great man?"

I blinked. "I guess I do," I replied with a shrug.

"You guess you do what?"

"You know what I mean. If I really want to remain married, Pee Wee will do."

"Dammit, Annette. That doesn't sound very hopeful, or very romantic!"

"Women of our age don't have many choices when it comes to marriage," I reminded.

"Woman of *any* age don't have many choices, girl," Rhoda pointed out. "Whatever you decide to do, I will support you all the way. I know I've said that a thousand times already, but I can't say it enough. I just hope you do the right thing." Rhoda finished her drink and set her glass back on the tray.

I glanced at my watch to check the time. For some reason, I suddenly got agitated. I was anxious to go back home now so I could hole up in my room. "I don't like to rush off, but I really should be getting back home. I don't like to leave Lillimae with the big bad wolves for too long. Old people can be pretty vicious. Daddy is not too dangerous, but Muh'Dear and Scary Mary can do more damage with their mouths than a school of piranhas."

"Tell me about it," Rhoda agreed. "But

let's get back to Pee Wee. I have a feelin' that once you get used to the idea of that baby, you'll make the right decision about where you want to go with your marriage."

I gave Rhoda a thoughtful look. "It's just that I don't know what the right thing is anymore, that's all. How right would it be for everybody involved if I took Pee Wee back feeling the way I do about that baby?" I finished my drink. "Let's put this subject on hold for a little while," I suggested.

Rhoda leaped up off the chair and clapped her hands. "Well, we've made a little progress. You don't sound as bad as you did when you called me up this mornin'. I'm glad to see that. I was afraid that I was goin' to have to have you put on life support."

"I feel all right, I guess. I just needed to get out of that house, even for just a few minutes."

We walked to the front door arm in arm.

"Call me later," Rhoda yelled as I shuffled off her porch.

The street cleaners were out, so I had parked two blocks from Rhoda's house. As soon as I made it back to my car, I realized I'd left my car keys on her living room coffee table. I rushed back up her walkway and onto the porch, but I didn't bother to knock. I let myself in, returned to the living room, and grabbed my keys. I had to blame my sudden urge to empty my bladder on the drink that Rhoda had served me. I made my way down to the end of the hall where the guest bathroom was located.

The house was still quiet. Just as I was leaving the bathroom, I heard voices in the kitchen, a few feet away. As soon as I realized one of the voices belonged to Jade, my breath caught in my throat, so I moved a little faster. I wanted to be out of the house before she saw me. An encounter with her, which was always hostile these days, was one thing that I didn't need right now. But then I overheard her say something that got my attention. It made me stop in my tracks. I held my breath and listened. I had to fan my ear with my hand, because what I was hearing made me sizzle with disgust.

"You know you want me," Jade purred. "You've been wanting to stick that big fat dick of yours in my pussy ever since I was a teenager. You look at me now like I'm something good to eat. And guess what . . . I am something good to eat."

"OW! No! No, that's not de way it is! I can't be with you this way, milady! You know I can't." It was the voice of Bully, Rhoda's long-time Jamaican lover. And it was obvious to me what was going on. I tiptoed to the kitchen doorway and peeped around the corner.

"I'm the woman you need," Jade continued. "Don't fight the feeling, sugar!"

I could not believe my eyes and ears! I prayed that I didn't hiccup or sneeze or cough. I didn't even want to think about what Jade would say, or do, if she caught me "spying" on her.

Jade was all up in Bully's face with her hands on his shoulders. What I saw next almost made me scream. She grabbed his crotch with one hand and wrapped her other arm around his waist. He was trying to push her away and begging her to leave him alone. It did no good for him to resist. That only made the scheming little tramp more aggressive. Right at the same time that she planted a big kiss on his lips, I heard Rhoda walking down the hallway humming a Luther Vandross tune. I quickly tiptoed in the opposite direction, hiding in the laundry room beyond the den. I was shocked at what I heard next.

"Aaarrgggh! Take your filthy hands off me — you pervert! You bastard!" It was Jade, yelling at the top of her lungs. "Mama! It's a good thing you got here when you did! Uncle Bully was trying to rape me!"

CHAPTER 17

Of all the things that I had experienced, being a rape victim was undoubtedly the one that I would never fully heal from. It had tainted most of my childhood. It was because of that abuse that I had developed self-esteem problems so severe that I didn't think I deserved anything worthwhile for years. I had even sold my body because I didn't think that I was good enough to be in a normal relationship with a man. And until I got involved with Pee Wee, and turned my life around, I had dated men who used me and took advantage of me.

In addition to myself, I had known several other females who had been either raped or inappropriately propositioned at one time or another; some more than once, or over a prolonged period of time like me. It was a traumatic experience for anyone unfortunate enough to be the victim of such a heinous crime. Girls like Jade gave us real victims a bad name.

"Mama! Oh, Mama! I'm so glad you got here in time! Uncle Bully was all over me! See how he ripped my good blouse?" Jade whimpered.

My jaw dropped and my eyes almost popped out of my head. I didn't even bother to wait around to see how Rhoda was going to react to Jade's accusation. I held my breath and tiptoed back to the living room door.

I was glad that I had parked a couple of blocks from Rhoda's house. I sprinted down the street to my car and scrambled into it so fast, I got tangled up in my seatbelt. I sped out into the street before I even closed my door. The way I was driving, weaving in and out of traffic and way over the speed limit, you would have thought that I was trying to get away from something. And I was. I didn't want any of the shit that was going to hit the fan to spatter on me. There was going to be a whole lot of that flying through the air in Rhoda's house.

There was just no telling what the outcome was going to be from Jade's latest "performance." This girl was one of a kind. Not only had she nearly driven me crazy by sending me a bunch of nasty letters and packages, and harassing me by phone, she'd tortured other folks as well. Her targets included her ex-fiancé and her ex-husband.

When she was in college, of which she flunked out in her freshman year, she accompanied some of her friends to Cancun to celebrate spring break. Two days after she landed on Mexican soil, she fell in love with a handsome young Mexican bullfighter named Marcelo and brought him back to Ohio with her. She treated him like a docile puppy most of the time, and he acted like one. But other times she treated him like a dog she didn't like. She made crude, racist remarks to him in front of her friends and family. She made him escort her to the beauty shop and the nail salon like a bodyguard. And when she went shopping, which was several times a week, she used to make that poor Mexican go with her just so he could carry her shopping bags. Nobody, except Jade, was surprised when Marcelo left her at the altar on their wedding day.

Less than a year later, Jade latched on to a nice young man named Vernie during a visit to her older brother's home in Alabama. She got Vernie drunk, and by the time he sobered up, they were married. She dragged him back to Ohio where she beat the dog shit out of him on a regular basis. And for some of the stupidest reasons! Once she attacked him because he'd smiled at a woman on the street. Another time she tossed a pan of hot water on his head because she didn't like the "stupid look" on his face. The weapons she attacked him with included lamps, rocks, frying pans, beer bottles, her fists and feet, and anything else that she could get her hands on during her tirades.

I had gotten to know both Marcelo and Vernie fairly well. They were both really nice young men. Jade didn't deserve either one of them.

Jade finally went too far one night. She attacked Vernie with a lamp upside his head; but Vernie finally fought back. She was the one who ended up getting the dog shit beaten out of her.

Now it looked like she'd gone too far again. I decided that if she had once tried to take my man, it was not that much of a stretch for her to try to take her own mother's man.

I took the long way home, driving the city streets instead of the freeway. I needed some time alone to think and clear my head. I didn't know how I was going to respond when Rhoda informed me about Jade's latest stunt. Knowing Rhoda, she had probably already tried to reach me on my cell phone, which was in my purse and turned off. This was a conversation that I was not looking forward to.

I drove down Main Street, and on into Roscoe's neighborhood. His car was in his driveway. I was tempted to pay him a surprise visit, but I didn't give that notion much thought. Sneaking up on men was not a wise thing for a woman to do. Not even dull men like Roscoe. The last time I'd snuck up on a lover, I'd overhead a telephone conversation between him and another woman in which I was the subject being discussed — and in the most unflattering manner. Roscoe might have had something else going on that I didn't need to know about, so I drove past his house without stopping. I was near the mall, so I ducked into a bookstore and browsed for about fifteen minutes. I would have hung around longer, but as soon as I spotted Scary Mary and two of her prostitutes strolling out of a lingerie shop, I bolted. I ran all the way back to my car.

I was glad to see that my house was empty when I got home. Even Lillimae was gone. She'd left a note saying that she had gone to get her nails done, and that she was going to treat Daddy to a night out. She included a P.S. informing me that my daughter had gone shopping with my mother.

Just as I had predicted, Rhoda had left me frantic messages on my cell phone and on my home phone. She didn't say anything about what she'd walked in on in her kitchen. Her message just informed me that "all hell has broken loose" and for me to call her back as soon as I could.

My hand was shaking so hard, I could barely dial her number.

"Annette, thank God it's you! I am so glad you called me back! Girl, I am goin' stone crazy up in this house!" Rhoda yelled.

"Uh, is something the matter?" I asked.

"Oh, you will never guess this one! Hold on so I can get myself another drink."

Rhoda was gone for several minutes. When she returned to the telephone, she was huffing and puffing like she'd been running.

"Sorry I took so long, but I had to check on Jade. She's in such a frantic state! I had to run to her bedroom and help her to the toilet so she wouldn't have another accident in her bed, or on my carpets. I was too late, but at least she didn't make as big a mess as she did a little while ago."

"Did Jade's infection get worse?" I had expected Rhoda to tell me right off the bat what had transpired between Jade and

162

Bully, but it seemed like she was dancing around that subject. I certainly was not going to bring it up, because as far as I knew, she didn't even know I was in the house when it happened.

"Annette, I know you've got enough problems of your own right now, and I am truly sorry that I have to burden you with more of my problems," Rhoda apologized. "But —"

I cut her off immediately. "But nothing. Don't you worry about burdening me. You ought to know by now that your problems are my problems, and vice versa. Now tell me what in the world is going on over there?"

"It's Jade. You are not goin' to believe what happened to her!" Rhoda paused and released several heart-wrenching sobs.

"Rhoda, please pull yourself together. You need to tell me what's going on."

"I . . . I . . . don't want to go into detail over the phone. I need you here in person in case I break down again."

"I'll come right back over there. But can you give me a hint? Is Jade in some kind of trouble?"

"Oh, Annette. She is! And so is Bully! This is the worst thing that has ever happened to my family." Rhoda stopped talking for about ten seconds. When she began to speak again, she sounded unusually calm. Not only did that surprise me, but it scared me too. "Like I said, I need to see you in person right away."

"I'll be there as soon as I can. But I need to know one thing: Is Bully still alive?"

CHAPTER 18

It took Rhoda a few moments to respond to my odd question. When she spoke again, her voice was weak and distant. "Of course Bully is still alive. I . . . I packed his shit and sent him to a hotel. The cab just left."

"Oh? Did . . . uh . . . you and him have a disagreement or something?" I felt guilty about concealing what I had witnessed; but I was feeling more overwhelmed by everything to be too concerned about feeling guilty.

Since my departure from Rhoda's house, I had added another bone to my plate. On my way home, before I drove through Roscoe's neighborhood, I had driven by the apartment where my ex-husband's lover now lived. I was surprised to see his red Firebird parked in her driveway. I couldn't wait to report this to Rhoda, but I had to hear what she had to tell me first.

"Annette, I've known Bully for most of

my life. At least I thought I knew him."

"What did he do? I've never known Bully to do anything to upset you."

"I wanted to wait until you got here to tell you. But I think the sooner you know, the better." I heard Rhoda sniffing and trying to catch her breath. Finally, she told me in a squeaky voice, "Bully tried to take advantage of my daughter. Right here in my own house! It happened just moments after you left! I never dreamed that Bully could be so stupid and brazen! You could have walked into the kitchen and witnessed what he was doin', just like I did!"

I waited until Rhoda let out a few more gut-wrenching sobs.

"You mean . . . uh . . . you actually saw Bully in the act, trying to mess with Jade?"

Rhoda hiccupped before answering. "Not exactly. I walked in on the tail end. She was hysterical. He had ripped her blouse and everything. Men are such dogs!"

I didn't know how to respond to Rhoda's comment, so I remained silent for a few moments.

"Annette, are you still there? Please hurry up and say somethin'," Rhoda ordered.

It took me a few more moments to respond. "Rhoda, I don't like to change the subject. But that's what I need to do for a

166

few minutes, so you can get a grip. I hope you don't mind."

"Change the subject? What — what is it you want to change the subject to? I thought you wanted to hear about what Bully did?"

"I do and I will. But I can tell that you are having a hard time talking about it. I just thought that if we talked about something else for a few moments, it would be easier for you to talk about Bully after that."

"All right. Just what is it that you want to talk about before I tell you the whole story about Bully?"

"Uh, there is something I need to tell you about Pee Wee." I heard Rhoda sniff and suck in her breath. "What is it?" she asked in a whisper.

"It's probably nothing serious, but I still want to run it by you," I croaked.

"What is it?" Rhoda asked again. I was glad that she had stopped crying, but now I was close to crying myself.

"I drove past Lizzie's place on my way home from your house. Pee Wee's car was in her driveway," I said, silently scolding myself for steering the conversation in another direction. My best friend clearly needed my shoulder to cry on right now, and here I was still bombarding her with my problems.

"Oh, like I just said, men are such dogs! If I had been in your shoes, I would have marched into Lizzie's place and whupped the daylights out of them both."

"It hurts me to know that he is still communicating with her," I admitted. "And now that she is pregnant, he's going to have to deal with her on a regular basis. I don't know if I can deal with that. That is, if I continue to work on my relationship with him."

"Are you afraid that if he sees her regularly again, that they might resume their relationship?"

The thought of that happening made me shiver. "I'm not afraid if they will or not. If they want to, they will do it. Nothing surprises me anymore. I used to think that Pee Wee was one of the 'good guys,' but look how wrong I was. That man has broken my heart into a million little pieces."

"Humph! I used to think that Bully was one of the good guys too! Look how wrong I was! Men are all the same after all, I guess. They think with their dick heads!" Rhoda hollered.

"I guess I'll have to wait and see just how involved Pee Wee is going to get with Lizzie now," I managed. "But a horny man does a lot of stupid shit."

"Tell me about it. But Bully couldn't have been that damn horny after what I'd done for him a few hours before he tried to jump my daughter! I could kill him!"

I tried not to get too upset about seeing Pee Wee's car in Lizzie's driveway, but I did. What bothered me was the fact that he had already met with her to discuss her condition. And until she gave birth, why else would he need to meet with her again this soon? I just hoped that he had a reasonable explanation to offer me when I spoke to him again.

"Uh, are you going to have Bully arrested or anything?"

"I damn near slapped his face clean off, but I don't see any reason to drag the cops into this. Jade is an adult, and well, she is kind of loose. And everybody in town knows that. I just can't believe that Bully was stupid enough to think that he could do me *and* my daughter, and get away with it!"

"Rhoda, I like Bully and I know you care about him a lot," I said in a gentle tone of voice. I didn't think that it would do much good for us both to be screaming and hollering like she was doing.

"Yes, I do care about him! His dick is good enough to be served on a platter, but if he thinks he's goin' to serve it to my daughter, he's wrong! I am not proud of the fact that I've been sleepin' with my husband's best friend all these years. But I have to draw the line somewhere. His relationship with me does not extend to my child."

"Don't shut the man out of your life this way until you know all of the facts about what really happened, Rhoda."

Rhoda let out a sharp cackle. "Girl, are you listenin' to me? Annette, I walked in on him practically attackin' my daughter! I am not blind!"

"I know you did, but can you tell me exactly what you saw in that kitchen, Rhoda?"

"I saw all I needed to see!"

"You didn't answer my question."

"What? I just told you. I saw all I needed to see."

"And *exactly* what was that?"

Rhoda sucked on her teeth and muttered something under her breath.

I had to speak quickly, because I didn't know if she was going to hang up on me or not. "You walked in on something, Rhoda. But you didn't walk in on Bully trying to rape your daughter."

"Annette, you were not here. You didn't see or hear what I saw and heard."

"I was," I mouthed.

"Huh? Was what?"

"I was still there."

The silence was frightening. "But . . . but you didn't see what I saw and heard, did you?"

"No, Rhoda, I didn't see what you saw and heard. And you didn't see or hear what I saw and heard either."

"You get back over here and tell me what the hell you are talkin' about," Rhoda ordered.

CHAPTER 19

After I ended my conversation with Rhoda and was about to leave and return to her house, my front door flew open. I was surprised to see my daughter, Charlotte, stumbling in. Behind her was Harrietta Jameson, one of my neighbors from across the street. Even though I'd been one of the first to welcome her to the neighborhood with a freshly baked plate of cookies the day she moved in a few weeks ago, I had not had a chance to get to know her.

"Your daughter was at my house," Harrietta told me. "My kids love her to death."

I gave Harrietta a puzzled look; then I looked at Charlotte. "I thought you were out shopping with your grandmother?" I said, looking from Charlotte to Harrietta with the puzzled look still on my face.

"I was, but I wanted to come home. Grandma walks real slow, and she wouldn't let me go into any fun stores. Besides, being around old people too long makes me feel old," Charlotte stated, making a face and shrugging her shoulders.

Harrietta and I rolled our eyes at the same time, and I offered her one of my warmest smiles. "Harrietta, I am sorry that I couldn't make it to your Tupperware party last week."

"Oh, that's all right. I'll be giving plenty more. I like to keep myself busy," Harrietta replied. There was an anxious look on her face. "I am not too good when it comes to making new friends, but with all these women on this street, I thought some parties would be a good way for me to get better acquainted with some of my new neighbors."

I nodded. "Well, I hope you like to eat, because I probably host more backyard cookouts than anybody in Richland," I laughed, forcing myself to push the incident with Jade, and my own problems, toward the back of my mind.

"Girl, just look at me!" Harrietta slapped her thick hip with a hand that looked about as big and wide as a small pie pan. "Can't you see that I have not missed too many meals?"

I liked this woman. I didn't know many women who had such a sharp sense of humor. She had a deep, husky voice, like some of those old-time movie stars. I knew that a lot of men found that attractive. I was curious about her love life, but that was one of the few things about new friends that I didn't touch until they brought it up first.

"Well, I'm glad to hear that. Uh, thanks for letting my daughter come stay at your house 'til I got home. I don't like to leave her alone for too long."

Harrietta nodded. "Tell me about it. I never leave my three alone for more than ten or fifteen minutes at a time. It's bad enough that the world is so full of devils these days looking for kids to corrupt, but most kids can find something destructive to get involved in on their own, if we don't keep an eye on them. I hope you don't mind, but when your mama came home to drop off your daughter and your sister was on her way out, I insisted that Charlotte come to my house to wait on you," Harrietta told me, talking so fast I couldn't interrupt her and excuse myself. I decided that if she didn't shut up soon, I was going to have to interrupt her anyway. I didn't want to keep Rhoda waiting too long. "I know I should have checked with you first. I got your cell phone number from your mama, and I tried to call you but you didn't answer. Your sister said you probably wouldn't mind. By the way, I introduced myself to Lillimae last week when I ran into her at the Grab and Go. We've chatted a few times these past few days at the corner supermarket, and we exchanged telephone numbers. She sure seems like a real nice lady."

"I'm glad you've already met my sister. I've been too busy to introduce her around the neighborhood. I'm glad she's here to spend some time with me, and help look after Daddy. He's becoming a real serious piece of work," I groaned. "Anyway, I appreciate you looking after my daughter. I hope she behaved herself and wasn't too much trouble," I said. "I just wish I could have checked with you first to see if it was all right for her to come over."

"Oh pshaw!" Harrietta chuckled, waving her hand. "I was glad to have Charlotte's company. She and my daughter Vivian are in the same class."

"I know. Thank you again." I squeezed Charlotte's shoulder.

"I wasn't no trouble, Mama. I could have stayed in this house by myself until you or Aunt Lillimae got back home. I am not a baby!" Charlotte snarled, padding across the floor toward the kitchen.

I shook my head and smiled at Harrietta.

"Don't mind her. She's at that age," I apologized.

"It's nothing! It comes with the territory. I go through the same thing with my three," Harrietta laughed, rolling her small, beady black eyes again.

Before I could excuse myself, Harrietta made herself comfortable on my couch. She immediately crossed her legs and kicked back like she was the host and I was the visitor! She seemed like a nice enough woman, but she also seemed kind of dense and presumptuous. I would never enter the house of somebody who I didn't know that well and make myself as comfortable as Harrietta had just done. I didn't even do that at Rhoda's house *or* my mother's house! I was standing in front of her with my car keys and my purse in plain view, and I kept glancing at my watch. Harrietta still couldn't see that she had caught me on my way out.

Other than what she'd just shared with me, I didn't know much about her background. She'd been a couple of grades behind me in high school and had lived on the opposite side of town. She had also been one of the "cool" kids back then, so she and I wouldn't have traveled in the same circles anyway. She had married a detective a month after she graduated from high school in such a lavish church ceremony people had talked about it for months. Like me, she was somewhat stout and ordinary looking. Unlike a lot of the plus-sized women I knew, who had the nerve to wear clothes that they had no business wearing, she wore a loose-fitting denim skirt and a loose-fitting white silk blouse that camouflaged the thickness of her body. She seemed to really have her life together. But according to the gossip making the rounds in Claudette's beauty shop, Harrietta's life was just as complicated as some of the other women I knew. Her husband had left her with three young kids and run off with another woman a few months ago.

"I guess you know about my husband leaving me," Harrietta continued, speaking in a voice so cold I was surprised that I didn't see fog coming out of her mouth. "And I set fire to everything he didn't take with him!" Her jaw started to twitch and her eyes suddenly looked empty, almost lifeless. Even though I didn't know this woman that well yet, something told me that she was the kind of sister who maintained a shit/ hit list that you didn't want your name to land on. I could just picture her burning up her man's belongings, or even throwing some acid into the faces of other victims on her shit/hit list. But just as suddenly as her demeanor had turned sinister, she softened again and offered me a smile that stretched from one side of her face to the other. "The Bates woman next door to me, she told me about how you chastised Pee Wee and Lizzie in your driveway the day he moved out. You and I have a lot in common. We don't take nobody's mess." I had to smile and nod in agreement. Because it dawned on me that I had become the kind of woman who had a shit/hit list that nobody wanted to be on. I was now a lot like the females who had terrorized me throughout my school years. Age sure had a way of equalizing things.

I plopped down on the love seat facing Harrietta. "I heard something about you and your husband breaking up the last time I was at the beauty shop," I admitted. "I'm sorry to hear that."

"Well, don't be sorry for me. Him and his whore deserve each other." Harrietta smiled and blinked a few times, but I could still see the red-hot anger in her eyes. "I don't miss him at all, or any other man for that matter. My man was no prize like your ex. He couldn't screw worth a damn."

CHAPTER 20

I gave Harrietta a curious look. "Excuse me?"

"Not that I know if yours could screw worth a damn either!" she laughed. "But he sure *looks* like he can. . . ."

"For the record, he is the best lover I ever had," I reported with a smug look on my face. It was true. Pee Wee was the best lover I'd ever had, and that was one of the reasons I missed him so much. "Uh, I've been meaning to invite you over for coffee or something so we could get better acquainted. Other than Margaret Bookman at the end of the block, you are the only other black woman on this street close to my age. But we'll have to get together at another time. I was just on my way out the door to go visit a friend who really needs to talk to me right now." I rose and started to move toward the door.

Harrietta finally took the hint. She leaped

up off my couch like a rabbit jumping out of a magician's hat. "Oh! I'm so sorry. I didn't mean to just barge up in here and get so comfortable," she chirped, looking embarrassed. "Girl, I don't know what the hell is the matter with me! I don't know where my manners are!"

"That's all right," I said, quickly glancing at the door and my watch again.

"You can come by anytime, and I already gave Lillimae my phone number for you or her to call me when you want to. And in case you didn't know, I provide child-care services. You ought to see how I decorated my patio for the kids," Harrietta revealed.

I nodded. "The best friend that I'm about to go see, she has been running a day-care center in her home for several years now."

"You mean Rhoda O'Toole? I know. I've run into her several times at the nail salon, at the mall, the Grab and Go, and Claudette's beauty shop. But please tell me this, if you don't mind, who does Rhoda's hair weave? I bet it's that white gay boy out on State Street. His work looks so natural."

I gasped. "Rhoda does not wear a weave. That's her real hair," I said proudly.

"Damn. She's hella lucky to have a head of hair like that. All that straight, shiny black hair looks like it belongs on an Indian woman. My grandmother was a full-blooded Cherokee, but as you can see by all these naps on my head, having Indian blood didn't do me a bit of good." Harrietta moaned as she tossed her head to the side, raking her fingers through her short, brittle curls. "That's why I own several wigs and hairpieces."

"I usually wear my hair in braids," I said, patting my two-week-old press and curl. "And by the way, for the record, my daddy has a lot of Indian blood too."

Harrietta looked at my hair. A mild frown crossed her face. "Umph, umph, umph! Honey child, I can see that having Indian blood didn't do you any good either, huh?"

"I guess not. But Rhoda's grandmother was a white woman. That's where she gets her straight hair from."

"So those great big green eyes of hers are probably natural, too, huh?"

I nodded.

"Black women who look like Rhoda usually think their shit don't stink." Harrietta laughed.

I shook my head. "Rhoda's not conceited about her looks at all. She takes it all in stride. One night I waited for her to join me at the Red Rose for a drink. I was sitting alone at the bar. When she walked in, all of the men at the tables near the entrance clapped — blacks, whites, Hispanics, and even a few Asians. Rhoda didn't even realize that they were clapping for her until I told her."

Harrietta shook her head. "If I walked into the same place naked, the men would probably *still* ignore me." For a brief moment, she looked so sad I felt sorry for her. "I don't need a man anyway."

I didn't know how to respond to Harrietta's last comment, so I took the conversation on a detour. "Uh, Rhoda loves taking care of those preschoolers," I said.

"I like the itty-bitty ones too. They sleep a lot during the day. However, I prefer them to be at least eight, or older. Kids that age don't require as much attention as the toddlers. But since the money is so damn good, I'll take them at any age."

"I'm glad to hear that, Harrietta. My daughter still needs to be supervised. So from time to time, I need somebody to keep an eye on her."

"I'll tell you what, if you'll scratch my back, I'll scratch yours. I'll look after your daughter for free when you need it, if you'll keep an eye on mine for free when I need to take a break."

"That's fine with me. Sounds like a good

plan. But my parents are usually available. And as long as I have my sister from Florida with me, I don't think I'll need to bother you that often."

I was disappointed, and becoming even more impatient by the second, when Harrietta sat back down. She crossed her legs again and unbuttoned the top button on her blouse. Then she suddenly gave me an anxious look. "I hope I don't sound too nosy, but is Lillimae your blood sister, or are y'all foster sisters, stepsisters, or play sisters?"

"We have the same biological father, but her mother was white."

"Oh. I figured it was something like that, because y'all do look like blood relatives."

"Harrietta, I really do have to leave right now," I said in a firm voice. I rushed to the door and held it open. I was not giving her a choice; she had to leave *now.* "I hope you'll visit again soon when I have more time." I liked this woman and I wanted to be friends with her, but a pushy new friend was one thing that I didn't need and was not going to tolerate this late in life. I had to nip this in the bud now. "As you can see, I was on my way out the door when you came." I raised my hand and dangled my car keys.

A contrite look crossed Harrietta's face. "Girl, I'm so dense. I'm just so tickled to be living on Reed Street, I don't know what to do with myself. I was raised right. I sure enough hope you don't think I'm always this rude!"

"That's all right." I opened the door wider.

"I need to get my ashy black ass on back home before my kids burn down the house." Harrietta shot up off the couch like a rabbit again. She was very agile for a woman who weighed over two hundred pounds. "Are you going to take your daughter with you now?" she asked, as she approached the door. She stopped and glanced around the room, then toward the kitchen where Charlotte had fled to.

"Oh! Um, no, I don't want to," I admitted. "I need to discuss a subject with Rhoda that is kind of sensitive. I don't want my daughter to hear any of it. You know how it is when kids hear something they shouldn't hear, and how they like to make a case out of it. My daughter has ears like a basset hound. And she loves to run off at the mouth about what she heard or saw some grown person do. I guess I'll have to take her with me anyway."

"Oh, girl, you don't have to do that." Harrietta grinned. "I got your back now," she

184

added, slapping a hand on her hip and rotating her neck. "You go on and visit with Rhoda. I'll take Charlotte back to my house with me. She'll be in good hands. I'll send her back home as soon as I see either you or your sister return."

I sighed with relief. I didn't want Charlotte anywhere near Rhoda's house because I had no idea how things were going to go when I got back over there. "Are you sure you don't mind? I really do appreciate you offering to look after her for a little while."

"Girl, if I minded, I wouldn't have offered."

"Thank you so much! I owe you one."

After I checked on Charlotte and told her that she had to stay with Harrietta, I had to spend a few moments arguing with her.

"I don't like that lady, Mama. She's not normal," Charlotte complained. She stood in front of the refrigerator with the door open, nibbling on a cold chicken leg.

"Well, you'd better learn to like her, because you are going to be spending a lot more time at her house. Now get back out to that living room and thank that nice woman for offering to look after your rusty behind."

Charlotte stomped back into the living room behind me, grumbling under her breath all the way.

I waited in my car until I saw Harrietta lead my daughter into her house, holding her by the hand.

CHAPTER 21

Rhoda didn't live that far from me. I could have made it to her house in a matter of minutes if I had taken my usual route. But I didn't. I don't know what I was thinking, but I drove two miles out of my way just so I could drive past Lizzie's apartment again.

There were so many "ifs" going through my head as I drove down one street after another. *If* I was going to continue working on getting back with Pee Wee, I needed to get used to the fact that Lizzie was going to be in our lives again. *If* it was going to bother me in the future as much as it did now, I needed to know so I could figure out how I was going to deal with it. *If* Pee Wee decided to resume his relationship with her, the sooner I knew that the better.

Lizzie lived in a predominately black and Hispanic area with Peabo in a huge red brick building on a street where I wouldn't walk a dog that I didn't like. The projects in

Richland's low-rent district didn't look as shabby as this neighborhood. The apartment buildings, especially the one that Lizzie lived in, and the houses on both sides of the street all needed some serious maintenance work. I had never seen so much despair. There were dozens of windows covered with cardboard. There were broken-down old cars parked in the driveways and on the street. Young kids with dirty faces, snotty noses, and hair that looked like it had not been combed in weeks were roaming around like stray dogs. Used Pampers had been strewn around the ground like fertilizer. Males and females of all ages who occupied the corners looked like they wanted to cuss out the world. I always kept the windows on my car rolled up, but I made sure that all of the doors were locked too.

I couldn't figure out what had made Lizzie choose a low-life creep like Peabo over a man like Pee Wee. Peabo was involved in a variety of criminal pastimes, even though he also had a respectable job driving the school bus for Richland's mentally handicapped kids. Another thing that I couldn't figure out was why he lived in such an undesirable neighborhood when he could easily afford something much better and safer. I answered my own question: Peabo lived in such a sorry neighborhood because the cops rarely bothered to patrol this part of town. It was a thug's paradise. People got robbed, shot at, cut up, beaten, and even killed over here on a regular basis.

I was happy to see that Pee Wee's car was gone from Lizzie's driveway.

I was glad when I made it back to my regular route and into Rhoda's neighborhood. As soon as I turned the corner onto her street, I saw her standing in her doorway with the front door standing wide open. This time I parked right in front of her house. She was so anxious to see me, she sprinted out to the car before I could even get out.

"I thought you'd never get here," she started, leading me into the house with her arm around my shoulder.

"Harrietta Jameson, my new neighbor, held me up for a few minutes," I explained. I looked around the living room, holding my breath. "Where's Jade?" I asked in a whisper.

Before Rhoda could answer my question, Jade slunk into the room. As soon as she saw me, she frowned. She wore a red see-through negligee, which seemed like an odd item of clothing for a woman who had just been "molested." She didn't have on a bra, so I could see the perky breasts that she liked to show off every chance she got. I was pleased to see that she had on a pair of panties. They were not the practical, loose-fitting cotton type that you would expect to see on a woman experiencing a urinary tract infection. They were a thong, and because of the amount of flesh that I could see, they had to be at least two sizes too small.

"What are *you* doing here?" Jade hollered with a grimace on her face. She looked me up and down with her brows furrowed and her eyes blazing with hostility.

"Jade, Annette was here when . . . when Bully . . . you know. She might have heard somethin'," Rhoda offered, giving her daughter a warm look as she gently rubbed her arm. "I want to get to the bottom of this situation as soon as possible." Jade looked like she had just smelled a rat. Her reaction must have puzzled Rhoda, because Rhoda let out a very loud gasp and moved a few feet away from Jade. Then she folded her arms and looked straight into Jade's eyes. "All right, baby?"

Jade's face froze. She looked as stiff as a telephone pole. "Huh? Heard something like what?" she asked through clenched teeth as she looked from me to Rhoda. The

190

grimace on Jade's face had been replaced with a look of fear.

I couldn't hold my tongue any longer. I sucked in some air and gave Jade a defiant look. "I was in the hallway when you were in the kitchen with Bully," I began. I turned to Rhoda. "I had left my car keys on your coffee table. I didn't knock when I came back into the house. I retrieved my keys, but I needed to use the bathroom before I left. I had to walk past the kitchen doorway. . . ."

It didn't take a mind reader to determine what Jade was thinking. "Shet up, you nosy old bitch!" she screamed, shaking a fist at me. "SHET UP, I SAID!"

There was a horrified look on Rhoda's face, but she remained composed. "No, *you* shet up," Rhoda said, wagging a finger in Jade's direction. "Go on, Annette. Did you hear or see Bully attackin' my daughter? Did you see him in the kitchen with her?"

"Yes, I saw him in the kitchen with your daughter. No, I didn't see him attacking her."

"I thought I told you to shet up!" Jade started to move in my direction, shaking her fist some more. I prayed that she didn't hit me. Even with Rhoda present, I would defend myself. When she spoke again, she

191

did so with her mouth stretched open so wide, I could see the base of her tongue. "Pig face, don't you stand here and make me look bad!" Jade shouted at me.

Rhoda grabbed Jade's wrist and stopped her in her tracks. "Girl, I advise you to get a grip. Keep your lips still until I hear what Annette has to tell me."

"But, Mama! Annette is crazy! She hates me! Please don't listen to her lies! She's always been jealous of me! She's been trying to ruin my life ever since I was a little girl!"

"If anybody was being attacked, it was Bully," I insisted, surprised that I was able to speak in such a calm manner. "Rhoda, I don't want to get too graphic and repeat what Jade said — and did — to Bully. But she was all over that man like a cheap blanket." Despite all of the pain that Jade had caused me, I didn't enjoy hurting her. But there were enough people in my life who were already in enough pain. It was not fair for me to stand by and let Jade get away with hurting Rhoda and Bully. I had no choice but to reveal what I had witnessed.

"Why you . . . you . . . big fat liar! You're a damn, fat-ass, middle-aged lying COW!" Jade hollered. Her eyes looked like they

192

were going to explode. Her lips were quivering like she'd just been Tasered.

"Jade, I *know* you, and that means I know what a low-down, dirty little tramp you can be," Rhoda said calmly, folding her arms. "You've ruined a lot of lives, but I won't help you continue to do so. Now, you tell me the truth. Did you or did you not come on to Bully?"

"NO! Do I look like the kind of woman who has to come on to a man like you two used-up old clucks?" Jade blinked hard and shifted her weight from one foot to the other.

"Do you mean to tell me that Annette is lyin' on you to my face?" Rhoda asked, sarcasm dripping from her lips like sap.

"SHE IS! SHE IS LYING, MAMA! HONEST TO GOD," Jade roared, tears sliding down her face like hot wax.

"Okay, if she's lyin', then please tell me why you think she's lyin' on you? What does she have to gain by tellin' such a bare-faced lie?" Rhoda asked. From the expression on her face, it looked like she was in as much emotional pain as Jade. And I could understand why. There was nothing worse than being in a situation in which a loved one was also the source of your pain. That was probably the only thing that Jade and Pee

193

Wee had in common these days. They both managed to inflict unimaginable pain on the people who loved them the most.

"I DON'T KNOW! I — I — feel like I'm going to faint — aaarrrggghhh!" Jade's eyes rolled back in her head. And just as I expected, she stumbled around for a few seconds like a newborn colt; then she hit the floor with a thud.

CHAPTER 22

For Jade to be as mean and feisty as she was, she sure fainted faster and easier than anybody I knew. As soon as she had hit the floor, she stretched out on her back like a baby seal. I helped Rhoda lift and haul her ass to the couch. Rhoda immediately began to fan and gently slap Jade's face, trying to revive her. Less than a minute later, Jade opened her eyes and started boo-hooing like a baby.

"I'll get a wet cloth," I offered. I started to leave the room, but before I could, Jade sat bolt upright. She stopped crying so abruptly, a few rapid hiccups flew out of her mouth. Then she looked from Rhoda to me, glaring at us with the level of hostility that I had become accustomed to. She jumped off the couch and started to hop up and down like a kangaroo. When she stopped hopping, she began to chant, "Ooo . . . wooo . . . wooo . . . I can't go on . . . I can't . . . go on!" She paused and rubbed the side of her face and wailed like a stuck pig for at least two minutes. It was a pitiful sight. What I couldn't understand was why she would want to make herself look even more ridiculous. Rhoda stood with her arms folded and a disgusted look on her face.

I didn't know what to say or do next. I was too stunned to speak.

"I don't know why you two old crows are picking on me like this again," Jade whimpered. "I haven't done anything wrong. I am the victim here! Annette is lying on me, Mama! Why would I want an old fart like Bully? I can get any man I want — I don't need *him!*"

"I'll ask you again, Jade, why would Annette tell such an ugly lie on you?" Rhoda asked in a steely voice with her hands on her hips. From the way she was tapping her toe on the floor, I could tell that she was running out of patience with her daughter. "Jade, I am not goin' to let you walk away from this. Not this time. You're goin' to come clean for once in your life."

"Huh? What do you mean, Mama?" Jade snarled, still glaring at Rhoda. I could see the rage simmering in Jade's eyes, threatening to boil over at any moment. "Don't you believe your own child?"

"Not if that child is you," Rhoda replied, with her lips snapping brutally over each word.

"But . . . I . . . Annette's had it in for me for a long time. Look at that smirk on her pie face." Jade waved her hand at me in such a melodramatic, sweeping manner, it made me feel like a used car that she was trying to sell.

I may have possessed what Jade called a pie face, but I was not smirking. If anything, I felt sorry for her because I knew that Rhoda was not going to let her talk her way out of trouble this time. And it had been a long time coming. I had always believed that a good dose of Rhoda's wrath would do Jade a world of good. But I never thought that I would be present to see it happen.

Rhoda moved closer to Jade. Jade stumbled back a few steps. "Jade, you tell me the truth or else," Rhoda said through clenched teeth.

Jade gasped. "Or else what?"

"Believe me, you don't want to find out, girl," Rhoda assured her.

Jade held her breath. A few seconds later, she exhaled with such a tight look on her face, you would have thought that somebody had punched her in her nose. "All right! I'll tell you why she's lying on me! She's still mad about me and Pee Wee! I could have taken him from her if I had really wanted him — but I was just playing!" Jade placed her hands on her hips and swiveled her head around, glancing from Rhoda to me. If looks could kill, Rhoda and I would have dropped dead immediately where we stood. "But . . . but she's still mad at me about it! She's mad at the world because Lizzie came along and took Pee Wee anyway. Annette couldn't hold on to him with Krazy Glue. Look at her, Mama! She's just a fat, miserable old cow. Make her leave this house!"

Rhoda massaged her forehead with the balls of her fingers; then she looked at her watch. "Jade, I don't have all day to deal with this. Now, this is your *last* chance to come clean. I want to wrap this up before your father comes home. I don't want him to know everything that happened here today, but he'll want to know why I sent Bully to a hotel. I am sure I'll come up with a good story to tell him, so I am not worried about that. Now, this is your last chance. You tell me the truth now and we'll go from here. But if you keep lyin' to me, *you will suffer!*"

"You — you're jealous of me!" Jade boomed. She was looking at me, so I assumed she was talking to and about me. But then she turned to Rhoda with a look in her eyes that I would never forget. It was a look that was a combination of pure evil and hatred. "You are the worst mother in the world! You're a bitch and I hate you! I have always hated you!"

I gasped so hard I almost choked on my own tongue. Now Rhoda was the one standing as stiff as a telephone pole.

I was shaking with rage. I didn't believe in striking children Jade's age, but if there was ever one who needed her behind whupped, it was her.

"Jade! How can you talk to your own mother like that?" I hollered, clapping my hands like I was addressing a disobedient pet. "Your mother has always treated you like a princess! She had your back when nobody else wanted to come near you! How dare you disrespect her this way!"

Rhoda held her hand up and shook her head at me. Then she turned back to Jade. "I want you to get all of your shit and get your ass up out of my house. Get out before I throw you out." Rhoda was talking in such a calm manner, I didn't know what to think. But I was so angry, I wanted to fly across the room and knock some sense into Jade's bone head myself.

"Fuck you!" Jade screamed at her mother. "You're just another old whore still trying to look and act young! Look at you! Standing there with more makeup on your face than Bozo the Clown! And your hair! All that long-ass hair, like you're still sixteen! And it'd be as white as snow if you didn't dye it!" Jade shot me another red-hot look. "And *you* — you still look like a freak show in my book. You're still fat! All you do is kiss up to my mother like a lap dog. Don't you know she only hangs around with a she-monkey like you to make herself look good? Are you so desperate for a friend that you would put up with that for all these years? You both are two straight-up dykes, I bet! All lovey-dovey all the damn time! I am ashamed for people to know that I know you two!" Jade turned back to her mother. "I have known about you and Bully since I was a little girl. I saw you with him on the beach in Jamaica one night, and I've been keeping tabs on you and him ever since. If Daddy wasn't such a fool, he would have figured out what was going on a long time ago."

"I told you to get out of this house," Rhoda said, still speaking with a lot of control in her voice. I was amazed at how she managed to restrain herself.

200

I was so stunned, I couldn't move my feet. But I could still move my lips and I had more to say. "Jade, you need to stop talking right now and do what your mother said. Let things cool off —" I suggested.

"Cool off, my ass!" Jade spewed. "I will leave this dump when I get good and ready. I am not going anywhere until I say what I've been wanting to say for years!" With her arms folded, Jade marched up to Rhoda and stood so close to her, their noses bumped. "Yes, I went after Bully! He needs a real woman like me! He's only with you because he feels sorry for you! Other than Daddy, what other man would be fool enough to stay with *a piece of a woman* like you? Nobody but a dickless, old dinosaur like Bully, that's who! Nobody else wanted you after that doctor cut off your titties! I was just trying to do Bully a favor. I wanted him to see what he was missing. . . ."

In all of the years that I'd known Rhoda, I had never seen the degree of hurt on her face that was on it now. She blinked hard a few times. Then she closed her eyes for a moment and slowly shook her head. When she opened her eyes, she blinked some more and slapped the side of her ear, like people do when they think their ears are deceiving them. But her ears were not deceiving her. I had heard everything that Jade said too.

"Rhoda, are you all right?" I asked. The reason I asked that dumbass question was because she looked like she was in a trance. When she swayed a little, from side to side, I thought she was going to faint. "Rhoda, maybe you should sit down," I suggested, gently grabbing her arm.

"I'm fine," she told me, slapping my hand away. She took a deep breath and looked at Jade in a way that made me sway a little from side to side.

"So? Are you just going to stand here and look stupid?" Jade hissed at Rhoda.

"Jade, you need to quit while you're ahead," I advised. "You don't know your mother as well as I do —"

"Didn't I tell you to shut the fuck up!" Jade retorted, wagging a finger in my direction. "My mother is a no-good witch and she knows it." What Jade said next made a chill shoot up my spine like a bullet. *She's the reason I am the way I am. . . ."*

It was a strange comment, even coming from someone like Jade. And that made it even more ominous.

CHAPTER 23

I was extremely concerned about what was going through Rhoda's head. There was a look of overwhelming sadness in her eyes. She was already a petite woman, but now she looked even smaller, and so fragile I thought she was going to crumble to the ground.

Jade's comment about Rhoda's breasts must have hurt Rhoda clean down to the bone, because Rhoda's lips began to quiver. Her hand, which was shaking like a leaf in a strong wind, suddenly stopped shaking and she began to slowly massage her chest. Her heart was beating with so much vigor that I could actually hear each thump.

Jade's comment even made *my* chest ache. I didn't even realize my hands were massaging my bosom, too, until I looked down at myself.

By making such an insensitive reference to her mother's surgery, Jade had crossed a line that she could not cross back over even if she attempted to do so with her feet strapped to a pair of stilts. One of the few things that even I knew not to bring up with Rhoda was the fact that she'd lost both of her breasts to cancer. The last thing that she needed to hear was someone referring to her as "a piece of a woman" because of that surgery — especially when it had literally saved her life. And especially when that someone was her own daughter.

I was flabbergasted and pleased at the same time to finally see a hint of acute remorse on Jade's face — a puppy-dog look that almost reduced me to tears. Maybe she was not as insensitive as she'd led me to believe all these years. If Jade had apologized to me for all of the pain that she'd caused me and improved her general behavior, I probably would have forgiven her. And for Rhoda's sake, I might have even eventually restored my relationship with Jade. I missed doing some of the things that I used to do with her. Like me taking her to the skating rink when Rhoda was too busy. Or the two of us going to the mall to shop and share a pepperoni pizza, and her referring to me as "Auntie Annette." It would have warmed my heart for me to hear her call me that again.

"Bitch, why are you looking at me like I'm crazy?" Those were the next words out of Jade's mouth, and they were directed toward me.

I was still stunned, but no longer pleased. The same puppy-dog look, which I had mistaken for remorse, was still on Jade's face. "Jade, apologize to your mother. If you don't want to do it for me or her, do it for yourself," I pleaded.

Jade snickered and then looked at me like I was crazy. "You are so crazy!" she boomed, with spit foaming in one corner of her mouth.

The next thing I knew, that heifer ran out of the room with the bottom of her negligee flapping behind her like a dragon's tail.

Within seconds I heard loud rap music coming from Jade's room. After all of the pain that this girl had just caused, all she could think about was herself, and listening to one of the late Biggie Smalls's final tunes.

"Are you all right?" I asked Rhoda, leading her to the couch. "You know she didn't mean any of that. She still has a lot of growing up to do."

"I . . . I don't believe what just happened in my own house," Rhoda whispered. "I must be dreamin'."

I shook my head. "You're not dreaming,

honey." I began to wonder if I had done the right thing by telling Rhoda what had really happened between her lover and her daughter in the kitchen. It took me less than a second to convince myself that I had done the right thing. Even though it had caused a firestorm like none I'd ever seen before in my life.

Rhoda jerked her head from side to side; then she looked at me with extreme hopelessness on her face. She looked like a woman in mourning. I'd only seen this degree of bereavement at funerals. And in a way, I guess you could say that one of Rhoda's loved ones had died. I didn't see how this mess could ever be repaired. "Did you hear what my daughter just said to me?"

"I heard every word," I rasped, words struggling to get out of my mouth. I had to clear my throat before I could continue. "But I honestly don't think she meant most of it."

"That girl has lost her mind!" Rhoda yelled with her fist clenched. "She must have!"

"She's just spoiled, Rhoda." I wasn't trying to defend Jade, but I didn't want to make the situation any worse than it already was by saying what was really on my mind. But the truth of the matter was, I firmly believed that Jade was the daughter from hell. And I believed that she was going to be the way she was until something or somebody knocked her off the high horse she'd been riding on for most of her life.

But the worst was yet to come.

"Annette, will you please fix me a drink?" Rhoda managed, coughing and massaging her chest some more.

"I'll get you a glass of wine," I told her.

"No, that won't do this time. I need a much more potent crutch. Pour me a double Jack Daniels on the rocks. And hurry!" Rhoda ordered. I could tell from the dazed look on her face that she was still in a state of shock. I was too. As much as I wanted other things to distract me to keep my mind off of my own messy life, I never expected something this extreme.

I ignored the portable bar in the living room and ran into the kitchen where Rhoda and Otis kept their hard liquor in a cabinet next to the refrigerator.

It took me only a few minutes to pour drinks into a couple of shot glasses. But by the time I made my way back to the living room, Jade had returned with her face fully made up. She even had on false eyelashes, coated with enough jet-black mascara to paint the side of a barn. She wore a pair of black stiletto heels, a white silk blouse, and a pair of jeans that were so tight, her crotch looked like it had toes. She had brushed out her long black hair and pinned it to one side with a heart-shaped barrette. Jade looked like she was on her way to a nightclub. "Mama, I'm almost out of my medication," she said. Her tone of voice was so casual you would have thought that she was ordering a cheeseburger. "And when you go to the pharmacy to get my refill, get me some panty liners too," she added.

"Go to the pharmacy and get what you need yourself!" Rhoda snapped.

Jade gasped. She rotated her neck and looked at Rhoda like she had just sprouted a beard. "What? I can't be going to the drug store and standing in those long lines in my condition," she pouted. "You know what a hard time I'm having with this damn urinary thing. Running to the john every ten or fifteen minutes and dripping puddles here and there. What's wrong with you? I am not going to go out in public and put myself through that."

"But you can get dressed to go out and hang with your friends — in public?" Rhoda asked.

"Going out to hang with my friends and standing in line at the pharmacy for God knows how long are two different things! You know that!" Jade rolled her eyes and gave her mother a hot, impatient look. Then she plopped down onto the chair facing the couch like she was Queen Elizabeth plopping down on her throne. "Well? Why are you two still just standing here looking at me? Get outta my face." Then she laughed. "Oh, Mama. You know I don't mean any harm when I get like this." Jade made a dismissive gesture with her hand before she began to fiddle with the strap on one of her stilettos, like everything was back to normal now. She had no idea how wrong she was.

Rhoda moved closer to where I stood by the door, still holding the tray with our drinks in my trembling hands. My hands were not shaking because I was afraid of Jade. They were shaking because I was afraid *for* her.

I set the tray on the coffee table as fast as I could because I was afraid that I was going to drop it.

"Jade, I thought I told you to collect your shit and get the hell up out of my house," Rhoda said as she plucked one of the glasses off the tray and immediately raised it to her lips. I had a feeling that she was going to need more than one drink.

Jade's face froze for a few seconds. She

gave Rhoda another hot, impatient look. Then her lips curled up at each end. For a split second, I thought she was going to laugh. But that impatient look returned to her face a split second later. "Mama, you can't be serious. This is my home," she said, her voice trembling. For the first time since I'd come back to the house, Jade looked truly worried. What I couldn't understand was how this girl had lived with Rhoda for her entire life and not known that Rhoda was nobody to mess with.

"Correction. This is *my* home. When you start payin' rent and some of the bills around here, and respect my rules, then you can call this your home again, girl. Until then, it's mine and I want you out of it RIGHT NOW!"

Jade turned to me with a desperate look on her face. I was surprised to see that she had tears in her eyes. "Fuck you, BITCH!" Jade hissed, looking at Rhoda with so much hostility in those same tear-filled eyes I had to blink to make sure my eyes were not playing tricks on me. Without saying another word, she snatched open the living room door and ran out like the house was on fire.

Rhoda and I remained silent until we could no longer hear the clip-clop of Jade's heels on the cement walkway leading from

Rhoda's front porch. My eyes remained on Rhoda. Her eyes remained on the door as she raised the shot glass to her lips again.

"Well, now! I guess she told us," I mumbled. My lame attempt to make light of the situation didn't amuse Rhoda. I walked over to her and gently rubbed her shoulder. Then I led her to the couch and we both sat down. "I had no idea that Jade had so much anger in her toward you. I know you better than your own mama knows you. I know you were, and still are, a good mother to that girl. These kids nowadays will take you to the river if you let them!"

"We were not angels when we were kids," Rhoda said with a weak, dry chuckle.

"Not even," I agreed. "And I hope it doesn't sound like I am trivializing the things we did, but there was never a time in my young years that I spoke to my mama the way your daughter just spoke to you. I feel sorry for the parents of the next generation. I don't know what we parents today can do to make our kids behave better."

"I do." There was a cold look on Rhoda's face, like her eyes had turned into ice cubes. She began to speak in a slow, mechanical manner that was as cold as the look in her eyes. "Sometimes you have to bite the bullet and fight fire with fire."

It was an ominous comment, even coming from a woman with Rhoda's history of homicide. I didn't know what she meant by it, and I didn't want to know. But I had a feeling that it was nothing positive.

"You want to stay for dinner?" Rhoda asked.

"I wish I could, but I need to spend some time with Lillimae so I can figure out what her plans are. Muh'Dear has made it clear that she doesn't want her in the house too much longer."

I didn't like the icy look that was still on Rhoda's face. And I was still wondering about the comment that she'd just made about fighting fire with fire.

Suddenly I became concerned about leaving Rhoda alone. She was in a lot of emotional pain. I couldn't imagine what it was going to be like between her and Jade now. I knew that if my daughter ever talked to me the way that Jade had talked to Rhoda, I'd put something on her that a witch doctor couldn't take off.

"Could you stay a little longer?" Rhoda asked, rising. She finished her drink and set the glass on the coffee table. "There is somethin' I need to do and I want you to be my witness. . . ."

CHAPTER 24

"Rhoda, don't you think you should cool off and then decide what you want to do next?" I asked. We were in Jade's lavishly decorated room across the hall from the master bedroom. It had been years since I'd been in Jade's room. Back then it had looked like any other young girl's room.

Rhoda's house was spectacular anyway, inside and out. But it was obvious that more time, effort, and money had been spent on Jade's room than any other room in the house. This girl had the nerve to have a canopied bed, antique tables, an old-fashioned chifforobe that must have cost a fortune, and flowered wallpaper. It looked like something from a scene in *Gone with the Wind.*

"I've cooled off as much as I'm goin' to," Rhoda told me, glancing at me over her shoulder as she snatched one expensive-looking frock after another from Jade's walk-in closet. She had already filled six large moving boxes with some of Jade's belongings. I had helped her set those boxes on the front porch.

"She's going to be totally pissed off when she comes back and sees what you, uh, what we've done," I warned, my voice cracking. It was too late for me to turn back now. I felt like this was as much my mess as it was Rhoda's. "She's probably off somewhere now feeling bad about what she said to you. You know she didn't mean any of that shit about hating you. I am sure that she was talking off the top of her head the way a lot of young people do."

"Don't make excuses for Jade. I did that long enough before I finally admitted to myself just how bad my child really is," Rhoda snapped.

"True, but I still don't think she really meant everything she said."

"It doesn't matter now," Rhoda sighed, looking around the room. "That's all of her shit. The furniture, the bedding, and everything else in this room stays here for now. Aunt Lola might be comin' up from Alabama for a visit soon, and this is the kind of garish shit she likes too."

"But Jade has no place else to go. She has

no job or any money of her own," I pointed out.

"That's her problem. Now she'll find out who her real friends are. Come on. Let's finish up here."

"I guess she'll fall back on all of those credit cards she has," I said. "And all of those belong to you too." That was one thing that I did not have to remind Rhoda of. She was already ahead of me.

"I cancelled every single one of them while I was waitin' for you to get here," Rhoda quipped. There was a wicked gleam in her eyes and a mysterious smile on her lips.

Just as Rhoda and I were setting the last of the boxes onto the front porch, a shiny black SUV rolled up and stopped in front of the house. I couldn't see the driver, but Jade was in the front passenger seat. She jumped out of the vehicle as soon as she saw Rhoda and me on the porch standing next to boxes piled up on both sides of the porch and on the patio.

"What the hell are you two up to now?" Jade asked in a casual voice, running up the walkway. You would have thought that the earlier events had been a tea party. Her eyes got wide as she looked at the boxes. "Mama, I . . . I hope you're not moving out! You

215

know I didn't mean those things I said! You don't have to move! This is your house!" Jade hollered. She attempted to wrap her arms around Rhoda's waist. Rhoda slapped her hands away and backed out of her reach.

"I am not goin' anywhere, but you are," Rhoda said firmly. "You're leavin' this house today. I am kickin' your useless ass out. I'm glad you brought some help with you." Rhoda nodded toward the van.

Jade gasped as she leaned down and lifted the lid off one of the boxes. "What — this is my stuff! You can't do this to me, Mama!"

"Correction! I can, and I did. If you don't move your shit off this porch today, I will throw it and you into the street," Rhoda threatened.

"I don't believe this!" Jade shouted, holding up one of her see-through negligees. "What the hell are you doing, Mama?"

"What the hell am I doin'? Are you deaf too? Didn't I just tell you that I am kickin' your ass out of my house, that's what I'm doin," Rhoda explained. "I'll be nice and give you the rest of today to move your things off this porch. Anything that you don't take with you today, I will have Goodwill come pick up tomorrow. Now get busy before I change my mind and call Goodwill today."

216

Jade's jaw dropped as she stood up. Tears and snot were streaming down the sides of her stunned face. I was not surprised to see a big round wet spot in the crotch of her jeans. Even before she had contracted that urinary tract infection, she had problems controlling her bladder. She had peed on herself on her wedding day when her fiancé jilted her, soiling her very expensive wedding gown.

I was standing several feet away from Jade, but I could still smell alcohol on her breath. Her eyes had looked mean enough a couple of hours earlier when she'd run out of the house, but now they were bloodshot and puffy.

"Mama, please don't do this to me," Jade begged. "I . . . I don't have any money, or anywhere to go. Give me a chance to make some plans."

"You've had more chances than you deserve," Rhoda insisted. "I don't want you in my house another day."

"All right! I apologize! I'm sorry for the things I said! Happy?" Jade's lips curled up into a shark-like grin. "Now, let's get these boxes back into the house and forget all this foolishness." She let out a loud breath and gave Rhoda a pleading look. It was so pathetic to see somebody as abrasive as she was suddenly cowering like a scared rabbit. "Oops! I need to get to the bathroom again."

When Jade attempted to enter the house, Rhoda blocked the door.

This infuriated Jade. "Mama, what . . . what's up? I said I was sorry! What more do you want me to do?"

"I want you out of my house, Jade," Rhoda said, looking Jade straight in the eyes.

Jade looked at me with her mouth hanging open. "Annette, can't you talk to her?"

I shook my head. "Not this time, baby girl."

Jade whirled around to face Rhoda. "You miserable old witch! My own mother throwing me out into the street like I'm a common bitch." The words spewed out of her mouth like vomit.

"*Like a common bitch?* That's exactly what you have become, Jade. This house is only big enough for one bitch, and that's me. Now you get the hell out of my sight while you still can," Rhoda advised.

I could not see this situation getting any uglier.

But it did.

"Okay! That's it! I'm tired of this shit — going 'round in circles with you! If you want to treat me like I'm just another rank stranger off the street, I can treat you the same way. I'll whup the dog shit —" Jade raised her hand and slapped Rhoda across the face. I was stunned, but Rhoda didn't even flinch. She grabbed Jade's wrist and twisted her arm back behind her. Words could not describe the look on Jade's face this time.

I almost fainted when I saw what Rhoda did next. She reared back on her legs and lifted her hand. She slapped Jade so hard across her left cheek that she left a complete handprint! Jade's complexion was as dark as mine and Rhoda's, so for a handprint to bloom on her face, Rhoda had to have delivered a blow that probably would have brought Muhammad Ali to his knees.

The sound that came out of Jade's mouth was not human. She sounded like a dying animal. "Eeeeeeyooow!" She began to rub her face with both hands. Her eyes rolled back in her head and she screamed again, "Eeeeeeyooow!" For the second time in the same day, Jade "fainted." She fell to the floor and landed on her back like a fallen tree.

CHAPTER 25

Rhoda and I didn't lift Jade off the floor and haul her to the couch like we had done earlier. And Jade didn't stay down for even a full minute. She wobbled up like an old woman with two broken legs. It took a lot of effort for her to get her balance with those insanely high heels she had on.

"Mama, you . . . you hit me," she whimpered. She gave Rhoda an incredulous look and repeated herself. "You . . . you hit me. You haven't hit me since I was a little girl!"

"And that's one of my biggest regrets," Rhoda admitted. "A few more whuppin's might have done you some good."

"I don't believe what you just did!" Jade croaked, looking more dazed than ever. "You actually hit me!'

"I'm goin' to hit you again if you don't get out of my sight, girl." I had never seen Rhoda as angry as she was right now. "Get out of this house before I kill you," she

220

seethed. Her hand was in the air, poised to strike her daughter again. Then, as if she had just come outside to do something as innocent as collect the mail from her porch mailbox, she sighed and strolled back into her living room.

Jade stood there looking like a deer caught in the headlights of an eighteen-wheeler. She seemed to be more stunned than I was. I was glad that I was not a mind reader, because I didn't want to know what she was really thinking. But the way she was glaring at me, you would have thought that I was the one who had just coldcocked her.

"You tell my mama that she won't get away with this!" Jade hollered. "You tell her that I said she's going to be sorry 'til the day she dies. You tell her I said —"

I interrupted Jade by throwing my hand up in front of her face. "Jade, if you have anything else to say to your mother, you go in that house and tell her yourself," I suggested. "Leave me out of this."

"Leave you out of this? Bitch, if you hadn't opened that hole in your face, none of this would have happened in the first place! You've been a meddlesome old busybody ever since I met you!"

"Jade, in spite of all the dumb things you do and say, you're still a smart girl. You

221

ought to know by now that every dog has its day. How long did you think you could push your mother around and get away with it? Now, if you've got something else to say to her, you do it. I am not your messenger."

"I don't have anything else to say to that woman! I wouldn't speak to her again if she was the last person on the planet. I am SO through with her. Nobody hits me and gets away with it. My husband was the last person who had the nerve to hit me, and I'll never speak to him again. Now I'm glad he divorced me!"

I nodded. "I'm sure he'll be glad to hear that," I sneered. "You'd better leave," I whispered, glancing toward the door. "Trust me, you don't want to find out just how far your mother can go."

Jade stumbled until she was backed up against the porch banister. She looked so pitiful and alone, and I could understand why. Rhoda had been her most important ally all of her life, but even I didn't think that Rhoda was going to "forgive and forget" all that had transpired today. Under the circumstances, I did feel sorry for Jade, but just a little.

"I could have her arrested for assault!" Jade growled, stomping her foot so hard she broke the heel on one of her stilettos. She sniffed and licked her lips, but it did no good. Tears and snot had formed a goatee around her mouth. And all of that makeup that she had applied was now sliding down her face like mud. Rhoda had slapped Jade so hard that her barrette had flown out of her hair and onto the porch floor.

"Jade, I know that I am the last person you want to take any advice from, but I'm going to give you some anyway. Leave. Leave here now before your mother comes back out on this porch! I hope I don't have to tell you again."

"Let her come back out here and hit me again. I swear to God, I'll have her arrested for assault!"

"You hit her, too, or did you forget that part? I witnessed *that* too. Your mama could have you arrested for assaulting her," I pointed out. "I saw everything."

Jade snorted. "That's the problem with you. You always seem to be around to witness something when it comes to my family!" The handprint that Rhoda had left on Jade's face was even darker now. And it must have been painful, because she kept rubbing at it, shaking her head and squinting her eyes. "And let me tell you one more thing" — Jade began to shake her finger in my face so close to my mouth, I was tempted to bite it — "one of these days you are going to see something you don't want to see. And it'll be somebody in *your* family! Charlotte ain't the angel you think she is. . . ."

"Now, don't go too far with me, Jade." I realized how stupid that remark was as soon as I'd said it. Jade had gone "too far" with me years ago. "For one thing, Charlotte has nothing to do with what's going on with you. She'd never disrespect me the way you did your mother here today."

"Uh-huh. Well, we'll see about that," Jade warned, removing her shoes and glaring at the one she'd just broken.

I had no reason to believe that Charlotte was up to no good, but because of Jade's ominous prediction, I planned to keep even closer tabs on my daughter. I had my family and now Harrietta Jameson on my team. And because of their support, I was confident that my experiences with my daughter would never be as ugly as Rhoda and Jade's. However, Jade's words still managed to give me a chill. "Jade, you should get your friend in the SUV to help you load up your stuff and leave," I urged, my hand already on the door and one foot inside the house. I glanced into the living room. Rhoda had sat down on the couch and was now sipping from a can of Pepsi. "Let your mother have some time to think about everything. I'm sure she'll come around before too long." I forced myself to smile.

"Shut up!" Jade shook her broken shoe in my face. I moved farther away from her because the heel on that shoe looked like a dagger. "You and my mother can go to hell! Now that I know what a cold-hearted bitch she really is, I don't need her anymore. And I don't need a useless old crone like you trying to tell me what to do!" Jade waved and beckoned to her friend in the SUV.

Within seconds, a stocky, light-skinned young man with his reddish brown hair in cornrows piled out of the van. He trotted up the walkway with an angry look on his moon face. I knew that he, and several of Rhoda's looky-loo neighbors, had watched the violent confrontation between Rhoda and Jade.

"Butchie, help me load up my shit so I can get the hell up out of here!" Jade commanded, snapping her fingers in her friend's stunned face as he chewed on a toothpick.

"What the fuck is going on?" Butchie asked, looking at the broken shoe in Jade's hand. An amused look suddenly appeared on his face. For a moment, I thought he was going to laugh. But when he looked at the handprint on Jade's face, he shuddered. "Damn! If your mama can pack a punch like that, you better get the hell up out of here, girl!" For a man dressed like a thug, and who weighed at least 250 pounds, Butchie didn't seem too brave to me. He began to sweat as he nervously looked toward the door. He was chewing on that toothpick like it was a stick of gum. "You always told me that your mama wasn't nobody to mess with. I see you wasn't lyin'. Let's load up your shit and haul ass, girl!"

"I told you that my mama was a straight-up bitch! Now you see for yourself!" Jade told Butchie. I didn't know Butchie personally, but I knew he was a small-time pimp. One of his hookers had shot him in his foot last year. He still walked with a slight limp. "And this fat-ass bitch here is always up in my business!" Jade barked, shaking her shoe in my direction again. "You won't have any good luck, bitch! You'll never get your husband back, and I hope that bastard baby of his that Lizzie is carrying pesters you every day of your life."

Jade's words pierced my heart like a sword. She could not have hurt me more if she had stabbed me with the sharp heel of that shoe that she was still waving in my face.

226

I dropped my head. I immediately slunk back into the house and joined Rhoda on the couch. I was glad that there was some Jack Daniels left. I poured myself a double; then I gave her a hug.

"Thanks. I needed that," Rhoda told me, almost choking on her words. She glanced briefly toward the door and sighed. I had shut the door behind me, but we could still hear Jade and Butchie cussing and fussing and stumbling around on the porch while removing that stack of boxes.

"It's going to be okay. I know everything is going to be okay. You and Jade just need some time away from each other," I insisted in a low, uncertain voice. I hoped that Rhoda believed what I had just said, because I was not sure if I did or not. What else could I say to ease her pain? I just hoped that my words made her feel better. I didn't feel too good myself right then. The chaos that I had just witnessed had affected me deeply. And if that wasn't bad enough, I was afraid of what I was going to face when I got home! I wanted to put that off for as long as I could. "Rhoda, if you don't mind, I'll sit with you just a little while longer."

She gave me a slight smile and a weak nod. She startled me when she lifted her Pepsi can and held it toward me. I raised my glass in a salute; then we finished our drinks.

CHAPTER 26

I knew that Lillimae and Daddy would probably be out for most of the evening. And since Charlotte was at Harrietta's house, I had nothing to hurry home to. Besides, I was afraid to leave Rhoda alone. I didn't know what was going to happen next. With her husband at the plant dealing with one union issue after another that could go on well into the night, and Bully holed up in a hotel room, I felt that it was imperative for me to remain with her at least until Jade had departed.

We looked at each other when we heard the SUV leave, but we didn't speak for a few moments. I ran to the window and peeped out, just to make sure Jade and her friend were both gone.

"They took all of the boxes, so I doubt if they'll come back," I said, returning to my seat.

Rhoda sniffed and blinked. "Annette, I

229

know you have other things that you need to attend to. I'll be fine, so I don't want you to think that you have to stay here with me," she told me. We had finished the bottle of Jack Daniels and half a bottle of wine.

"I don't mind staying a little longer," I said. "I can at least stay here until Otis gets home, in case you want me to be around when you tell him what happened. But if you'd rather be alone now, I understand."

"Tell Otis what happened? What . . . what do you mean?" Rhoda stammered. "Do you think I'm goin' to tell my husband what happened here today?"

"Well, yeah. How are you going to explain to Otis about Bully being in a hotel, and Jade and all of her things gone?"

"Oh, I'll think up somethin'," Rhoda assured me.

I gave her a wan look. "Well, whatever you tell Otis, please call me up right away and tell me, so I'll know what to say in case I run into him. And since we're on the subject, make sure you tell me whatever you tell Pee Wee in case it comes up the next time I see him." I wanted to talk to Rhoda some more about me seeing Pee Wee's car in Lizzie's driveway. But that was one thing that she didn't need to deal with at the moment. That was another big can of worms that I would eventually open and dump in her lap anyway.

"Let's finish the wine and then you can go. I think I need to turn in early tonight. It's been one hell of a day," Rhoda decided.

I called home to check my voice mail before I left Rhoda's house. Other than a few ambiguous messages from my mother complaining about one ailment after another, and a call from Roscoe, nobody else had called me. The telephone rang as soon as I got back home. It was a few minutes past eight.

It was Harrietta. "The girls just started putting together a pizza. And after that, they want to play Monopoly. Do you mind if Charlotte stays a little longer? It would be nice if she stayed the night. The girls want to get up early in the morning to make pancakes."

"If she wants to stay the night, it's fine with me," I said, knowing that if Charlotte had a choice, she'd come home — but I hoped she'd stay with Harrietta. I enjoyed being alone when I was feeling as tense as I was now. And after everything that I'd been through today, I could barely sit still. "Uh, tell her I said for her to stay the night. I'll bring her sleepwear over in a few minutes."

"You sound tired. Is everything all right?"

231

"I'm fine, but I am a little tired."

"Well, you get some rest, then. And we've got plenty of sleepwear over here, so don't you worry about bringing anything over. I'll send Charlotte home after we eat breakfast in the morning. The girls and I have to be at church for Sunday school by ten anyway."

"Tell Charlotte I said she'd better behave herself," I said, anxious to get off the phone.

"Don't worry. I got everything under control," Harrietta assured me.

Less than a minute after I had ended my conversation with Harrietta, my telephone rang again. It was Charlotte.

"Mama, I don't like this woman! I do not want to spend the night over here," she whispered.

"Why are you whispering?"

"Harrietta doesn't allow us to use the phone. She's in the bathroom, so I have to talk fast. Unlock the front door. I'll be home in a minute."

"No, you won't. You're spending the night."

"NO!"

"Look, you'd better watch your tone of voice, Miss Thing. I'm raising you, you're not raising me."

"Mama, please . . ."

"You are spending the night at Harrietta's

house, Charlotte. Now this conversation is over."

"Mama, I — I gotta go! She's coming!"

I heard some scrambling around on Charlotte's end; then I heard her hang up. I shook my head and chuckled. I was so glad that the "problems" between my child and me were so trivial. But I was determined to streamline my relationship with her even more.

Charlotte was so used to having her way that she had a hard time observing other people's rules. I did not have a problem admitting that my child was not perfect. As a matter of fact, she was just as spoiled as the next. But I thanked God that she was not even close to being as spoiled and volatile as Jade. However, she was still spoiled enough for me to keep her on a fairly short leash. I regretted the fact that I was partly responsible for my daughter being slightly bratty, but there was still time for me to turn her around. I was glad that I had a friend like Harrietta now who seemed to know how to approach children with equal amounts of authority and compassion. That was the way my mother had raised me.

When the telephone rang again a few minutes later, I assumed it was Charlotte calling back. But this time it was Pee Wee.

"I need to see you as soon as possible. Tonight," he said.

"I've had a very long day. Can't whatever it is wait until tomorrow?" I asked. The image of Pee Wee's car parked in Lizzie's driveway flashed through my mind. "Whatever it is, it can't be that important," I said, wondering if he was going to tell me why he had visited Lizzie today.

"It could wait until tomorrow, but I think the sooner you hear what I have to say the better," he responded.

He had my attention.

"Can't you tell me what it is over the telephone?" It was bad enough that I had to hear his voice while I was so distressed; I wasn't too wild about seeing his face too.

"I could, but I don't want to," he declared. "Look, you've been avoidin' my calls since the last time I saw you. You know that we are goin' to have to sit down and talk sooner or later anyway, so why don't you just do it now and get it over with."

"Is the something that 'could wait until tomorrow' about that woman?"

"Yes, it's about Lizzie."

"I will tell you now that I am not in the mood for any more surprises. If this is something that is going to piss me off, I don't want to hear it tonight."

"I can't say if it's goin' to piss you off or not. But I would like to see you anyway. I miss you. . . ."

"All right. I'll be up for another hour," I replied. "If the lights are all out when you get here, you're too late, so don't bother to knock. Once I get in the bed, I don't want to get back up."

"I'm on my way," he said quickly.

A few minutes after I had hung up and kicked off my shoes, I heard somebody stomping up on my front porch. Before I could make it off the couch to see who it was, the door flew open. Lillimae waddled in, huffing and puffing. She sat down hard at the other end of the couch, making it squeak and tremble like somebody had dropped a piano on it. Even though she looked tired and somewhat sad, she didn't waste any time telling me about the good time that she'd had with Daddy. They had dinner at an Italian restaurant and visited a nearby jazz club. They went in Daddy's truck, and I was happy to hear that Lillimae did the driving. She dropped Daddy off at home and parked his truck in front of my house.

"Your mama wasn't too happy about me and Daddy goin' out without her," Lillimae told me. "We invited her, but she said she had to stay home and scrub her kitchen floor. Daddy said she must have forgot to tell me that she'd just scrubbed that same floor the day before. . . ."

"As long as you had a good time anyway, that's what's important." I smiled, which seemed to put Lillimae more at ease. For one, she knew I was her strongest ally when it came to my mother. But it was a difficult position for me to be in. On one hand, I was glad that she and Daddy were enjoying each other's company so much. On the other hand, it made me sad to know that it was also hurting my mother, and that there was not a thing that I could do about it.

"How did your visit to Rhoda's house go today? You and that pit-bull daughter of hers didn't lock horns again, I hope," Lillimae said with a sharp chuckle. I was glad she had changed the subject, but it was another painful one.

"Girl," I began, shaking my head and rubbing my forehead with the ball of my thumb. "It was no picnic," I groaned. "Are you sure you want to hear about it?"

CHAPTER 27

"Oh yes, I do. I want to hear all of the details!" Lillimae yelled, giving me an impatient look.

After I had told her everything that had transpired in Rhoda's house, she stared at me in slack-jawed amazement. I had left no stone unturned. I even told her about Rhoda's handprint on Jade's face. However, I didn't see any reason to tell Lillimae about Rhoda and Bully being lovers.

"Some folks get more pissed off at the messenger than they do the perpetrator. Do you think I should have minded my own business and not told Rhoda what I witnessed?" I asked, rubbing the back of my head. "I keep asking myself that so much now, that each time I get light-headed."

Lillimae gave me a guarded look. "I really don't know how to answer that."

I glanced at the floor, then back to Lillimae. "Rhoda didn't get mad at me for get-

237

ting in her business, but Jade sure as hell did. But no matter what, I probably did do the right thing. Rhoda feels the same way. If she didn't, she would not have confronted Jade the way she did."

"Well, I'm glad to hear that Rhoda reacted the way she did. I would hate for you to lose her friendship over somethin' that crazy-ass daughter of hers did. But from now on, before you get involved in other folks' business, think about it long and hard first. Rhoda and her daughter may never be close again because of what you told Rhoda."

"That's good advice, but I don't know how I will react if I'm ever in another situation like this one." Now it was my turn to look tortured.

"What's the matter, sugar?" Lillimae asked, looking alarmed. "All of a sudden you look like you want to cry."

I did want to cry, but I managed to hold back my tears. I had done enough crying lately. "A lot of people knew about Pee Wee and Lizzie way before I did. Nobody cared enough about my feelings to tell me," I whined.

Lillimae gave me a surprised look. "Would it have been better to hear it from a third party or from Pee Wee and Lizzie the way you did?"

"I guess it was better that I heard it from them," I admitted.

"If one of your friends had told you first, I guarantee you that Pee Wee would have denied it."

"No matter what, I think I did the right thing by Rhoda," I insisted. "And Bully too. He was the real victim in this mess."

Lillimae slapped the side of her head. "What I can't figure out is, why would a young girl like Jade want a man like Bully? He's handsome, sexy, and well-built. But when I met him that other time I was up here, his personality seemed kind of dull to me," Lillimae said as she began to cornrow braid her shoulder-length blond hair.

"Who knows why Jade went after Bully. You know how crazy young folks are these days," I replied.

"Well, from what you've told me, it sounds like the girl is on drugs. Why else would she go off on her own mother like that over a man? Especially a man who has been a friend of the family for so long. Rhoda told me one time that Bully used to change Jade's diapers!"

"Uh-huh, that's true," I said with a nod.

Lillimae shook her head. "But for Rhoda to throw Jade out on the streets, even after what the girl did, that sounds a little extreme to me."

I was taken aback by Lillimae's comment. "What would you have done if your child had talked to you the way Jade did to Rhoda, and then got violent too? I think a lot of mothers would have done the same thing that Rhoda did. Lord knows I hope I am never put in the position to find out. . . ."

"I don't know how I would react if one of my kids went off on me like Jade did Rhoda. And I hope I never have to find out," Lillimae said with a heavy sigh and a yawn. "On that note, I'm goin' to bed."

Pee Wee arrived thirty minutes after my telephone conversation with him. I let him in and waved him to the living room couch. "You want a plate? Lillimae cooked enough for an army," I said dryly.

"No, I'm not hungry. I went by that rib shack on Noble Street and had a combo a couple of hours ago." Pee Wee let out a loud, heavy sigh as he sat down and crossed his legs, tapping his knee with his finger. "I heard about Jade," he told me with a disgusted look on his face. "Rhoda called me up a little while ago. I am glad you happened to be there when that ruckus took place."

Pee Wee and Rhoda communicated on a

regular basis. They had been close friends for so long that sometimes I wondered why they had not become lovers.

"It was ugly." Just thinking about that nasty scene made me cringe. "But I told Rhoda to give Jade some time and she'll come around. I'm going to get myself a beer. You want one?" I asked, already moving toward the kitchen.

"Don't mind if I do," Pee Wee said.

I handed him a can of Bud Light. As soon as I popped open a can for myself, he started. "Annette, I went to talk to Lizzie today." He took a long drink and let out a mighty belch. Without excusing himself like he usually did, he continued talking, "Me and Lizzie had a real long talk."

"I know you were over there. I saw your car in her driveway on my way to Rhoda's house this afternoon," I said with a sneer. I eased down on the love seat. One thing I was glad of was that I was not nervous. If anything, I was defiant — ready to do more battle with him if I had to. But I knew that he knew better. It was to his advantage not to provoke me.

"She is pregnant, but not by me." He put a lot of emphasis on the last part of his sentence, and that piqued my interest. If there was something he knew that I didn't

241

know, I wanted to hear what that something was immediately.

Pee Wee drank some more beer and gave me a look that I could not interpret.

"You don't think that baby is yours? And how did you come to that conclusion?" I asked.

"I don't think, I *know* that baby is not mine," he insisted.

"You screwed her, didn't you?"

He raised his hand and twirled his index finger around a few times. "Look, let's try and have a nice, calm conversation. You don't have to be usin' no crude language like that. I know you might not believe me, but this is just as painful for me as it is for you. I'm just as nervous as you are." He didn't hear me snicker, because I covered my mouth with my hand. He cleared his throat and tapped his knee with his finger some more. "Do you think I'd want to be raisin' another child at my age? I'm old enough to be a grandfather."

"I did give that some thought," I admitted. "Technically, we were old enough to be grandparents when Charlotte was born."

Pee Wee shrugged and nodded. "That's true. But let's keep this conversation on track." He paused and sucked in some air and maybe some more courage because his voice got hard and direct. "See, this is the thing; I looked over that doctor's report some more this mornin'. And from what I could see, Lizzie is due to give birth in March."

"So?"

"You do the math. A woman carries a baby for nine months or less. Lizzie left me in May. If she was pregnant then, she'd be havin' her baby no later than January or as late as February, not March."

"Maybe she miscalculated," I said.

"She sure did. She and I had not been, uh, *close* since the end of May, so there is no way that baby is mine."

I stared at Pee Wee with my lips pressed together for a few moments. "How long did you visit her today?" I asked.

"Just long enough to say what I had to say to her. Look, if you think that there is still somethin' between Lizzie and me, you are wrong. I hope you believe that, and I hope you believe what I just told you."

"I still say that maybe she miscalculated. Maybe her due date is before what she told you and what the doctor's report says. Charlotte came a week later than the doctor said she'd come, or did you forget about that?"

Pee Wee shook his head. "A baby comin' a week late is one thing. A baby comin' two whole months late is a horse of a different color. And a real dark horse at that. This baby mess with Lizzie gets stranger and stranger."

"How come you are so sure about that baby not being yours? How do I know you didn't sneak around with her after she left you for Peabo Boykin?"

"Because I didn't sneak around with her after she left me for Peabo. Once it was over with her, it was over; and not soon enough if you really want to know. Leavin' you for her was the dumbest thing I ever did in my life!" Pee Wee leaped up off the couch and rushed into the kitchen. He returned a few moments later with another can of beer. "I don't know what else I have to do or say for you to believe that I regret leavin' you and causin' you all these headaches." He drank and then released another belch. "I don't know what was wrong with me." He snorted and wiped his lips with the back of his hand. "But I hope I don't have to pay for my foolishness for the rest of my life."

I considered Pee Wee's words carefully and took my time responding. I finished my beer first and then set the can on the coffee table. Then I gave him one of my harshest looks. "You seem to be so certain that this baby is not yours. There must be *something* you can say to me that will convince me that it's not." I folded my arms and waited. "And it's got to be something that's solid. So unless you can tell me that you didn't have sex with Lizzie at all while you were involved with her, I can't imagine what other foolproof thing there is."

His body stiffened and a scowl appeared on his face. Something was up. . . .

"Can you hurry this up, please," I rasped, holding my breath and praying that I wouldn't snap. I was already at a point where I felt I could no longer be responsible for my actions.

"Annette, I really don't know how to tell you what I have to tell you next. I don't know how you're goin' to react to it."

"There's only one way to find out, and I'd like to hear what it is," I said, cocking my head to the side.

"It's somethin' I had been hopin' that I would never have to tell you," he muttered, with his eyes searching the floor like he was looking for something he'd lost. I was glad that he had stopped tapping his knee with his fingers. But I knew that he was still nervous by the way he kept blinking his eyes and clearing his throat. He sniffed and looked at me with puppy-dog eyes and quivering lips.

245

"Something like what? Were you impotent during all that time you were involved with her? That's about the only way I can see you being one hundred percent sure that you didn't get her pregnant."

"It's worse than that," he managed, hardly moving his lips. "Annette, I can't make no babies. *I shoot blanks.*"

CHAPTER 28

I had heard a lot of stupid comments and remarks over the years. And from time to time, I said a few things myself that made people roll their eyes. But what Pee Wee had just said was one of the most off-the-wall things that I'd ever heard. "You've been shooting blanks? What the hell is that supposed to mean?" I demanded, glaring at him with my eyes stretched open so wide I thought my eyeballs were going to pop out.

"It means just what I said," he murmured, speaking in such a low voice that I had to turn my ear to the side to hear him clearly. He cleared his throat and kept talking, speaking louder. "As much TV as you watch, and as much as you read, I know damn well you've heard that phrase before."

"Yes, I have heard something like that before, but not coming from you. Do you mind explaining to me exactly what you are trying to say?"

"My sap is useless."

"Your *what?*"

Pee Wee looked embarrassed. He started speaking in a low voice again. "My jizzum," he practically whispered. I knew what he meant, but from the look on my face, I assumed he didn't know that I knew. So he offered further clarification. "My *sperm*."

Now it was time for my jaw to drop, and it did. It dropped open so wide that I thought my bottom lip was going to touch my bosom. "What's your sperm got to do with all this?" I asked. "Are you forgetting that we have a child together — or do you think that another man might be her daddy?" I was tired, but I still had enough energy to get angry.

"I know Charlotte is my daughter, but we made her a long time ago. Things were different back then. The truth is, my baby-makin' batter is about as potent as Gatorade these days. . . ."

"Pee Wee, will you please get to the point and tell me *exactly* what you mean!"

He held up his hands as if to protect his face from the sting of the harsh look I gave him. He could see that I was getting angrier by the second. He knew that I'd been somewhat involved in a violent confrontation already a few hours ago at Rhoda's house and I assumed he didn't want to be part of one that I initiated against him. And even though it was one of the many things in our past that we didn't talk about, I had no doubt in my mind that he still remembered the rolling-pin smackdown that I'd administered to him and Lizzie the day that they had come to my house to tell me that they were in love. He still had a scar on the side of his forehead where the tip of my rolling pin had slammed into him.

"Now, I know you remember that situation I went through last year? The male-related condition that Dr. Stoney treated me for."

"How could I forget that?" I muttered. I was nervous now and anxious for this meeting to end. My throat was dry and I was thirsty, but now I couldn't even finish my beer.

Last year, Pee Wee had been diagnosed with a mysterious prostate ailment. It had temporarily wiped out his sex drive. He had endured an aggressive treatment procedure, and within a year his doctor had given him a fairly clean bill of health.

"I didn't tell you everything," he confessed. "There was more to that situation. I was hopin' that I'd never have to tell you everything, but I have to now."

A lump immediately formed in my throat. All I needed now was for Pee Wee to tell me that he was preparing for the afterlife. That would have pushed me over the edge for sure. "Are you telling me that the treatment didn't work, or is there something else wrong with you now?" It pleased me to see that he recognized the concern on my face and in my voice. I bit my bottom lip, but I didn't even try to hold back my tears this time. "Is it terminal?" I choked.

He held up his hand again, but he didn't respond right away to my question. "Uh-uh," he finally said.

"Well, what is it?" I managed. "Look, my heart is beating like it's about to bust out of my chest. My nerves are shot and my blood pressure is sky-high. If you keep beating around the bush and don't tell me everything I need to know, you might have to arrange my funeral." If I was going to lose my husband for good after all, I didn't want death to be the thing to take him from me this time. "Do you mean . . ." I rose, trembling in my tracks. My legs wobbled and before I knew what was happening next, I involuntarily plopped back down on the couch. "Are you . . . going to . . . die?" I whimpered.

He laughed and I considered that to be a

good sign. "Yes, I am goin' to die . . . eventually."

"I need another drink," I mouthed. I rose up off the couch again and stumbled back into the kitchen. I didn't get another beer. I fixed myself a double shot of bourbon this time. One thing I promised myself was that as soon as things settled, I'd reduce my alcohol intake. I had drunk more in the past few days than I normally did in a month.

"You don't have to worry, Annette. I ain't dyin' no time soon. Not unless I get hit by a bus, or you finish me off for me actin' such a fool." He laughed again, but I didn't see the humor in his words. "Uh, see, Dr. Stoney told me that the treatment I was gettin' might have a few side effects. . . ."

"Such as?"

"Well, as you recall, my sex drive was on life support durin' that time. I was no more interested in pussy than I was in mud pie."

"How could I forget that part," I managed.

"There was another side effect that was worse," he said, looking at the floor.

"What could be worse than you not wanting to touch me?"

"The medicine that I was taking diminished my sperm count." He looked up at me with an expression of unbearable despair on his face. It made him look even older and more unattractive. In fact, that look on his face made him look sick. "It was already low when I started the treatment. By the time I finished the treatment, it was at ground zero."

As devastating as this news was, I was relieved to hear that it was not something worse. But what Pee Wee had just revealed overwhelmed me anyway. A great sadness came over me. I wanted to cry some more, but that was one of the many things that I was sick and tired of doing. It never did any good, and I always ended up with red, swollen eyes — which gave the busybodies something else to gossip about. "So you are telling me that you can't have any more kids?"

"Didn't you ever wonder why you never got pregnant again?"

"For one thing, my eggs were old by the time we got busy. And your juice was just as old. I didn't spend any time wondering about why you hadn't made any more babies since Charlotte until . . . until Lizzie called me up and told me she was having your baby."

"Lizzie is havin' a baby, like I just told you, but it's not mine, like I just told you. When I showed her the papers that I got

252

from Dr. Stoney, she changed her tune. She broke down and cried like a baby herself. That's when she told me that she knew that Peabo is her baby's daddy, and that she knew it all along! But when she told him she was pregnant, he went off on her and told her that he already had five kids and wasn't about to support another one."

Lizzie was an even bigger fraud than I originally believed. Nothing that woman could do or say would surprise me now. "So she decided to pin it on you?"

"She said she knew I'd be a better daddy than that asshole she's with now," Pee Wee said, giving me a sheepish look. That didn't help his case any. I wanted to slap that look off of his face. I wanted him to be as angry as I was about the fact that Lizzie had tried to pull the wool over his eyes.

"Did it occur to her that you might count up the months? I know she's stupid, but is she that stupid?"

Pee Wee shrugged. "I guess she figured it was worth a shot. People do some of the stupidest shit around here!"

"Pee Wee, are you telling me the truth?"

"You want to see the papers from Dr. Stoney? I told Lizzie, and I'm tellin' you, when that baby comes, we'll get a blood test done. I know that's not one hundred percent accurate to prove if a man is a baby's daddy or not, but it's the best I can offer. The bottom line is, there is no way that baby can be mine." Pee Wee paused and rubbed the side of his neck. "You know how I got around before me and you got married. Didn't you wonder how come none of my exes got pregnant by me?"

"That's not something that I spent a lot of time thinking about either. As a matter of fact, that's not something I gave any thought to at all. I had a busy life back then myself. I was engaged to another man before you and I got serious, remember?"

Pee Wee gave me an exasperated look, but that didn't bother me at all. I was just as exasperated as he was, if not more.

"Annette, like I said, just to be sure, I will still go through with a blood test after Lizzie has her baby anyway. I will do whatever I have to do to straighten out this mess. I want you and me to resume what we had started, because I do want to give our marriage another chance. Don't you?"

I took my time responding because by now, I didn't know what I wanted anymore. "I still don't want to rush into anything. I still think we should date other people for a little while until we decide whether we really want to reconcile," I allowed. Before I could stop myself, I yawned.

"I'm goin' to get out of here so you can get some sleep. After that mess you went through with Rhoda and Jade today, I know you must be worn out. I'll be in touch. You want to go out to dinner one night next week or somethin'?"

"I don't want to make any plans for next week just yet. I need to spend some time with Lillimae, and I know Rhoda's going to need a shoulder to cry on for a while."

"Your birthday's comin' up real soon. How about then? We can have a nice dinner at that Italian restaurant you so crazy about. Or any other place you want to go."

"I'll think about it."

"Well, I'll be in touch anyway. But if you want to talk to me, you got my new phone number."

Immediately after Pee Wee left, I stumbled upstairs to Lillimae's room. I told her everything that Pee Wee had told me.

"Well, I guess that's good and bad news," she told me, lying in bed on her side like a seal. "I am so glad you came up here to tell me this right away. I was worried about you and what he was up to now. Eowww!"

Even though I felt slightly better, I didn't sleep much that night. There were so many

255

thoughts dancing around inside my head, I didn't know which one to address first.

CHAPTER 29

The following Sunday afternoon, I joined Lillimae in the kitchen to help her finish off a barbecued chicken that she had cooked earlier.

"While you were still upstairs, your boyfriend dropped off a basket of dirty clothes for you to wash and iron for him," she told me.

I jerked my head up from my plate and looked at her. "What boyfriend?" I asked.

"Oh, you got more than one?" Lillimae's eyes got big and an amused look quickly appeared on her face.

I gave Lillimae a sheepish grin. "Uh, I have been dating a couple of men. Roscoe was the one you met the night you got here. It's nothing serious, though," I said with a shrug. "I only see them every now and then."

"Yeah, I did meet that Roscoe. He's the one that dropped off his dirty clothes this mornin'."

"I'm kind of seeing another guy, every now and then. Ronald Hawthorne is a personnel representative for the water department. He's a nice enough guy."

"Uh-huh." Lillimae gave me a cautious look. "That's nice, I guess. I'm glad to see that you didn't let Pee Wee's departure stop you from livin' it up."

"Like I just said, it's nothing serious with either one of them — and they know that. I just like to kill time with them," I mused.

"These two boyfriends are just *maintenance* men, huh?" Lillimae asked with a double wink.

"Yeah, something like that."

"Uh-huh. And I hope they do good work." I blinked, wondering what Lillimae would say if she knew about Roscoe's problem, something that I had only shared with Rhoda. I had regretted telling Rhoda, because she had tried to talk me into sneaking some Viagra into Roscoe's drinks, which I thought was ridiculous. As far as I was concerned, that was a variation of date rape. "There is nothin' wrong with us women keepin' our female machinery tuned up," Lillimae decided.

I looked at my watch and gasped. "Shit! I just remembered that I told Ronald I'd call him today." I skittered across the floor and grabbed the telephone on the wall. My call went straight to Ronald's voice mail. I hung up and gave Lillimae a thoughtful look. "I'm worried about Rhoda. I've left her a few messages too. Has she called today?"

"Uh-uh. After what she went through with that useless daughter of hers, she's probably too upset to do much of anything these days. Maybe you should call her again," Lillimae suggested.

I lifted the telephone again and dialed Rhoda's number; this call went straight to voice mail too. I left her a message to call me when she felt like it.

Charlotte had spent the night at Harrietta's house again. She came home about an hour after I'd left Rhoda a voice mail, and marched up to me in the kitchen with a scowl on her face.

"I keep telling you that I hate that strange lady, Mama. Please don't make me go back to her house again," Charlotte said through clenched teeth.

"What in the world happened over there?" I asked, stirring the batter for the sweetbread I was making for dinner to go with the smothered pork chops Lillimae had already cooked.

"She's a sick puppy, that's what. I don't

like her, and I don't want to go over there anymore," Charlotte told me.

Lillimae was humped over the counter by the sink, peeling potatoes for a salad.

"Unless you can tell me something other than Harrietta is 'strange' and a 'sick puppy,' you'll go over there when I tell you to. Is that clear?" I told my daughter.

"Yes, ma'am. . . ." Charlotte slunk back out of the kitchen like a whipped puppy with her bottom lip sticking out like a nipple.

Lillimae got my attention by loudly clearing her throat and moving closer to the table. "Do you mind if I say somethin'?" she asked, wiping her hands on the tail of the white duster she wore.

I looked up at Lillimae. "You can say whatever you want to say. But I'll tell anybody that these kids today think they can call the shots. Well, I am not going to let my child get as out of control as Rhoda let hers," I vowed.

There was a mysterious expression on Lillimae's face now. "Darlin', I think I need to stick my nose into your business right about now," she told me. "I didn't want to bring this subject up and get you all worried, but I can't hold my tongue any longer." A strange look suddenly crossed her face.

That alone was enough to make me worry. I held my breath as she massaged her brow. With a straight face, she looked directly in my eyes and asked, "Just how well do you know this Harrietta woman?"

CHAPTER 30

I didn't want Lillimae to know that her question had surprised me. I gave her a surprised look anyway. "What do you mean by that?" I asked, hoping she couldn't tell how much the question had also disturbed me.

"I mean, do you know her as well as you should? Wolves got all kinds of sheeps' clothin' to choose from these days. . . ."

I shrugged. "I think I know Harrietta well enough." I shrugged again and Lillimae's brow shot up.

"You think you know her well enough, or you *believe* you know her well enough?" Lillimae asked.

I didn't shrug this time, but I tried to speak with a more authoritative tone. "I know her well enough to feel comfortable leaving my daughter with her. Harrietta's not just some wild woman off the street. She's got kids; she runs a child-care business. She's just a little stricter than Charlotte is used to, that's all." I glanced toward the window over my sink. From it, I could see Harrietta's house across the street. "One thing that I can say about Harrietta is that she keeps a clean house. And she pays her bills on time. I've seen delinquent credit documents come across my desk on just about everybody I know except her." I turned back to Lillimae with a concerned look on my face that I couldn't explain. "I just can't figure out what she does or says to her kids for them to be so . . . I don't know . . . humble."

Lillimae gave me a puzzled look. "Humble? Now that's an odd word to describe kids as young as hers."

"Well behaved, I mean. I never see them outside in the yard playing like all the other kids on this street. And when they come over here, they are so quiet and, oh, I can't think of a better word to describe their behavior. Humble is the best word that I can come up with."

"Well, that's not the right word, if you ask me." Lillimae let out a loud breath and gave me a serious look. "Remember that old movie *The Stepford Wives?* The one where the men had some kind of eerie thing goin' on where they were programmin' their wives to act like robots?"

"Robot? Now, that's another odd word to describe kids. Maybe we're not being fair to Harrietta. She's a real good mother and she deserves credit for that."

"You're probably right. But if you don't know her that well, maybe you should make it your business to get to know her better soon. Let's start invitin' her over on a regular basis." The look on Lillimae's face was too serious now, and that had me worried. "If you don't mind me stickin' my nose even deeper into your business, I suggest you visit her house on a regular basis too. If she's puttin' up a front for your benefit, and the benefit of all the other kids' parents, the best way to find out for sure is to pay her a few surprise visits. That way, if she's up to no good, you'll catch her."

"I don't like where this conversation is going. You would think that we were discussing somebody suspected of spying for the Russians or something." I forced myself to laugh. Lillimae gave me such a stern look that it made me stop laughing right away.

"I just think you need to pop in on her when she does not expect it, that's all," she told me.

"She didn't know that I was coming over there when I dropped in on her a couple of nights ago," I reminded. "There was nothing out of the ordinary going on. I felt so comfortable there, and everything was so pleasant and well arranged, I didn't want to leave." I sniffed. "One thing I'm glad to know is that she doesn't have a bunch of men parading in and out of her house. She'll never have to worry about some devil putting his filthy hands on one of her girls, or any of the girls she takes care of, under her roof the way Mr. Boatwright did me."

"Boatwright is probably burnt to a crisp in hell by now, so we can forget about him," Lillimae snapped. She rubbed my shoulder and patted the side of my head. "You've been through too many ugly situations to ever let your guard down again, girl."

I had always thought of myself as a smart, practical person. I managed a fairly large group of employees at the collection agency that I worked for. One of my toughest job responsibilities was that I had to go after some pretty hardcore deadbeats to get them to pay their delinquent bills. Therefore, I had to be on my toes all the time, so keeping my wits about me was essential.

I had experienced so many ups and downs in the past few years that I couldn't afford to ever let my guard down again. And I didn't plan to. Especially when it came to my personal life.

But even being alert had not been enough for me to avoid a catastrophe. I was alert back in March — or so I thought. But I didn't even know that Lizzie was having an affair with my husband until Pee Wee and Lizzie told me! Losing my husband to another woman was a hard thing for me to live with. It wasn't something that I couldn't get beyond, though. But when it came to my child, it was a different story. I knew that if something bad happened to her, I would never get over it the way I could get over losing my husband to another woman. I knew that there was never enough parents could do to protect their children. My mother had watched me like a hawk when I was a child, but I had still been victimized by a man my mother and everybody else had trusted.

Shortly after Pee Wee had left me for Lizzie, I'd dated Jacob Brewster, one of my former boyfriends. When I felt that he was getting too chummy with my daughter, I severed my relationship with him immediately. Well, other things had occurred that had also prompted me to make that decision, but my daughter had been the main reason. I knew that the world was full of sharks and wolves, and unless I could spend every minute of the day with my daughter, there was no way that I could protect her from them all.

But I would *never* let her get too close to the men I socialized with. Other than Pee Wee and my daddy, no other men slept over at my house. Roscoe seemed more comfortable taking me to his place. And Ronald only visited me at my house for about an hour each time when he came. And sometimes he didn't even stay that long. The last couple of times that I was with him, it was at a motel. The last time Ronald paid me a visit at my house, Muh'Dear quietly and unexpectedly showed up. Without alerting me that she was even on the premises, she walked into my bedroom while Ronald was on top of me. I thought I'd never hear the end of that. Visiting Ronald's house had never appealed to me. He had five frisky dogs and several free-loading relatives. That was why I had no problem meeting him in other locations.

Charlotte ate her lunch in her room, but I couldn't stop thinking about what she'd said about Harrietta earlier in the day, and all of the days before. I took Lillimae's advice and invited Harrietta and her daughters to eat dinner with us that evening, and I planned to do so a few times a month.

If this woman was going to be looking after my child from time to time, I did need to know more about her. One thing I needed to know was *exactly* what her relationship was with men. I tried not to be nosy, but I did notice that the only men I'd ever seen at her front door were her ex, the mailman, and the pizza delivery guy. Since I worked during the day, and I didn't peep out of my windows on a regular basis when I was home, like some of my other neighbors, I couldn't keep close tabs on her. But I had no reason to believe that there was anything going on in Harrietta's house that I needed to know about. It was not possible for me to know everything about her, anyway; just like it was not possible for people to know everything there was to know about me.

For all I knew, Harrietta might not have wanted to be friends with me if she knew how much alcohol I consumed. And since Harrietta didn't date, if she knew how often I thought about sex, and how easily I slid into bed with three different men, it might have a profound effect on what she thought of me.

Jade had kissed up to me for years and had fooled me into thinking that she was my friend. But that was because I had something she wanted: my husband. I had nothing that Harrietta wanted, so she had no reason to kiss up to me, other than the fact that she wanted me as a friend.

CHAPTER 31

Lillimae had plans to go out with Daddy again that evening. When I told Charlotte that I had invited Harrietta to eat dinner with us, her eyes bulged out like she'd seen a ghost. "Dang, Mama! Ain't it bad enough that I have to be around that lady in her gloomy house? Do I have to be around her in our house too?" she complained.

"If you don't want to eat in the dining room with Harrietta and me and her girls, you can eat in the kitchen or your room," I suggested. "I really want to get to know this woman better, so I can figure out what it is you don't like about her." I rubbed my daughter's back. "Now, she'll be here soon, so go wash your hands and remove that stupid look off your face."

Charlotte chose to eat dinner in her room, but when I suggested Harrietta's girls join her, Harrietta protested. "I don't ever let my girls manipulate me. I told them before we left the house this evening that they were going to stay where I could see or hear them," she told me as we set the table in my dining room. Her girls were in the living room.

"But they'll just be upstairs," I pointed out. "I am sure that if they get into something that they shouldn't be into, we'll find out soon enough."

"Not this time," Harrietta told me, shaking her head. She let out a mild snort. She continued talking with her face contorted like she had just sat on a tack. "Last month I let them visit with those Johnson kids around the corner. It hurts me to talk about what happened. Lucy, with her clumsy self, knocked over Mrs. Johnson's expensive vase that she brought back with her from Spain. I don't have to tell you, but it cost me a real pretty penny to replace that damn thing — ugly as it was. Besides, my girls tell lies when they are not around me."

"All kids lie." I chuckled. "I know my daughter tells a fib when it suits her." I cleared my throat and became more serious. "Listen, uh, there is something I need to discuss with you, and the sooner I do it, the better," I stated.

Harrietta's eyes got big, her face froze. "Uh, what is it?"

"My daughter gets along with just about everybody I know. She, uh, likes everybody we know . . . except for you. She gets hopping mad when I send her to your house. I don't know exactly what it is about you that she doesn't like because she doesn't tell me anything specific."

"Annette, you are making me nervous. I wouldn't do anything in the world to harm your child, or anybody else's child," Harrietta told me, her voice cracking.

"I hope not. But sometimes kids are too scared to reveal too much information when somebody is abusing them in some way."

"Abusing them? Annette, I am not abusing any child! Why —"

I held up my hand. "I didn't say you were. But there has to be a reason why Charlotte doesn't like you. I know my girl is spoiled, but she's always been spoiled. However, she has never felt the way she feels about you with anybody else. You seem like a good person to me. But Mr. Boatwright, the man I told you about the other day who abused me when I was a child, he had most people believing he was a saint."

"Well, he was a *man* and we females know how those *devils* can be. Look, if you don't want your child associating with me, that's fine with me. I know I have a strong personality and that rubs some people the wrong way. But I would still like to be friends with you. We have a lot in common and I enjoy your company." Harrietta managed a weak smile, but there was a sad look in her eyes.

"I didn't mean to upset you, but I figured that the sooner I addressed this issue, the better. And just so you won't think I am not being fair to you, I know my daughter acts a fool when she has to do something she doesn't like. So, it could just be that you are a little more rigid than she is used to. And the way kids are these days, it could also be that she gets a kick out of saying things to hurt people she doesn't like — whether they are mistreating her or not."

Harrietta shook her head again and let out a heavy sigh. That sad look was still in her eyes. "If one of my kids ever tells me they don't like a particular person, I will say something to that person about it, so I do understand you bringing this up. We can't afford to be naïve when it comes to our babies like some mothers are."

"I am not going to be as naïve as my mother was," I vowed. "She never wanted to hear anything bad about my abuser, so he was able to rape me on a regular basis right up under her nose. Had she confronted that man and really tried to find out why I didn't like him, it would have given me more courage. I might have exposed him before he died so that something could have been done about what he did to me. Do you understand where I'm coming from? Nobody, and I mean *nobody,* is going to abuse my child and get away with it. If my daughter even hints that somebody is abusing her, they will regret the day they were born," I warned. I noticed how Harrietta's body stiffened.

"And I don't blame you one bit, Annette. That's why I would only trust my girls with a woman like you. I know you have some men friends since Pee Wee took off; I've seen you around town with a couple. But I know you would never put my girls in a position where one of your men could take advantage of them — like your mama did with you . . ." Harrietta dropped her head and stared at the floor. "I swear to God, I would never do anything to hurt your child." She snorted and started to fan her face with her hand. The room was not that hot, so I could not figure out why there was so much sweat on her face. But the things I had just said had me feeling kind of warm, too, and the next thing I knew, I was fanning my face too. "Maybe I should leave . . ."

"You don't have to leave," I said, holding up my hand. "I personally don't have a problem with you, so I still want us to be friends. If Charlotte doesn't change her opinion of you in the next couple of weeks, I will send her to one of the other neighbors like I used to do. I don't want her to get too much more worked up over this, and I don't want her to cause any friction between you and me."

"Charlotte will get used to me — if she gives me a chance. All of the other kids I take care of did, and there were a couple that hated my guts!" Harrietta said. "They both came around, and now they love me to death. . . ." Harrietta blinked and gave me a dry smile. "And I'm glad you let me know what was on your mind," she added with a dismissive wave of her hand.

I breathed a sigh of relief. I was glad that everything was out in the open. "Uh, now that you and I are on the same page, I hope this is something we won't have to talk about again."

"I hope we won't have to either," Harrietta said firmly. "But if you feel the need to do so again, don't hesitate. You can talk to me about anything."

"I'm glad to hear that." I sniffed. "I don't want the girls, especially Charlotte, to know what we just talked about. For the time being, I think this is something we should keep between us."

"Don't worry. I won't say anything to Charlotte about our little discussion. But now that I know how she feels about me, I will try to be a little less rigid with her." Harrietta gave me a broad smile. "Okay?"

"Okay," I said with a nod. From the way she turned away from me, I assumed she didn't want to continue the conversation. I knew I didn't.

I excused myself to check on the food still on the stove. When I rejoined Harrietta, she was standing in the middle of the living room floor with her arms folded like a drill sergeant, glaring at her children. Vivian, Lucy, and Diane were twelve, ten, and nine, respectively. They were attractive kids, but unusually quiet. They were not just "quiet"; those girls were like mutes. Dressed in the typical attire for girls in their age group — ripped jeans and loose-fitting T-shirts — they sat side by side on my couch looking like they were conjoined.

During dinner, I tried to draw the girls into the conversation several times, but it was like pulling a dragon's teeth. Not a one of them spoke without first looking at her mother. Each time, she would give them a grim look and a sharp nod; then they would speak with so much control it was disturbing. It was the first time that I allowed myself to think that maybe Harrietta was a little too rigid. Her kids *were* like the robotlike women in *The Stepford Wives,* like Lillimae had suggested.

After dinner, Harrietta finally allowed the girls to join Charlotte in her room. I saw them smile for the first time that evening.

"Uh, are your girls always this quiet and well behaved?" I asked Harrietta as we cleared the table.

She didn't reply right away. But it looked like she was considering my question. Finally, she said, "Always. My girls are always quiet and well behaved. They'd better be . . ."

Fifteen minutes later, when I went upstairs to check on Charlotte and the girls, I found them sitting on the floor at the foot of Charlotte's bed watching cartoons. "Aren't you girls a little old for cartoons?" I asked, standing in the doorway with my hand on the knob. "I thought kids your age liked those music videos."

"We are not allowed to watch videos or anything on cable," Vivian said in a weak voice, her eyes on the floor.

"Well, I don't allow Charlotte to watch

whatever she wants to either. But as long as it's not obscene, or too violent, you girls can come over here and watch whatever you want." I entered the room and gently closed the door behind me, and moved closer to the kids.

"I keep telling you their mother is not normal," Charlotte said, giving me a smug look. "Tell her, y'all. Tell my mama that your mama is not normal."

CHAPTER 32

Vivian turned to me with a frightened look on her face. She resembled Harrietta the most. "We hate her," Vivian said, looking at her sisters for support. They both nodded.

"Why?" I asked.

"We just do," Diane said. This was the first time that she had spoken since I'd met her. I was amazed at how deep her voice was. She was the youngest, but looked and sounded the oldest.

"She don't beat us or nothing like that," Lucy quickly offered. "We just don't like her. We wanted to live with our daddy. He's real cool. When he lived with us, he let us do whatever we wanted to do, and Mama didn't like it. That's why he left."

So that was it! They missed their father. Now it all made sense. Harrietta's kids "hated" her because she'd divorced their father.

I didn't like to discuss certain subjects

with children. I didn't like to get too personal with people I didn't know that well anyhow, so I didn't continue the conversation. Now that I knew a little more about Harrietta's situation with her children, I couldn't help feeling a little bit of sympathy for her. But knowing what I knew now still didn't give me a clue as to why my daughter disliked Harrietta so much. It was something that I was going to have to keep at the front of my mind.

I was glad to see that Lillimae had returned home by the time I made it back down to the living room. She and Harrietta were chatting away like old friends.

"Did you know that Harrietta teaches Sunday school at her church, and she used to be a Girl Scout troop leader?" Lillimae said as I dropped down into the La-Z-Boy.

"Oh," I mouthed. "You spend a lot of time with kids, huh?" I said, looking at Harrietta. She was beaming like a lighthouse. "Honey, I love kids. We don't spend enough time with them, if you ask me. But it's something I've always enjoyed. I had to help my mama raise my nine younger brothers and sisters. We were all raised the old-fashioned way, so none of us ever got into trouble the ways these kids do nowadays." Harrietta shook her head. "One of the little boys that I look after now, he's so grown and arrogant, you'd think he was paying the bills in his house. His mama and his daddy act like they are afraid of that little boy! You wouldn't believe how they pamper that little devil when they drop him off on their way to work. But I've got his mannish little ass under control now."

"I raised my boys with a firm hand too," Lillimae said with a proud sigh. "Kids need to always know who has got the upper hand."

"I won't argue with that," I said with a nod.

The more I talked to Harrietta, the more sympathetic I felt toward her — despite Charlotte's feelings. I had to be honest and admit to myself that when I was a child, my mother had had a few female friends whom I didn't like. With that in mind, I realized my daughter's feelings were not that un-usual. Even though Harrietta was younger than me, I thought that maybe I could learn a few things from her about "tough love" childrearing methods. Maybe I'd avoid problems with my daughter later on, and she wouldn't do some of the dumb shit that I'd done as a youngster — prostitution be-ing the worst. I was only sorry that Rhoda had not met a woman like Harrietta in time to "save" Jade.

"Annette, I can't believe how much we have in common. The bitch that stole my husband was supposed to be a close friend too." Harrietta seemed eager to discuss the break up of her marriage. Lillimae and I shared a bottle of white wine, but since Harrietta didn't drink alcohol, she clutched a glass of Pepsi in her hand. She took a long swallow and burped.

"I hope you didn't take it too hard," Lillimae told Harrietta, giving her a pitiful look.

"Oh, it hurt like hell!" Harrietta shouted, balling her fist.

Harrietta and I did have a lot in common. She was about my size, which was a fourteen these days. She was dark like me, but she could have used a few makeup tips to enhance her beautiful chocolate complexion. At least I knew how to hide the fine lines around my eyes with the right concealer. I also knew how to enhance my best feature, which was my eyes, with the right shade and quantity of eyeliner and mascara. Harrietta's makeup, which was at least two shades too light for her complexion, ended abruptly at her jawline, like an ill-fitted mask. She had more candy-apple red lipstick on her teeth than on her lips. A short, curly black wig snugly covered her head like a bathing cap.

Harrietta had eagerly accepted my dinner invitation when I called her a few hours ago. As a matter of fact, she didn't even wait until dinner was ready. She had come over as soon as she got off the telephone.

Now she seemed so comfortable she couldn't stop talking.

"Girl, I came home from my job at the post office that day and I —"

"Post office? I used to work for the post office," Lillimae blurted, cutting Harrietta off.

"Yeah, I had been there for nine years. Anyway, I was supposed to go out of town after work for a church retreat that Saturday, day after my birthday. Would you believe that that snake I was married to had the nerve to take me out to dinner on my birthday, give me a gorgeous new bracelet, and make love to me like it was for the last time — which it was — that night. All the while knowing what he had planned."

My stomach tightened. Pee Wee had made love to me hours before he left me. I nodded for Harrietta to continue.

"Anyway, I had eaten some tuna salad for lunch that Saturday, and it must have been bad, because I got sick on the way to the retreat. I had to turn around and come back

283

home. The kids were with a sister from church. When I got home and saw Derrick's car in the driveway, I got scared. He was supposed to be on a fishing trip with one of his buddies. Naturally, I thought that he must have gotten sick from that same tuna salad because he had eaten some of it too. I eased into the house, went up the stairs to our room at the end of the hall, and opened the bedroom door. That motherfucker was sick all right! And even sicker when I got through bouncing lamps, books, and my fists off his head. That bastard had the nerve to have his bitch in my house — in my bed!"

Lillimae squawked like a dying chicken. I groaned so loud, I almost fell off the love seat.

"Men ought to know better than to bring their whores into their wives' homes!" I offered. "I'll bet mine won't do it again." I had already shared bits and pieces of my story of betrayal with Harrietta before tonight. But from the disgusted look on her face, you would have thought that she was hearing it all for the first time.

She whooped and hollered louder than me and Lillimae put together. "Damn! Damn! Damn! Annette, you went through hell. Well, Paulette had been my home girl since junior high! Now there she was — in a gown that I hadn't even worn yet! Stretched out in my bed with my pink sponge rollers on her nappy head! She left my house running, wrapped up in one of my best sheets. I chased that heifer all the way down the block. When I caught her, I whupped her ass some more for running off with my four-hundred-thread-count sheet." Harrietta seemed to be enjoying her rant. There was a dark, hollow look in her eyes and a cruel smile on her lips.

"And what did you do to Derrick?" I asked.

"There was only one thing I could do. I divorced him. A woman would have to be crazy to stay married to a man who pulled a trick like that." Harrietta paused and gave me a wan look. "I know your situation with Pee Wee was a little different, and I know you and him are trying to work things out, but Derrick didn't want to work anything out. He couldn't wait to marry Paulette. That's what hurt the most. He wasn't even sorry. He didn't even want to be with me after that — even though I told him we could work things out!"

"My man has his faults, and I will overlook all of that eventually and go back home," Lillimae confessed. "It's so hard to find a truly righteous man these days."

"Well, I have not dated much since I divorced Derrick. The last man I did go out with was so useless in the bedroom, he couldn't turn me on with a pair of pliers," Harrietta laughed. "I am so glad I got my kids to keep me company. People thought I was a fool for quitting my job at the post office to start doing child care. But taking care of kids is my calling. I don't have to worry about them hurting me. *They are so easy to control. . . .*"

"Not all kids are easy to control," I pointed out. I hadn't told Harrietta about Jade, and I didn't plan to. The last thing Rhoda needed was for all of the town gossips to be discussing her business before she resolved things with Jade. Besides, Harrietta would hear about Jade soon enough anyway. And I was sure that when she did, she would toot her horn some more about how well she was raising her kids.

I just hoped that she didn't toot it in Rhoda's face.

"That's true, but we have to control our kids for as long as we can. Regardless of whether we do a good job or not, only the good Lord knows how they are going to treat us when we get old," Harrietta said with a frightened look on her face. "Speaking of getting old, Annette, Charlotte told me that your forty-eighth birthday is coming up soon."

I nodded and swallowed a lump that had suddenly formed in my throat. "Uh-huh. Next week," I practically groaned.

I didn't know where Harrietta was going with this conversation, but from what she'd said so far, it didn't sound like it was going in a positive direction. "Well, just be glad that you are still able to take care of yourself," she told me, giving me a look of pity — and I didn't know why. She didn't waste any time telling me why. "Turn on the TV and watch *Cops* or any other true-crime show. Read any issue of *Essence* magazine. Good black men are as scarce as hen's teeth. Half of them are either in jail or in a hospital dying of AIDS or a drug overdose. Half of the half that's left, who are not with women of other races — or other men — they don't want old crones like you and me. Our chance of landing a good man is next to none. That just leaves our kids to keep us company. Ha! That's a joke within a joke. The way kids are turning on their mamas and daddies these days, killing them for insurance money or dumping them off in some nursing home where they'll get abused, neglected, raped, and beaten, there is no telling what we have to look forward to. Either we put up with all of that or we bite the bullet and grow old alone. . . ."

CHAPTER 33

It saddened me to hear that Harrietta had such a grim outlook on life. Even though what she said was true for some people, I didn't like to think about the comments she'd made about some of the problems that we would probably face as time moved forward. Other than that, I didn't mind getting old — even if it meant I wouldn't have a man.

I felt so sorry for women like Harrietta. She seemed to be in control of her life and her children, so I couldn't understand why she felt the way she did. But like a lot of women in our age group, she was confused and frightened. Her kids would probably remain in her life once they reached adulthood, but from what she'd told me, she'd never have another serious relationship with a man. *She* was probably going to grow old alone.

A week after the dinner with Harrietta,

my mother called me up at seven in the morning. It was my birthday. Instead of wishing me a "happy birthday," she greeted me with, "I just wanted to remind you that you ain't gettin' no younger, girl. The older you get, the harder it's gwine to be for you to keep off all of that blubber that you lost. And with Lillimae cookin' up a storm all the time now, you're gwine to end up lookin' just like her, maybe even worse. Lord help you!"

"Lillimae does not hold a gun to my head to make me eat, Muh'Dear," I said with a yawn. "Charlotte loves her cooking so much she doesn't even complain when Lillimae cooks collard greens like she does when I do."

"Uh-huh." Muh'Dear suddenly started to cough, and she did that for a full minute. The same way that Pee Wee did the last time he was in my bedroom.

"Are you all right?" I asked.

"Don't you worry none about me," my mother whined.

I sat up in bed, still slightly hungover. Pee Wee had delivered a bouquet of red roses and a birthday card the evening before. Even if he had invited me out that night, which he hadn't, I probably would have declined. I had decided that the less I saw of him in an intimate setting, the better. I had enjoyed a candlelit dinner with Roscoe at his house last night. While we'd slow danced in his living room, he had surprised me with a few quick pecks on my cheek. Other than him pinching my butt a few times, that was as far as our "lovemaking" went this time. And as usual, Roscoe had apologized. He told me again that he was no "lover boy" and that he was glad that that didn't bother me. However, he did tell me this time that if we got more serious, he would get some professional help with his "problem" if I wanted him to. I didn't want Roscoe to do anything special for me. As long as I had Ronald, I was all right for the moment. Ronald had some flaws too. He was going through a bitter divorce, so he didn't want to flaunt our relationship. Very few people knew we were seeing one another. I went along with that because I enjoyed his company and he was a fantastic lover. "If that greedy bitch I married found out about me and you, she'd be trying to get even more of the shit I worked for for so many years," he told me the same day we began our relationship. I had met him two months ago in a coffee shop while I was having lunch.

I knew of women like Ronald's estranged

wife, so I understood where he was coming from. But I had been around the block enough times to know that Ronald probably had other reasons for wanting to keep our relationship quiet. He was no doubt dating other women and probably wanted to avoid any public embarrassments by running into one while he was with one of the others. I didn't have a problem with that either. As a matter of fact, I preferred to keep my personal life somewhat quiet. I was tired of being fodder for the Richland gossips.

Yes, I was trying to restore my marriage, but until that happened, I wanted to have as much fun as I possibly could. An hour after Roscoe had brought me home last night, I went back out to meet Ronald at the hot tubs out on Sawyer Road.

Roscoe wanted to see me again on the upcoming Friday night, but I had not decided yet if I wanted to see him again so soon. The main reason was because Ronald had hinted that he wanted to see me again on that same night.

Muh'Dear interrupted my thoughts with more coughing.

"Muh'Dear, you don't sound too good to me. Have you been taking those vitamins that Dr. Green gave you? I'm about to get up and get dressed. Is there anything you need me to do for you?"

"Naw, you stay home and keep that Lillimae company . . . like you been doin' since she got here."

I sighed. "I'll come over later today."

"You don't have to. I'll be all right, somehow, God willin'. . . ."

"Well, if you do need me before I get over there, just call me and I'll come over right away."

"I don't want to bother you if I need help. That's what they got the ambulance service for. . . ."

I got off the telephone in a huff. Then I got up and dressed. I was on my way to my parents' house fifteen minutes later.

Muh'Dear must have had a miraculous recovery, because by the time I let myself in to her house through the back door, she was hovering over the sink like a horsefly. "Frank, is that you?" she asked without turning around. Then she started to hum her favorite B.B. King tune, "The Thrill Is Gone." That told me that she was not feeling as badly as she sounded on the telephone. She paused again and yelled over her shoulder. "I'm fixin' to make some more buttermilk biscuits. Then we can check with Sister Miller to see what time bingo starts this evenin'. I —" She whirled around and

293

stopped talking as soon as she saw me standing in the middle of the floor with my arms folded.

"Shouldn't you be lying down? You sounded awful a little while ago," I said in an accusatory tone.

Muh'Dear responded with a loud cough. "I still don't feel too good," she croaked. "Uh, you didn't have to rush over here. And how come you didn't bring Charlotte with you?"

"She wasn't up yet," I answered, easing into a chair at the cluttered kitchen table. "And she wanted to stay around the house to help Lillimae make me a birthday cake. Are you and Daddy going to come over this evening to get some cake?"

"Well." Muh'Dear wobbled across the floor, wiping flour off her hands onto her apron. She sat down hard in the chair across from me. "Well, we might and we might not. You know I don't eat everybody's cookin'. Is that Lillimae clean?"

"Lillimae is as clean as you are, Muh'Dear. If you and Daddy can make it, come around six," I said. I rose and headed back toward the door, even though my mother had plastered one of her puppy-dog looks on her face.

Muh'Dear didn't come to the house that

evening, but Daddy did. And so did Rhoda and Scary Mary. We had a nice quiet dinner to help me celebrate my birthday. Afterward, Rhoda and I went to the Red Rose for a few drinks.

I wanted us to enjoy our night out, so I decided not to mention Jade or Pee Wee unless Rhoda brought them up. We ordered a bottle of wine and sat in a booth near the bandstand, enjoying a new band that the club owner had brought in from Toledo. We even got up and danced a few times with some of the club regulars. But it was hard to ignore what we obviously wanted to talk about.

"I haven't seen or heard from Jade since I kicked her out of the house," Rhoda told me. She didn't display any emotion at all. But when Pee Wee's name came up, she got anxious. "Have you seen him lately?"

"He dropped off some roses and a birthday card last night, but he didn't stay long. He's been by the house a few other times lately, but we haven't made love since the day Lizzie called me up and dropped her bombshell in my lap," I reported.

"Oh. How are you feelin' about all of that now?" Rhoda asked with a stiff look on her face.

I shrugged. "I guess I feel as good about

Pee Wee as you feel about Jade."

"That's pretty grim," Rhoda decided.

From that point on, we talked about everything except those two.

Daddy and Scary Mary had left the house by the time I got home from the Red Rose, but Harrietta had come by. Earlier in the day I had invited her to join us to help celebrate my birthday, but she had declined. She told me that she had planned to do something else with some church members that evening. When that fell through, she came to the house anyway, but I had already left.

Lillimae had taken Daddy home and not returned yet. She had left Charlotte in the house with Harrietta before I returned. Harrietta's girls were with their father. The whole time that Charlotte had been alone with Harrietta in my house, she stayed in her room.

"I apologize for my daughter's rudeness," I told Harrietta. "She should not have left you sitting in the living room by yourself. She knows better."

"Oh, that's all right. She'll get used to me eventually," she said, helping herself to what was left of my birthday cake.

CHAPTER 34

The next morning, I called Rhoda's house several times every fifteen or twenty minutes. Each time the call went directly to voice mail. When I had not been able to reach her by Monday morning, I drove to her house on my lunch hour, after I'd gulped down half of a Big Mac.

When I arrived, Rhoda seemed surprised but happy to see me.

"I haven't been takin' any calls," she began as she waved me to the wing chair on the side of her living room couch. There were pillows and a blanket on the couch where I assumed she had been sleeping. There was also an empty wine bottle and a wineglass on the coffee table. "Uh, Otis doesn't know everything. He just thinks that Jade got on a rant and moved out on her own. That's all he needs to know."

"I won't tell him anything," I promised.

"He'd been after her to get her own place

for a long time now anyway. He didn't want her to get married last year and have us support her and a husband. Then she ups and marries Vernie, and we ended up supportin' her and a husband any damn way! Well, at least until Otis gave Vernie a job at the mill. But Otis feels — and I agree with him — that it's high time for Jade to be on her own. I had already removed her name from our credit card accounts. But did I tell you that her daddy took her name off our bank accounts too? She was our primary beneficiary."

"No, you didn't tell me about that. That was a smart thing to do." Smart was an understatement. As far as I was concerned, Jade was the last person in the world who deserved to be on any account as a primary beneficiary.

I gave Rhoda a pitiful look. She looked so sad and weak. I could certainly understand her being sad. But one thing that I could say about Rhoda was that I had never known her to be as weak as she appeared to be now. She had faced a lot even before she had to deal with breast cancer and a stroke. She'd been present when an out-of-control cop shot and killed her beloved brother when she was still a child. Her second-born child had died in her arms, and she'd given birth to a demonic child like Jade. Her list of unpleasant things was just as long as mine, if not longer. I was once weak, but I'd grown stronger over the years. But Rhoda had rarely shown any signs of weakness.

Until now.

"Don't keep givin' me those pitiful looks, Annette. I don't want any pity," Rhoda advised. "As much as you and I have been through over the years, you should know me well enough by now to know I don't like people feelin' sorry for me."

"Rhoda, I don't pity you any more than you pity me. I am just concerned. I know you are hurting. And for the record, so am I. It seems like we can't get away from turmoil, huh?"

"Maybe that's why we are such good friends."

We sighed at the same time. Then we looked in each other's eyes for a long time.

"Do you want to talk about Jade?" I finally asked.

Rhoda gave me a thoughtful look. Then, to my surprise and concern, she laughed and shook her head.

"Well, when you are ready to talk about what happened some more, you know I'll be ready to listen," I told her.

"I'd rather talk about you and Pee Wee," she said with a sniff.

I read Rhoda like a book. I knew that her main concern was her daughter. Despite all of the mean and nasty things that Jade had yelled at Rhoda, I knew enough about young people to know that they usually meant only half of what they said. And at the end of the day, the parents usually forgave the children no matter what they had said or done. I had just finished a true-crime book about a man who had forgiven his son who had conspired with two of his friends to kill his entire family for insurance money. The father was the only survivor of the bloody massacre that occurred in the family's mansion in an upscale Cleveland neighborhood on Christmas Day last year. The boy had been found guilty and sentenced to life without parole. But the father had been all over the TV news and on the radio professing his love and forgiveness of his son. Rhoda had read the same book. As a matter of fact, she was the one who had passed it on to me.

"There are some people who can forgive a person for just about anything, huh?" I said. "Like that boy in Cleveland who tried to have his whole family killed, and a certain person we both know . . ."

300

"I guess some people deserve to be for-given. I'm sure Pee Wee is one of those people," Rhoda mumbled. "But that's for you to decide. Me, I'd probably forgive him."

I had meant Jade, but I didn't correct Rhoda. And since the ball was now in my court, I took it and ran with it. "Rhoda, I don't think Lizzie's baby is really Pee Wee's," I stated.

"And when and why did you come to that conclusion?" she asked, giving me a curious look.

"Pee Wee finally told me something that he should have told me a long time ago."

"About him and Lizzie?"

"About him." I paused and gave Rhoda a pleading look. "Did you know he had a low sperm count? And always has?"

Rhoda held up her hand. "Whoa now! Where is this comin' from?"

"How many men close to fifty do you know with only one child?"

"Now that you asked, quite a few. I know a few middle-aged men who don't have any children at all. What's your point?"

"Pee Wee told me that he's always had what they call a low sperm count. That prostate thing that he went through a while back, that and the treatment reduced his

301

sperm count even more so. It is very unlikely that he can father any children because of that."

Rhoda gave me a suspicious look. Then she looked around. When she looked back to me, she spoke in a whisper, "Do you mean to tell me that Charlotte is not his child?"

I shook my head, rolled my eyes, and laughed. "Now, you know better. Sure, she is his daughter, and I am one hundred percent sure of that. If what he told me is true, back then when I got pregnant, he was still able to father children. Now the possibility is slim to none. More than likely, it's none." I had no proof that what Pee Wee had told me was true, but I believed him anyway. I couldn't see him telling me such a barefaced lie, knowing that I would eventually find out the truth.

"Hmmm. Well, somebody got Lizzie pregnant!"

"Yeah, somebody did, but it probably was not *my husband.*"

Lately, when I referred to Pee Wee as "my husband," a mild pain shot through my chest. I had first noticed it the day after Harrietta told me that her children hated her because she'd divorced their father. Even though divorce was a possibility in my future, now I had to step back and consider how it was really going to affect Charlotte if I went through with it. The last thing I wanted was for her to tell people that she hated me. But the other side of the coin was that Rhoda's husband had always been in Jade's life, and look how she turned out anyway. I'd heard Jade with my own ears tell Rhoda that she hated her. Life was becoming too complicated for me. But I was determined not to let it destroy me or make me more bitter than I already was.

"And you are sure of this? I mean, you believe Pee Wee about this low sperm count thing?" Rhoda questioned.

I nodded. "There's more." I pressed my lips together and massaged my scalp with all five fingers on one hand. I could feel another headache brewing. "Lizzie's baby is not due until March. If that's the case, she didn't even get pregnant until after she'd moved in with Peabo."

"And she's still claimin' that Pee Wee got her old fossil ass pregnant?"

"He said that when he told her about his so-called low sperm count, and the fact that the baby was due eleven months after they broke up, she changed her story."

"What a conniving bitch!"

"She knew it was Peabo's baby — or

somebody else's — all along. But being the conniving slut that she is, she decided to finger Pee Wee because she's no fool. She knows that Pee Wee is the kind of man who takes care of his responsibilities. Had he fell for her lie, that baby would have been treated like royalty."

Rhoda rubbed my shoulder. "Annette, I'm so sorry."

"Sorry? About what?"

"I'm sorry that you had to go through this mess in the first place. You've been through enough. I ran into your mother yesterday mornin' at the Grab and Go. She held me hostage for twenty minutes talkin' about how disappointed she was with you about you lettin' that *white* woman stay at the house."

I sighed. "I wish Muh'Dear would stop referring to Lillimae as a white woman. She keeps referring to Lizzie the same way no matter how many times I remind her that both of those women have black fathers. You know Muh'Dear."

"I do and that's why I know she'll eventually come around. She got used to Lillimae when Lillimae was up here that other time."

"Yeah, I remember. If we're lucky, she'll come around this time too."

"Guess what? Jade sent that Butchie guy

over here this mornin' to get her medicine," Rhoda said, looking at the wall. "She's still got that damn urinary tract infection."

"If she'd slow down and stop drinking margaritas like a fish, that medicine would probably be more effective," I replied.

"I must have told her that a dozen times, but she didn't listen to me. Butchie wouldn't tell me where she's stayin'." Rhoda's eyes narrowed and she gritted her teeth. "With creeps like that Butchie in the mix, she's probably holed up under a bridge in a cardboard box, or some flop house, and eatin' her meals in a soup kitchen."

"I doubt that. Butchie is a thug. Most thugs always have a hustle going. You saw that big SUV he rolled up in."

"Yeah, you're probably right. Jade is the kind of girl who always lands on her feet." A crooked smile formed on Rhoda's face. "My husband is so sweet. When I told him that Bully checked into a hotel to give us some privacy, he insisted on havin' him move back into our guest room."

"Bully's moved back into your house?"

"Uh-huh." Rhoda sighed and gave me a strange look. "I hope you don't think I'm choosin' a man over my daughter. That's not the case here."

"Rhoda, I've told you before, I would

never judge you. I know how important Bully is to you, and I know you still love your daughter. But the girl is out of control, Rhoda. Don't let her destroy your life," I said.

"Oh, she won't destroy my life, Annette. Or anybody else's." Rhoda snorted and gave me a hopeful look. "You'll see. . . ."

CHAPTER 35

I had never tried to encourage or discourage Rhoda to end her relationship with Bully. I had no right to even suggest such a thing. Even though she was married and loved her husband, her lover was just as much "family" as I was. He filled a void in Rhoda's life that even I, or her husband and kids, could not fill.

Bully had an ex in London where he owned and managed some high-end hotels. The only child he had fathered, that I knew of, was Rhoda's deceased son, who had died when he was a toddler. I was *still* the only other person in the world who knew that Bully and Rhoda had had a child together. Bully didn't even know that he was, or had been, a father.

I knew that Rhoda would probably always have a special attachment to Bully because of their child. And the fact that Bully still found Rhoda attractive enough to fly across the Atlantic several times a year to sleep with her, even after she'd lost her breasts to cancer.

"I'm glad to hear that Bully's back in the house. With Otis working all those long hours and even some weekends, you don't need to be alone. And I know how much you care about Bully. He's a good man," I told her. "Uh, I hope that little stunt Jade pulled on him didn't upset him too much."

"Bully's fine. He doesn't even want to talk about it anymore. He's even forgiven her."

"Hmm. I guess he really is a good man."

"Speakin' of good men, what's goin' on with you and Roscoe and Ronald? You haven't mentioned either one of them much lately."

"Roscoe is fine. I had dinner with him at his house the other night."

"Was that all? Was food the only thing he ate? He's got a mighty long tongue. . . ."

I gave Rhoda a wan look. "You know it was, you nasty thing, you." I laughed. "I tried to help him out a little, you know, warm him up with my hands, if you know what I mean."

"Unfortunately, I do," Rhoda snickered. "That's about all I get to do with my husband these days."

"Anyway, after a few clumsy minutes, I

stopped and offered to fix us some drinks. He told me to make sure I washed my hands. . . ." I chuckled as Rhoda gasped; then she chuckled too. "That was the end of that. That's the one thing about having a husband living in the house that I miss: sex whenever you want it."

"Humph! Like hell! Havin' a husband livin' in the house is no guarantee that you're goin' to get some lovin'. I can't tell you the last time Otis made love to me — not even some hand or tongue action."

"Thank God you've still got Bully to fall back on."

"And you still have Ronald as a backup, right?"

"Yeah, but I haven't seen or heard from Ronald since our little get-together at the hot tubs." I suddenly felt like my old self again, whatever that was. As hard as it was for me to believe or accept, I was getting used to life without Pee Wee. I was not as angry or confused as I'd been when I got that devastating call from Lizzie. I felt fully alive again. I felt like celebrating by getting into some kind of mischief. "Uh, I think I'll give Ronald another call as soon as I get home."

I didn't even wait to get home to call Ronald. As soon as I got to my car, I dialed his number from my cellular phone. He answered after the fourth ring.

"Hey, baby boy," I cooed. After that fiasco with Louis Baines, a man young enough to be my son, I had decided that I would never get involved with a younger man again. I called Ronald "baby boy" sometimes because he looked young, even though he was going to be forty-nine soon.

"Um . . . hello," he said with caution. "Who's calling?" His hesitation and the fact that he didn't recognize my voice alarmed me.

"This is *Annette,*" I said firmly, putting a lot of emphasis on my name.

"Oh! Yeah, yeah. How have you been doing, sugar! I have been meaning to call you, but I've been so damn busy."

"Uh-huh. Well, I've been busy, too, so that's why I haven't called you until now." I didn't want to know about Ronald's social life, so I never stuck my nose into his personal business. I knew all I wanted to know about him.

"Uh, I'm still thinking about that night we spent at the hot tubs. I hope you are too," I teased with a giggle. "I didn't mean to put all those scratch marks on your back."

This time he hesitated so long it scared me. "Oh! Annette, *that was you?*" he asked.

If somebody had bounced a brick off my head, I could not have felt more stunned. It had been less than a week since I had hooked up with Ronald at the hot tubs and he had forgotten me already! "Um . . . I was just calling to see if you still wanted to get together next week? The last time I saw you, you said you couldn't wait to see me again."

"Uh, yeah, but I'm going to have to take a rain check. I've got company coming from Detroit in a few days. My cousin Nola and her kids. They'll be staying with me for a while . . . personal family reasons that I don't want to get into right now . . ."

"Oh, I didn't know you had family in Detroit."

"I thought I told you."

"No, you didn't. Well, my sister from Florida is visiting me anyway, so maybe now is not such a good time anyway."

"I would like to see you soon, though," Ronald admitted.

"Uh-huh. How soon do you mean?"

"Well, can you get away for a little while now?"

One thing that made my relationship with Ronald so convenient for me was that it was very casual. I cared about him, and I assumed he cared about me, but we were not committed to one another. If we could find time to get together, it was okay. If we couldn't, that was okay too. We got together when we could, no questions asked. Despite our loosey-goosey relationship, I was still very much interested in Ronald, or to be more specific, I was interested in that package between his firm thighs. I was a woman who still enjoyed sex very much, which was one of the reasons I was still sleeping with Pee Wee. But because of all that had happened, I was not that eager to jump back into bed with him anytime soon. And since Roscoe was my only other option, I wanted to hold on to Ronald for as long as I needed him.

One thing I could say about Ronald was that he and I were very compatible under the sheets. Next to Pee Wee, he was the best lover I ever had. Even so, I still tried to keep things with Ronald in perspective. I might have been an old fool, but I didn't want to be so obvious. There were times when that was easier said than done. I had been a prize-winning fool when I got involved with Louis Baines. That sorry-ass gigolo had played me like a fiddle. Now when it came to an intimate relationship with a man, I wanted to get as much out of it as I could. And that even applied to the times when I slept with Pee Wee. I didn't know when, or if, that would ever happen again. Even though my relationship with Ronald was flimsy, I still chose to run with it for as long as I could.

I couldn't believe how much I had lowered my standards. After Pee Wee had forgiven me for having an affair, I had promised myself that I would never stoop low enough to let another man use me. But in this case, I decided that I was using Ronald just as much as he was using me. There had been several times when Ronald invited me at the spur of the moment for a quickie in a motel or a romp in the hot tubs. Once when neither of us had much time to spare, we made love in the backseat of his Lincoln. Each time I'd felt like a cheap whore and a sex-starved old fool, which to some people is probably what I was acting like now.

As hard as I had been working to keep things in perspective, in every area of my life, I was losing my grip after all. And that made me feel sad and sorry for the woman that I had become. With those thoughts dancing around in my head, my latest urge to be in a man's arms suddenly didn't seem so appealing anymore.

"Maybe some other time, Ronald," I replied. I hung up before he could talk me

into behaving like a sex-starved old fool
tonight.

CHAPTER 36

As it turned out, I was a sex-starved old fool after all.

Despite the thoughts that I'd been having about Ronald, he broke me down anyway later in the month. He caught me at a weak moment on that sunny, bright Sunday.

Lillimae and I were in the living room on the couch watching TV. We were in the middle of *Family Feud* when a news bulletin interrupted the show to report the tragic death of Princess Diana in an automobile accident in Paris earlier that morning. We watched in horror and silence. When the news ended, I promptly turned off the TV.

"My Lord. What a mess! Who would have thought that a beautiful, sweet, beloved woman like Princess Diana would die in such an ugly way," Lillimae commented, her voice full of emotion. "And just last month, she was sittin' on a pew attendin' the funeral of her friend Gianni Versace! I

315

am so glad I got him to sign that napkin for me!"

"This is going to be all over the news for the next few days. I don't think I can stand to see it again today," I said, returning to my seat on the couch.

"I can certainly understand that. But it's such a shame. Famous folks are droppin' like flies," Lillimae lamented, shaking her head. "First Versace and now that pretty little Princess Diana. I wonder who's next. Life is so short." Lillimae stopped talking and gave me a sorry look. "Annette, we shouldn't put off doin' anything 'til tomorrow that we can do today. Especially women our age. The older we get, the fewer chances we got to have some fun."

I blinked at Lillimae. "Are you trying to tell me something, or are you having second thoughts about leaving your husband?"

"Both. I have been thinkin' about my husband a lot lately. When I talk to him, I miss him even more." Lillimae glanced away, but within a few seconds she returned her attention to me and that sorry look was still on her face. "Have some fun before it's too late, Annette. Have a good life."

Before I could respond to Lillimae's comments, the telephone on the end table rang. I leaned sideways on the couch and grabbed it on the third ring. It was Ronald. "Hello, baby. Can you get away for a little while?"

Just the sound of his voice made my crotch tingle. "For what?" I asked. My head was swimming because he had taken me by surprise.

"I'd rather show you. Meet me at the Princeton Motel," he told me. "Can I go ahead and check into our usual room?"

Lillimae gave me a conspiratorial smile and started bobbing her head up and down like a rooster.

"I'll be there in twenty minutes," I told him. I hung up and blinked at Lillimae. "Uh, I'm going to go out for a little while," I explained, wobbling up off the couch. "Ronald wants to talk to me."

"That's what I'm talkin' about," Lillimae said with a wink. "Do enough 'talkin' ' for me." She laughed and gave me a dismissive wave.

The following week while I was with Ronald again in the same motel, same room, another news bulletin interrupted the movie that we'd been watching. This one was to report that Mother Teresa had died of a heart attack. "Damn! Famous folks are dropping like flies," Ronald exclaimed, with an unlit cigarette dangling from his lip.

"That's the same thing my sister said just

last week when Princess Diana died," I remarked.

Ronald slapped my naked rump and then pulled me into his arms. "That's why it's important for us regular folks to live each new day like it's our last."

Ronald didn't make thought-provoking comments that often. But the comment he'd just made was not something that I had not heard before. As a matter of fact, I thought about things like that almost every day now. I was going to live each new day like it was my last.

I was cordial to Pee Wee every time I saw him now, but as far as me attempting to get intimate with him again, that was one thing that I had a problem with. I just couldn't bring myself to do that yet.

I was thankful that he came to the house almost every week now to see Charlotte, and to give me some money. Most of the time during his visits, Lillimae, Muh'Dear, and Daddy were also present. But even if they had not been present, I had no interest in pulling Pee Wee upstairs to the bedroom.

Now that Pee Wee had spoken with Lizzie about her predicament, she had no reason to call my house again and get me all upset. And she had not called since that morning back in July. But whenever I saw her on the street with her belly poking out like a horse's behind, I got upset all over again.

Roscoe called me up at work the Monday after Thanksgiving and invited me to go to the movies. Before I could even accept or decline his offer, he added, "I've been dying to see you again! See, I've got a couple of pairs of pants that need the legs hemmed. I'll bring them with me."

"Uh, don't do that. I'm going to be very busy the next few days," I protested.

"Oh, that's all right with me, baby. I am in no hurry to get them back. And when you wash them, don't use a whole lot of starch like you did last time."

"I don't think I want company tonight, Roscoe. I'll take a rain check on that movie."

"Okay, then." He sounded disappointed, but I didn't care. So was I. I was disappointed that he was still treating me like a maid. "Well, do you mind if I drop my pants off tonight anyway? You can hem up the legs whenever you get a chance."

"Do you know that dry cleaner on Alice Street?"

"Yeah, what about it?"

"I always go to them when I have clothes that need to be altered. They do all my cleaning too."

"Oh, but they have some high and mighty prices," Roscoe complained.

"Yeah, but it'll be worth it in the long run. You'll get what you pay for."

Roscoe didn't waste any more time talking to me that night. I had wanted some company, even his, but not bad enough to agree to another one of his domestic requests. But the next couple of times that I called him up, he was too busy to see me. And I couldn't even catch up with Ronald at all. He had changed his home telephone number, and no matter how many times I called his cell phone number, my calls went straight to voice mail. He did not return any of my calls.

It didn't take long for me to really begin to feel the pinch of loneliness. I cooked a huge dinner the next Sunday evening that I ended up eating alone. Muh'Dear and Daddy had been invited to eat dinner with some church members. They had taken Charlotte with them. Scary Mary had invited Lillimae and me to spend the day at her place to help celebrate her birthday. Lillimae eagerly accepted the invitation, but spending the evening in a brothel with a madam and her prostitutes didn't appeal to me at all.

After I'd eaten as much as I could stand, I

curled up on the couch to watch some of the pre-Christmas programs. I couldn't remember the last time I'd felt so abandoned and lonely.

Lillimae had begun to spend so much time with Daddy that she was out of the house more than I was. Charlotte had a busy social life, so her disappearing acts were as frequent as Lillimae's.

I had called up Rhoda every day since the last time I visited her house a couple of weeks ago. Each time she declined my offer for us to get together for drinks or lunch.

Today, when she finally found time to have lunch with me at a burger stand near my work, she seemed unusually depressed. "I guess you've heard about my daughter," she choked, ignoring her cheeseburger.

I was not hungry. I'd only ordered a cup of tea and some fries. I took a few sips of my tea and swallowed a few fries before I responded. "What has she done now? Have you heard from her? Do you know where she's staying?" Rhoda had not seen or heard from Jade since that fiasco on her front porch last summer. There were rumors about Jade floating all over Richland. One busybody told Rhoda that she heard Jade was living with a rich Arab guy in Akron.

Another person said she had seen Jade entering a halfway house with her suitcase. No matter where the girl was residing, she was still partying up a storm. A lot of people, including me, had seen her staggering in or out of one bar after another.

"She's stayin' with Cecil Thigpen," Rhoda said with a profound groan. "That's where she's been all this time."

"Hollywood? The fool who runs the Liberty Street projects?" I wailed. Cecil Thigpen was a thirty-five-year-old thug who had been in and out of jail since he was ten years old. His crimes included everything from purse snatching to pimping. Because of his flashy outfits, manicured nails, and Diana Ross–like hair weave, we all called him Hollywood.

"Uh-huh. He's been shot so many times his body must look like a sieve. It's just a matter of time before somebody else tries to take him out."

"Oh Lord. I am so sorry to hear that, Rhoda. I thought Jade had a little more class than to associate with a lowlife like Hollywood. I heard he beats on his own mama!"

"Well, at least him and Jade have that in common."

"I'm sorry. I didn't mean to go there," I apologized. I know you are trying to forget about Jade hitting you."

"Annette, there are a lot of things in my life that I want to forget. Jade slappin' me is not one of them. I will never forget that. And I am goin' to make sure she never forgets it either."

"I just hope that she comes to her senses before she gets into some serious trouble. Living with a criminal is not going to improve her life in any way. She needs to get up off her butt and find a job."

"She did. That's the other thing I wanted to tell you."

"Well, at least that's one step she's made in the right direction," I said with a forced sigh of relief. "Who hired her?" That question came out sounding a bit harsh, so I tried to soften the blow. "Maybe a job will help her mature faster."

"You remember Chet Stargen, that young bank manager at Richland First National? Pee Wee, Bully, Otis, and a few of their buddies took him to a strip club for his bachelor party last night. Chet is about to marry one of the Brice girls."

"Uh-huh. But what does that have to do with Jade?"

"Jan Brice is one of Jade's home girls."

"And?"

"And the bachelor party was at that funky

strip club over on Willow Street. The one they call The Cock Pit — and believe you me, that's an appropriate name for that damn place," Rhoda snarled.

I didn't know much about the other strip clubs in Richland, but I had heard a lot of nasty things about The Cock Pit. This hell-hole attracted some of the lowest forms of humanity in the city of Richland. In addition to the horny old businessmen and frisky frat boys, the other patrons ran the gamut from dirty-looking old men to pornographers in town looking for some fresh new small-town talent. The last time I drove past it, a dirty-looking old man was standing outside in the parking lot masturbating in broad daylight. A woman I knew who worked in the taco stand next door to the strip club complained about having to step over used condoms in front of the building on her way to work each day. What could be more skanky than that? In addition to the used condoms littering the parking lot, there was a lot of drug activity, prostitution, and violence associated with that dump. Because there was an elementary school two blocks away, a few religious groups had been trying to get that club to either shut down or relocate to a seedier part of town. Church members from various congregations paraded around town on a weekly basis with signs and passed out flyers condemning that place. But, unfortunately, none of those protests had done any good. And when a camera crew followed some protesters into the club one evening, the strippers and the club owner not only taunted them with insults, but a few of the strippers threw rocks and mooned them, shaking and patting their naked behinds like it was going out of style! The place was still as rowdy as ever.

"Guess who's doin' nude lap dances at that sleazy hole in the wall?" Rhoda said, her voice so weak now I could hardly hear her.

"I'm afraid to ask." My chest tightened. I knew Jan Brice and her two younger sisters. They were from a pretty wild family; Daddy was in prison for robbing a bank, Mama sold bootleg liquor, both of the younger sisters had several kids all by different men. Dorothy Brice, the youngest, was just four years older than Charlotte! "One of the Brice girls, and I am not surprised."

"Close. Jade is workin' there. She's been workin' there ever since I kicked her out of the house."

CHAPTER 37

As corrupt as Jade was, I had a hard time picturing her performing nude lap dances, stripping, and doing whatever else females that desperate did in front of a room full of horny men. As a matter of fact, those were the last things that I expected her to do. One reason I felt that way was because she looked down on people she referred to as "skanky." That list included the low-rent community, people who shopped at thrift shops and discount stores, women who wore tacky hair weaves, and anybody who went to the low-end bars.

Despite the fact that Jade had participated in and won a "hot body" contest one night in her favorite high-end bar, she despised the women who entered the monthly wet T-shirt contests at the bars that catered to the ghetto crowd.

"Oh my Lord in heaven! Has Jade truly lost her mind? I am surprised they haven't closed that place down yet," I hollered. "They get raided several times a year!"

"I know. But they pay a fine and are back in business the next day. Truly shady people are way too sly to get caught in criminal acts. And when they do, the charges mysteriously disappear. I heard that The Cock Pit owners have mob connections and lawyers who can perform more magic tricks than David Copperfield. And half of the cops on the Richland force go there, and so do a lot of Richland's most prominent businessmen. In addition to all that, the club's owner have to be payin' off somebody downtown. In this world, that's all it takes. When you grease the right palms, you can practically get away with murder. Or any other crime you're involved in. You've been around enough thugs to know that by now."

"Yeah, but people have been making a lot of noise about that particular strip club. We rarely hear anything about the other three in this town."

"Well, those other places are tame compared to that damn Cock Pit. The girls can't even remove their G-strings in those places. They can only go topless. I heard that the men can get whatever they want in one of those Cock Pit private rooms, and not have to worry about gettin' arrested or anything.

And since you brought it up, what about Scary Mary? She's been pimpin' women out of her house for years, and she's been raided more times than I can count. You and I both know she's payin' off the right people downtown. She'll be in business for as long as she wants, just like that damn strip club."

"I never thought Jade would stoop this low," I allowed, shaking my head in disgust. "Especially in a disgusting place with a name like The Cock Pit."

"The young mother of one of the kids in my day-care center, she used to work at The Cock Pit," Rhoda revealed. "Her stage name was Hot Stuff. Can you believe that?"

"You mean Debbie Young? I had heard about that, but she seems to have turned out all right," I replied. "Working at The Cock Pit didn't do her much harm."

A sad look crossed Rhoda's face. "Yes, it did. That's where she contracted HIV. . . ."

"Damn. Well, I know that Jade will protect herself if she's going to be having sex with any of those perverts. She's smart."

"She's not smart enough, Annette. She's makin' some bad choices right now that she'll never be able to live down." Rhoda let out a mournful howl and shuddered. "Dammit to hell! I never thought my own child would end up doin' some shit like strippin' and lap dancin'. That's one step from bein' a skanky-ass prostitute!" Rhoda was one of the few people who knew that I'd turned more than a few tricks during my teens. I had been so desperate to get money to leave home with, I didn't care how I got it. But I was one of the lucky ones. I'd gotten out of the business before it destroyed me.

"I'm sorry. I didn't mean that the way it sounded," she said. "I never thought of you as a skanky-ass prostitute."

"Well, that's what I was. But that just goes to show you that anybody can make a bad choice. And I don't know if what I'm about to say next will make you feel any better, but it's because of the bad things that I went through that made me the woman I am today. Looking back on it now, I think that my being a teenage prostitute made me see firsthand just how ugly that lifestyle, or anything close to it, can be. I'm a stronger woman because of it, and I am proud of myself."

"Well, you should be. I'm proud of you, too, girl." Rhoda cleared her throat. "Annette, you don't have to call to check on me every day, or visit with me. I'll be fine. You get on with your life. I know things are movin' real slow between you and Pee Wee, but you've still got Ronald and Roscoe to keep you busy. Enjoy them both while you still can."

"I will," I chuckled. I planned to do just that.

However, something told me that things between Pee Wee and me would soon speed up. I knew that it was just a matter of time before we ended up back in bed. I knew that grooming another man to be a possible replacement for Pee Wee was not going to be easy. I had not met another man I liked in months.

As much as I liked Roscoe, I had almost reached my breaking point with him. Last week when I refused to wash a basket of clothes for him, he went to the Laundromat on his own. But he still had the nerve to bring that same basket of clothes to my house for me to iron. And I had refused.

I was proud of the fact that the last couple of times I went to his house, I refused to wash his dishes or "hit a few spots" in his living room with a dust rag and his Dirt Devil.

I really missed being intimate with Pee Wee. I saw Ronald a few times in the interim, but knowing that I was never going to have a real relationship with him made me miss my husband even more. But it was impossible for me not to miss him. We had known one another for over thirty-five years. We had had a great relationship at one time. He had been a good childhood playmate first and then a good husband. And I had been a good wife, until a smooth operator derailed my common sense and talked me into his bed.

As hard as I tried, especially lately, I still couldn't see myself being married to another man. From the looks of things, if Pee Wee and I didn't resume our marriage, I was going to grow old alone after all.

I was surprised when Ronald called me up an hour after I got home from work that dreary Monday after my lunch with Rhoda. Christmas was still three weeks away, but Lillimae had already begun to cook up a storm. Today, she prepared turkey wings, green beans, and cornbread stuffing. After she and I and Charlotte ate dinner, I went to my bedroom. I was tired and my plan was to turn in early. It was only eight o'clock, and I was about to get into my nightgown when the phone rang.

"Hey, beautiful. I've been thinking about you all day. Can you get out of the house for a little while?" Ronald didn't beat around the bush when he wanted something. That was one of the things that I liked about him.

"Uh, I guess I could," I said, twirling the telephone cord around my finger. The truth of the matter was, I didn't want to go back out. All I really wanted to do was crawl into my bed. But I hadn't been intimate with a man since my last tryst with Ronald. Since it was hard enough to hook up with him anyway, I had to see him when I could. "What about your cousin Nola and her kids from Detroit?"

"They are at that church tent revival that's been going on off and on for months. Can you meet me at the Come On Inn?"

"If your relatives are at the revival, why can't we get together at your place?"

"Because I don't like surprises. You know that. At least at a motel or the hot tubs, we don't have to worry about unexpected company disturbing us — like that time your mama caught us in the act in your bed. Now, can you meet me at the Come On Inn or not?"

Ronald had become a little too aggressive for my tastes lately, and I didn't like that at all. For the first time, I began to seriously consider breaking off my relationship with him. As much as I enjoyed his body, I couldn't tolerate his attitude as much as I used to. "Do you mind if I think about it for a little while? I was doing a few things around the house," I lied.

"That's fine with me, but if you can't spare some time for me tonight, I don't know when I'll be able to see you again." Ronald stopped talking, but I didn't respond soon enough. "I am going to start working a different shift, so it might be months before I can see you again," he added.

I still didn't respond soon enough. "Annette, I really need to see you tonight. Don't you want to see me more than you want to do a few things around the house?" he whined in a voice that sounded like it belonged to a child.

"All right. I'll meet you in about half an hour," I agreed. I gave in because the way things were going, my days with Ronald were numbered anyway. What harm could it do to me for me to see him at least one more time?

CHAPTER 38

I did a lot of things with and for men that I was not proud of. One of the things that I wasn't proud of was the fact that I had given money to Louis Baines, the man I'd cheated with. Another thing in my past that I was not proud of was that I had agreed to marry Jerome Cunningham, a man I did not love. For one thing, he was so cheap, he used to cruise restaurants just to steal condiments. When I met him, he showed me enough packets of sugar, salt, and pepper stacked up in his kitchen pantry to last him for years. And his family had hated me on sight. They made a lot of snide remarks implying that I was too "dark" to be with Jerome, who was almost light enough to pass for white. I was glad when we broke up, because the only reason I was going to go through with the marriage in the first place was because I wanted to show everybody that I could land a good-looking man.

I had struck a gold mine when I landed Pee Wee, and had botched that relationship big time. In the meantime, I was somewhat happy to be involved in a sexual relationship with Ronald. He was a good backup for Roscoe. As a matter of fact, he was more than just a backup. He was handsome, which made me proud to be seen with him in the out-of-way public places he took me to — even though the only people who ever saw us together were strangers. But he was more "laid-back" than any man I had ever known. He admitted that he didn't like to do anything that he didn't want to do, which probably had a lot to do with the fact that he was always getting reprimanded and put on probation at his job. I called that being lazy. He was usually too lazy to come pick me up when he wanted to get together. I tolerated his behavior because I enjoyed his company, and because he was so temporary that I expected the relationship to end at any moment. As long as I was having fun, I saw no reason not to see him when I could.

That was why I was on my way to see him now.

Ohio was having one of its worst winters in decades. Even though one of the neighborhood teenage boys had shoveled mounds of snow off my walkway and driveway a few hours earlier, fresh snow that was still coming down covered the ground like a white blanket. I had to drive as slow as possible to get to a street that the city workers had cleared some of the snow off of and sprinkled some kind of salt to melt the ice.

My gas tank was almost empty, so I had to stop at a gas station along the way. It was just my luck that the meddlesome cousins Wyrita and Lizel had also stopped to get gas at the same time.

"Annette, where you off to?" Wyrita yelled, walking up to my car with her hands on her hips with Lizel marching next to her. Wyrita had on a knitted brown wool cap with matching mittens, ear muffs, and boots.

"You usually don't get out by yourself much these days," Lizel added. She was even more bundled up than Wyrita. A red muffler was around her neck, chin, and the lower part of her cheeks. There was a goofy-looking cap on her head that was pulled down so far on her face, it looked like she had on a ski mask.

Wyrita and Lizel were nice women and young enough to be my daughters. And even though they were both bright and attractive, they had just as many man troubles as the rest of us. But that still didn't stop them from getting in everybody else's business.

"You don't look as bad as I expected you to look after finding out about Pee Wee and that baby," Lizel commented. "I expected you to be prostrate with grief. I would have bet money on it."

"Me too," Wyrita said, adjusting her cap and muffler so I could see more of her face.

"I'm sorry I disappointed you, but I don't have time to be sitting around feeling sorry for myself. I've got things to do, places to go," I quipped. From the looks on the cousins' faces, I got the impression that they were disappointed to hear what I'd just said. Yes, I was still in distress somewhat, but Pee Wee and Lizzie were not the only things going on in my life.

"What do you think about that Jade?" Wyrita asked. "She really cooked her own goose this time, huh?"

"That's really none of my business," I answered. "But I do hope that things between her and Rhoda work out somehow."

"You got enough problems of your own anyway," Lizel sniffed. "I wouldn't want to be in your shoes, or Rhoda's. By the way, I ran into Lizzie last night. She looks like hell. Her face is all bloated and pale, and her hair is as limp as a wet dishrag. She's got enough gray strands to cover a pillow."

"I saw her too." Wyrita paused, sucked on her teeth, and shook her head in pity. "It's a damn shame she let herself go this quick. And imagine a woman her age getting herself pregnant! That's asking for trouble. Our Aunt LuAnne had a change-of-life baby, and it came here with a hole in his heart and water on his brain," Wyrita clucked.

"Well, Lizzie's baby is none of my business. But I do hope her child is healthy," I allowed. "You two have a nice night."

I finished pumping my gas, put my credit card away, and jumped back into my car.

Somehow I took a wrong turn and ended up back on the street where the gas station was. Lizel and Wyrita were just leaving and ended up right behind me in Lizel's aging Toyota. I didn't know if they were following me on purpose or not, but they stayed right on my tail for the next four blocks. When I got to the motel, I drove right past it and pulled into the Grab and Go parking lot. Another thing about Ronald was that he often forgot to bring condoms with him. And because of all that was going on, the last thing *I* needed was to get pregnant at my age. Even though the store was as crowded as it usually was, by the time I got up to the cashier to pay for a package of condoms, Lizel and Wyrita had stumbled in and caught me in the act. The way that they were looking at my purchase, you would have thought that I was buying illegal drugs.

"I hope he's worth it," Lizel teased, jabbing me in my side with her elbow. "Whoever *he* is." She cleared her throat and gave me a conspiratorial look. Then added with a wink, "If you need them *king-size* raincoats, he *is* worth it."

"I wish I had a reason to buy them in that size," Wyrita snickered, and so did Lizel, the cashier, and a few people in line behind me.

Even though my face was burning, I managed to maintain my composure. "I hope you two ladies have something fun planned for tonight too," I said, turning to leave.

"Me and that fool I was with broke up, and I haven't had a date in two weeks," Lizel whined. "You know any single men you can introduce us to?"

"No, I don't," I said as I slunk back out the door, praying that they wouldn't follow me again. I sprinted to my car and jumped in, speeding out of the parking lot with my lights still off. I didn't realize that until an ongoing car blinked its lights at me.

It seemed like fate was against me meeting up with Ronald at that motel. Two cars had collided in front of the motel's entrance, so I had to drive to a parking lot a block away and walk back to the motel. By the time I rounded the corner, another ten minutes had passed. When I arrived at the motel, Ronald was standing in the parking lot with his arms folded and an impatient look on his face.

"I was just about to give up on you, girl. You were supposed to be here half an hour ago," he told me, pulling me along by the arm.

I told him the reason for my delay, but he continued to complain about my tardiness anyway. He didn't even stop when I reminded him about the times he'd been late to a rendezvous with me. Between him and Roscoe, if I had to settle with one for a husband, as hard as it was to believe, I would choose Roscoe. Being in a sexless marriage with him wouldn't kill me. I didn't know at what age people generally stopped having sex, but I'd already had more than my share in my forty-eight years, so I could live with abstinence *if* I had to.

I dismissed the thought of Roscoe and being married to him as fast as I could. Like Lillimae had told me to do, I was going to have my fun while I still could.

Ronald was a considerate lover most of

the time. As soon as I made it inside the motel room at the end of the building, he practically threw me down on the bed, mounted me like I was a mule, and snatched off my clothes. It was over before I could even get wet.

"Mmmm, that sure was good," Ronald rasped with a cigarette already dangling from his lip. Then he lifted his head off the pillow and gave me a puzzled look. "You gaining weight?"

"I've put on a few pounds lately. My sister likes to cook up a storm every day." Ronald had moved to Richland from Columbus just a few months ago. He was so easy on the eyes. If I had to describe him, I would say that he was an older version of the late Tupac Shakur: shaved head, cocky attitude, hot-as-hell body and all. He didn't know that I used to walk around wearing size twenty-four muumuus. And I didn't see any reason to tell him that I'd lost over a hundred pounds in the last couple of years.

"That extra meat looks good on you." He slid his hand across the top of his shiny scalp and smiled. Then he looked at me with the interest of a cannibal. "I got a few more minutes to spare. Don't put your clothes back on yet. I'd like to do a little nibbling. . . ."

A *little* nibbling was all Ronald did for the next two minutes. Just as I was getting excited, his cell phone rang. He answered it, told whoever was calling "yes" once, and that he would "be there soon." He told me that he had an emergency to go take care of. He got up, got dressed, and was out the door within minutes. I felt soiled and cheap by the time I left the motel, which was as soon as I put my clothes back on. And the worst part of this little liaison was that I had not enjoyed it. I was just as horny when I got back home as I was when I went to the motel.

Pee Wee had left a voice mail message and since it was still fairly early, I called him back.

"I was wonderin' if I could take you out to dinner tomorrow evenin'? You and Charlotte," he said.

Because of that unsatisfactory little episode with Ronald, my guard was down. I was in a weakened state, so Pee Wee could not have called at a better time. Not only that, but it had been months since Pee Wee, Charlotte, and I had gone out together. I missed that.

"I'd like that," I said, hoping he didn't detect the eagerness in my voice. "I'm glad you asked."

CHAPTER 39

There were times when I regretted living in a city as small as Richland. Especially with the kind of folks who liked to stay in other folks' business. And it seemed like all of the black folks in Richland did that in three shifts. One night somebody I didn't even see saw me coming out of a restaurant with a white man. Before I made it home, which had taken only ten minutes, Scary Mary had left me a voice mail message asking if I was dating white men now. My "date" was one of the process servers my collection agency worked with. He had treated me to dinner to show his gratitude for all the work I sent his way.

The next evening after my conversation with Pee Wee, while I was upstairs trying to decide what to wear out to my dinner with him, Scary Mary barged into my bedroom. She startled me as I stood in front of my mirror wearing only my underwear. She wore one of her many brocade dusters and was leaning on her cane. I was glad to see that she had on a new and better-looking wig: a short gray bob with bangs covering the many lines in her forehead. Despite the fact that it was an improvement compared to the other wigs she wore, it didn't complement her mulish face. I didn't even know she was in the house. That was another thing I didn't like about small-town life. People showed up unannounced, uninvited, and usually unwelcome on a regular basis. This kind of behavior was something that I'd known all my life, even when we lived in Florida, but I was still not used to it.

"I didn't know you were here," I gasped, grabbing my bathrobe off the bed and quickly slipping it on.

"Well, you know I'm here now," Scary Mary crowed, looking around my cluttered room. "You look like you just seen a ghost. I ain't gwine to bite you, girl, so get that spooked look off your face." Scary Mary was the kind of woman who said whatever was on her mind. And nobody was exempt from her sharp tongue. You couldn't embarrass or intimidate her no matter how hard you tried. She lived by her own rules. But the main thing about her was, she had always helped Muh'Dear and me when we really needed it. It was for that reason that I put up with things from her that I wouldn't have put up with from anybody else.

"It's just that you scared me," I told her.

"That's why folks call me Scary Mary, girl," she chortled, looking me up and down as I rolled and pinned my hair into a French twist. "You done finally come to your senses and realized that Pee Wee is about the best you ever gwine to do with a man?"

"What's that supposed to mean?" I asked, my eyes still on my reflection in the mirror.

Scary Mary plopped down on my bed with a groan, placing her cane across her lap. "Now that Lizzie done come clean about that bun in her oven bein' Peabo's, you ain't got to worry about your man bein' connected to her no more. If I was you, I'd move him back up in this house as soon as possible."

"I'm in no hurry, and Pee Wee isn't either." I lifted a pair of black slacks off the dresser. It was a struggle to get into them because of the bothersome pounds that I had regained. I got the zipper to go all the way up, but even though I sucked in my gut, I was unable to button the waistband.

"I hope you don't mind me sayin' so, but seems like you havin' a mighty hard time gettin' into them britches. And you lookin' right plump these days, if you don't mind me sayin' that neither." Scary Mary paused and turned her head to the side. She looked at me out of the corner of her eye. "Lord have mercy. *You* ain't expectin' no little newcomer in a few months, too, I hope." She sucked on her teeth and shook her head. Then she gave me a look that made my flesh crawl. She pressed her lips together, furrowed her brow, and shook her head some more. "What a mess you would have on your hands if that was the case. You and that Lizzie woman both bein' pregnant at the same time! Both of y'all with one foot and a big toe in the grave."

"I'm not pregnant by Pee Wee," I said quickly, sliding my arms into the sleeves of a loose-fitting, blue and black plaid blouse.

"You ain't pregnant by Pee Wee? Oh." Scary Mary looked disappointed. "But you didn't say you wasn't pregnant. . . ."

"I am not pregnant, period," I snapped. "Let's go downstairs so I can fix you a drink before I leave."

"Oh, you ain't got to worry about fixin' me no drink. That was the first thing I did when I got here. I could find my way to your alcohol with my eyes closed. But since you mentioned it, I wouldn't mind havin' another one for the road. I know I ain't supposed to drink hard alcohol when I'm driving, but believe it or not, being drunk sharpens my senses. I make my best decisions when I'm buzzed. You ought to try that sometime when you tryin' to get through some difficulty."

I was glad when I got downstairs to see that Pee Wee had already arrived. And since Scary Mary made herself comfortable on the couch with another drink, and was looking from me to Pee Wee like she wanted to bite us, I thought it would be in our best interest for us to leave right away.

"We better be on our way," I told Pee Wee.

"But our reservation is not until eight o'clock," Pee Wee blurted, looking at his watch. "It's not even seven yet. I came early so we'd have a little more time to kick back and just visit," he said. It took him a few moments to read my face. I rolled my eyes and bit my bottom lip, and he finally got the hint. "Oh! You said somethin' about stoppin' by the mall on the way to the restaurant to pick up some frock they holdin' for you at that boutique next to the shoe store, didn't you? I almost forgot!"

"Uh-huh," I said quickly, beckoning for Charlotte. She sat stock-still on the arm of the couch, facing Scary Mary. From the pinched look on Charlotte's face, I could see that she was as eager to get away from Scary Mary as I was. Lillimae was in the kitchen, cooking a "snack" for herself and Scary Mary. Despite the fact that my mother was not too fond of Lillimae, Scary Mary had become quite fond of her.

"We better hurry if we want to beat the traffic," Pee Wee suggested, ushering Charlotte and me out the door.

Since we had some time to kill, we actually did go by the mall on our way to the restaurant. I didn't have anything on hold at that boutique, and I had purchased all of the Christmas gifts that I could afford, so all we did was a lot of aimless window-shopping.

"Mama, can we go in that toy store next?" Charlotte asked, pointing toward a window that displayed everything from video games to black Barbie dolls.

Just as I was about to respond, I saw something that made me freeze. Walking toward us was Ronald, and he was not alone. There was a plump, attractive woman in her late thirties walking beside him. Trailing behind them were four kids. The youngest was an adorable little boy who appeared to be around six. The other three, all girls, were in their early teens.

Pee Wee was well aware that I was seeing

348

a couple of other men, but Roscoe was the only one whom he'd seen me with. He used to cut Roscoe's hair until Roscoe started going to his competitor, who was Lizzie's new employer, and the nephew of the man she dumped Pee Wee for. Roscoe had told me early in our relationship that since he and I were together, he no longer felt comfortable letting Pee Wee cut his hair. A "conflict of interest," he called it. Pee Wee was disappointed to lose a long-time client, and when I told him the reason Roscoe had deserted him, he laughed about it.

Since Ronald had a bald head, he didn't need a barber, but he went to one anyway to get his scalp oiled and massaged. He worked in Akron, so he went to a barbershop there. As far as I knew, Pee Wee didn't even know Ronald.

I was wrong.

Chapter 40

Pee Wee clapped his hands, threw his head back, and yelped like he was being reunited with a long-lost relative. He rushed up to Ronald and shook his hand, then slapped him on the back. "My man! I haven't seen you in a while! Merry Christmas!" Pee Wee yelled, grinning like a fool. Ronald just stood there blinking and trying his best not to make eye contact with me. "Baby, this is Ronald Hawthorne from the pool hall. I used to whup the drawers off his ass at the pool table so many times he stopped comin' to the pool hall." Pee Wee grabbed my arm and pulled me forward, like he was proudly putting me on display. My face got so warm it felt like somebody had just wrapped a hot towel around my head. "This is my wife, Annette," he introduced. Then he smiled at the woman standing next to Ronald. "This must be the lovely wife you was always braggin' about. And I recognize your kids from the pictures you used to flash all the time."

Ronald and his wife were dressed in expensive, casual outfits. She wore a dark blue wool coat over jeans and a loose-fitting light blue blouse. Ronald had on an ankle-length leather coat, jeans, and a maroon turtleneck sweater. The kids all had on jeans and hooded jackets, buttoned all the way up to their necks.

"Hey, brother," Ronald finally managed, looking at the ground when I tried to look in his eyes. "Uh, this is my wife, Nola, and these are our kids. . . ."

"Where are the other two?" Pee Wee asked.

"Huh? Oh! The older kids are out with their friends this evening," Ronald replied. I couldn't remember the last time I'd seen a human act this nervous.

"Well, you've got a beautiful family, man." Pee Wee paused and turned to me. "Ain't this a beautiful family, baby?"

"Sure enough," I responded. It was hard for me to keep a straight face, but I managed. "You look familiar, Ronald. Have we met before?"

He finally looked me in the eye. "Uh, I don't think so!" he said, talking so fast spit flew out the side of his mouth.

I stepped closer to Pee Wee, my eyes still on Ronald's face. "Pee Wee, as soon as the

351

weather breaks, we need to have a cookout and invite Ronald and his family," I said, tugging on Pee Wee's arm. Ronald looked like he wanted to sink into the ground.

"Yeah, that's a good idea. I know our daughter, Charlotte, would love to meet your girls, my man," Pee Wee grinned. It had been a while since I'd seen him this jovial, and it made me feel good.

"I'd like that," the wife said. "Now that the kids and I are back in Richland for good, I'd really like to get back into the swing of things. Annette, I make some mean barbecue sauce — I add lime — so having a cookout would be right up my alley."

"I'm glad to hear that," I said stiffly.

"Six kids!" Pee Wee said, like it was something that nobody else had done. Now that I knew about his low sperm count and the fact that he would never have the large family he used to tell me he wanted, I could understand why he was in such awe of Ronald having so many kids. "And I know you must be proud of them all. Six kids are such a blessin'!"

"Seven soon," Nola chirped, patting her stomach. "Two more months to go. We tried real hard for this one."

"Seven!" Pee Wee yelled. "Brother, no wonder you stopped comin' to the pool hall.

Sounds like you didn't have time to put your pants on!"

Nola smiled in my direction. "I've been up in Detroit with my baby sister since June. She was pregnant with her first and so frail things didn't look too hopeful. She'd already miscarried three times. Anyway, the doctor put her on bed rest to see if that would help. The kids and I stayed with her until the very end. She now has a beautiful baby girl." Nola paused and wrapped her arms around Ronald in such a way that from the painful look on his face, you would have thought that he was now wearing a straightjacket. "Poor Ronald. He was so lonesome he cried like a baby each time we talked on the telephone." Nola paused again and caressed Ronald's face, which must have been as hot as a campfire by now. "Ronald was on the verge of a nervous breakdown being so alone. He called me every night, and he drove up to Detroit every chance he got. It's a good thing I got back home when I did. Women would love to get their hands on my boo; but I know I can trust him, so I didn't worry about him, uh, doing anything crazy while I was gone." Nola jabbed Ronald's side. "Right, baby?"

"Right," he mumbled, glancing at me.

Nola leaned forward and winked at me. "I

told Ronald to be careful because there are a lot of skanks in Richland." She was right about that. And the way I was feeling right now, Ronald must have thought of me as one of those skanks his wife had warned him about.

"Tell me about it," I snorted. "Well, I'm happy for you, Nola." I turned to face Ronald. "What was your name again?" I asked, snapping my fingers.

"Ronald," he practically growled.

"You're a lucky man, and your wife is a lucky woman," I said. "I hope you will always be good to her."

"I . . . I intend to," he managed, looking at me with defiance — as if I was the one who had been deceiving him!

"Can't we go in the toy store?" Charlotte said, tugging on my hand.

"Oh! What's wrong with me! This is my daughter, Charlotte," Pee Wee introduced.

Charlotte had met Ronald just once when he came to the house to pick me up. She had only glimpsed him as she rushed to her room with a couple of her friends. From her reaction now, she didn't remember meeting him. And for that I was glad.

"It was nice meeting you all," I said, already walking away.

"Hey, man, let me give you my phone

number in case you want to get together some time. You still go fishin'? I know some good spots up around Cleveland with some bass that will bite anything." Pee Wee scribbled his phone number on a scrap of paper. By now I was ready to pass out. My relationship with Ronald was over.

I did not sleep with other women's husbands.

After we left the toy store, with video games for Charlotte that I'd never heard of, we went to the restaurant, even though we were a half hour ahead of our reservation. Charlotte and Pee Wee sat down on the velvet couches in the waiting area. I made a beeline to the bar and by the time the waiter led us to our table, I'd drunk two glasses of wine.

I was glad that we'd been seated in a booth near the back exit. I didn't like sitting out in the open in any restaurant. It seemed like every time I went somewhere and sat by the entrance, somebody I didn't want to see saw me.

Right after our waiter took our order — we all requested steak and veggies — I looked at Pee Wee and then at Charlotte. I had to blink to hold back my tears. This was the first time the three of us had been out in public together since Pee Wee had left me for Lizzie. As disappointed as I was with him, I was just as disappointed with myself. I wondered if I had not had the affair with Louis Baines, would Pee Wee have gotten involved with Lizzie. I couldn't change the past, but because of it, I would not be as stupid in the future. It saddened me to know that some people who had good lives didn't realize it until it was too late.

"What's wrong, Annette? You look kind of sad," Pee Wee noticed. "You got tears in your eyes."

"I'm all right," I said. "Just some dust or lint got caught up in my eye." I dabbed at my eyes with the tail of my napkin.

"She must get stuff in her eyes all the time," Charlotte chirped. "Every time I look up she's crying like a baby."

Pee Wee and I looked at Charlotte at the same time.

"Like I just said, I got something in my eye," I insisted.

"But, Mama! What about last night? I heard you crying in your room — all night!"

"I cry sometimes myself too, Char," Pee Wee said, blinking hard. He had tears in his eyes too.

"Yes, I do cry sometimes," I admitted. "There's just been so much going on in my life lately."

"Like what, Mama?" There were times when I wanted to strap a muzzle onto my daughter's mouth. This was one of those times.

"For one thing, my daddy is getting to the point where he needs somebody to look after him more. Having Lillimae around is a double blessing, but I still worry about him. And then there are some work-related issues that have me concerned. We've had some dangerous situations at the office with hostile debtors. So you see, my life is not so simple anymore," I said, giving my daughter a sharp, threatening look. I had to keep reminding myself that kids noticed more than we thought they did.

"Don't I know that. One thing you and I both need to do is be there for Rhoda and Otis." Pee Wee shook his head. "They are goin' to need some serious emotional support."

Charlotte blinked and looked from me to Pee Wee. "Why? Did Jade already quit that cool stripping job?" she asked.

Pee Wee and I looked at Charlotte again at the same time. I couldn't tell which one of us displayed the biggest frown. He took the next words right out of my mouth. "Char, strippin' ain't a cool thing for any female to do. If you ever do somethin' like

357

that, I would never get over it."

"But why are strip clubs so bad if so many men go to them?" Charlotte asked.

"Because they don't know any better," I said, glaring at Pee Wee.

"That's right. We don't know any better," he muttered, looking like he wanted to melt into the floor.

CHAPTER 41

By the time we left the restaurant, the weather was so bad that several streets had been closed. The detour we took only led us to another detour.

Pee Wee had to drive through an unincorporated area, swing back through downtown, and then onto the freeway to get back to our side of town. Once we got there, we saw several traffic accidents, and people slipping and sliding on the icy ground, falling down like bowling pins.

"What a mess of a night," I complained. "It's never taken this long to get to my house."

"We are closer to my place than yours," Pee Wee mentioned, in a cautious voice I noticed.

"So?" I mouthed. I already knew where this conversation was going, and I didn't like it one bit.

"So? Well, *so* it might make more sense

for y'all to come home with me tonight." Pee Wee glanced at me as he wrestled with the steering wheel to avoid hitting a stalled car in front of us.

"Yeah!" Charlotte hooted from the backseat, pumping her fist like she'd just won a prize.

"I don't think so," I said quickly. "I'd really like to get home and sleep in my own bed tonight."

I didn't know what Pee Wee thought I meant by the last part of my comment, but he gave me a weird look. "You can sleep in my bed. I'll sleep on the couch." He peered at Charlotte through the rearview mirror. "Char, you know your room is already available for you."

I looked at Pee Wee like he had lost his mind — and he must have! Did he actually think that I was going to sleep in the same bed that he'd slept in with the woman who had ruined our marriage? The only reason I didn't ask him that question out loud was because Charlotte was in the car. I still had not even set foot in the apartment that he had shared with Lizzie, and I didn't plan to ever do so! "No, that's all right," I said firmly.

He must have read my mind because his face looked like it was about to crack. "I'm just tryin' to help, Annette."

"Then help me get home, all right?"

After several more delays, Pee Wee finally parked in front of my house. He leaped out of the car. After a lot of slipping and sliding, and almost falling on the ice, he opened the back door for Charlotte. They hugged one another for a couple of minutes. It gave me enough time to open my own door and scramble out before he got to me. But he still followed me up to the porch, with his hand on my shoulder. Even with his support, I slipped on some ice on the steps. Had he not been there to keep me from falling, I might have injured myself.

"I would come in for a nightcap, but I'd better get back on the road. There's just no tellin' how long it's goin' to take for me to get back to my side of town," he said.

"Daddy, why don't you just spend the night with us?" Charlotte suggested with a hopeful look on her face. Like I said, there were times when I wanted to strap a muzzle on my daughter's mouth. I gave her one of my stern "What's wrong with you, girl?" looks. She promptly got the message. "Uh, maybe some other time, huh, Daddy?" she amended.

Pee Wee laughed and tickled her chin. "Yeah, maybe some other time." He hugged

Charlotte again. Then he gave me a dry look and a playful tap on my shoulder. "Have a blessed evenin'," he told me as he ran back to his car.

The only light on in the house was the lamp on the end table in the living room. I assumed Lillimae was in bed.

Even though Charlotte was on the Christmas holiday break from school, I still sent her to bed right away.

About an hour later, I heard a commotion on my front porch. Before I could set my glass of hot tea on my living room coffee table and get off the couch to go investigate, the front door flew open like a tornado had suddenly dropped down out of the sky. To my surprise, in walked Muh'Dear with her arm around Lillimae's shoulder.

I gasped. "What the hell? What's going on?" My first thought was that something bad had happened to Daddy and that he had sent for Lillimae. "What's wrong with Daddy?" My heart was racing, my eyes were burning, and I was having a hard time breathing.

"There ain't nothin' wrong with that old billy goat," Muh'Dear answered, padding across the floor with her arm still around Lillimae's shoulder. My second thought was that my mother had suddenly slipped into some rare state of delirium. The way she trashed Lillimae, I never expected to see her with her arm around her shoulder — unless she was about to choke her!

"Annette, don't get all upset. Everything is under control," Lillimae informed me. She eased away from Muh'Dear and immediately started fanning her face with one hand and brushing snow off her slick black leather coat with the other.

"I wanted to get Lillimae back home before too late. You know I don't like to be out drivin' after dark. I was gwine to send her home in a cab," Muh'Dear told me, fanning her face with her hand too. It was only then that I noticed they both had sweat on their faces.

"What's wrong?" I asked again, standing in front of my couch with my legs shaking. I had to sit to keep from falling.

"We just excited, that's all. That's why we both been sweatin' like wrestlers for hours. See, we had a little problem at the restaurant this evenin'," Muh'Dear said, still fanning as she plopped down on the couch next to me, unbuttoning her coat. She kicked off her round-toed oxfords and started rubbing her ankles together like a cricket. Her thick support hose, rolled down to below her knees, looked like donuts at the top. "Lillimae, don't put too much ice in that rum and Coke you're gwine to fix for me. And just a dab of rum. The last thing I need is to get pulled over by one of them brutal- izin' cops."

"What problem did you have at the restau- rant this evening?" I asked, looking at Muh'Dear.

"The head cook at Muh'Dear's restaurant had a nasty fall on a patch of ice this eve- nin' and broke her hip," Lillimae informed me, speaking over her shoulder as she moved toward the kitchen.

Muh'Dear? I had to shake my head and pinch my arm to make sure I was not dreaming. Lillimae had never referred to my mother as Muh'Dear! Every black child, even the ones who had a lot of white blood, knew that the title Muh'Dear was sacred. And the way my mother talked about Lilli- mae to her face and behind her back, I knew that there was no valid reason for her to encourage Lillimae to call her that! My mind was in a tizzy. I hadn't even had enough time to process the things that I had experienced this evening. The run-in with Ronald and his wife, and Pee Wee's request for me and Charlotte to spend the night with him were still heavy on my mind.

"And the assistant cook was out sick,"

Muh'Dear added. "Mayor Walker and his party of twelve had a reservation for a private Christmas party tonight. The mayor's secretary had made the reservation a month ago. They was celebratin' somethin'. You know how white folks like to gallivant in and out of restaurants all the time, and you know how they like to spend money after a few drinks. I love doin' business with rich crackers!"

I cut a sharp look in Lillimae's direction. She rolled her eyes, stumbling across the floor with two drinks in her hand. She had removed her coat and left it in the kitchen.

"Miss Gussie Mae was at her wit's end wonderin' what she was goin' to do with that hungry mayor and his party sittin' up in the VIP room waitin' to get fed," Lillimae said, sitting down on the love seat across from me and Muh'Dear. She wasted no time kicking off her shoes too. She never wore stockings or pantyhose. Unfortunately, none of the stores in Richland carried sizes large enough to accommodate her stovepipe-wide legs. She had to wear leg warmers like I used to.

"Lillimae, didn't I tell you to stop actin' so formal with me. You call me Muh'Dear like I told you, hear?" Muh'Dear gave Lillimae the kind of affectionate look that she gave to me when she was in a good mood. I couldn't believe my eyes or ears.

"Oh, yeah. Anyway, Muh'Dear had a major crisis on her hands and I had to help her out," Lillimae said with a triumphant look on her face.

I didn't know what to think now. There was nothing that I wanted to see more than my mother and my half sister getting along better. I certainly never thought that it would happen when I least expected it.

"I called the house for you," my mother continued. My mother wasn't looking or acting drunk. She appeared to be lucid. And that made this new development even more of a mystery. I was not one to look a gift horse in the mouth. But until I knew all of the facts involved in this incredible turn of events, I decided to remain skeptical. Muh'Dear paused and snorted, and gave me a wide smile. "Anyway, I thought that between me and you, we could whup up a decent meal for the mayor and his folks. You wasn't here, so I called my day cook, hopin' I could get her to turn around and come back to do another shift. That lazy heifer had made plans for the night — or so she claimed. It's a damn good thing Lilli-mae was home! Otherwise, my goose would have been cooked well done — just like the one the mayor had ordered for his meal!" My mother smiled at my sister for the first time since she'd arrived from Florida — at least in my presence. "Lillimae saved the day and my butt!" Muh'Dear was beaming like a lightbulb. "I didn't know you was such a good cook, Lillimae. This girl sure enough put her foot in that corn she fried. When I tasted it, I wanted to put my *face* in it! This was the first time the mayor ever ate at my restaurant *and* took an order to go too!"

"I'm glad the night turned out all right," I said, smiling. "I hope your cook recovers soon." In spite of everything that I had just heard and witnessed, I chose to remain skeptical. Yes, Lillimae had saved the day and Muh'Dear's butt. But would Muh'Dear feel the same way in the future that she was feeling now? Just the day before, she had delivered a few unflattering remarks to me about Lillimae's weight again.

"I hope so too. But it won't be no real big disaster if she don't now! I told Lillimae that she can fill in for Donna Jean for as long as she wants to." Muh'Dear finished her drink and rose. "Lillimae, we'll talk salary tomorrow. If you don't mind, please come around four before the day cook leaves so she can show you the ropes, and so I can serve you up a mighty big plate of my fried okra that you enjoyed so much tonight." Muh'Dear gave me a pleading look. "When Charlotte goes back to school after the holiday vacation, have her take the bus to my house like she used to. Lillimae won't be at the house to keep an eye on her no more durin' the time she waitin' on you to get home from work. Charlotte can sit with her granddaddy until you pick her up."

"Oh, you don't have to worry about that. My new neighbor across the street offered to look after Charlotte when necessary. She'll be in good hands," I said.

Charlotte must have been eavesdropping, because just as Lillimae was about to walk Muh'Dear to her car, Charlotte came trotting back downstairs.

"Mama, please don't make me go to that Harrietta woman's house every day after school! I hate her! I'm old enough to stay by myself," she hollered, waving her arms like somebody signaling for help. Her outburst and the category five look of anger on her face startled me. She had on her Cookie Monster nightgown and a cutoff stocking cap on her head, to hold her recently permed curls in place. She looked so young that I still worried about her being alone in the house.

"I don't want you to be in this house

alone, girl. Now you are going to have to stop this mess about Harrietta." I gave Charlotte an exasperated look, but that didn't seem to faze her. She still looked like she wanted to cuss out the world. "Oh well, I was hoping I wouldn't have to tell you this, but I had a talk with her that evening she had dinner with us. She knows you don't like her. And now that she knows that I know you don't like her, I doubt if she'd ever do anything to upset you."

"She already has," Charlotte whimpered. "She — oh, never mind!"

"She *what?*" I demanded. "If you can't tell me exactly what you hate about this woman — other than her being too strict — shut up and behave yourself. Yes, Harrietta is strict and I can understand you not liking that — I didn't like grown folks being strict with me when I was young either. But her being strict when you are in her house will keep you out of trouble," I declared. "You'll get used to her."

Even though my daughter was twelve and very responsible, I didn't like to leave her alone too often. Last year she had fallen in with a bad crowd, and I was determined to prevent that from happening again anytime soon. And there had been a few daytime break-ins on our street lately. I didn't want to think of what might happen if a burglar broke into my house when my daughter was home alone.

"But Harrietta . . . she's . . . she's not normal," Charlotte insisted, looking at me with a desperate look on her face. It seemed like the older she got, the more she over-reacted to the littlest thing. I didn't like that, and I was not going to let it influence my decisions.

"Not normal how?" Muh'Dear wanted to know. "She looks as normal as the rest of us to me."

"She's just real, uh, creepy, that's all," Charlotte said, hunching her shoulders and making a face.

"Charlotte, go back to bed," I ordered, pointing toward the staircase. "Now!"

Charlotte rolled her eyes and started stomping across the floor like a mule. "You're going to be real sorry one day, Mama," she warned.

"These kids," Lillimae sighed, shaking her head.

"Charlotte needs a little more structure in her life. I wish she was more like Harrietta's girls," I said in a low voice.

Muh'Dear gave me a strange look. "I ain't never seen Charlotte this fractious. Maybe you ought to get to know more about that woman, just in case."

Just in case. Those words rang in my ears. In spite of how I felt about Harrietta, it was at that moment that I realized I needed to be a little more concerned about Charlotte's feelings and the impact that Harrietta had on her.

Charlotte's prediction that I would be sorry one day sounded ominous and made me more than a little concerned. What if she was not being rebellious and troublesome just for the heck of it? After that thought, I decided right then and there that the best thing that I could do was keep Charlotte away from Harrietta unless I was around.

CHAPTER 42

As soon as I was alone again, I padded into the kitchen and called up Harrietta.

"It's Annette," I began with hesitation. "Um, I've given it a lot of thought and I think it's in everybody's best interest if I don't leave my child with you anymore."

"I see. Well, that's fine with me, Annette. After that conversation we had, I was thinking that same thing myself," Harrietta told me, sounding relieved. "I know some kids think of me as a beast, but I can live with that," she chuckled. "No hard feelings on my part."

"I don't have any hard feelings either, and you and I can still be friends if you want," I told her.

"I'm glad to hear that, Annette, because I really like you. The girls will be sorry to hear that Charlotte won't be friends with them anymore."

"Oh no! I didn't say that she couldn't be

friends with your girls. As long as your girls don't take a dislike to me, they are always welcome to come here, if you don't mind. And you can still come here too. I am trying to be fair to my child and to you. If Charlotte changes her feelings toward you . . . well, we will deal with that when and if it happens. Now, you have a blessed evening, and I hope you and I can get together again soon," I said, meaning every word.

Right after I hung up, I went upstairs, got into my nightgown, and crawled into my bed. It had been a pleasant evening. Part of it had to do with my decision to sever the relationship between Harrietta and Charlotte, not to mention the fact that I would no longer be involved with Ronald. After what had happened tonight, there was no way I was ever going to see him again.

I knew that Rhoda would get a good laugh when I told her about Ronald getting busted, and if there was anybody who probably needed a good laugh right about now, it was Rhoda.

Her husband, Otis, answered the telephone when I called a few minutes after I'd come to my room. "Haylo, Annette. It's always a treat to hear your voice," he said, speaking so slowly his Jamaican accent didn't sound nearly as thick as it usually did. There were times when I spoke to Otis that I almost needed an interpreter. There was sadness in his voice now.

"Otis, I heard about Jade working in that nasty-ass strip club," I said. "I'm sure she'll be all right." I don't know why I made that last statement. My voice was weak, so I didn't sound too confident. In fact, I didn't really believe that what I had just said was true myself, so Otis probably didn't either. I didn't think that anybody working in a strip club like The Cock Pit was going to be all right. But what else could I say to make Otis feel better and have a shred of hope?

"I pray for my child. She's diggin' a dark hole. In my country, we say, 'If you gonna dig a hole, dig it deep.' It means what you Americans mean when you say that 'God don't make no mistakes' thing."

"I think you mean 'God don't like ugly,' " I corrected. "But I like what you just said too."

"Maybe so. But God *don't* make no mistakes. Everything happens for a reason. However, I give God thanks that my girl is finally on her own and no longer living off me and her mother's earnings. Everybody should make his or her own way in life after a certain age. We will all learn from Jade's behavior." Otis paused. "And Pee Wee's behavior. Buh'lieve me, milady, somebody will benefit in some way. I know you realize what a good man you had with Pee Wee now that he's gone from de house. You never miss your water 'til your well runs dry, eh?"

"Yeah, that's for sure," I mumbled. I couldn't get over the fact that everybody assumed I was missing Pee Wee. Sadly, it was true. He had been out of the house for almost a year now, and I missed him more than ever.

"Annette, let me say again that somebody will benefit from all de trials and tribulations we are dealing with now."

"I hope so, Otis."

"Pee Wee is a good man, you know. Sometimes we good men, *and* you good women, make mistakes. But like I said, God don't make no mistakes." Otis liked to talk. I knew that if I didn't shut him up, he would yip yap into my ear all night.

"Otis, I have a few things that I have to get done tonight. But I just wanted to chat with Rhoda for a few minutes before I got busy," I said quickly. "I'm glad I got the chance to chat with you, though, and I am happy to hear that you are doing all right with . . . you know. The things going on in your family right now."

The next voice I heard belonged to Rhoda. "Annette, I'm so damn glad you called. I've been feelin' like shit all day," she told me. "This is the first year that we didn't even put up a Christmas tree, or do any Christmas shoppin'. I am not in a holiday mood. I am so glad I have Lizel and Wyrita takin' care of all my child-care responsibilities. I can't even deal with that right now."

This was worse than I thought. I was not in that much of a holiday mood either, but I had put up a tree, purchased a lot of gifts, and was looking forward to celebrating the last holiday in the year. Every year since I'd known Rhoda, she had celebrated each Christmas like it was her last. She bought the largest Christmas tree that she could fit into her living room, and she spent days on end decorating it with expensive ornaments. She bought elaborate gifts for everyone from her family members on down to her paperboy. And she had always gone way overboard with her child-care activities during this time of the year. Rhoda, Lizel, and Wyrita, and the young children exchanged gifts. They also decorated Rhoda's den with wreaths and a second Christmas tree, sang Christmas carols, baked cookies, made snowmen, and did all kinds of other wonderful things associated with the holiday.

The week before Christmas last year, Rhoda had produced and directed a nativity play in our neighborhood community theater. Of all people, *Jade* played the part of Mary, the blessed virgin mother of Christ! I didn't know if that was an honor to Mary or an insult.

"I can imagine how you must be feeling. But I am really sorry to hear that you and Otis are not celebrating Christmas this year. Would you like to get together for lunch, or maybe a quiet dinner and some drinks tomorrow?"

"I'd like to, but I can't. I don't like to leave the house unless I really have to. In case . . . in case Jade decides to come home. I want to be here when that happens."

"I see. I understand."

"I've left messages on her cell phone for her to call me so we can talk, and she hasn't returned a single one. I don't like what she did to me, but I don't like what I did to her either. Even when she was a naughty little toddler, I only whupped her a few times. I've never been so violent with her before."

"But she's never hit you before either. And she's never disrespected you the way she did that day last summer, Rhoda. She is still your child, and I know you still love her. I will support whatever you decide to do."

Rhoda sniffed. Her prolonged silence for the next few moments frightened me. I was afraid of what she was thinking. "I'm glad to hear that. I've got an idea," she chirped.

Uh-oh, I thought to myself. "And what is it?" I expected to hear her say something outlandish. And she did.

"I'm goin' to go to that shithole strip club and force her to talk to me. Otis is afraid that he'll tear the place down if he goes. I'd feel better if you went with me. Pee Wee said he would go, too, but I really don't want to drag him into this. Thanks to Lizzie, Pee Wee's got enough mess on his hands."

I didn't want to remind Rhoda that the Lizzie mess on Pee Wee's hands was also the same mess on my hands. It was better for us to deal with one mess at a time. "I'll go with you if you think it'll help. But you know how Jade feels about me. I'm probably one of the last people on the planet that she wants to see."

"I'm sure she probably feels the same way about me these days. Maybe even worse. I won't know for sure unless I go. If I am able to get through to her and get her back on the right track before Christmas, it would be the best gift I ever got."

"All right. Just let me know when you

want to go. I'll go with you if you think it'll help."

"Thanks." Rhoda sniffed again. "How did dinner go with Pee Wee tonight? Have you two made much more progress?"

I took a deep breath and the following words rolled out of my mouth like dice: "Dinner was fine. But guess who we ran into on the way to the restaurant?" I didn't wait for Rhoda to respond. "Ronald was at the mall with his wife and four of their six kids."

"Wife? Six kids? Why — why that bald-headed motherfucker! He's *married?* I thought he was divorced! Are you sure it was his wife and not that Nola woman cousin he told you was comin' to stay with him for a while?"

"Oh, it was the Nola woman all right, but she is not Ronald's cousin. Ronald introduced her to us as *his wife.* Apparently, she's been in Detroit all this time taking care of her pregnant sister. Pee Wee knew that lying jackass from the pool hall. You should have seen how nervous and uncomfortable Ronald was when Pee Wee introduced him and his family to me. All this time, I thought Ronald was divorced, or at least going through a divorce. From the looks of things, there never was a pending divorce on his end, but he knew about Pee Wee and that we were separated. I never lied or tried to hide anything from Ronald. I can't believe he never even told me that he knew my husband. I guess he didn't want me to mention the fact that he and I were dating to Pee Wee, because at some point Pee Wee would have mentioned Ronald's wife to me."

Rhoda laughed. "Oops! I'm sorry! I didn't mean to laugh, but this is kind of funny."

"I figured you'd get a good laugh out of this. I couldn't wait to tell you." I laughed myself now.

"Maybe you should check up on Roscoe now. How do you know he's not married?"

"I have a key to Roscoe's house, and he never hesitates to take me home with him or out in public. I doubt very seriously if he's hiding a wife and a bunch of kids."

"Maybe Ronald really was goin' through a divorce. And maybe later, they patched things up and he didn't want you to know because he wanted to keep seein' you."

"It doesn't matter now."

"I guess not. I'm just sorry you had to find out about Ronald the way you did. I think we both need some drinks. Let's get together for a few at the Red Rose tomorrow night around seven. Then . . . then we can decide on when we can pay a visit to that strip joint."

"All right," I said with hesitation, hoping that Rhoda would change her mind after thinking it through more thoroughly. "But I hope going to that club is what you really want to do, Rhoda."

"No, I don't want to go there. But if it's the only way that I can see my child face-to-face, and get her to talk to me, then that's what I am goin' to do."

CHAPTER 43

I didn't like to lie to Lillimae, but I didn't want her to know that Rhoda and I were planning to visit that strip club. Lillimae had loose lips, and I didn't want her to blab our plans to some other big mouth and have the information reach Jade before we got to her. The last thing we needed was for Jade to hear that somebody was going to attempt an intervention on her behalf. Especially when that "somebody" was her mother and me, two women she now hated with a passion.

We had decided to go the following Saturday night. To throw people off, I had casually mentioned to a few that Rhoda and I were going to go to the latest tent revival on Franklin Street on that night.

Rhoda had wanted to go the night before, but I declined that offer right away. I had never told her about how so many unpleasant things seemed to happen to me on

Fridays. But that was the main reason that I insisted we go on Saturday night.

That night arrived too soon for me, but I couldn't disappoint Rhoda and back out now.

"I sure wish I could go with you and Rhoda to the tent service tonight. I know that tent group comes and goes on a dime, so I hope we can all go again real soon," my mother said when I told her during a telephone conversation. Rhoda was waiting for me to pick her up.

"I wish you could go with us, too, Muh'Dear. But I am sure we'll all get to enjoy some services together soon," I replied. "And I just want to let you know that I am very happy about the way things are going between you and Lillimae."

"Me too. She's a sweet woman." Muh'Dear snorted the way she usually did when she was about to say something mean. I held my breath and waited. "And Lillimae is such an accommodatin' person to work with. She never complains and she is always eager to do whatever it is I need her to do. And the girl can cook up just about anything! I need to be here tonight so she can show me how to make that screamin' gumbo she served the other day," Muh'Dear said, speaking into the phone so loud my eardrums ached. "And one more thing — you don't have to worry about cookin' nothin' for Christmas. Me and Lillimae got that one covered."

"Oh! That's good to hear." I sighed.

"Okay, baby. I know you and Rhoda will remember me and Frank, and Charlotte and Scary Mary in your prayers tonight, but please include Lillimae too."

Even though Muh'Dear and Lillimae were getting along much better now, I knew that my mother had different motives than Lillimae. Even though they were now as thick as thieves, she still sputtered a few choice words about Lillimae when she got a notion to do so. For one thing, I knew that my mother would never get over the fact that Lillimae was the daughter of the woman my daddy had deserted us for. And Muh'Dear made sure I didn't forget.

"I'm surprised that that off-white gal, raised by a fully white woman, knows how to cook so good!" Muh'Dear exclaimed. "You know how them folks like to eat half-cooked vegetables and blood oozin' from their rare-cooked meat like jelly. And I ain't met a white woman or man yet who knows how to season a pot of greens properly. Every black person I know knows that you need to season greens with some smoked turkey necks, or some neck bones, or a big ham hock — any kind of meat product! Oomph! Oomph! Oomph!"

"I guess Lillimae inherited a lot of Daddy's traits," I suggested. "I'm glad she has a real appreciation for good food."

Muh'Dear laughed. "And that's another thing! I don't mean to criticize, but Lillimae needs to do somethin' about her weight. Every time I go in the kitchen, she is in there gnawin' on somethin'." Muh'Dear didn't sound as harsh as she usually did.

"Muh'Dear, you don't have to keep her working for you if you don't like her," I said.

"I ain't said nothin' about not likin' that gal! Even with that limp, stringy blond hair hangin' off her head, them blue eyes, and that flat-ass bootie of hers, she reminds me a lot of you, so she's all right by me. I'm glad I did get to know her better. But I'm just sayin' she needs to stop feedin' her face so much. Uh-oh!" Muh'Dear chuckled and began to whisper. "I think I just heard her come in! I don't want her to hear me yip yappin' about her. The poor thing. And you better not rat me out to her." Muh'Dear laughed some more, so I didn't feel too badly about her ranting and raving about Lillimae again. "You know how dainty and sensitive white women can be. She'll bust

385

up cryin' if you told her what I just said about her."

"You don't have to worry about me telling Lillimae anything. Now, I don't mean to rush you off the phone, Muh'Dear, but I need to go and get ready for the revival. We want to leave early enough to be on time, in case we run into trouble with all this snow and get delayed."

I had decided to send Charlotte to another neighbor's house. Mrs. Pickett was a widow and loved having company.

"You mean you are not making me go to Harrietta's house tonight?" Charlotte asked.

I shook my head. "As long as you don't want to go to Harrietta's house, you don't have to," I assured her. "I had another talk with her. I told her that I don't want her to look after you anymore. You don't have to go over there at all. Happy?"

A pensive look appeared on her face. "Good. I just wish . . . I just wish that her kids didn't have to live with her."

"Well, what that woman does with her own kids is none of my business."

"If she was doing something real bad to them, would you turn her in?"

"I don't know what you're getting at, but, yes, I would. If I had *definite* proof that Harrietta, or anybody else, was abusing kids in any way, I would contact Child Protective Services immediately. So, can you prove she is abusing her kids?"

Charlotte just stared at me and slowly shook her head. "Uh, maybe . . ."

"Maybe what?"

"Nothing, I guess."

"All right, then. When you think you can, then you let me know. For now, you go get your coat and boots on and get over to Sister Pickett's house."

CHAPTER 44

I didn't like to think about the fact that Charlotte disliked Harrietta with such a passion, even after I told her she no longer had to spend time with her. The more I thought about it, the more it baffled me. And Charlotte's ranting and raving was not the only reason why. Recently, when Harrietta and I were together, I did notice something that seemed a little strange, even to me. I had visited her house for coffee a couple of days ago. Afterward, I invited her and her girls to my house to watch a recent showing of *The Wiz* that I had recorded. During our walk back to my house, with the kids running ahead of us, the old Collie tied to a buckeye tree in the yard next to her house started to bark and howl like the world was coming to an end. I had always thought that the poor creature was mute. But now he was also growling and gnashing his teeth too. He seemed so agitated that I thought he was going to break loose and attack Harrietta and me. The odd thing was, I had never heard this dog bark or howl or behave in an aggressive manner before. This dog was very docile and so old that he stumbled when he walked. And he was blind in one eye.

"I wonder what provoked that old dog? He never barks or gets excited about anything. Not even with all these cats strutting up and down our street," I remarked to Harrietta.

"Oh, I've heard him bark before. Every time he sees me he goes crazy," Harrietta replied. "It must be my perfume."

I gave Harrietta a confused look. "Your perfume? Why would perfume make a dog so angry?"

"It happens. Didn't you read about that case in Vermont with that woman who got attacked by her neighbor's dog because her perfume irritated him?"

"Oh yeah. Now that you mention it, I vaguely remember reading something about that a few weeks ago," I said. "By the way, your perfume is a fragrance I'm not familiar with. Exactly what is it so I'll know not to ever wear it?" I chuckled, but I was serious. The last thing I needed was to get mauled by a dog because he didn't like my perfume.

"Don't laugh, but it's called Run Devil Run," Harrietta told me with a proud sniff. "It's supposed to protect me from evil forces."

I couldn't stop myself from laughing.

"I get it from that candle shop over on Weekes Avenue. See, I used to live in Louisiana when I was a little girl. My family lived in the bayou where a lot of us believed in lotions and potions and a few other good-luck devices. Miss Gertrude, the old woman who runs the shop on Weekes Avenue here in Richland, she's a good friend of mine, so I like to give her a little business from time to time."

Harrietta had seemed like a conservative, no-nonsense kind of woman to me. I was shocked to hear now that she had ties to a mysterious woman who everybody I knew, even Scary Mary, thought of as a witch doctor.

"Hmmm. Well, if it agitates a normally quiet dog, maybe you should try another fragrance," I suggested. That was all I could think to say on this subject. I didn't like to discuss certain things with anybody; witchcraft was at the top of my list. But because of my rural southern background, and the fact that Scary Mary dabbled in voodoo from time to time, I knew that a lot of people took things like this very seriously. I couldn't hide the concerned look on my face. Harrietta noticed it right away.

"Annette, I don't light up candles, or go around chanting gibberish and other shit like some of the people I know do. The only thing I buy from Miss Gertrude is my perfume. And I only do it to keep her happy. She's old; she won't be around too much longer. It's the least I could do. I don't really believe in all this hocus-pocus stuff anyway, so I don't want you to think this is a big deal with me. And I sure don't want you to think that I involve any of the kids in this. My girls don't even believe in simple little things like horoscopes or fortune cookies."

"I'm glad to hear that. My daughter is even afraid of the dark. She's the only kid I know who is afraid to watch movies with vampires, werewolves, or any other thing associated with the occult. I don't want her to be exposed to anything connected to that candle shop," I said firmly. I didn't feel like laughing now, so I dropped the subject.

A day later, the same thing happened. The same dog went crazy when Harrietta and I walked by. I was glad his owner had him on a leash, because the way he was showing his teeth, with spit dribbling out of both sides of his mouth, I knew that if he got loose,

391

Harrietta and I would be dog meat. A few steps later, when we got in front of the Mortons' house next door to me, their little Chihuahua started barking and jumping up and down like he'd seen the devil. I had never seen this dog act so agitated before either.

"I hate dogs and they hate me," Harrietta commented. Until she'd made that statement, it had never occurred to me that the two dogs barked only when I was with *her.* Even the times when she didn't have on any of her Run Devil Run fragrance. . . .

I didn't have the time or desire to dwell on this subject anymore tonight. What I needed to focus on at the moment was Rhoda and me going to that strip club.

I had never been to a strip joint before in my life. From what I'd seen on TV and in the movies, I expected to see just about every freaky thing in the world once we got inside. And that was just about what I saw.

As soon as we paid our fee to a cross-eyed midget in a booth by the entrance door — we had to pay to get into this damned strip club — a half-naked woman in her early thirties led us to a table right in front of the round stage with a metal pole in the middle of the floor. From that point on, I was appalled to say the least. I felt sick! I couldn't order a drink fast enough from our waitress, a bored woman who looked more like a man. The next thing that turned my stomach like it was on a rotisserie was the smell of cigars, cigarettes, and sweat. That all slapped me in the face like a mallet. The insides of my nostrils felt like somebody had stuck burning matches up in them. Even my eyes burned.

The men were absolutely out of control. You would have thought that they had never seen a woman before in their lives. Some were whooping, hollering, and waving their arms in the air like they were at a rodeo. One man, in an expensive-looking suit at that, was on his hands and knees on the floor in front of the stage barking like a dog. Some of the "dancers" looked like teenagers, but the majority of the strippers appeared to be between the ages of late twenties and early forties. I almost choked on my wine when a woman with breasts the size of basketballs went up to the man at the table next to ours and grabbed his dick with both of her hands.

"My Lord in heaven!" I said, my eyes almost rolling out of their sockets. "I can't believe that Jade is working in a dump like this!"

Before Rhoda could respond, the DJ introduced the next stripper: Juicy J. The applause from the men was thunderous. You would have thought that the late, world-famous, exotic dancer they called Gypsy Rose Lee had returned from the dead and was about to perform again. It was Jade who pranced out onto the stage and started dancing to "Ice Ice Baby" by Vanilla Ice. I thought I would faint dead away! From the smirk on Jade's face, you would have thought that she owned the club. She was dressed like a nurse, but within minutes, she had removed everything except her black thong panties and her thigh-high boots. After Jade twirled around upside down on that pole for a few minutes, she crawled like a crab to the front of the stage and stretched out on her back. She spread her legs open, stuck her finger inside her panties, and frantically masturbated, with a spotlight aimed at her crotch. Good God!

CHAPTER 45

I was in such a state of shock and disbelief that I didn't even realize Rhoda had leaped out of her seat and run up to that stage. She stood right smack dab in front of it, with one hand on her hip and her other hand in the air, shaking a finger in Jade's direction. The music was so loud I could not hear what Rhoda was trying to say to Jade. But whatever it was, it only made Jade mad because she shook her head and danced toward a trio of young men waving money at her off to the side. I couldn't believe what I saw next. Jade sat on the edge of the stage, with her legs gapped open as far as they could go. Then she slowly pulled her thong panties to the side, exposing her shaved vagina. A drooling man ran up to her and stuffed some bills into the leg of her panties. I don't know how she did it, but Jade leaned forward and plucked the money from her panty leg with her teeth.

The song ended and I heard Rhoda say loud and clear: "Jade Marie O'Toole! You ought to be ashamed of yourself!" Jade ignored her mother and moved to the other side of the stage, where another man slid another bunch of bills into her other panty leg.

To my amazement, Rhoda placed her hands on the edge of the stage and was about to climb up on it. Within seconds, a huge man wearing a ripped wife beater and black leather pants appeared out of nowhere. There was a menacing scowl on his face. He wrapped his meaty arms around Rhoda's waist and lifted her off the floor as if she weighed nothing. He returned her to her seat with a thud and a warning. "Now, you listen; you dykes can't be comin' up in here actin' a fool, touchin' and grabbin' on these girls! If y'all want some pussy-on-pussy action, you have to go in the Diamond Room." He paused and nodded his pumpkin-shaped head toward a door off to the side of the stage. His thick rubbery lips remained open, revealing blunt yellow teeth that looked more like corn. He whipped a large white handkerchief out of his pants pocket and honked into it. He cleared his throat and wiped his forehead with the same handkerchief before he spoke again. "And y'all have to pay for a lap dance like every-body else. If y'all want to act like men, you're goin' to behave like men! Shit!"

"That's my daughter up there on that stage makin' a fool of herself," Rhoda whimpered, giving the bouncer a pleading look.

"I don't care if that's yo' mama. You ain't comin' up in here breakin' the rules. Now, you sit still or I will throw both of y'all dykes out of here!" the scowling bouncer told us. Not only did this creature look like a huge frog, he sounded like one too.

The bouncer left, grumbling cuss words under his breath. People at nearby tables were whispering among themselves and giv-ing Rhoda and me hostile looks.

I felt totally offended by what that bouncer had just said to us. I wasn't upset about him telling us that if we wanted a lap dance we had to pay for it, but I had a problem with him assuming we were lesbians. There were a few other women in this dump who were not with men. I didn't assume they were dykes.

"I don't like this place, Rhoda. I don't see how anybody could stand to be in here for more than a few minutes," I complained. "It stinks like hell in here!"

"I don't like this *toilet* either. It's much

worse than I expected," Rhoda complained.

Jade continued to perform her act, glaring at me and Rhoda.

"Well, now I don't think this was such a good idea. I don't think you are going to be able to talk to your daughter in this place after all," I said, gently placing my hand over Rhoda's. Her hand was shaking so hard, I had to hold on tight to keep her knuckles from hitting against the top of the metal table. "Let's go," I begged. "That same mean-looking bouncer keeps giving us dirty looks."

"I'm not leavin' this place until I talk to my child," Rhoda insisted. "If you want to leave, I can't stop you. I'll go home in a cab."

"I am not leaving this place without you. But if you don't want them to make another scene with us, you'd better stay in your seat."

By now Rhoda was in tears. She wiped her eyes and blew her nose into the napkin that had come with her drink, which had an illustration of a naked woman on it.

"Rhoda, if you do get to talk to Jade, exactly what are you going to say to her? You can't force her to leave this place."

"I don't know what I'm goin' to say to her. But I can't leave her here like this. She's still my baby and I still love her; so I'm stayin' until I talk to her, no matter how long it takes. There is nothin' else that girl can do that'll hurt me more than what she's doin' now," Rhoda said, making a sweeping gesture with her hand toward the stage. She looked so sad and helpless, but other than me being with her, I didn't know what else to do to help her.

I knew I couldn't say what I was thinking, but I didn't agree with what Rhoda just said. I had a feeling that Jade was going to do something that would hurt Rhoda even more. My prediction would come true a few minutes later.

"Honey, the way Jade keeps glaring over here at us, I don't think she wants to hear anything you or I have to say."

Rhoda whirled around to face me. "I want to let her know that she can leave this place tonight with me. I can't rest until I do everything I possibly can to bring her to her senses. I owe that much to her . . . and to myself." Rhoda mopped more tears off of her face; then she rubbed her nose and sneezed. "But this place is so despicable, I'll be glad when we can leave."

"I'll be right behind you. Just say when," I said with a sigh of relief as I sneezed into one of those sleazy-looking napkins. Three men had plopped down at the table a few feet behind us. Within seconds they were all smoking cigars, and whooping and hollering as Jade continued to degrade herself up on that stage. Now she was dancing to "Kiss from a Rose" by Seal. Seal was one of my favorite entertainers. He was such a class act that I couldn't imagine how horrified he would be to know that his music was being used in such a degrading way.

I locked eyes with Jade. The smirk on her face had intensified. I was convinced that if it got any worse, it would melt that metal pole. If this kind of "entertainment" was what the people in this place called sexy, I knew that Rhoda didn't have a chance in hell of talking some sense into her daughter's head. And by now the stage floor was almost covered with bills that the men had tossed to Jade. A few moments later, Jade was dancing a jig and giving herself a single slap on the side of her butt every three or four seconds. She was completely naked now; even the boots had been removed.

"Oh, Lord have mercy," Rhoda moaned, her head in her hands. She looked up, right into Jade's eyes. Jade gave Rhoda a major smirk. When the song ended, she snatched the pieces of her costume and the pile of tips up off the floor, and pranced off the stage like a drag queen. The last thing I saw of her was her naked ass jiggling like brown Jell-O.

A different waitress came to our table and asked if we wanted more drinks. Except for a short heart-shaped apron, a G-string, and red high heels, she was completely naked. I shook my head. Rhoda beckoned for the woman to lean closer to her and Rhoda whispered something in her ear. The woman whispered something back to Rhoda and nodded toward a door on the other side of the room. As soon as the waitress left, Rhoda rose from her seat so fast her chair fell against me.

"Come on. We're goin' to the dressin' room," Rhoda told me, grabbing me by my arm. She started moving before I could protest. I stumbled along behind her like a lamb until we were off the main floor. We crept down a dimly lit hallway that smelled like urine, marijuana, and stale cigarettes.

Before we could enter what I assumed was the dressing room, the door flew open. A buxom blond woman almost knocked us down trying to get out of the room so fast. "Move, bitches! I need to get my ass out on that stage!" she yelled in a hillbilly accent. Rhoda shook her head and proceeded to

enter the room with me still right behind
her.

Chapter 46

Jade's place of "employment" was more disgusting than I thought. The so-called dressing room was a sight to behold. The stench in it was worse than the one out on the main floor. In addition to smoke and sweat, I smelled marijuana smoke, cheap perfume, and the unholy stench of stale farts that seemed to be bouncing off the walls. One wall contained a row of gray lockers. Some had padlocks, some had been pried open. Outfits that I would not have worn during my stint as a prostitute, even if I had had a stripper's body, dangled from hooks in the lockers that were standing open. A large pink plastic penis was hanging like a piñata from a gold chain that had been placed in the middle of the ceiling. Scattered about the dressing room counters were dildos, whips, vibrators as long and thick as my arm, thong panties, makeup, wigs, and hairpieces. And as unbelievable as it was, there was a rosary dangling from a mirror right next to a wallet-sized picture of a man licking a naked woman's breast.

Jade sat in front of a full-length mirror with a cigarette dangling from her lip and a champagne glass in her hand. Except for a towel draped around her shoulders, she was still naked. She didn't see us right away, so she seemed to be in a frisky mood. "One of my regulars wants me to give him a blow job without a condom, but I told him like I tell them all, I am not sucking on your joystick bareback for less than five hundred bucks." Jade threw back her head and laughed like a drunken sailor. "I am no —" She looked in the mirror and froze at the sight of Rhoda and me standing a few feet away from the doorway. Her head whirled around so fast she almost fell off the chair. The cigarette fell from her lips and onto the floor. There was a look of hatred on her face that was so intense it made the hair on the back of my neck rise up from my skin like needles.

"The soup kitchen is next door," one of the women yelled, looking from me to Rhoda.

"Listen, if y'all are the new cleanin' ladies, that damn shower is full of water bugs and ants," another one yelled.

"Shet up!" Jade ordered, her hand up in the air. "This is my mama!" The other strippers started buzzing; some even snickered and shook their heads. "What the hell are you doing here?" Jade snarled, rising from her seat with a hand on her hip.

Rhoda swallowed so hard she had to bob her head. "I want to talk to you, baby," she said in a voice that sounded unnaturally gentle coming from her. "You don't have to do this to yourself. Please let me take you back home so we can talk about what you really want to do with your life."

"I'm twenty-one. Remember how you reminded me of that time and time again? You wanted me to get out and be on my own. Well, I did." Jade stopped talking long enough to pick up her cigarette and suck in some more smoke and then blow donut-shaped smoke signals in Rhoda's direction. Rhoda flinched, and for a second I thought she was going to dismember Jade with her bare hands; or at the very least, slap that damn cigarette out of her mouth. And if there was anybody in the world who could get mad enough to do that, it was Rhoda. I was relieved when she didn't. All of the other women present, and there were at least a dozen, remained silent and watched this exchange as if they were spectators at a sporting event.

"Jade, I know better. This is not what you want to do. Come home and let's have a cup of coffee and talk. We can find a school where you can learn a real trade. With your looks, you could even look into a career in TV or the big screen. You are way too good to be involved in crap like this like the rest of these . . . these tramps!" Rhoda insisted, looking around the room from one angry face to another. She wrapped her hand around Jade's wrist.

The other strippers rolled their eyes and snickered. One mumbled a few obscene phrases under her breath.

"Don't you touch me," Jade warned, slapping Rhoda's hand away. "What the hell do you care what I do anyway? You . . . you threw me out of the house I grew up in like I was some bum off the street. And now you come up in here trying to talk shit to me? And by the way, you called me a tramp the day you kicked me out, so I guess I'm in the right place."

"No, you're not a tramp, and you are not in the right place —" Rhoda declared.

Jade held her hand up to Rhoda's face. "I know you want to ease your conscience, but I won't help you. I can do whatever the hell I want to do now!" Jade snapped. "Now

406

take your lap dog and get up out of here! Be nice and go have a drink on me. Tell the bartender to put it on my tab. We got everything you two would like — oops, everything except Geritol." Jade didn't crack a smile at her last comment, but the other women guffawed like hyenas.

"I don't want a drink, thank you," Rhoda said, using that unnaturally gentle voice again. "Can we go somewhere so we can speak privately?"

Instead of answering her mother's request, Jade smashed out her cigarette in a heart-shaped ashtray; then she began to drag a brush through her hair. She went on about her business like Rhoda and I had suddenly become invisible. "Lorna, can I have some of that glitter?" Jade said, addressing the woman in the mirror next to her.

"Jade, please don't do this. For your own sake, you can at least come outside and talk to your mama," I suggested.

Jade stomped her foot on the floor, grabbed a see-through gown and a pair of clear, open-toed high heels from the counter, and ran out the door. She came back a few seconds later with the same bouncer who had manhandled Rhoda and two more who were just as ferocious look-ing. "Get these women out of here," Jade said to the men, snapping her fingers.

"Come on, Heckle and Jeckle! Y'all GIT! GIT UP OUT OF HERE!" yelled the first bouncer who had accosted us in the main room. He grabbed Rhoda by one hand and twirled her toward the door.

The other two bouncers each grabbed one of my arms and escorted me out, leading me by my elbows like I was a lamb on the way to be slaughtered. By the time they got Rhoda and me out of the club, through a back door into a parking lot that was full of men just lurking around, I was overwhelmed beyond belief. My head felt like it was going to spin clean off of my shoulders!

It was a good thing that we had parked two blocks down the street from the club. The brief walk gave us time to breathe in some fresh air and collect our thoughts.

"We could file complaints about those fuckers being so rough with us, you know," I offered. "We were not doing anything bad enough for them to grab on us like they did." The two bouncers who had pounced on me had been so rough, both of my arms were throbbing like I had been wrestling with a bear.

Rhoda shook her head. "This is as far as I go. I don't want to involve the cops. I'm through."

"Honey, you did all you could. Whatever happens next is up to Jade," I said.

"Is it?" Rhoda croaked, looking straight ahead.

I was glad that it had stopped snowing. By the time I drove Rhoda back to her house, almost in complete silence, she was so upset I offered to spend the night with her, or take her home with me.

"I'm fine, Annette. I'm just a little shaken, that's all. I just can't believe what happened back there. You can go on home."

"Rhoda, leave the girl alone for a while. When and if she wants to talk to you, she'll do so when she's good and ready. You and Otis can't do any more than you've done already. Let it go. Let her go. . . ."

"I wish I could, Annette. I . . . I just want to talk to her . . . hold her one more time." Rhoda put her head in her hands and cried like I'd never seen her cry before. Not even when her baby boy died.

I walked her to her front door and gave her a big hug. I felt so helpless. But I had done all I could.

I took my time driving home. My feet felt like they weighed ten pounds each as I practically dragged myself up onto my front porch. As soon as I made it inside and removed my coat, the telephone rang. I let the answering machine catch the call. I didn't feel like talking to anybody else tonight unless it was Rhoda.

"Annette, if you in that house, and if Rhoda is with you, pick up this telephone right now!" It was Scary Mary. She was the last person in the world I wanted to speak to at a time like this. I was not in the mood for any of her busybody antics. "Well, when you get this message, you call me back right away. I just left a message on Rhoda's machine. If you know where she's at, you let her know that her daughter is at my house and she wants to come home and talk to her. . . ."

Chapter 47

Just as I was about to dial Rhoda's number, she called me. "Annette, I just came out of the bathroom and there was a message from Scary Mary! Jade is ready to talk to me!" The excitement in her voice was incredible. I could just picture the huge grin she must have had on her face.

"She left me the same message. Do you want me to come back over?" I asked Rhoda. "I can be there in a few minutes."

"No, I'll call Scary Mary's place and see what's goin' on and then I'll call you back."

"Oh shit, somebody's at the door. Rhoda, hold on." I was surprised to see Pee Wee standing on my front porch. I didn't have time to explain anything to him, and I didn't want to keep Rhoda on hold for too long. I just waved him in. He stood next to me as I resumed my conversation with Rhoda. "Uh, Pee Wee's here. If you want me to come over, maybe I should bring him with me. There is no telling what kind of thugs Jade might have with her, so you might need some men around. Is Otis home?"

"He's already in bed. He's been so distraught because of all this mess, all he wants to do is sleep," Rhoda told me.

"Well, like I just said, Pee Wee and I could come over there if you want us to."

"No, I don't think either one of you should come," Rhoda decided. "And I don't want Otis to know about you and me goin' to that strip joint tonight," she added. "Tell Pee Wee that right now in case he sees Otis before I tell him what you and I did."

I held the telephone away from my ear and turned to Pee Wee. I told him as briefly as I could about Rhoda and me going to that strip club, and what we had tried to do. I also told him how rudely we had been treated.

"Y'all ain't had no business goin' over there to that place without me and Otis as backup anyway!" Pee Wee yelled, talking so hard the veins on the side of his neck were poking out like worms.

"Pee Wee, with all due respect, those bouncers are twice as big as you and Otis, and at least twenty years younger. They would have mopped up the floor with you

412

two if you had gone over there with us," I said. "I'm sure Rhoda feels the same way." I returned my attention to Rhoda. "You were saying?"

"Scary Mary said that Jade will only talk to me if I come alone. She wants to meet me at that bar across from the nail shop on Willow Street," Rhoda announced. She suddenly seemed as giddy as a schoolgirl, and I could understand why. It looked like there was some hope for a reconciliation with Jade after all.

"Are you all right to drive your SUV? You can drive it over here and leave it, and I can drive you to the bar," I offered. "I'll park around the corner from the bar so Jade won't know I came with you."

"Annette, please let me handle this," Rhoda whimpered. "Now, I'll call you back as soon as I can."

As soon as I hung up, Pee Wee told me that somebody at that strip club had already called him up and told him about Rhoda and me being there, and the uproar that we'd caused. "I came over here as fast as I could. I am gettin' real worried about you, Annette."

"You don't have to worry about me," I snapped. Then I purposely changed the subject. "I'm out of Pepsi. Could you drive me over to the Grab and Go so I can pick up a few liters?"

We were out the door within five minutes. When we got to the convenience store, Pee Wee decided to go inside too. We went separate ways as soon as we got inside. I grabbed two liters of Pepsi, and when I attempted to join him in the next aisle where the beer was, I bumped into another customer. I didn't recognize her at first because she had on a pair of big round-rimmed eyeglasses, and a woolen cap covered most of her head. It was Lizzie, the same woman who had ruined my marriage.

"Annette," she mumbled, unable to look me in the eye. "I haven't seen you in a while."

My eyes immediately rolled down to get a look at her stomach. She had gained about fifty pounds, and most of it was around her middle. I knew that she was supposed to give birth in three months, but from the size of her belly, it looked like she was going to go into labor at any minute. "So," I said, looking at her from the corner of my eye. She looked whiter than ever. As a matter of fact, she didn't look like she had a trace of black blood in her now. "You look well," I told her. "Better than I did when I was at the stage you're at now when I was pregnant with Charlotte."

"Yeah, but I've had a lot of complications. Water retention, gas — you know, stuff like that. I've moved back home, too, so my mama can take care of me." She offered me a tight smile, but that was not enough for me to smile back at her. "Things didn't work out between me and Peabo." Things were probably not going to work out between her and any man that she got involved with, I thought with a smugness that I had to force myself to contain. I could tell she was uncomfortable about running into me after all this time. I hadn't seen her this close up since that day back in March in my kitchen, the day Pee Wee moved out of my house and in with her.

"Uh, well, my stepdaddy is back there in the snack section. I'd better go check on him before he fills up the cart with Fritos and pretzels," Lizzie said, already backing away.

"Yeah, you'd better do that," I sneered. I didn't see Pee Wee in the beer aisle. He was at the checkout counter when I got there, and had already paid for his beer.

"What took you so long?" he asked, looking at his watch. "We need to get back to the house so we can be there when Rhoda calls."

"You know me. I can't walk past a magazine rack without stopping," I lied as I paid for my Pepsi.

Before Pee Wee pulled out of the parking lot, I saw Lizzie peeping from the store's front window. He didn't see her, so he didn't see the unbearably vacant look on her face. She looked like she didn't have a friend in the world, and after the way she'd betrayed me, she probably didn't. As much pain as that sad sack had caused me, I still felt sorry for her. In her search for love and happiness, she had sacrificed a lot: her friendship with me, then Pee Wee, and only God knew what else. But now she was right back where she was when I had tried to rescue her from her drab life. She was living back at home with her elderly mother and stepfather with no daddy for the baby that she was about to bring into the world. My life was no bowl of cherries, but I wouldn't have traded places with her for any amount of money in the world.

"Why you so quiet?" Pee Wee asked as we neared my street, driving about five miles an hour because it had begun to snow again.

"Oh, nothing. I was thinking about Rhoda and how I hope things work out between her and Jade," I replied.

Five minutes after we walked into the

house, Muh'Dear and Daddy brought Lilli-mae home. Daddy was hugging a pile of beautifully wrapped Christmas presents. He squatted down and set them under my tree, moaning and groaning because he had such a hard time standing back up. Then, wiping his forehead with the sleeve of his plaid jacket, he looked at me and shook his head. "We heard all about you and Rhoda causin' a ruckus up in that tittie bar," he told me with a grimace on his face as he removed his coat and draped it across the back of the couch. Lillimae removed her coat and helped Muh'Dear remove hers.

"I don't know what the world is comin' to for women to even want to take off their clothes for a livin'," Lillimae exclaimed, hanging the coats on a wall rack by the front door. "If those strip-club owners came up to me, they couldn't pay me enough to show my shame in such a public way!"

I had to press my lips together to keep from laughing at the thought of 280-pound Lillimae stripping. I gave her a pensive look. It was only then that I realized that my half sister, unfortunately, looked like the human version of Miss Piggy; all the way down to the floppy blond hair, snout-like nose, and pinkish complexion.

"Lillimae, I don't think you have to worry

about that," I said, hoping that it didn't sound like I was trying to be funny. But everybody laughed anyway, especially Lillimae.

"I don't know why you and Rhoda lied about gwine to the revival tonight. You should have been up front about that tittie bar. I would have gone with y'all in case some of them goons up in there got ugly and y'all needed some protection," Daddy said, still huffing and puffing from squatting down to place the Christmas presents.

"Frank, you can barely walk from one room to the next without walkin' into the wall. You wouldn't have been no good in that tittie bar up against all them young, big ox bouncers," Muh'Dear said, giving Daddy a pitiful look. Then she gave me the same look. "Annette, I hope you and Rhoda don't never do nothin' that reckless again. If y'all had told me, I would have gone over to that place and talked some sense into Jade."

We were all sitting in the living room sipping on iced tea when Rhoda steamrolled through the front door without knocking — just thirty minutes after I'd spoken to her.

"Did you meet with Jade already?" I asked, motioning her into the house. "Did your daughter talk to you?"

Rhoda looked so depressed and defeated.

There was just no telling what Jade had said to her. "Yes, my daughter did talk to me. It didn't go well. It didn't go well at all."

CHAPTER 48

Rhoda dropped her car keys and purse onto the coffee table. She exhaled as she sat down hard on the arm of the couch where Muh'Dear and Daddy sat with anxious looks on their faces.

Pee Wee stood next to Rhoda, rubbing her back. "You don't look too good, sister," he noticed.

"I don't feel too good either." Rhoda exhaled again. "I told Jade she could come home and all would be forgiven, if she agreed to my conditions. I told her she had to get a real job, respect me, be more responsible, and help me keep the house clean." Rhoda's eyes rolled back in her head; then she laughed in a strange and eerie way. It was disturbing to say the least. "Then she tells me that she will only come home if I agree to *her* conditions. She earns anywhere from five hundred to a thousand dollars a night in tips at the club, so she

420

claims. She will quit the club only if I give her an allowance equal to half of what she's makin'. Can y'all believe the nerve of that girl?"

There was a horrified look on every face in the room, especially mine. Every feature from my forehead to my chin felt like it had frozen in place.

"I'll say she's got some damn nerve!" Muh'Dear shouted, almost jumping off the couch. "Who in the world does that little chicken-leg hussy think she is?"

Rhoda laughed in that same eerie way again. "Oh, this is the best part. She said I had to agree to let her come and go as she pleases, let her smoke weed in the house, hire a maid to clean her room, and let her entertain her boyfriends in her bedroom, no questions asked."

"I hope you didn't agree to any of that shit!" Lillimae snapped. There was a disgusted look on her face as she handed Rhoda a glass of rum. "Take this, sugar. You look like you need it."

Rhoda sipped from her glass and then sucked in a deep breath. "Fuck no, I didn't agree to her demands! So I guess she won't be comin' home. There is nothin' more I can do. I realize that now."

"Rhoda, you ain't done all you could do.

She is still your child, and you got to be there for her and love her unconditional," Daddy suggested.

"Oh, shet up, Frank! You didn't have no trouble raisin' your girls. I don't know about your other daughter Sondra that you had with Lillimae's mama, but Lillimae is one of the most upstandin' women I know. Jade ain't right. There comes a point in time when a bad child can cause more damage to a parent than a serpent's tooth," Muh'Dear said. "Rhoda, you got a King Kong–size mess on your hands, girl." She shuffled over to Rhoda and gave her a long bear hug.

"Well, y'all, I'm goin' home to my husband now," Rhoda said, looking strangely serene.

"If Jade was my child, I'd teach her a lesson she'd never forget," Muh'Dear said. "I'd straighten her out once and for all. It's been years since I had to whup Annette, but I still know how to swing a mean switch. Shoot!"

Rhoda didn't want me to, but I went home with her anyway. Otis and Bully were snoring like bulls in the living room. Otis was stretched out on the couch; Bully was slumped in the love seat. I wondered how things would be if Jade came home while

Bully was still occupying the guest room.

Rhoda and I went into the den to watch the eleven o'clock news. The lead story was about a teenage boy who had robbed the Grab and Go, threatening the cashier with a baseball bat. The whole crime had been caught on the store's security camera. An announcer for Channel Four asked viewers if they could identify this stupid-ass boy. Before they could even finish the story, they reported that the switchboard had just lit up like a Christmas tree. The very first call had come from a viewer who identified the boy without hesitation: the boy's own mother.

"Damn! Can you imagine a mother turning her own son in knowing he's probably going to jail?" I gasped.

There was a blank expression on Rhoda's face. At first I thought she was asleep with her eyes still open. "Oh my God! Rhoda, are you awake?"

"I'm awake." Rhoda's voice was barely audible.

"Girl, did you see what was just on the news?" I asked.

"Mmm-huh. Sure I saw it. Some woman turned her own son in for robbin' the Grab and Go," she said with a shrug. "I don't blame her one bit. . . ."

We didn't mention the strip club or Jade anymore that night. We talked about the Grab and Go robbery, some upcoming sales at the mall, the latest gossip from Claudette's beauty shop, and a new movie that had been recently released. "So you think *Titanic* is goin' to be a box office hit?" Rhoda asked. We had both seen the new movie a few days ago.

I shook my head. "I'm sure that it won't be half as big of a hit that *Jaws* was. That Kate Winslet might make it big some day, but that Leonardo Di— whatever his name is — looks too much like a teenager for anybody to take seriously. He'll be waiting tables this time next year." We spent a little more time talking about a few things we'd seen on TV, and how glad we'd be when Christmas was over. Before long, we had forgotten all about the report about the woman turning her son in for robbing the Grab and Go. At least I did.

"That woman must really love her son to turn him in like that," Rhoda said in a hoarse voice.

It took me a moment to realize what she was talking about. "Oh, you mean that mother the news said turned her son in? Well, that boy cooked his own goose. He's going to jail for sure. And at least his mother will know where he is for a while. Yes, I would say she loves him. If she didn't, she wouldn't have turned him in. And he would have continued to commit crimes. That fool would probably end up killing some innocent person, or getting himself killed."

Rhoda nodded. "Uh-huh. I agree with you on that one. At the rate that boy is goin', he would be much better off in jail than on the streets."

CHAPTER 49

"That's it! I've got it!" Rhoda said. It was the first thing out of her mouth when she called me up on Sunday morning.

"You've got what?" I asked, glancing at the clock on my nightstand. It was only seven A.M.

"I know how I can save my child!" I couldn't remember the last time I'd heard Rhoda sound this giddy. "I'm goin' to send Jade to jail," she announced. "I don't know why I didn't think of this sooner! But after seeing that TV news report about the woman who turned her son in last night, I know that I need to send my daughter to jail to save her."

"You want to send Jade to jail? For slapping you? I don't think she'll get much time, if any, for that. And don't forget, you slapped her back. Not to mention the fact that this happened last summer," I pointed out.

"She's goin' to get herself killed, or end up in prison anyway, Annette. With the people she's runnin' with, it's just a matter of time."

"I won't argue with you on that, but what can you do to her to send her to jail? From what you keep telling me, she wants nothing else to do with you, so you won't even be around her to know what she's up to."

"I think I know a way." Rhoda paused and snorted. Rhoda was not the kind of woman who snorted much; that was more of a guy thing. Or something you'd expect from Muh'Dear or Scary Mary, or even me. But this time she snorted like Mr. T. "Poppy is dyin'." Poppy was Rhoda's elderly father-in-law. "Jade adores him. That old Jamaican lives and breathes for that girl. He taught her how to fish, scuba dive, and how to spit halfway across a room. Last week she told Scary Mary that she plans to go to the islands after the New Year to spend some time with Poppy while he's still alive. The doctor says he's only got a few more months."

"So?"

"Otis and I are goin' down there too. Jade's goin' to get busted at the airport when she attempts to reenter the States."

"Oh? And what is she going to do to get

herself busted?" I wanted to know.

"She's goin' to get caught with drugs in her luggage."

I wasn't sure that I'd heard right. "What did you just say? I know it's not what it sounded like you said."

"What did it sound like I said?"

"Rhoda, it sounded like you said Jade is going to get busted at the airport coming back from the islands with drugs in her luggage. Now, either I'm hearing things or you did say that. And if you did, why did you say that?"

"They don't search everybody. But if an anonymous tipster calls the right person and tells them Jade is a mule, she'll get searched."

I still didn't know if what I was hearing was what I was hearing. I could have sworn that Rhoda had just told me that her daughter was going to get busted at the airport for transporting drugs from Jamaica to the States. That made no sense at all to me. If Jade was not even speaking to Rhoda, how did she know what Jade was planning to put in her luggage?

"Rhoda, what are you talking about? I know that your daughter is a little off, but I don't think she'd be fool enough to try and smuggle drugs out of Jamaica into the

States. It's too risky. They've got dogs sniffing all over the airports and DEA agents running around like headless chickens." I had to pause to catch my breath. "How do you know Jade is going to have drugs in her luggage?"

"Because I'm goin' to put them there."

The room got frighteningly quiet. Even so, I could hear a ringing noise in my ears. "Rhoda, have you lost your mind?"

"No, I have not lost my mind; but if I don't do somethin' to save my child, I will lose what's left of my mind. I love Jade, and I'd rather send her to jail than let her continue doin' all the crazy things that she's doin' now."

"And where will you get the drugs?" I asked dumbly. "Wouldn't you have to go to a lot of trouble?"

"Where would I get drugs?" Rhoda cackled. "Honey child, that's the least of my worries! I know more ganja farmin' Rastafarians in Jamaica than Bob Marley knew. Half of them are my in-laws. I'd have no trouble gettin' my hands on what I need."

"But even if they find the drugs on Jade, they'll have to prove that they are hers, won't they?"

"The drugs will be in her possession. It will be up to her to prove they are not hers."

"I don't know about this, Rhoda," I said, shaking my head. "They come down really hard on smugglers. Jade could get sent away for a long time."

"I know. . . ."

"But is that what you want for her? Wouldn't that be like cutting off your nose to spite your face? If they find drugs on her, she's probably going to go to prison!"

"Annette, my daughter is already in prison if you ask me."

"Rhoda, I —"

"Let me finish! She's livin' with drug dealers, pimps, strippers, and who knows what else. And from what we both heard her say in that strip-club dressin' room about her givin' some regular a blow job, she's obviously involved in prostitution too! At least if she was in prison, she would *have* to follow somebody's rules. Her daddy and I would know at all times where she was and what she was doin'."

"Rhoda, you really need to think this through. This could really backfire on you. I do read the news and I watch a lot of true-crime TV. People get killed, raped, and abused in prison."

"People get killed, raped, and abused on the street too. What would you do if Jade was your daughter?"

"But I —"

"What will you do if Charlotte turns out like Jade? If you had the chance to shake some sense into her by settin' her up to get arrested, wouldn't you do it? If this was the only way you could save her?"

"I don't know, Rhoda. And I hope I never have to find out."

"I hope you don't either."

I prayed that Rhoda would change her mind. There *had* to be a better way for her to turn her daughter around. But after all Jade had done and said, I honestly didn't know if such a thing was possible.

Had I not known any better, I would have sworn that Jade was going out of her way to antagonize her family on purpose. She had behaved in such an atrocious manner in that strip club that I didn't think she could outdo herself.

But it wouldn't be long before she did.

CHAPTER 50

About three weeks into the New Year, there were several news reports on TV about a woman named Paula Jones, as homely as she could be, accusing President Clinton of sexual harassment. Everybody I knew was laughing about it. Even me. Clinton was a handsome man. And with his cute Southern accent and charisma, he could have done much better than Paula Jones. If what that woman named Gennifer Flowers was saying in the tabloids was true, she'd had a very long affair with Clinton. She was a pretty woman, and I could see why the president would have been attracted to her. But this Paula woman was such a straight-up dog.

"It's a damn shame how far a female will go to get attention," Lillimae said after one of the TV broadcasts with that Paula woman grinning into the camera. "This heifer's nose looks like a man's elbow. She needs a heavy dose of spiritual guidance."

Spiritual guidance was one thing that we all needed on a regular basis to nourish our relationship with God. I couldn't remember the last time I'd been to church, or even to one of the frequent tent revivals. Now seemed just as good a time as any for me to do so.

The tent revival folks had left Richland the last week in December, but they had returned a week ago. This time they had pitched the huge tent in the parking lot of the Second Baptist Church, the church that I went to when I did go to church. Muh'Dear, Pee Wee, Daddy, and almost every other black Baptist I knew belonged to this church.

This was the fourth time in the last six months that Reverend LeRoy Pritchard, a roving assistant pastor from Columbus, had brought his popular revival to Richland. He and his staff usually set up the tent, which was large enough to accommodate at least a couple of hundred people. Until the beloved reverend replaced the reverend he assisted, or got a church of his own, he would roam around with his tent, spreading the gospel for several weeks at a time each year. And since he had grown up in Richland, and was a first cousin to Reverend Crutchfield, my preacher, he spent more time here than in

433

any other city in Ohio.

Each week of the revival, the Reverend Pritchard and his associates printed up flyers inviting people to attend the evening services that lasted from seven to nine P.M. The flyers only contained program information that pertained to each individual night. Well, "that modern-day Sodom and Gomorrah," as Reverend Pritchard called the strip club that Jade worked for, had become such a huge thorn in the side of Richland's black community that the elders had spent more time condemning it than any other place. Every other day for the past two weeks, the flyers had displayed "guaranteed salvation" to anybody connected to The Cock Pit. All they had to do was attend the service and atone.

Last Sunday evening, two dozen church members paraded around in front of the strip club with signs condemning it, begging the patrons to "come to Jesus" before it was too late. The bouncers chased them away, but some of the protesters returned later that night during the club's busiest hour. They blocked the entrance, discouraging dozens of patrons from entering the club. It made the front page of *The Richland Review* newspaper the following Monday.

On this particular Sunday evening, just as

people were moseying into the tent's front and only entrance, two SUVs pulled up and parked across the street in front of a deserted feed store. Somebody had built a huge snowman in front of the feed store, complete with a carrot nose and pieces of coal for eyes. What was about to take place would have made that snowman melt, if such a thing could happen.

Before Scary Mary, Rhoda, Muh'Dear, Daddy, Lillimae, Charlotte, and I could get into the tent and find enough metal folding chairs where we could all sit together, all of the doors on each SUV flew open. It was fairly dark, but there was a lot of light from the streetlights, so we could see everything taking place across the street. And it was a sight to behold. Several half-naked young women, and the same three mean-looking bouncers who had accosted Rhoda and me in the club, piled out. They marched out to the curb like soldiers.

"Wolves! Nothin' but the big bad wolves!" Muh'Dear gasped, clutching a thick black muffler around her neck.

"And them wolves didn't even bother to dress up in sheep's clothin'!" Daddy noticed. He wore a black fedora, black suit, and white shirt. And with the grim expression on his face, you would have thought that he was a funeral director.

This pack of wolves was being led by none other than Jade. There was a mischievous look on her face that could have stopped a clock.

"Rhoda, ain't that your girl?" Lillimae gasped, attempting to usher Charlotte inside.

Charlotte had been very reluctant to attend the tent meeting. As hard as she tried to bargain her way out, volunteering to do laundry and other unpleasant household chores, you would have thought that she was trying to talk her way out of a whupping. Most of the kids who attended the meetings did not do so by choice. My daughter quickly changed her tune when I told her that she had to go either to the revival or to Harrietta's house.

There was an amused look on Charlotte's face now, the kind you see only on the faces of youngsters her age. Had the same look been on my face, people would have thought that I was crazy. "Dang! Jade looks hella cool in that outfit!" Charlotte yelled, admiring Jade's micromini and halter top. We were still in the middle of one of our worst winters in years, and Jade was dressed like she belonged on a beach. I wore my knee-length, blue wool dress with a thick, lined

436

plaid coat on over it, gloves, boots, a muffler around my neck, and I was still cold.

"Young'un, you better save your praises for the Lord," Scary Mary warned Charlotte, using her gnarled fingers to thump the side of my daughter's head like a cantaloupe.

"Let's get inside," I insisted, standing behind Lillimae. But nobody was moving forward, and I couldn't because Scary Mary and Lillimae were blocking the way.

Rhoda's jaw had dropped so low that her mouth looked like a dipper. In her cream-colored silk dress with matching wool coat, her face beautifully made up, and her hair pinned into a neat French twist, she looked like a supermodel who had just stepped off the cover of *Vogue* magazine. But from the sudden look of horror on her face, it seemed like she'd gone from looking like a *Vogue* cover girl to one who belonged on *Mad* magazine. She looked like she wanted to cuss out the world. "That's it. I'm not goin' to let my child go on like this," Rhoda said in a low voice.

What happened next was so outrageous, cars driving down the street stopped.

One of the bouncers produced a boom box and fired up one of the raunchiest rap CDs that I'd ever heard in my life. I didn't appreciate any of that trash anyway; most rap music was disgusting to me. But this one crossed the line. Whoever the "singer" was, started out chanting *"pop that pussy, pop open that bootie . . ."* Jade lifted her skirt and began to perform a slow bump and grind. Then the other strippers did the same thing as the bouncers clapped, whistled, and cheered them on.

CHAPTER 51

Reverend Pritchard was a big man with hard, menacing features. He was not happy with what was taking place, and I knew he was going to attempt to stop it before it got out of hand. He walked out to the edge of the sidewalk with his hands on his hips.

"Uh-oh," Daddy said in a low voice. "Reverend Pritchard's gwine to put the fear of the Lord into that mob."

I agreed with Daddy. And if anybody could put the fear of the Lord in somebody, it was Reverend Pritchard. But as soon as he got close enough, Jade and the rest of her crew looked at him like he was crazy.

"We done already called the law, so you devils better get back in them hoopties and get the hell out of here! This is private property," the reverend roared, waving his arms like he was directing traffic. "I don't know what y'all trying to prove, but you ain't rackin' up no points here!"

"Are you saying that we can't come to this revival?" Jade jeered, still bumping and grinding. "We need some spiritual guidance. We are sinners and everybody knows that even sinners need love."

"Girl, you need way more than spiritual guidance," Reverend Pritchard hollered, shaking his fist at Jade. He crossed the street and stood right in front of her.

"Jade, you need a whuppin'!" an unidentified voice yelled from the entrance area of the tent.

I didn't realize that I had put my hand over Charlotte's eyes until she pushed it away.

"Us Cock Pit folks got religion too!" one of the bouncers chortled. At the same time, this same man was sipping from a can of Budweiser beer!

"Amen! And a COCK-A-DOODLE-DO!" one of the other strippers yelled.

"We can do what we want, wherever we want, and when we want," another one added, giving us the finger. She used that same finger to pat her crotch. Then, with a sinister giggle, she licked her finger and gave it to us again.

"Save us! If y'all can parade around in front of our club, we can parade around here!" Jade screeched, laughing and dancing so hard it looked like she was having a spasm. Then she threw back her head, stretched her mouth as wide open as it would go, and roared with gut-wrenching laughter. She went too far when she wrapped her arms around the reverend and started *humping* him!

"I don't think so," Scary Mary said with a look on her face that would have frightened the Devil. Looking from the spectacle across the street to my face and around to the others in my party, she continued, "Y'all move back. This one is mine. I know just how to straighten out this mess," she said, speaking calmly now, despite the fact that she was obviously just as outraged as the rest of us. "I may be a she-pimp, but even I know there is a time and a place for everything. A sex sideshow don't belong this close to hallowed ground!" To this day, none of us knew Scary Mary's full background. I didn't know how old she was, or even where she had come from. But one thing I did know was that this old sister had earned her nickname. She had been involved in criminal activity since the age of nine, when she and her outlaw mother lived in a chicken coop on a white man's sugarcane farm in south Florida. She had only one biological child of her own, despite the fact that she'd been married several times, but she treated me and all of my friends like family. In spite of her age, which was at least late eighties or early nineties, and her declining health, people feared her. She wouldn't hesitate to bat somebody's head with her bamboo cane or bite off somebody's finger (she'd done that to one of her unruly male clients a few years ago). People feared her because she knew where all the bodies were buried, so to speak. She had so many connections that she never had any trouble getting her way, good or bad. She was like a cross between Oprah and John Gotti; she could be your "best friend" or your "worst enemy." Every Thanksgiving and Christmas she donated dozens of bushel baskets of food to poor families, and she helped serve food at the local soup kitchen on a regular basis. I was glad that I was on her good side.

We all stood back as the fearless old madam sauntered over to the strippers with her hands on her hips, the tail of her butterscotch-colored tweed coat almost touching the ground. Reverend Pritchard turned around and headed back toward the tent, wiping sweat off of his face with his sleeve.

Scary Mary stopped with her face inches in front of Jade's. Jade gasped. Her body was suddenly as rigid as a tree. "Shame, shame, shame! Shame on you, Jade! SHAME!" Scary Mary chanted. "If you was my girl, I'd skin you alive!"

Jade looked around at her friends and rolled her eyes. Then she looked up into Scary Mary's face. Jade looked like a midget standing in front of Scary Mary, who was at least six feet tall.

"What . . . what is your problem, old woman?" Jade asked Scary Mary in a voice that displayed a great deal of fear. "Can't y'all take a joke?"

"You can call yourself jokin' all you want to, Devil, but I can assure you that I AIN'T JOKIN'! And who you callin' an old woman? I ain't *that* old, so don't you call me no old woman, girl. I can still do anything you can do, and better. You think you got this poontang thing sewed up? Pshaw! Sex is my business, always has been. You ain't lived long enough to know the ropes like you think you do! You wouldn't know a real dick from an Oscar Mayer weenie. I done been where you tryin' to go. I got more experience in any form of the sex business in one of my baby fingers than you got in your ass and mouth put together! You can provoke me if you want to and I promise you, *you will suffer!*" Scary Mary told Jade.

"I . . . I . . ." Jade stuttered.

"I . . . I . . . I — nothin'!" Scary Mary hollered, mimicking Jade's shaky voice. "I . . . I . . . I!"

The only other sounds that I could hear were of the cars driving down the street. Nobody was laughing, talking, blasting that rap music, or doing anything else, except breathing.

"You know I was just playing," Jade stammered, backing a few steps away from Scary Mary.

With each step that Jade took backward, Scary Mary took one forward. "And what's my problem? Girl, I ain't got no problem. But if I had to choose one, I'd have to say my problem was *you!*"

Scary Mary kept talking, but in a voice that was too low for any of us to hear now. From the frightened looks on the faces of the strip-club gang, especially Jade's, what Scary Mary was saying had to be pretty potent because it did the trick. Jade and her cohorts scrambled back into their vans and shot back off down the street like they had just robbed a bank.

"Rhoda, I was gwine to include you in my prayers this evenin' anyway, but now I'm gwine to devote my entire prayer request to you," Muh'Dear said, rubbing Rhoda's back.

We all waited until Reverend Pritchard and Scary Mary composed themselves before we filed into the tent and took our seats.

I had seen the reverend do some serious preaching, jumping up and down and sweating like a pig, even falling off the pulpit once. But I had never seen him preach the way he did that night.

"He talked about them strippers and that strip club like it was gwine out of style," Daddy said later that night after we had all gone to my house. "I'll be the first one to sign that petition he's about to draw up to get the city to shet that hellhole down."

"Once they shet that place down, maybe Jade will come back to her senses and drag her slap-happy ass on back home," Lillimae said, not sounding very confident.

From the look on Rhoda's face now, I had a feeling she no longer wanted her daughter to simply "drag her slap-happy ass on back home." That was when I recalled what Rhoda had told me the other night, but I didn't say anything to her about it.

Later that same night, at my dining room table during a feast of fried cat fish and black-eyed peas that nobody, except Lillimae, seemed to be enjoying, Rhoda whispered in my ear, "Remember what I said I was goin' to do?"

At first, I pretended like I didn't know what she was talking about, but I did. She was going to set up her own daughter to go to jail. "You're going to plant drugs in Jade's luggage when you guys go to Jamaica," I replied.

Rhoda didn't answer. She didn't have to.

"Rhoda, do you watch much cable TV?" I asked. "Those documentaries on true crimes?"

"Yeah. Why?"

"A lot of the channels do documentary-type shows about people who get caught up in foreign jail situations. Those Jamaican jails are brutal."

"I know that. She won't get caught in Jamaica. I told you, she's goin' to get caught comin' back into the States. Don't you remember me tellin' you that?"

"Maybe you did, Rhoda, but I am going to be honest with you; I didn't think you were serious about this. Even now I am wondering if you really mean to go through with this thing."

"Well, you can stop wonderin' about it. I really do mean to go through with this thing."

CHAPTER 52

About an hour after all of my company had gone home, I moved from my dining room into the living room and curled up on the couch with the TV on. I watched a *Golden Girls* rerun and then the news. They were still reporting Bill Clinton and Paula Jones stories.

It was past eleven and I had sent Charlotte to bed. Lillimae had turned in for the night, and I was glad to have some time alone to organize my thoughts, again.

Just as the news was about to go off, Pee Wee knocked on the front door. He had called earlier and told me that he was coming over to bring money for Charlotte.

Despite the fact that I had spent the evening with family and friends, I now felt so lonely that I was glad to see Pee Wee. He usually called before he came over. But when he didn't, his unexpected visits didn't bother me as much as they used to. As a matter of fact, I was happy to see him these days.

To me, my glee meant that we had made some significant progress. It looked more and more like we would live as man and wife again after all. It had been quite a while since we'd had any close contact, meaning some "action in the flesh," as the revival reverend had referred to sex. And quite frankly, I needed some now. Especially since I had severed my relationship with Ronald. I had not spoken to him since that clumsy night at the mall. But I had seen him on the street a few times with his wife and children. Each time, he'd looked at me like I was a stranger. I had also finally dropped Roscoe completely from my agenda. That was one relationship that had become useless, to me and to him. For one thing, I was of no more use to him when I stopped doing domestic chores for him. I missed him, but not enough to continue the relationship.

"I'm glad you had some time for me," Pee Wee said as soon as he came in and made himself comfortable on my couch. "I know you are one busy lady."

"I'm not as busy as you think," I admitted. "At least not with other men." I sniffed. "But I do have a lot going on."

"Don't I know it."

I didn't know how much Rhoda had told him about how she was going to plant drugs on her daughter, and I was certainly not going to tell him. But I felt that I needed to know what Rhoda had shared with him on this subject. I didn't want to slip up and reveal information she didn't want anybody else to know.

"Uh, have you talked to Rhoda lately about Jade?" I asked, giving him a cautious look.

He shrugged and shook his head. "Not really. I ran into her at the gas station on my way over here, and she told me about that mess at the tent revival this evenin'. I told my girl she needs to drag that little heifer of hers into the woods by her feet and whup the dog shit out of her."

"A lot of people feel the same way you do. But I think it's too late for that. Whuppings didn't faze Jade at all when she was growing up. Rhoda only whupped her a few times. But Otis didn't hesitate to chastise her when she misbehaved, which was a waste of his time. One time I saw him lay into her with a switch like he was whupping a man. After he turned her loose, that little hussy ran out of that room laughing so hard Otis and I had to laugh too. You want a drink?"

"A beer would be nice."

Right after I handed Pee Wee a can of Bud Light, I excused myself and ran upstairs to use the telephone in my bedroom. I wanted to make sure I didn't say something to him about Rhoda that he didn't need to know. I knew that he was her best male friend, but there were some things that she and I shared that nobody else on earth needed to know. If Rhoda was really serious about sending her daughter to prison, for Rhoda's sake, I didn't want the world to know.

"Pee Wee's downstairs," I told her, speaking in a low voice even though he couldn't hear me down in the living room. "I don't want to say anything you don't want me to say. But, uh, did you say anything to him about what you told me you're going to do to Jade? That, uh, thing with her luggage?"

"HELL NO!" Rhoda boomed. "Of course I didn't tell Pee Wee what I am goin' to do. And don't you ever breathe a word of it to him, or anybody else! I didn't think I needed to tell you not to."

"Rhoda, I don't want you to go to jail. But if this thing backfires and you get caught, you might be the one to get locked up. Have you thought about that?"

"I got it all figured out. Don't worry."

"That's easier said than done. I honestly don't think I can not worry knowing all of what I know." I sniffed and rubbed my nose. My bedroom door was closed, but I glanced at it anyway to make sure I didn't have an audience. The floor in my upstairs hallway was hardwood. From the landing at the top of the stairs all the way to my bedroom at the opposite end of the hall, the floor creaked when somebody walked on it, even if they tiptoed in their bare feet. I hadn't heard anybody approaching, but I lowered my voice to a whisper anyway. "But I'll try."

Rhoda chuckled. I couldn't figure out why because I didn't think anything we had said so far was amusing.

"I'm worried about you," I told her.

"You worry about yourself and Pee Wee. I got my shit under control. I'm goin' to be real busy shoppin' for clothes to take with me, and makin' sure Lizel and Wyrita have everything under control with my child-care obligations. I don't want to leave the children or their parents in a lurch. I might not get to see you much before I leave for Jamaica, but I'll call you from down there as often as I can."

"Rhoda, I can't afford to lose you. Please be careful," I pleaded.

"You do the same tonight."

"What do you mean?"

"Girl, you know damn well what I mean."

"Rhoda, if I knew, I wouldn't be asking," I said with a hiss.

"Look, I know you better than your own mama. I know your pussy has been itchin' for weeks. Right now you've got the only man you know who can get the job done right sittin' in your livin' room. From what he's been tellin' me lately, he hasn't been with another woman in weeks, so his dick is probably as hard as a lead pipe by now. *Get you some tonight.*"

When I went back downstairs, Pee Wee had unbuttoned his shirt. I was glad to see that he'd lost part of that pot belly he'd had a few months ago. He had also kicked off his shoes and propped up his feet on my coffee table. He looked right at home.

"You want something else?" I asked, meaning another beer.

Pee Wee looked me up and down and smiled. "Well, since you asked . . ."

I did "get some" that night. And it must have been pretty obvious, because the next morning as soon as Lillimae saw my face, she started grinning.

"Somebody got lucky last night," she teased. "I heard that ruckus comin' from your room. It sounded like you were tearin' down the house. It's about time you got some. . . ."

452

I faked a gasp. "Lillimae, I don't know what you mean," I said, not looking at her. I poured myself a cup of coffee and joined her at the kitchen table.

"You got some what last night, Mama?" Charlotte wanted to know, creeping into the kitchen with her backpack.

"Uh, nothing," I mumbled, wiggling in my seat.

"Some new clothes," Lillimae offered. "Your mama got herself some new clothes last night."

"Is that all?" Charlotte said with a bored look on her face. "Mama, I hope you didn't get any more of those old granny goose–looking blouses and dresses that you already have enough of."

"Uh, you'd better hurry up and eat so you can get out there to meet your school bus. Make sure you have your lunch money and all your homework," I said sharply. "And don't forget, I'm going out to dinner tonight with Daddy, and your aunt Lillimae is going to be at the restaurant helping your grandmother." Charlotte was about to grab a piece of bacon, but her hand froze in midair when she heard what I had to say next. "Do you want to go to Harrietta's house when you get off that school bus after school?" Because I had had that talk with

Harrietta about Charlotte, I was confident that Harrietta would work extra hard to make Charlotte like her. But now I'd let Charlotte decide whether or not she wanted to give Harrietta another chance.

"I'd rather go hang out at the church!" Charlotte hollered. "Mama, I don't want to keep going to that old woman's house. I keep telling you she's not normal!"

"Exactly what does she do that makes you think she's not normal?" Lillimae asked.

Charlotte dropped her head. "It don't matter. Y'all grown folks stick together anyway." With a slight smile on her face, she said, "Mama, if I'm good and don't complain so much about Harrietta, can I go to the Valentine's Day dance at my school coming up?"

"I'll think about it," I replied, relieved that she had directed her attention toward something more pleasant.

CHAPTER 53

I had visited Harrietta at her house a few times since my decision not to depend on her to look after Charlotte anymore, but she had stopped coming to my house — even when I invited her. We discussed a lot of different things when we were together, but there was now some tension between us. I knew that our relationship would never be the same again.

I was surprised that she still let her daughters spend time with Charlotte in my house. She had even allowed Vivian to go to the skating rink with Charlotte the day before.

When I told Charlotte that she could attend the Valentine's Day dance at her school a couple of weeks after the fiasco that Jade had participated in during the tent revival, she was ecstatic. But when I told her that Harrietta had volunteered to be one of the chaperones at the dance, she decided not to go. I didn't try to change her mind. When

Harrietta called me up and asked if Charlotte wanted to ride to the dance with her and Vivian, I lied and told her that Charlotte had suddenly become sick and wouldn't be going to the dance. I don't know if she believed me or not, but I found out the next day that Vivian had suddenly changed her mind about going to the dance too.

Harrietta called me up around eight the next morning. I had just finished cooking breakfast and was anxious to dive into the buttered grits on my plate.

"Is Vivian at your house?" Harrietta asked, sounding frantic.

I was puzzled to say the least. Harrietta was very particular about when she let her girls out of her sight. "No. Why would she be here? Especially this early in the morning. Didn't she come home with you after the dance last night?"

"She didn't go to the dance last night."

"Oh? But she was even more excited about it than Charlotte was. Did she get sick too?" I stopped chewing on the piece of bacon that I had just speared with my fork. I didn't feel so hungry anymore.

"When I told her that Charlotte was not going to the dance, she changed her mind. When I went to her room to wake her up for breakfast a few minutes ago, she was gone. So was her backpack, her cell phone, and a few of her clothes."

"Hmmm. Maybe she's with her daddy," I offered.

"No, she's not. That porch monkey is on a two-week cruise with his whore."

"Oh. Well, she's not here. I do know that she spent some time on the telephone with Charlotte yesterday evening. Hold on and I'll run upstairs and ask her if she knows anything."

When I entered Charlotte's room, she was already up, which was unusual for her on a Saturday morning.

"Do you know where Vivian is?" I asked.

Charlotte was sitting on the side of her bed reading a comic book.

"Nope," she replied, shaking her head.

"Her mother's on the telephone. Vivian didn't go to the dance last night either, and when Harrietta went to get her for breakfast this morning, she was not in her room."

"Well, I don't know where she is," Charlotte answered with a shrug.

The thought that Vivian had run away was the next thing that entered my mind. I didn't want to mention that to Charlotte and I didn't mention it to Harrietta, but she brought it up as soon as I returned to the telephone.

"Oh my God! I think she's run away!" Harrietta screamed.

"Oh no! I hope not! Have you called up her other little friends?"

"I've called up everybody I know. Somebody knows where she's at, but nobody's talking!" Harrietta choked on a sob.

"If she's not back home within the next hour, I think you should call the police. Do you want me to come over? Do you want to send Diane and Lucy over here while you go out and look for her? Or if you want me to, I'll go with you."

Harrietta let out a groan. "Thanks, Annette. I'm going to make a few more calls and if I don't have any luck, I'll let you know."

Charlotte entered the kitchen a few minutes later.

"Can I eat in my room?" she wanted to know, not looking at me as she fixed herself a plate.

"Charlotte, if you know where Vivian is, you'd better tell me," I said, shaking my fork at her. "Her mother is beside herself!"

"I don't know nothing," she replied, still not looking at me.

"Running away from home is way out of character for a girl like Vivian," I insisted.

"Don't you think so?"

"I guess," Charlotte mumbled. She stumbled out of the kitchen with a plate that contained a large portion of grits, several pieces of toast, and *two* spoons.

I waited a few moments and then followed her, holding my breath as I tiptoed up the steps.

She had locked her bedroom door, and that was something she never did. She was taking too long to open it when I knocked, so I trotted to my room and got the key. Before I could get all the way into Charlotte's room, I saw Vivian scrambling to get into the closet.

I called Harrietta immediately. A few minutes later, she stormed into my house clutching two switches. She didn't whup Vivian in my presence, but I was sure that the girl was going to catch hell when she got home. And I didn't blame Harrietta one bit for being so angry.

"How could you get involved with that girl running away like that? What is the matter with you kids?" I hollered at Charlotte as soon as Harrietta and Vivian left.

Lillimae came galloping into the living room in her housecoat.

"What in the world is all the hoopin' and hollerin' about?" she asked, looking from me to Charlotte.

"Vivian ran away from home last night and Charlotte was hiding her in her bedroom," I snapped, glaring at Charlotte.

Lillimae gasped; then she began to speak in a very gentle voice. "Charlotte, honey, don't you know better than that? You can't let a runaway stay in this house."

"She was going to go someplace else after today," Charlotte whined, with a look of terror on her face. From the way she was trembling, you would have thought that I had two switches in my hand too. "I was just trying to help. . . ."

"Well, you've helped her enough, young lady. You won't be going to that skating rink at the mall, riding your bike, or doing much of anything else for a while," I declared. "And I don't know what Harrietta is going to do about this, but outside of school, I don't want you to communicate with Vivian again until I say you can. I won't be surprised if Harrietta stops you two from associating with one another ever again!"

Harrietta didn't return any of the calls that I placed over the next few days. I didn't even see her or any of her kids outside their house, or anywhere else. I decided to stop leaving messages for her. I felt that if she

ever wanted to communicate with me again,
she would.

CHAPTER 54

It was the last day in February; two weeks
since I'd last spoken to Harrietta. But I had
seen her and her girls going in and out of
their house during the last few days. Everything appeared to be all right, so I didn't
bother her. I could understand her being
upset with Charlotte for hiding Vivian in
her bedroom. And if I hadn't found Vivian
when I did, there was no telling what she
might have done next. Just thinking about
that made me mad, so I could imagine what
it did to Harrietta. If and when she ever
wanted to communicate with me again, I
would welcome her. In the meantime, I
would stay out of her business. I already
had enough on my plate anyway.

I left work a few hours early that Friday
to drive Rhoda to the airport in Cleveland.
Jade had left for the islands the day before,
and Otis was going to join them a few days
later. Before Rhoda and I parted, I asked

her again if she was serious about planting drugs in her daughter's luggage.

"I wouldn't have told you what I was goin' to do if I didn't mean it. I feel like I have no choice now," Rhoda told me, sounding exasperated. I knew she was exasperated and overwhelmed. But she seemed more determined than ever to go through with her bizarre plan.

"Rhoda, you do have a choice. Jade will get locked up for a crime that she did not commit. That boy who robbed the Grab and Go committed a real crime. That's why his mama turned him in," I reminded. "I just wish that you'd give this thing some more thought."

"Some *more* thought? You think I should give this thing some more thought? This is all I've been thinkin' about since I first mentioned it to you, Annette."

"Well, I don't think you've thought about it enough. Sending your own child to jail? Do you really want to do *that* to her?" I was talking so fast I had to cough to keep from choking on my words. "What you're proposing to do is a crime. I hope you realize that."

"Annette, do me a favor and let me handle my business. Now, let me get in line so I can go get checked in." Rhoda looked at her travel documents in her hand and groaned. She was clearly distressed and I could understand why. Going to wait for somebody to die, then attend their funeral was stressful enough. But with everything else that was going on, I was surprised that Rhoda was still able to speak in a coherent manner. I could not imagine what it would be like to set up my own child — or anybody else for that matter — to go to jail! Especially for a crime they did not commit. It was wrong any way you looked at it — ethically, morally, and legally. But in a twisted way, as a desperate mother, I could see a glimmer of logic in Rhoda's plan. Since I had already expressed my thoughts about this insane situation to Rhoda, it was not necessary for me to say it again this late in the game. But I knew that I would again eventually.

Rhoda seemed like she was in a fever of anxiety. She kept glancing at her watch and looking around. Every time there was a loud noise, she jumped.

"Are you all right?" I asked.

She rolled her eyes and gave me a weak smile. "Of course I'm all right." She sucked in some air and offered me another weak smile. "Lord, I hope they can switch me to a window seat. I would not want to sit for hours on end in a middle seat if my flight was on the Concorde." She paused, gave me a pitiful look, and glanced at her watch again. "You may not think that my daughter is committin' any crime, but I do. Her life-style is a crime." I got the feeling that Rhoda was trying to convince herself that she was doing the right thing more than she was me.

"If you feel she's already committing crimes, don't you feel she'll eventually get caught and go to jail legitimately?"

"True. I'm sure she'll eventually get caught up in some mess and get arrested anyway. But what if she's involved in some-thin' like a shootout with the cops, or some of those thugs who have a grudge against those snakes she's workin' for? What if she overdoses on drugs? What if she gets in-volved in somethin' she can't get out of? Now I'm through talkin' about this." Rhoda patted her hair, which was in a ponytail. "Any of my gray roots showin'? I didn't have time to make it to the beauty shop."

"I don't see any," I answered. "You look fine."

Rhoda didn't want to continue the conver-sation, and in a way I was glad. Her sending Jade to jail was one thing that I wished she had not told me about. I couldn't stop thinking about it now. And when we parted in front of the entrance to her flight's departing gate, she hugged me like she was hugging me for the last time.

I didn't sleep much that night. All I could think about was Rhoda's plan going awry, and her going to jail, and me losing the best female friend I ever had.

I kept myself as busy as possible for the next few days. That Friday, on my way home from work, I ran into Wyrita at the Grab and Go. I was two people behind her in the express checkout line. When I got outside, she was waiting on me, leaning on the hood of my car. She had already dropped her purchases into her car, two vehicles over from mine, so I knew she meant business. She was not about to let me get away unscathed. Wyrita would have made a good spider. She was the kind of woman who could spin an imaginary web and get you caught up in it before you knew what was going on. I felt like a trapped fly.

As soon as Wyrita opened her mouth, my chest tightened, and I began to ache in several parts of my body. "I seen Lizzie's little baby boy a couple of hours ago," she began with glee. "He looked so sweet and innocent," she added, giving me the kind of look that people give to women they feel sorry for. I couldn't understand why she was feeling sorry for me. "I was at the hospital visiting my aunt Mildred. She just had hip surgery."

"Oh, I hope she recovers soon," I said, ignoring her comment about Lizzie's new baby boy.

I attempted to leave, but Wyrita jumped in front of me. The way she grabbed my arm you would have thought that she was a security guard trying to subdue a shoplifter.

That baby looks just like Pee Wee," Wyrita reported, looking at me like I had just announced I had a fatal disease. And what she had just said made me feel like I had a fatal disease. But I was getting tired of people feeling sorry for me. I was still a strong woman. I had survived more crises than five other women put together. I didn't need any more pity.

"Is that right?" I replied, trying to sound and look like I was not interested. "I'd better get home before my ice cream melts." I sighed. "It was nice seeing you again. If you and Lizel need any help with the kids at the child-care center, I'll take some time off work to help out until Rhoda gets back from Jamaica." I rushed off before she could get another word in edgewise, but the words that had already slid out of her mouth rang in my ears all the way to my house.

Until I inspected that baby's features with

my own eyes, I refused to accept what Wyrita had just said. I would decide for myself if the child looked "just like Pee Wee." If he was really telling me the truth about him not being with Lizzie since their breakup last May, he was not that baby's daddy. However, if Pee Wee did sleep with Lizzie after their breakup and even though his sperm count was extremely low, there was still a possibility that he could be that baby's father. I knew that because I had spent a few hours on my computer Googling information on the subject one night a few weeks ago.

The uncertainty of the baby's paternity was going to haunt me until I knew for sure. But I made up my mind to let Pee Wee bring it up the next time I saw him.

CHAPTER 55

Pee Wee showed up at my house unexpectedly around ten that same night. He sat on one end of the living room couch, and I sat on the other. We made small talk and drank a few beers as we watched two episodes of *The Cosby Show* that I had recorded. Lillimae was with Muh'Dear, and Charlotte was in bed.

He seemed uneasy. He kept scratching his head, the side of his neck, and his face. He also cleared his throat a lot. Finally, he said, "I don't like to get in your business, but are you seein' anybody else right now?" He paused and did some more scratching. This time it was his arm. "You seem nervous and jumpy. And your mind seems to be on a thousand other things."

To say that I was nervous and jumpy and that my mind was on a thousand other things was an understatement. I had a lot on my mind right now. The issue of Lizzie's

469

baby was on my mind, but that was not what I wanted to deal with tonight. I had to deal with what Rhoda was up to. I could always deal with Lizzie and that baby later. The baby had been conceived and was here, and I had to live with that knowledge. I couldn't do a damn thing to change the outcome of something that had already happened. I could do something about a situation that had not happened yet — but could I? Other than pray, what else could I do? Rhoda's mind was made up, and one thing I knew about her was that when she decided she was going to do something, nobody could talk her out of it. Trying to do so was a waste of time. Her mind was as pliable as a slab of concrete. With each passing day, I became a little more concerned about what Rhoda was threatening to do to Jade.

"I'm not nervous or jumpy," I defended, rubbing the side of my arm even though it was not itching.

"You didn't answer my question. I want to know if you seein' anybody else right now?" Pee Wee asked again.

"We're still separated, and as long as we are, I will see other men if I want to. Why do you ask?"

"Like I just said, your mind seems to be a thousand miles away. Your eyes are glassy and you look nervous. I know you were not expectin' me, but if you want me to leave so somebody else can come, I will. The last thing I want to do is cause you some embarrassment with one of your other men friends."

"I think it's a little too late for you to be worrying about embarrassing me," I said, sounding more hostile than I meant to.

"What's that supposed to mean?" Pee Wee growled, leaning sideways with his head turned so he could see my face better. "You got another man lined up for tonight or not?"

I shifted in my seat and turned so that I could see his face better too. "That's none of your business," I snapped.

"I know, I know," he moaned, rubbing his cheek. "Well, I guess we should change the subject, huh?"

"Sounds like a good idea to me," I quipped, folding my arms.

"How is work?" From the bored look on his face, I knew that he was about as interested in my work as I was in his.

"Work is fine, Pee Wee."

"That's nice, Annette," he muttered.

We remained silent for a few moments. During those sounds of silence, I realized that I could no longer ignore the "elephant" in my living room. And it was a mighty big one too. It had to be addressed. "Did you know that Lizzie had her baby last night? A little boy?"

Pee Wee's eyes got big, and his jaw twitched. He blinked and looked at the floor before looking back at me. "Who told you?" Now he was the one looking nervous and jumpy.

"I ran into Wyrita at the store this evening and she told me. She said that little boy looks just like you. . . ."

"All newborns look alike," he defended, patting his pockets.

"I didn't say anything about that baby looking like other newborns. I said I was told that he looks just like you."

Pee Wee pulled a joint from his jacket pocket and lit it. I could tell that he really was nervous by the way he was sucking in that potent smoke and blinking his eyes. I shook my head when he tried to pass the joint to me. I had not indulged myself with drugs in months. I had no desire to do it again anytime soon, if at all. Even though the only time I ever smoked that shit was in the privacy of my own home, and only in the presence of Pee Wee, I knew it was something I didn't need in my life, and I would never smoke another joint again unless it was for medicinal purposes. I had seen it destroy too many people. And now it was about to destroy Jade. I shook that thought out of my mind.

"I was told that that baby looks just like you," I said again, fanning smoke out of my face. I was glad that I had placed fresh room deodorizers in several locations in each room, even the kitchen. No matter how strong that smoke was, the deodorizers took care of it. So far, my nosy parents and my inquisitive daughter had never suspected that I condoned anybody I knew doing anything "illegal" in my house. I wanted to keep the deep dark secrets that I harbored to myself for as long as I could.

"People think Lizzie's baby looks like me? Shit! I don't see how! Annette, if this is goin' to keep comin' between us, we don't need to even try to be friends no more! I'm tired of goin' back and forth with you on this! I told you what my doctor said. I told you I didn't fuck Lizzie after we broke up." Pee Wee rose off the couch, his legs trembling like the hooves on a clumsy ox. "I'll set up a blood test if that's the only way I can prove to you that that baby is not mine."

"You don't have to have a blood test done for me. Don't *you* want to know for sure?"

"I know for sure. But if a blood test will

satisfy you, when I get it done and show you the results, maybe we can move forward."

"Maybe you should go on and have the test done — I don't know — I don't care!" I wailed.

Pee Wee took out his car keys. "I'm sorry I ruined your evenin' and I promise it won't happen again. I came over here to invite you to that bed and breakfast in Cleveland that me and you and Rhoda and Otis like so much. I thought it would be nice for us to get away from it all and just relax for a change . . . the way we used to." Even though the news about Lizzie giving birth was now the biggest thorn in my side, his sudden invitation softened my heart. If I ever needed to "get away from it all" and relax, it was now. "With Rhoda gone for a while, I thought it would be nice for you and me to spend some time alone." He started to move toward the door.

My heart began to beat faster and my pulse rate accelerated. I had been, and would probably always be, a fool on some level. But I was still human. And like every other human being sharing this imperfect planet with me, all I really wanted in life was to be happy — at least as often and for as long as I could. "Pee Wee, you don't have to leave," I bleated. "I wish you would stay and keep me company."

"What for? So you can eat on my black ass about that baby?" He waved his hands. "What do you want from me, Annette?"

"Why don't you sit back down and have another drink," I suggested, waving him back to the couch. "With Rhoda out of town and Lillimae working late nights with Muh'Dear at the restaurant, I am feeling kind of lonely these days. Let's be a little nicer to each other," I suggested.

Dragging his feet like they were bowling balls, he returned to the couch and put his keys back in his pants pocket, mumbling gibberish under his breath.

"I am tryin' to be nice. I try to be nice every time I see you or talk to you. You are the one that won't let up on this baby mess," he said in a firm voice. I could see that he was trying to contain his anger, so I decided that I was going to be a little nicer.

"I hope that Lizzie's baby is healthy," I offered.

"I am goin' to get that blood test done, no matter what. And I will give you a copy and I want you to frame it. Just promise me you won't bring this shit up ever again," Pee Wee told me, slamming his fist on the coffee table.

I chose to ignore that. I was going to "be nice" for as long as I could.

"I don't want to talk about Lizzie and her baby anymore. I have other things on my mind tonight," Pee Wee added.

I nodded. "I have other things on my mind too," I said gently.

We gave one another a nervous look. He shrugged first; then I did the same thing.

Then we both laughed.

"Oh, well." Within seconds he seemed like the upbeat, jovial man I had known most of my life. "Got any good gossip?" When we were teenagers, back when we all thought that Pee Wee was gay, he was the best source of gossip in town. He had changed drastically over the years. He obviously was not gay, and he no longer spewed gossip the way he used to. To hear him ask if I knew any good gossip now made me nostalgic. The news that I had to share was somewhat dreary, but it had to be discussed sooner or later.

I decided to steer the conversation back in its original direction, which was more neutral. Not that it was a more pleasant subject, but at least it was one that was not as upsetting as Lizzie. I glanced at the floor first. Then I looked him in the eyes again. "Uh, I think our girl Rhoda is going off the deep end."

"Oh? In what way? I know she's been beside herself about Jade. But I think it's a good idea for her to go to Jamaica at the same time Jade is goin' to be down there for Poppy's last days. I have a feelin' that them both bein' in the same place at the same time might make a big difference in their relationship."

"I have a feeling it will too," I muttered, offering a mysterious smile.

Pee Wee smiled back. As a matter of fact, he licked his bottom lip and gave me a look that I had not seen since our wedding day. "Girl, I ain't told you lately, but you are still the sexiest full-figured woman I ever laid eyes on. . . ."

CHAPTER 56

The day after Pee Wee's visit, he called me up on my cell phone. It was almost midnight, but I was happy to hear his voice again so soon. We had made love for hours the night before. And during that time, I had felt so good that I didn't even think about all of the pain we had caused one another in the last couple of years.

I had taken a long bubble bath and slid into my nightgown around ten. Charlotte was in bed with cramps. She had never had them before, but for some reason they'd attacked her this evening with a vengeance. She even refused to help me eat her favorite Chinese takeout items that I'd picked up on my way home from work.

Lillimae was in her room talking on her cell phone to her husband. He was getting more frantic by the day for her to come back to him. She had just come home from The Buttercup after helping Muh'Dear with another affair for some important clients. This time it was a wedding reception for Muh'Dear's banker's daughter.

"I've been tryin' to get in touch with you," Pee Wee said, sounding frantic and almost out of breath. "Your cell phone and your landline went straight to voice mail every time I called this evenin'. I'm glad you finally picked up."

"What's up?" I asked, sitting up on my living room couch. It had been raining all day. I didn't like to sleep in my bed when I was alone during a big storm. There was something scary to me about the way the heavy wind howled and made the branches on the trees tap and scrape against the outside of my windows. It reminded me of the hurricanes I had survived in Florida. I had planned to sleep on the couch all night.

"I . . . I heard from Otis a couple of hours ago. Poppy passed. The funeral was yesterday," Pee Wee told me, choking on a sob. "I lost my daddy a long time ago, but I'm still hurtin', so I know how Otis feels. Him and Rhoda need us now more than ever. Please try to be available when they call you."

I had been around Rhoda's father-in-law only a few times since she married Otis, but he seemed like a really nice old man. And a wealthy old man to boot. Errol "Poppy"

O'Toole and his family had once owned several orange groves in Florida, and he had left behind a considerable fortune. Not that Rhoda and Otis were hurting for money, but I knew Jade couldn't wait to get her hands on whatever Poppy left her.

"The man's body is not even cold yet and them folks down there are fightin' like cats and dogs over who gets what," Pee Wee snarled. "Otis said Jade got so drunk she fell on the old man's death bed the day before he passed, makin' him roll to the floor." Pee Wee paused and sucked on his teeth. "If that wasn't bad enough, while everybody else was still at the hospital, Jade and a couple of her greedy female cousins went to the old man's house and took all of his wife's jewelry. One granddaughter had the nerve to roll up in a movin' van with four movin' men. She had them load up half of the furniture in the house! If Otis and some of them big strappin' male relations hadn't stepped in, them fools would have cleaned out that whole house that Poppy lived in all these years with his wife."

"What? But Poppy's wife didn't die too. She's still going to need everything in that house until she does!" I yelled.

"No, but Otis said that Jade whooped and hollered loud and clear that that old lady was goin' to go soon, too, and she didn't want to have to come back down there again so she was takin' the jewelry now. What a mess."

I could not believe my ears. I suddenly didn't care if Jade went to jail for a crime she didn't commit. Jail seemed to be the best place for somebody like her. She was guilty of enough things that it didn't matter what she went to jail for! "Did you speak to Rhoda?" I asked.

"Uh-huh. She seemed real calm about all the mess Jade's pulled lately. Poor thing. And I don't know why, or what she meant by it, but she said somethin' about she wasn't worried about Jade because she'd get what she had comin' real soon."

"Karma," I mouthed.

"Karma? Is that one of them New Age things or somethin' that Oprah came up with?"

"It's an Eastern belief that . . . well, it basically means 'what goes around comes around.' "

"Well, you and me both know that's true. Look at all the mess we got ourselves into by givin' in to temptation and ignorin' our weddin' vows. I hope Louis Baines's dick was not worth all this turmoil to you that we tryin' to put behind us, because that crack between Lizzie's thighs sure wasn't."

"I think we need to stay away from those two subjects for now," I warned. I didn't wait for Pee Wee to respond to that. "I would have gone to Montego Bay with Rhoda and Otis for the funeral, but I had some really important audits and meetings on my calendar," I said, almost out of breath. I was having a hard time getting air in and out of my lungs. I knew that I wouldn't breathe right again until Rhoda made it home safe and sound.

"Annette, uh, honey, I need to tell you somethin' before you hear it from one of them busybody nurses at the hospital. . . ."

I didn't like the tone of Pee Wee's voice. It told me that whatever he had to tell me this time, it was going to be unpleasant, at least to me.

My breath caught in my throat. "Please . . . please don't tell me you've got another medical condition. I don't think I can stand to hear more bad news for a while," I managed.

"I know you just said we need to stay away from this subject, but we need to talk about it again."

Lizzie! The "bad news" had to be about her!

"So you've got more bad news for me

after all, huh?"

"I wouldn't exactly call this bad news, so you don't have to worry about that." Pee Wee coughed and muttered something unintelligible under his breath. From the tone of his voice, I knew that whatever he had to discuss with me, it was probably going to be something that I didn't want to hear. And to me that was equal to more bad news. He began to speak slowly. "I need to come clean about somethin'. I seen Lizzie and I seen that baby. I was with her when she gave birth to her son, March seventh." He had to cough deeply and long to clear his throat. "Uh, that was the same day as my mama's birthday. . . ."

"I see," I said with my cheeks throbbing like every tooth in my mouth was aching. "Then I presume you've been with that woman again?"

"Um . . . yes and no."

"Well? Is it yes, you've been with her, or no, you have not been with her? Which one is it?"

"I haven't been with her the way you think," he said quickly.

"Then what way have you been with her?"

"Her mama called me up right after Lizzie went into labor. She damn near begged me to drive them to the hospital. Peabo had a big fight with Lizzie a little while back, so she moved back home with her mama and stepdaddy. The stepdaddy got a ticket for drunk drivin' the other day and they suspended his license. Lizzie's mama is recoverin' from a mild stroke, so she's too nervous to drive anywhere for the time bein'."

"Why did she call you? Lizzie and her folks have other friends. They've got neighbors. Why didn't she just call a cab or an ambulance? Neither one of them is on strike that I know of."

"Uh, Lizzie's mama said I was one of the best things that ever happened to her daughter. She knew they could count on me."

"Pee Wee, it is one thing for you to be the kind of man that everybody can count on, but you've got to draw the line somewhere. If you don't, people will continue to run to you every time they need some kind of help. You are not Mother Theresa or the Wizard of Oz. You need to start saying no when people come to you for favors."

"This was different. I would have done this favor for anybody. You didn't make a fuss when I took that Puerto Rican woman down the street to the hospital when she went into labor."

"You didn't sleep with that Puerto Rican woman — or did you?"

"Annette, please don't go off on a tangent on me. You and I both need to keep our wits about us so we can be there to support Rhoda and Otis when they get back from Jamaica. Besides, I'm still tired. I was up most of the night that Lizzie gave birth. She had a real rough labor. There were some complications because of her age, and they thought she needed a Cesarean. Things eventually worked out in her favor and she had her son the natural way, praise the Lord."

Lord! I wished he had not mouthed those last few sentences! The words that pertained to Lizzie bounced off my head like bricks. I held my breath to keep from choking, but holding my breath led to something worse. I began to gasp and hyperventilate. I even felt dizzy. If I hadn't been lying on the couch already, I would have fallen onto it.

"Annette, you all right? It sounds like you havin' some kind of attack or somethin'! You want me to come over there?"

"I'm fine!" I snapped. "You don't have to worry about taking *me* to the hospital."

CHAPTER 57

"Maybe I shouldn't have brought up this subject, huh?" Pee Wee sounded so contrite now, you would have thought that he was the recipient of bad news instead of me. And as far as bad news went, this was worse than I had expected.

"But you did bring it up." I swallowed hard as I glared at the telephone in my hand like it was the source of my discomfort. I wanted to stomp it to pieces and then throw it out the window into the street. "Do you mean to tell me that once you got that woman to the hospital, you stayed until she gave birth?"

"Lizzie didn't want me to, but her mama practically begged me to stay with her until it was over. It was the least I could do. That old lady ain't never been through somethin' like this, and this bein' her first — and probably her only — grandchild, she needed somebody there to support her, I guess."

"Pee Wee, *why* did you take Lizzie to the hospital when you know how I feel about that woman and her baby — and how she tried to make you her 'baby daddy'? Why are you telling me that you escorted her to the hospital and stayed with her during her labor — like you were the baby's daddy?"

"Another reason I went was because I wanted to let her know as soon as possible that I want to get a blood test done. I know if I don't prove to you, and all your gossipy friends, that that baby ain't mine, I'll never hear the end of it."

"You don't have to prove anything —"

"I do! Anyway, right after the baby came, I told her that I was goin' to talk to the doctor to see how soon I could get that blood test done. Lizzie didn't want to hear that. She got all huffy and puffy, almost leaped up off the bed. She told me she was not goin' to let me do a blood test because she knows I ain't that baby's daddy."

"Then why are you doing it?"

"Because it seems like that's the only way I can convince you that I'm tellin' the truth. And by the way, that baby don't look no more like me than none of them other babies in that hospital nursery."

"Most newborns look alike," I mentioned. "You said so."

"I didn't mean it." He got silent. I remained silent, too, because I didn't know what to say next. I was glad that he was the one who spoke again next. "Where's Charlotte? I haven't chatted with her in a few days and I'd like to."

It was a good thing that he changed the subject. Had he not, I would have ended this conversation. He was beginning to annoy me. "She's in her room. Hold on." I laid the telephone on the coffee table and trotted to the foot of the stairs and yelled for Charlotte. She didn't answer. I called again. She still didn't answer. Annoyed at her too now, I took the stairs two at a time and stomped down the hall to her room. She was not in her room and her bed was still made. She had gone to her room more than four hours ago. . . .

Just as I was about to go back downstairs, Lillimae came out of the bathroom, grinning and shaking her head and waving her cell phone. "That man of mine is about to drive me up the wall with his whinin'. He didn't treat me right when I was there. But now he calls me up and tells me when I come back, he'll treat me like a queen. He just told me that one of his sisters came to the house and stuck some of those yellow Post-its on everything she wants if I don't come back home. That heifer!" Lillimae grinned some more. "I guess I need to start gettin' myself ready to go back home soon. I swear to —"

"Lillimae, is Charlotte in your room?" I asked, cutting her off.

"No, I haven't seen her since I came upstairs. You checked her room?"

"Yes, I did, and she's not in it. She hasn't even been in her bed." Lillimae followed me back to Charlotte's room. I was just about to check her closet when I noticed the typewritten note on top of her dresser.

It read:

Mama, I am running away from home. I love you and my daddy and my auntie Lillimae and everybody else. But I can't stay here no more. You don't want to listen to me, and I can't keep trying to talk to you about Harrietta. I thought that after Vivian ran away, you and everybody else would finally believe that something is wrong with Harrietta and get in her face! That woman is a freak and a skank witch! When the bank sends my Christmas Club money, give it to the church. Maybe when I get grown up, I will come home and maybe you will listen to me then because you grown folks only listen to and believe what other grown folks say. Even though you are the way you are, I still love you anyway. It's real late and I know you and Aunt Lillimae are probably asleep by now. But I am sneaking real quiet out the back door downstairs.

Love, Char

P.S. I have been hiding a hamster in a shoe box in the basement for a long time. Please feed him and hug him every night like I did.

After Lillimae had read Charlotte's note, she immediately started punching numbers on her cell phone. "Harrietta, this is Lillimae! Now Charlotte has run away! Check with your girls to see if they are hidin' her! Take a look-see around your house and call me back! Listen — I have to go!" Lillimae whipped around and looked at me. "Annette, let's call the police!" she hollered.

I screamed and swayed from side to side. If I had not been so close to the dresser, I would have fallen to the floor. My head felt like it was about to burst wide open. I made it back to the living room telephone in record time. I had forgotten that Pee Wee was still on the line so I attempted to dial 911 as he started yelling.

"What's all that whoopin' and hollerin' about?" he wanted to know.

"Charlotte is gone!" I hollered.

"Gone where?"

"She's run away!"

"What the hell do you mean by that? That girl ain't had no reason in the world to be runnin' away!"

"I punished her for letting Harrietta's runaway daughter hide in her room, but I'm sure there's more to it than that. She left a note, but it doesn't make a whole lot of sense! I . . . I thought she was in her bed! She went to her room like she always does! She slipped out while Lillimae was in her room and I was taking my bath. I need to call the police!"

"I'm on my way!" Pee Wee yelled.

"If I don't call you back on your cell phone in a few minutes, meet us at the police station!" I hollered. I ended the call with Pee Wee and dialed 911.

Lillimae stood behind me, wailing like an injured lamb.

I could not have reached a more disinterested dispatcher on the line if I had tried. "What's your emergency?" she asked, like it was painful for her to speak. I could just picture the look of indifference on her face and it made my blood boil.

"My daughter has run away!" I croaked. "You need to send a policeman to my house. My address is —"

"Ma'am, calm down. Your name, please?"

"Annette Davis! I think —"

"Address?"

"Uh, 1028 East Reed Street! I —"

"Your daughter's name and age?"

"Charlotte Davis. She's almost thirteen —"

I didn't like the fact that every time the dispatcher asked me something, she cut me off before I could finish answering her.

"I'm sure your daughter will turn up. You know how these young kids are today. A runaway is not considered an emergency."

"Look, lady! Stop cutting me off and let me finish before you ask me another dumb-ass question! My daughter is missing! She snuck out of the house tonight *in this storm* and she left a note. Now, if you don't send somebody out here, I am coming down to that station and I might end up in jail for kicking your fucking ass!" I yelled.

"Ma'am, if you don't get a hold of yourself, I am going to end this call. Now, if you —" I cut the woman off in midsentence, hanging up the telephone so hard my hand vibrated.

Lillimae and I threw on some clothes and

our coats, and we ran out the door of our house. We piled into my car and shot off down the street like a cannonball.

There was an elderly couple, walking like they were taking their last steps, and a younger woman holding a baby wrapped up in a dark brown receiving blanket like a burrito. It was Lizzie and her parents. She looked right in my face. I guess she didn't know right away that it was me because she smiled. But that smile didn't stay on her face for more than a couple of seconds. She pressed her lips together and rushed across the street, still looking back toward me. I didn't have time to react to seeing her with her baby for the first time. None of that mattered to me anymore. I had much more important things to deal with tonight.

As soon as I sped on down the street, I almost sideswiped a hearse coming from the opposite direction, and that scared the hell out of me. I took that as a bad omen, but I didn't know who it was meant for. My daughter and my best friend were both in trouble.

No matter what happened, and to whom, my life would never be the same again.

CHAPTER 58

The rain was coming down so fast and heavy, even with my windshield wipers on full blast, I had a hard time seeing my way. I drove down one street after another, driving like a bat out of hell. Thankfully, I didn't encounter or cause any accidents, or any other mishaps that would have delayed me.

The wind was howling like a wolf and blowing so hard, the few people I did see out walking on the streets were losing umbrellas left and right. I even saw the wind blow one woman's wig off her head.

For Charlotte to run off at night in a storm she had to be mad as hell about something. I knew that when we did locate her, I was going to get the full story from her as to exactly what it was she'd been trying to tell me. And since she'd been so vague in her note, I imagined the worst! Everything from her contracting a venereal disease to her being pregnant.

Good God! The thoughts running through my head were unbearable.

I almost slammed head-on into the side of the police department building when I arrived. I thanked God that I didn't. In addition to my latest crisis, the last thing I needed was to injure myself and Lillimae, and wreck my car.

Lillimae and I scrambled out of my car and were stumbling up the steps to the building entrance within a matter of seconds. We didn't even bother to get the umbrella that I kept in the trunk of my car.

The lobby was more crowded than I expected it would be on such a stormy night. There was the usual mob of hand-cuffed criminals being detained: belligerent hookers, two thugs with bloody noses and other facial injuries, and even a prosperous-looking man in a three-piece suit.

The woman behind the front desk was black, so I couldn't claim racism when she rolled her eyes at me and Lillimae when I blurted out the reason for our visit.

"You'll need to file a missing persons report," the woman informed us, tapping her multicolored fingernails, which were almost as long as her tongue, on the top of the desk.

"The girl is not missing, ma'am. She's run

away and she could be in serious trouble," I wailed, trying hard to remain reasonably composed.

"She's only twelve," Lillimae pointed out, looking at that woman like she wanted to slap her. If Pee Wee hadn't arrived when he did, I would have slapped that bitch myself. While I was standing there crying and sweating like a pig, this woman began to fiddle around with the pens and pencils in a cracked coffee cup in the middle of her desk.

"Don't y'all look for missin' kids no more?" Pee Wee asked, his arm around my shoulder. It was a good thing he was supporting me, because my legs felt like they were about to collapse like a defective folding chair.

"Was your daughter kidnapped?" the woman asked, looking from Pee Wee to me.

"No, she was not kidnapped. She ran away on her own," Lillimae said. "She even left a note."

"And she left a note?" the woman asked, rolling her eyes again. "Oh, well, technically that's not a missing person situation. A voluntary runaway and a missing person are two different things."

"Sister, this might just be another statistic to you, but this is my daughter we are talking about!" I shrieked. "Now, what are you people going to do about it?"

Without speaking, the woman's hands shuffled around on her messy desk until she located a form under a pile of other papers. Looking bored, she grabbed one of the pens out of her cracked coffee cup. Had she rolled her eyes again or said the wrong thing, I was prepared to put a crack in her head to match that damn cup.

My daughter had run away and all the authorities were going to do was fill out a report! I could not believe what I was hearing. Pee Wee was even more furious than Lillimae and I were. He demanded to speak to somebody with more authority.

"Sir, you might as well calm down and let me do my job. This is not the first time somebody has come here to report a runaway child, and it won't be the last. We don't have the manpower or the time to go off looking for runaway kids. This is not Hollywood, so we don't send officers out to get cats out of trees either —"

"If something happens to my child, I am holding you responsible!" I threatened. But even that didn't faze this woman. She just blinked and tapped the tip of her pen on her desk. She asked the pertinent questions and filled out the report; then she told us to come back if Charlotte had not returned after forty-eight hours and sent us on our way.

Pee Wee, Lillimae, and I didn't speak until we got out to the visitors' parking lot. "We'll do all we can on our own. I am not goin' to sit around waitin' on these bastards to do their jobs," Pee Wee said through clenched teeth.

"Annette, you want me to call your mama and daddy?" Lillimae asked, rubbing my shoulders. We stood between my car and Pee Wee's.

"Yeah," I managed, so shaken I could barely speak.

"I'll call them as soon as I get back to the house. Annette, I can drive your car. You ride with Pee Wee," Lillimae told me, bless her heart. I was so glad that she was still with me. "As soon as we get to the house, I am goin' to get on the computer and print up some flyers. I am goin' to go out myself tonight and tack 'em up in store windows and on telephone poles all over town."

"I need a list of all Charlotte's friends so I can pay each one a visit tonight," Pee Wee said, his voice trembling. "In the meantime, let's all try to stay calm. This might not be as bad as it seems. She could be layin' low at one of her little friend's houses like I did one time when I took off."

498

"Things have changed since we were kids, Pee Wee. I was a crazy kid, too, like almost everybody else. I ran away several times. By the grace of God, nothin' bad ever happened to me. But thirty years ago, people were not as crazy as they are now," Lillimae stated, her voice trembling like it was about to crack. Her face was as red as a tomato, and dark circles outlined her eyes. Her hair, which was even more askew than mine, was saturated with sweat.

I had shed a lot of tears since I'd read Charlotte's note. I didn't realize that a few more had begun to trickle down the sides of my face until I tasted them on my lips.

"Maybe we should wait a while before we tell Muh'Dear and Daddy. If Charlotte comes home tonight, or tomorrow morning, we will have worried them for nothing," I said, folding and unfolding my arms.

"You're right. They don't need to be gettin' upset if they don't have to," Lillimae decided. "But I will print up some flyers tonight anyway. We're goin' to do everything possible to find that child."

After we got back to my house, Pee Wee decided to stay the night. It was the longest night of my life. The three of us must have drunk ten cups of coffee each. I wanted something stronger, like a double shot of

Jack Daniels, but this was one time that I wanted to be as lucid as possible.

Every time I heard a siren or a car drive past the house, I ran to my front window. I went out to my porch a few times, looking up and down my street. At one point I looked up at the sky, wondering if the Devil had finally overpowered God. It was getting harder and harder for me to believe that God didn't make mistakes.

My chest tightened, and for a moment it felt like I couldn't breathe. I stood up and paced back and forth throughout the living room. I knew that I couldn't stay in the house too much longer not knowing where my child was. We had called up all of her friends and nobody knew where she was. At least that was what they told us. I didn't have much faith in our police department, so I knew we had to do whatever we could on our own.

Pee Wee went out and visited the homes of some of the same friends of Charlotte's that we had already called. Still, none of them had seen or heard from her, or so they claimed. Not even Harrietta and her kids.

After Pee Wee returned, Lillimae offered to go back out with him and search the malls and the video arcades and any other place we thought she might be, and to post the flyers she'd printed with Charlotte's picture and our telephone number. I had to stay in the house close to the telephone in case she or the police called. I firmly believed that she would call home soon, scared and desperate.

By morning, I was too frantic for words. Pee Wee and I were still on the living room couch. He had fallen asleep around seven A.M., still sitting in an upright position. I had slept in snatches; a few minutes during one hour, a few minutes during another hour. I had eventually dozed off for about an hour. I almost leaped out of my skin when the telephone rang around eight-thirty. I was already awake, but the telephone startled Pee Wee. His body jerked and he let out a shrill yelp. Then his eyes flew open in such a quick and mechanical manner that it seemed like they'd been programmed.

It was Rhoda on the other end of the line. I was glad to hear her voice. If I ever needed her emotional support it was now. Charlotte was more like a daughter to her than Jade. But Rhoda started talking before I could get a word in edgewise. We were running neck to neck in the crisis department with our daughters and since she'd called me, I felt I needed to hear what she had to say first.

"Girl, I'm a stone wreck," she murmured in a disembodied voice. "My family is unravelin' like a ball of yarn." She stopped talking and blew her nose. She sobbed for a few moments before she continued, "I won't keep you long, but I just wanted to let you know that I'm back home."

"Uh-huh. I'm glad to hear that. I know you must be tired, but I'm sure you're glad it's over. I wish Pee Wee and I could have come down for the funeral. Poppy was a real nice old man. How was the service?"

Rhoda ignored my question. "It's done," she whispered. Her voice sounded so weak and hollow it made me shudder. Grief was so contagious. But I didn't need any from her; I had more than enough of my own.

"What? What's done?"

"You know . . . what we talked about before I went to Jamaica."

"Uh, let me call you back from the kitchen," I told Rhoda. "I don't want to wake up Pee Wee."

"Oh? He spent the night?"

"It's not what you think. Not this time," I muttered. I hung up and quickly padded to the kitchen and called Rhoda back.

I couldn't even think straight. My mind

had already spun out of control, so I was confused as to what Rhoda was talking about. "Now, tell me exactly what you mean." It took me a few moments to process what she'd just said; then it hit me like a ton of bricks. "Oh! You did do that . . . that thing you said you were going to do to Jade?"

"I tipped the authorities off two days before we left. I had to make sure they searched Jade's luggage."

"I can't imagine how difficult it was for you to do all what you did. I just hope that things go the way you want them to," I mumbled.

"If they don't, I don't know what to do next, Annette. Listen, I can't tell you how much it means to me to be able to confide in you. I don't know what I would do if I didn't have you. Thank you for bein' my friend."

"I feel the same way, Rhoda." I was still trying to decide at what point I should let Rhoda know about Charlotte. That was hard to determine because I didn't know whose mess was more critical: hers or mine. At least she knew where her daughter was. I didn't know where my daughter was, or even if she was dead or alive. "Things will

work out. You did . . . uh . . . what you had
to do."

Chapter 59

"Why does it seem like we are talkin' like the characters in the *Mission Impossible* movie? My phones aren't tapped," Rhoda said.

"My phones are not tapped either, but maybe we should watch what we say anyhow," I replied. "You never know who is lurking around a corner."

"Well, it's cool on my end. I'm the only one up," Rhoda said with a noisy sigh.

"All right. Tell me everything. You said you did what you said you were going to do?"

"I did. My daughter was detained by Cleveland customs agents a few hours ago." Rhoda sniffed. "Annette, she didn't say a single word to me the whole time we were in Jamaica. Not even during Poppy's funeral! When she found out we were on the same flights, she downgraded from first class to coach — she has *never* flown coach — so she wouldn't have to sit anywhere near her dad and me. If she had given me just a hint that she wanted to make things right, I probably would have changed my mind about what I did. But she didn't. By the time we were packed up and ready to come back to the States, she was lookin' at me like she wanted to kill me, mumblin' all kinds of obscene shit under her breath. That did it. She cooked her own goose. I knew then that I had to go through with my plan."

"If she wasn't even speaking to you, how did you manage to get access to her luggage?" I asked.

"I didn't. Every time I attempted to go into the room where her luggage was, somebody walked in on me." At this point, Rhoda's voice became hard and menacing. I was glad that we were on the telephone because I didn't want to see what kind of look she had on her face. "And when I did get into the room without any interruptions, I found out that she had already packed all of her bags and locked them! Everything but the zippered leather container that her boogie board was in." Rhoda paused and let out a loud breath.

"Boogie board? Who goes to Jamaica for the funeral of a loved one and feels good enough to go to the beach to ride a boogie board?" I asked. I could have answered that question myself, but Rhoda didn't hesitate to do so.

"Jade." She let out another loud breath. "She left Poppy's funeral early to go attend a reggae concert on the beach. That little witch wouldn't even ride in the same limo with Otis and me to go to the funeral, or to the airport to come back to the States!"

"I thought Poppy's passing might soften Jade a bit, make her relax," I stated.

"A ton of Ex-Lax couldn't relax that girl. Anyway, after they, uh, searched her luggage and found a five-pound plastic container of high-grade marijuana underneath her boogie board, they took her into a room and strip-searched her. As a matter of fact, they strip-searched Otis and me, too, since we were traveling together. It was so humiliating!"

"Oh Lord! Well, obviously they didn't find anything on you or Otis, or did they? On Otis, I mean? I know he smokes ganja big time when he's down there with his relatives. I hope he didn't forget to check his pockets before he left."

"Oh, you don't ever have to worry about that man. He's a lot of things, but he is not stupid. He'd never get caught with any shit on him, in the islands or anywhere else."

"I'm glad to hear that. Are you all right?"

"Don't worry about me. I'm fine for now," Rhoda assured me. "Thank God Otis is holdin' up. But my in-laws are fallin' apart."

"I figured they would. It's a shame that you had to do this while they are still mourning Poppy. How is your side of the family handling this?"

"I just got off the phone with my parents. They are the only ones that I've told so far. After all the havoc Jade wreaked when she lived with them in New Orleans, my daddy said jail is where her ass belongs. My mother is fit to be tied. She's threatenin' to crawl out of her sick bed and come to Ohio to beg for Jade's release."

"Oh Lord. I didn't realize how many folks were going to be impacted by what you did, Rhoda. Are you sorry about it now?"

"Annette, I am not sorry about anything. I agree with my daddy. Jade belongs in jail."

"For something she didn't do?"

"Let's not go there again," Rhoda snapped.

I could feel her exasperation, so I decided to tone down my responses. "Um, I am just glad you're all right. So what happens next?"

"I'm not sure."

"Well, since they found something on Jade, did they take her to jail?" I watched a lot of true-crime shows on TV. I read books written by some of the most popular crime writers. And I kept up with the news. Even with all of the knowledge they provided, I still didn't know what the general procedure was for someone attempting to smuggle drugs into the States. But I did know that it was a *very* serious situation.

"They took her into custody. She's in the county jail for now. I do know that she will face a judge soon." Rhoda mumbled something that sounded like a dying person's last words. For a moment, I thought she was going to slip into a coma. "I had to do it, Annette. I had to save her."

"I know you did," I said, with my voice cracking and my heart beating like a bongo drum.

"Annette, I will call you later after I get some rest. But before I let you go, are *you* all right? You sound kind of strange."

It was a little while before I was able to respond. Before I could get the words out, I had to rub my eyes and cough to clear my throat. Doing that didn't seem to help much. My eyes felt like they were on fire, and my stomach was in knots. "My daughter disappeared last night."

"WHAT? Oh my God! Why didn't you say somethin'? How could you sit there and listen to me go on and on and not say somethin' before now?"

"I am having a hard time dealing with it, and it's hard for me to talk about. I was going to tell you before we got off the phone!" I replied, my voice fading in and out like a cheap cellular phone. I'd had a lump in my throat for so long that I had almost forgotten about it. But it began to throb again immediately.

"Damn, Annette! Well, are the cops lookin' for her?"

"Rhoda, she's a runaway. She left a note and snuck out in the rain while I was in the bathtub and Lillimae was in her room. All the cops did was file a report."

"They've got to do more than that! Charlotte is a minor! A child, for goodness sakes!"

"They didn't say it in so many words, but I got the impression that they won't contact me until they need me to identify her body. Lillimae printed up some flyers last night, and she and Pee Wee posted them everywhere they could."

"SHIT, SHIT, SHIT! I'm on my way over there!"

"Rhoda, I am sorry about your daughter, and I am truly sorry about your father-in-law's passing. I know you've got enough on your plate, so don't get too worked up about

Charlotte. She's a smart child. I know she won't go too far for too long. I'm glad that she's only a runaway, and not caught up in some mess like Jade . . . if you know what I mean."

Rhoda remained silent for so long I got even more concerned. Finally, she said, "I know exactly what you mean. They've already run a report about Jade on the local TV news. I can just imagine what a gossip buffet this is goin' to cause at Claudette's beauty shop."

"I am so sorry you had to do what you did. And you know that I am behind you all the way. I am glad you're home, and as soon as I freshen up, I'll call you back to let you know what's going on with Charlotte."

"How is Pee Wee handling this?"

"Not well at all. Oh, by the way, Lizzie gave birth to a little boy."

"Does Pee Wee know?"

"He's the one who took her to the hospital when she went into labor, and he stayed until it was all over," I snapped.

"My God, girl. You must be devastated with all this shit goin' on. I'll be there as soon as I can. I need you, but I think you need me more."

"Rhoda, please. Stay home and get some

rest," I insisted. "I will see you later in the day."

Right after I got off the telephone with Rhoda and returned to the living room couch, Lillimae came galloping down the stairs, waving her arms. "Eeeeow! Turn on the TV news! You will not believe what they just reported!" she hollered. I was surprised to see a woman as large and heavy-footed as Lillimae move with so much agility. Every picture on my living room walls, the ornaments on my end tables, and even the Venetian blinds on the windows shook and rattled as she sprinted across the floor with her housecoat flapping like a bat's wings.

I held up my hand. "I already know," I said with a heavy sigh.

"Well, will somebody tell me?" Pee Wee asked, straightening his shirt as he rose up off the couch.

"Rhoda's daughter was caught trying to smuggle marijuana into the States from Jamaica," I said, easing up off the couch with a moan. I was thoroughly exhausted from being awake off and on for most of the night, but I had to keep my wits about me somehow. I was slightly disoriented, and the inside of my mouth was so dry that my tongue kept sticking to the roof of my mouth. I had to flick it a few times like a snake before I could speak again. "That's what she called to tell me a few minutes ago."

Lillimae gasped. "That's not what I —" Instead of finishing her sentence, she shot across the floor and turned on the TV. She flipped through several channels before she got to the local news, but the newscaster was signing off, with a grim expression on his face as he shook his head.

"I am sure they'll be repeating the story off and on all day," I predicted. "I didn't know Jade was stupid enough to pull a stunt like this."

"My Lord! You think — honey, you better brace yourself. Be still! Don't nobody move! Because if you are not careful, you're goin' to faint. The news I'm talkin' about is not about Jade! I didn't catch the whole news program, so they must have already reported on Jade before this, but . . ." Lillimae paused and looked from me to Pee Wee. "Harrietta, the woman across the street who has been running a day-care center and looking after Charlotte . . . she . . . that woman has been arrested for child pornography!" Lillimae announced.

I didn't faint, but the news was so devastating that it brought me down to my knees.

Chapter 60

Lillimae was so upset she couldn't stop crying. She had blown and rubbed her nose into a tissue so much that her nose was now swollen and her nostrils had expanded, making her look even more like Miss Piggy.

After hearing about Harrietta, Pee Wee and I were even more worried about Charlotte. It didn't take a mind reader to know that we were all thinking the same thing: Did Harrietta have something to do with Charlotte's disappearance?

Within an hour after we had heard the news about Harrietta's arrest, Muh'Dear, Daddy, Rhoda, Otis, and Scary Mary arrived at my house; all were equally horrified, angry, and shocked into stunned disbelief. I could not decide what upset them more: Charlotte's running away or Harrietta's arrest.

Muh'Dear looked like Medusa. Her long

gray hair was standing up on her head, shooting out in different directions and dangling like snakes. Scary Mary's wig was on backward. Daddy had his glasses on so crooked that the lenses covered more of his cheekbones than his eyes. They had all seen a brief news report about Jade on the same TV news station, but the major news was about Harrietta Jameson, the woman whom I had trusted to look after my only child.

Scary Mary calmed down long enough to give her version of a full report on Harrietta that she claimed she got directly from a "reliable source" on the police force. "They tell me that an anonymous tipster sent a package to a reporter at *The Richland Review* newspaper that contained all kinds of incriminating evidence against Harrietta! The reporter went straight to the district attorney's office with that shit! That she-devil has been in cahoots with a child pornography ring with associates not only in the United States, but in places as far away as Nigeria and Amsterdam!" Scary Mary was so overwhelmed and angry, she had to pause to catch her breath. But she had more to say. "Anyway, y'all, it was on account of that tip-off that they jump-started an investigation into that woman's activities. Come to find out, she done even pimped out her own young'uns! The child protective folks done placed all three of 'em in protective custody. The cops snatched Harrietta's computer, and all kinds of tapes and pictures done been confiscated."

While Scary Mary was still talking, I peeped out the front window a few times. I had been so preoccupied since yesterday, I had not paid any attention to anything going on in my neighborhood. I hadn't even noticed any police cars in front of Harrietta's house. Who would have ever dreamed what was going on across the street inside that lovely house with the lavender wind chimes on the front porch, and those two cute little peach trees and birdbath in the front yard? This was a mess and a half! The quiet residents on Reed Street would never get over this! Other than my friend Jean Caruso's little girl getting kidnapped, raped, and murdered about twelve or thirteen years ago, we had never experienced any major scandals in this neighborhood until now.

"I ought to hire somebody to blow that sleazy bitch to kingdom come!" Scary Mary yelled. "If she ever gets out of jail, she'll never smile again — unless she's smilin' at me! That lowdown sexpot." I was glad to know that even though Scary Mary made her money pimping other women, she drew the line when it came to sex and children. "My top girl June Ann, she had Harrietta lookin' after her little girl Bonnie Sue. Now June Ann is so prostrate with grief, there's no tellin' when she'll be able to get back to work. That's money I'll be short! Regardless, money or not, I do not tolerate grown folks messin' over itty-bitty young'uns!" Scary Mary paused and gave me a look of pity. "Annette, child, there is somethin' I never told too many people. But back when you told us about Brother Boatwright takin' advantage of you all them years that you was growin' up, I had my handyman Jude take me out to the cemetery where we buried Boatwright." Scary Mary paused again and looked around the room. It seemed like Lillimae's hand came out of nowhere and handed her a large drink. She took a quick swallow and continued, "Anyway, I went up to Boatwright's grave. And guess what — I squatted down and pissed on it! I didn't tell Jude why I was emptyin' my bladder on that asshole's final restin' place, but he knew it had to be somethin' unacceptable, so he peed on it too!"

All eyes were on Scary Mary. The living

room got so quiet that all I could hear was a faint humming noise coming from my refrigerator in the kitchen. I had never thought to desecrate my rapist's grave, but it didn't bother me one bit that Scary Mary had done it. If what they had said about Harrietta was true, then I couldn't think of a punishment severe enough for her that would satisfy me.

"My God, my God!" Muh'Dear managed, looking like she was going to faint. "How in the world can so much mess happen right up under our noses all the time? No wonder my granddaughter took off! Lord, I hope she gets her little behind back here before somebody else gets their hands on her!"

"I don't know what this world is comin' to," Daddy moaned. "Young kids and sex don't mix!" He had adjusted his glasses, but they were still on crooked. The left lens covered only half of his eye.

I heard the paperboy toss *The Richland Review* daily newspaper on my front porch. I rushed out to get it and started reading it before I went back into the house. First of all, there was a report about Jade's arrest. Located at the bottom of the front page was a four-paragraph article with the heading:

Daughter of Prominent Richland Family Detained at Cleveland-Hopkins International Airport for Allegedly Smuggling Marijuana from Jamaica

I only scanned the first paragraph. It didn't tell me anything that I didn't already know. I was more interested in the lead story on the front page. The headline immediately made me sick. It was much more upsetting than the one about Jade. I couldn't believe my eyes as I read:

Local Woman Arrested in Worldwide Child Porno Ring

It was a major struggle for me to finish that first paragraph that followed the headline. And there were so many additional paragraphs that the story took up two whole columns. Even though Scary Mary had revealed all she knew about Harrietta, the newspaper report brought it all home. Harrietta had photographed and videotaped those poor children in sexual situations, including bondage and S&M. Young kids involved in something as sinister and depraved as sadomasochism was something I couldn't even begin to fathom. I knew there were some young kids from horrific backgrounds who willingly got involved in this kind of shit, but I knew that none of the kids in Harrietta's care had even heard of such foolishness until she entered their lives. All of the parents of the other children, and I, had practically handed over our children to this monster on a silver platter! I was glad that I didn't have access to a gun. I was so angry, I wanted to storm the jail and shoot that bitch dead.

Harrietta Jameson had advertised and sold the pictures and videos of the children over the Internet. The article went on to say that according to several sources connected to the case, she'd kept a huge supply in her own home for her own perverse pleasure. No wonder that sick bitch didn't date! I could not read the whole article. Black bile oozed out of my mouth like tar, spattering onto my feet.

When I got back inside, waving the newspaper in my hand, tears and sweat sliding down my face, Lillimae grabbed the newspaper and read the front page headlines out loud. She let out a scream that could have woken up a dead man. She stomped her foot and flung the newspaper to the floor.

To this day, I don't remember all of the harsh things that my family and friends said about Harrietta that morning. Everybody agreed that she was the reason Charlotte had run away. We were all confident that now that Harrietta had been exposed, Charlotte would be home any minute now. But that wasn't the only subject we discussed. Somebody, I don't remember who, made a few comments about Jade's arrest. Otis clearly didn't want to discuss it. He snorted and stumbled toward the kitchen, waving his hands in the air. Rhoda grimaced and shook her head, making it clear that she didn't want to discuss it further either. However, she did say for my ears only, "She had it comin'."

Jade had a lot of shit coming her way and she deserved it. But my twelve-year-old child did not deserve to be involved in a sex scandal! Had I been able, I would have kicked my own ass. As a survivor of sexual abuse, how could I have not known something was not right with Harrietta? How could I have not questioned the fact that my child, other kids in the neighborhood, and even Harrietta's own children were terrified of her? And what about the neighborhood dogs barking at only *her?* The mess that she had fed to me about those dogs barking at her because of her unusual perfume was bullshit. Animals sensed a lot of things, and now I knew that one of the things they sensed was the presence of evil.

During my nightmare with Mr. Boatwright, I had never complained to my mother about me not liking him. As a matter of fact, everybody, including my mother and Scary Mary, had regarded that nasty bastard as a saint, and he had acted like one — except with me. He not only fucked me on a regular basis, he controlled almost everything I did. He decided what friends I could have, what I could do, where I could go, and so on. I had not thrown up any red flags, and the reason for that was my abuser had threatened to kill me and my mother. He even went so far as to stick a gun in my mouth on more than one occasion. That was all he needed to do for me to keep my mouth shut. My daughter had tried to tell me something about Harrietta, and I had chosen not to listen. Had Harrietta threatened her too? The thought made my flesh crawl and my blood boil.

There were no words to describe how frightened I was. Another foul predator had turned my life upside down, and the fact that this time it was a *woman* made it even worse.

My daughter had been "missing" since the night before, and I had no idea where she was or whom she was with. I knew that there were a lot of other predators out there just waiting to get their paws on a naïve twelve-year-old.

"I need to let the cops know Charlotte was one of the kids in Harrietta's care," I said, the words burning my mouth like acid.

"Honey, you ain't got to worry about that. Dem investigators will be comin' to you," Otis said, returning to the living room and still waving his hands in distress. "Maybe de same ones who took Harrietta's children to protective custody . . ."

Otis's remarks gave me something else to worry about! If this mess really got out of hand, would the child protective people remove my child from my custody when she turned up? "I don't want my child taken to a foster home!" I hollered. "How could I have been so blind and stupid?"

"Annette, don't jump the gun. Until we locate Charlotte and find out how she was mixed up in Harrietta's mess, we don't have to worry about them child-care folks puttin' our child in no foster home. Baby, you didn't do a damn thing wrong!" Pee Wee assured me.

"Yes, I did," I muttered. "My child was crying out for help, loud and clear, and I didn't listen to her."

Chapter 61

We all kept our eyes glued to the TV monitor, waiting to see what the news was going to report next on Harrietta. Each report was bad, but to me it seemed like each new one was more disgusting than the one before it. One broadcast stated that that low-down bitch had even made videos of some of those poor kids masturbating and performing oral sex on one another!

"If they ever release that bitch, I am goin' to take care of her for good," Rhoda growled. She gave me a conspiratorial look and I knew exactly what she meant. I wanted to kill Harrietta myself, but I didn't want to suffer any more consequences for my actions; because if I did kill her and ended up in jail, I really couldn't protect my child the next time. And I didn't want Rhoda to end up in jail either. Not with all of the mess that she had going on in her life with her own daughter.

My head was throbbing so badly by now that I had to hold a cold compress against my forehead to relieve the pain. That helped a little, but then my stomach and my chest began to cause me even more pain.

"Annette, why don't you go upstairs, take a relaxin' bath, and lie down in your bed for a while. That couch can't be too comfortable," Lillimae said. She stood over me as I lay sprawled on one end of the couch with that cold compress still pressed against my forehead.

"Annette, take an aspirin," Rhoda suggested. "Then get in your bed where you'll be more comfortable too."

"No, I don't need any aspirin, and I'd rather stay right here," I declared. I was aggravated even more because now the inside of my mouth tasted like shit. There was also an even larger lump in my throat now. It seemed like every few minutes, a different part of my body felt under siege. "I . . . I guess I need to go back to the police station soon and tell them that my daughter was one of the kids who had been in Harrietta's care," I said. Everybody looked at me. Before anybody else could speak, the telephone rang. The caller ID flashed Wyrita's name and phone number. I almost didn't answer, but it was a good thing I did.

It was Wyrita's cousin Lizel on the other end of the line, with some *more* disturbing news. "Annette, I heard about your girl. I seen the flyer they put up in the window at the Grab and Go when I stopped there on the way home from my aerobics class," Lizel informed me. "Did she come home yet?"

"No," I mumbled. "I have no idea where she is or who she is with," I sobbed, rubbing my forehead.

"Well, I think I saw her over on Lymon Court last night," Lizel said in a low voice. "It sure kind of looked like her."

Lymon Court was one of the shabby areas where a lot of Richland's lowlifes hung out. It was also the main stroll for the street prostitutes.

"What?" I rasped. "You think you saw her?"

"Uh-huh. Something tells me it really was her — I could be wrong, though. I didn't have my contacts in. But when I drove closer to the curb and slowed down my car to get a better look, she saw me. She turned so I couldn't see her face."

"But you're still not sure it was her?" I asked. Charlotte was well aware of the high crime in that area and it frightened her. As a matter of fact, she didn't even like it when she was with me in the car when I had to drive through there to get to Claudette's beauty shop.

"Oh my Lord," I moaned. I stopped rubbing my forehead because I was afraid I was going to rub a hole in it. "What was she . . . doing?"

"Don't start me to lying. But if I had to guess, I would say that she was trying to get paid, if you know what I mean. She was sure enough dressed the part. She had on one of them straight-up hoochie-coochie woman outfits: real short skirt, makeup, some kind of halter top, and sky-high heels with toes so sharp they looked like missiles."

"No! That couldn't have been Charlotte! She doesn't even like to go near that place in a car. She's not allowed to wear makeup yet, and she doesn't own any clothing and shoes like that!" I immediately wished that I had not included that last sentence. I was not naïve. I knew that if Charlotte, or any other young girl, wanted to wear makeup and hoochie-coochie outfits, she would. When I was young, I used to sneak around and wear makeup before Muh'Dear gave me permission to do so. And the only reason I didn't wear sexy outfits back then was because muumuus and other loose-fitting frocks were the only things big enough for me to fit in.

"Well, she might not own nothing like that, but she was sure enough wearing it. Or I should say all that mess was wearing her. She looked like she was eighteen, going on nineteen," Lizel clucked.

"NO!" I screamed.

"Yes! And that pimping hound dog that they call Hollywood was with her. I don't know if he done already turned her out, but I doubt if they was over there window-shopping, if you know what I mean. Lord help us!"

"Thanks, Lizel," I muttered, clumsily placing the telephone back into its cradle. "That was Lizel. She saw Charlotte on Lymon Court last night with that pimp they call Hollywood."

Every jaw in the room dropped.

"Hollywood? Oh, hell no! His butt is mine! He's been tryin' to steal my girls from me for years! I told him the next time he stepped on my blue suede shoes, I was gwine to teach him a lesson he would never forget!" Scary Mary screamed. She got so excited she started pacing the floor, swinging her cane in the air with every step.

"Ain't he that same nasty-ass thug that Jade moved in with when Rhoda kicked her out?" Lillimae gasped, giving Rhoda a pitiful look.

"He is. But I ran into one of her stripper friends at Claudette's beauty shop a few weeks ago. She told me she and Jade have been sharin' a place since the end of August," Rhoda reported.

"So your girl traded one devil for another, huh?" Daddy hollered.

Rhoda dropped her head and didn't respond. She had not mentioned Jade's current living arrangements before now. At one time I could not imagine the pain she was going through because of her child. Now I knew. . . .

I sucked in my stomach and picked up the telephone again. "I need to call the cops." Then I looked at Rhoda. "I need to have them go over to Hollywood's place and arrest my daughter for her own good. . . ."

I could see the tears forming in Rhoda's eyes as she nodded at me. "You're goin' to set up your own daughter to get arrested?" she asked, cocking her head to the side.

"Something like that. If they take her to jail, at least I'll know where she is," I managed, locking eyes with Rhoda. Now I knew how she felt! Now I felt that her setting Jade up to be arrested was the best thing she could have done to save her child. I was convinced that if I wanted to save my daughter, I had to have her locked up too.

My hands were trembling so hard I couldn't hold the telephone still. I had tears in my eyes, too, so my vision was blurred. I had to blink several times and wipe my eyes just so I could see the numbers on the dial.

"I hope them folks take you seriously this time," Pee Wee said.

Scary Mary hobbled across the floor and stood in front of me, leaning on her cane. She was leaning so far to the side, I thought she was going to fall over, but she didn't. She was so old, her bones so weak, she rarely stood up straight anyhow. "Annette, hand me that telephone," she ordered. "*This is mine.* I'm gwine to straighten out this mess!" Scary Mary grabbed the telephone out of my hand and punched in some numbers. "Let me speak with Detective Robert Donnelly, please . . . uh-huh. Horse feathers! I ain't gwine to tell you the nature of this call! You just tell him that Scary Mary is on — uh-huh. Bless your soul. Yes, I'm *that* Scary Mary. Put him on . . . Hello, Bobby — what you mean 'who's callin'?' You know *who* this is, goddammit! Thank you . . . Yes, I'm fine, too, even though I'm still recoverin' from grippe, shingles, and gout. Uh-huh. Listen, my godchild's daughter is missin'. She's shackin' up with that low-down funky black dog they call Holly-

wood — a PIMP. . . . Uh-huh . . . that's the
one. One of my spies seen her with him on
the Lymon Court stroll last night and the
word is she's stayin' at his place. . . . Uh-
huh. Oh, she's a minor all right . . . twelve
— ain't even cut all her teeth yet. You send
somebody over there to that poontang-
palace Hollywood works out of lickety-split.
Have one of your boys grab a hold of him
and cuff him up real good. Then I want you
to take the child to juvie for a wake-up call.
I bet that a few nights with the rest of them
hardheaded heifers in that big doll house
will do her a world of good." Scary Mary
paused; then she cackled like a setting hen,
laughing so hard tears rolled out of her eyes.
"Don't worry . . . my girl Lola will be available when you bring your happy white ass
by the house for your weekly visit. . . . Bye,
baby." Scary Mary exhaled a loud breath,
looked around the room, and snapped her
gnarled finger. "Somebody pour me another
drink."

"What was that phone call about?" Daddy
asked dumbly, scratching his chin.

Otis handed Scary Mary another glass of
Jack Daniels. With her chin tilted up and
lips pursed like a goldfish, she took a long
drink before she turned to me. "Case
closed," she said with a wink.

CHAPTER 62

The next day went by in a haze. There were times when I thought that I was walking in my sleep. I had no appetite, and I didn't even want a glass of alcohol, my usual pacifier. All I wanted was for things to be back to normal again. Whatever that was.

That evening around six-thirty while I was alone, two male investigators in suits, accompanied by a husky policewoman, came to my house to tell me that Charlotte was in custody. Despite all of the glamour of TV, where these kinds of folks usually looked like George Clooney and Charlie's Angels, these three people looked more like the sour-faced types that appeared on *Cops*. I had never had cops in my house before, and after the way I'd been treated when I went to the station to get them to help find Charlotte, I didn't like them that much. And from the looks of these three, I didn't have too much confidence in their abilities. I would have bet good money that they could not investigate a serious case, or even protect a piggy bank.

As soon as they started to talk, my doubts and fears went away. The older man — I forgot their names as soon as they told me — did most of the talking. "Mrs. Davis, you can rest assured; we've got everything under control. Your daughter is safe and sound, and happy that things turned out the way they did. She's been checked out by a doctor, and she's fine . . . physically at least. But I strongly advise you to take her to talk to a therapist as soon as possible."

The two men occupied my couch, the woman sat on the love seat. I chose to remain standing in the middle of my living room floor as the younger man went on to tell me what had happened. I knew I was only hearing what they wanted me to hear, but I was glad for that. The gist of their report informed me that a task force had raided Hollywood's house last night. He'd been arrested for a variety of offenses, including drug possession, stolen guns, and contributing to the delinquency of minors. My daughter was being held at the county juvenile facility where she'd been singing like a rock star, long and loud, about Harrietta and her sordid business. Charlotte had told anybody who would listen that she would tell them everything that Harrietta had made her and the other children do.

Shortly after the investigators left, Pee Wee arrived. He and I rushed down to Juvenile Hall. A trustee led us to a small room with no windows and waved us into seats at a low, metal table where Charlotte had already been seated. She looked so young and confused. Her hair was askew, and her eyes were red and swollen. And the gray smock she had on made her look like an unwanted creature that somebody had thrown away. I could not believe that my life had come to this!

"I'm sorry," Charlotte muttered, looking at the floor. She looked so frightened. As soon as the trustee left us alone, Pee Wee and I jumped out of our seats at the same time and ran to her, covering her with hugs and kisses. We were all crying and talking at the same time. Charlotte was so scared she was shivering, but once she started talking, we didn't stop her. "Mama, Daddy, I am so sorry for worrying y'all the way I did. I ran away because I was scared of what all Harrietta told Vivian she was going to do to me if I ever told what she was doing to kids — and what she made me do when I stayed at her house. Vivian ran away for the same reason. She was going to try and get her daddy to believe her because we didn't know what else to do! The night I ran away, I was hanging out at the Grab and Go when Hollywood came in and told me to come with him because he was going to take care of me. I was just going to stay out for that one night, but, well, once I hooked up with him, he made me stay with him. He made me put on those hoochie-coochie clothes, and some makeup and stuff. He said he was going to be good to me so I had to be good to him." Charlotte stopped talking and stared off into space. "I knew that what Harrietta was making us do was wrong, and I knew that what Hollywood was telling me I had to do was wrong. I was going to run away from him, too, and come back home anyway, but I was so scared. I was glad when I heard they had arrested that nasty, stinking Harrietta woman!"

"Baby, you should have told me what was really going on over there at that woman's house!" I scolded. "I've always told you that there was nothing you couldn't talk to me about."

"And you ain't never ever got to be scared to come to me when you got a problem," Pee Wee told her.

"I *tried.* From the first time I had to go to

her house, I knew she was crazy. I tried to tell you then. But every time I tried to tell somebody that that woman was not normal, nobody wanted to listen," Charlotte hollered. "What's the point of you grown folks telling us kids to tell if somebody does something nasty to us, if you don't want to listen? And even if I had told you, you probably wouldn't have believed me, and I would have been in a worse mess with Harrietta!"

"I tried to pry the information out of you each time, now didn't I? I asked you point-blank why you didn't like Harrietta and why you thought she was strange. Why didn't you tell me then what she was making you and those other children do?" I asked.

"She said if we ever told, she'd shoot us," Charlotte whimpered. "She even showed me and one of the other kids her gun. I was scared and worried that if I told you and you didn't believe me, she would shoot us dead."

A gun threat was one of the things that old Mr. Boatwright had used to control me during my ordeal with him. Once, when I was only seven years old, he told me that if I ever told anybody about our "love affair," he'd use that gun to shoot me and my mother. I had been so frightened that I remained silent for years. Had Rhoda not smothered him to death during our senior year in high school, I don't know how long he would have abused me.

"Uh, I'm the one that sent that anonymous package that ratted Harrietta out," Charlotte said in a small voice.

Pee Wee and I looked at one another, then back to Charlotte with our mouths hanging open. "You?" I mouthed, keeping my voice low. Even though we were alone, I didn't feel confident that our conversation was private. I'd seen enough TV shows to know about hidden cameras and microphones. I looked around the room; then I leaned closer to Charlotte, whispering, "You were the one who sent that anonymous package to that reporter? The detective told us that they were still investigating that, and that they were almost sure that the informant was one of Harrietta's disgruntled associates."

Charlotte nodded. "I guess you could say I was one of her disgruntled associates." A puzzled look crossed Charlotte's face. "What does disgruntled mean?"

"Somebody who is not happy with a situation," I explained. There was a lot more to the definition than that, but I didn't want to go into it at the moment.

"Well, then I really was a disgruntled associate," she said, putting a lot of emphasis on her words. It seemed like she had matured a lot since the last time I saw her.

Pee Wee looked around the room; then he leaned closer to Charlotte, speaking in a voice that was even lower than mine. "Did you tell anybody else that it was you who sent that package to that reporter?" he asked.

Charlotte shook her head. "I didn't tell any of the other kids because I didn't know who I could trust. They were all too scared of that woman, so I didn't want to take a chance on telling them what I was going to do."

"And exactly what all did you send that newspaper man?" he asked. "You don't even read the newspaper. How did you know about this man?"

"I saw him on TV talking about how he had helped expose some people who were running scams on old people, cheating them out of their life savings and everything else they owned. This year he helped them shut down that funeral director that was stealing jewelry off dead folks just before he had them buried. He mentioned a lot of other good stuff that he'd done, so I knew then that he was the right person for me to get in touch with. First I thought about sending him an e-mail, but I know they can trace e-mails. So I called up that reporter first, but as soon as he heard my voice and realized I was just a little kid, he told me to stop playing around on the telephone, so I hung up real fast. I had called him from a pay phone at school." Charlotte paused and rubbed her nose with the back of her hand. Her hands were so ashy and her hair looked so limp. I didn't know much about juvenile facilities and how they took care of the kids, but I knew that this was one place that my daughter did not want to be.

"I didn't know you even watched the TV news programs," I managed.

"There are a lot of things you don't know about me, Mama."

Chapter 63

What I had just heard out of my daughter's mouth made my ears ache. Her words broke my heart because what she had just said was true. Oh, I had my work cut out for me. Now I not only had to work on being a good wife, I had to work on being a good mother! I knew that I had been a much better wife and mother than a lot of women, but that didn't make me feel any better.

"Well, we are goin' to fix that. Me and your mama are goin' to find out everything we need to know about what's goin' on with you. Now go on and finish tellin' us your story," Pee Wee said.

Charlotte let out her breath and then sucked in some air. She looked from me to Pee Wee before she continued. "Anyway, the next day after I tried to talk to that reporter on the telephone, a better idea came to me. I got it from that old Morgan Freeman movie that I wasn't supposed to watch. . . ."

Charlotte confessed.

Pee Wee and I looked at each other again. "What Morgan Freeman movie?" I asked.

"*The Shawshank Redemption.* Morgan Freeman's friend broke out of prison and then he sent a package to a reporter that told everything that mean warden and his guards were up to. I took some pictures with my cell phone and I downloaded them on my computer. I printed out a lot, but I only sent that reporter the ones that Harrietta was in. She used to get so confused, she couldn't keep things straight. I typed up a four-page letter to go with the pictures. I had my mittens on so I wouldn't leave my fingerprints on anything. Then I sealed up the letter and the pictures in a big brown envelope, and I sent the package to that reporter by registered mail. I put a fake name and address on the return address."

I was stunned to say the least. Who would have thought that a Morgan Freeman movie would turn out to be so important in this mess?

"But if you did all that, why did you still run away?" I asked.

"I sent that package two weeks ago and when nothing happened, I didn't think it would. That's why I ran away."

"Well, I hope you never run away again.

You pretty much was jumping from a frying pan into a fire. Harrietta and Hollywood are two of a kind," Pee Wee pointed out. "What did you think Hollywood was goin' to do for you?"

Charlotte rolled her eyes, not the way she usually did, but in a gentler manner. It was so subtle that Pee Wee didn't even notice, but I sure did. A stern look from me brought her back down to earth. There was a contrite look on her face. By her blinking her eyes, which had tears in them now, I decided that this gesture was part of her apologetic position.

"I didn't plan on hooking up with Hollywood. I was just going to hang out for a while until I figured out what else to do." Charlotte scratched her arm and sniffed. "I . . . one other thing is . . . uh . . . I want y'all to know that . . . um . . . I'm still a virgin. Hollywood was going to give me a week to get myself ready to make him some money," Charlotte said quickly. "I know y'all might not believe me, but you can have a doctor check me out."

"We know. One of the investigators told us you'd been examined," Pee Wee said.

"The important thing now is that you are all right," I told her, squeezing her hand and then patting the side of her head.

"All I had to do for Harrietta was help her take those nasty pictures and hold the video camera when she . . . you know . . . filmed the kids doing nasty stuff," Charlotte said, looking at the floor. "She said I was too old to do most of the stuff she made the other kids do. She said her Internet clients liked real, real young kids the most." At this point Charlotte paused and a very angry look crossed her face. "Mama, she even showed us some video somebody sent to her of real little kids in Asia talking about how they enjoyed doing nasty stuff! She kept telling us that the whole world had gone sex crazy — even President Clinton. She said that the sooner we learned about sex, the better prepared we'd be to deal with it when we got older!"

Pee Wee and I looked at one another at the same time. I could see my reflection in his eyes. I never felt or looked so helpless and hurt before in my life.

"Oh my God!" Pee Wee yelled, clenching his fists. "Do you mean to tell me that there is pictures of *you* doin' *God knows what* that some sick bastards are gettin' their freak on over? And some of them pictures might even be on the Internet for the whole world to see?"

"NO! I wouldn't let her take no pictures

of me. She made me take pictures of some of the real young kids, doing all kinds of nasty stuff with their fingers and those fake, uh, penis things. By me taking the pictures, she said I was as guilty as she was, so that's another reason I was scared to tell on her."

"What about Hollywood? Did he . . . what all did he . . ." I couldn't even finish the sentence. If my daughter had lost her innocence before her time the way I had, I didn't think I could stand to hear that and not lose my mind.

I could tell that my daughter was uncomfortable talking about what she'd been through, but I wanted it all out in the open as soon as possible. I wanted her to know that no matter how ugly something was, she should still talk to me about it.

"All Hollywood did was kiss me and play with my titties. That's all Harrietta did to me too. But Hollywood did say that he would have to do the nasty to me before I . . . you know . . . got with my first man," Charlotte managed.

I didn't know how much more I could stand to hear without throwing up. I was amazed that I hadn't already done that by now.

"Lizel told me she saw you on the stroll with Hollywood," I told her, massaging the

544

tsunami taking place in my stomach.

"I know. I seen her spying on me. Hollywood took me out that night so I could see where I'd be working. Then he took me to McDonald's to get a Happy Meal. Just before the cops busted down his front door, he was getting ready to, uh, test me, he called it. He said he had to see how much I was worth." Charlotte paused again. "Before we did it, he was going to take a bath after I took one. I was going to sneak out while he was in the tub. I wasn't going to let him do nothing nasty to me. Honest to God."

"That cheesy-ass son of a bitch! If that nigger ever walks the streets of this town again, I am goin' to kill him with my bare hands!" Pee Wee threatened.

"Pee Wee, let's try to be calm about this."

"Calm my ass! My daughter has been violated by two grown-ass people! And I don't know which one was worse! If I ever see Hollywood or that bitch Harrietta on the street again, I am goin' to go to jail for homicide!" I had known Pee Wee for over thirty-five years. This was the first time I'd seen him this angry.

"Well, it's all over now. Let's keep things in perspective so that something like this will never happen again," I advised.

"You damn right nothin' like this is ever

goin' to happen again! Not to my child! I am goin' to be watchin' her like a hawk from now on!"

"Does that mean you're moving back home, Daddy?" Charlotte asked, smiling and blinking with hopeful anticipation.

I didn't wait long enough for Pee Wee to respond. "Charlotte, are you sure Harrietta didn't do anything to you except make you take pictures of those other kids? You have to tell us everything. There are not going to be any more secrets in this family."

"She used to feel up and down my titties and squeeze and rub my butt, but that's all; honest to God," Charlotte admitted, hunching her shoulders. "Every time I threatened to tell on her, she said nobody would believe me. She said that sooner or later she'd make me do more stuff . . . be in the pictures doing all kinds of nasty things with some of the other kids, and even to myself so she would have something to hold over me and keep me in line. Am I in trouble?"

Pee Wee and I gasped at the same time. "No, you ain't in trouble, baby. If anything, you're a hero. If you hadn't done what you did, there is just no tellin' how far Harrietta would have gone with this mess!"

"It was wrong for you to run away, Charlotte. That's why you are in here. And I want you to know that I was the one who told them to bring you here."

"You wanted me to go to jail?" Charlotte whispered, her voice as weak as a newborn kitten's.

"I wanted you to see what it's like for kids who break the law. Running away from home is a crime. I hope you never do anything else to wind up back in a place like this," I said. "If being in here doesn't scare you straight, nothing will."

"And I couldn't agree with your mama more," Pee Wee added.

CHAPTER 64

From the way that Charlotte's face screwed up into an extreme pout, I could see that she didn't like what her daddy and I had just said.

"Can I come back home, or do I have to go to live with foster folks or something, or Hollywood? When he picked me up on the street that night I left home, he told me that from now on he was going to be my daddy, because y'all didn't want me anyway. He even took me to the video arcade so I could play games while he talked to me."

"That mangy dog is in jail, and will be for a while! You're comin' home after we finish up with that social worker and do whatever else we need to do. I've already set us up for our first meetin' with a family counselor." Pee Wee paused and gave me a pitiful look. "We all need some professional help. The sooner we get it, the better off this family will be."

All I could do was nod, but I managed a weak smile too.

"The trustee told me the news about Harrietta and how her bail was set so high even God couldn't afford to bail her out. But . . . what about Hollywood? Did they set a real high bail for him too? He was real mad when the cops kicked down his door. I hope he don't bail out and come to our house to start some mess," Charlotte said in a low, worried tone of voice.

"With his long criminal record, they ain't even set his bail yet. You don't have to worry about Hollywood comin' to that house. If he ever does, it'll be the last time he makes a house call!" Pee Wee boomed. "Like Harrietta, he's got enough charges against him, they might put him *up under* the jailhouse, let alone set him a bail he can afford. But you have to be strong, baby girl. If you have to testify, you can't let his ugly face or threats stop you from tellin' the law what he tried to make you do. Did he give you anything illegal?"

"You mean like beer?"

"Yeah, that too. But I meant somethin' stronger."

Charlotte shook her head. "No, he didn't give me nothing stronger than beer. All he would give me and the other girl that he had picked up was a few puffs on a joint, that's all."

I hadn't eaten since the news about Harrietta broke. My stomach felt like somebody had vacuumed out all of my insides. But after what Charlotte had just revealed, yet another knot suddenly formed in my tortured stomach. I had to bend over and grab my knees to keep from throwing up my intestines.

"You see what you've done to your mama," Pee Wee said, rubbing my back.

"I am so sorry for causing all this mess. I will be good from now on. I want people to be proud of me. I don't want to be another Jade. . . ." Charlotte wiped a tear from her cheek. "I never thought Jade would be stupid enough to come over to that tent revival and act a fool like she did that day."

I looked up, blinking so hard my eyes felt like somebody had splashed some bleach in them. "Well, now Jade is where she needs to be."

"Huh?"

"You don't know about the mess she's in now?" Pee Wee asked.

Charlotte shook her head again and rolled her eyes from Pee Wee's face to mine. "Uh-uh. What did Jade do? Where is she at?"

"She's in jail too. But she is in a worse

place than you're in, and for a far more serious crime," I said. Charlotte stared in slack-jawed amazement as I told her about Jade's arrest for smuggling drugs. "If you don't straighten up and fly right, you *will* be where Jade is," I warned. I don't know why I added, "And I will make sure of that." Yes, I was willing to do what Rhoda had done to Jade if I ever felt that jail was the only way to save my child.

It was another Friday, a few days after we had first visited Charlotte. And black Friday in my life. Lillimae had taken Daddy to see his doctor. Charlotte was still in custody. Pee Wee and I had visited her again the evening before. She had practically foamed at the mouth because she was so anxious to get back home. But Pee Wee and I agreed with the social worker that a few more days in custody might send a very strong message to Charlotte. One thing I was convinced of was that once she got home, she would walk a chalk line and be as pliable as a pile of Silly Putty until she was old enough to get a job and move out on her own.

Even though it was just past noon, the sky was almost pitch-black. We were in the middle of one of the worst thunderstorms that season and it seemed to fit everybody's mood. Muh'Dear was at the house when the same two male investigators came to talk to me again so that they could finalize their investigation. She eyed them with contempt and hovered over them like vultures, clucking and mumbling stuff under her breath, shaking her head in disgust, and rolling her eyes. She caused so much tension that the investigators rushed through their final meeting with me and practically left my house running.

As soon as the investigators drove off, Muh'Dear broke loose. "I don't trust none of them folks," she complained. "If that anonymous person hadn't blew the whistle on Harrietta, there is just no tellin' how far that wench would have gone." Muh'Dear paused and gave me a puzzled look. "You reckon the tipster was one of them kids?"

I gasped and shook my head. There was no way I was going to tell my mother, Lillimae, or anybody else, other than Rhoda, that Charlotte was the one who had broken the case wide open. I didn't want this situation to be drawn out any more. If Harrietta changed her plea and hired a lawyer, I didn't want some sharp-talking fool yelling and screaming at my child, making her feel like a criminal, the way some defense attorneys did.

"The investigators are pretty sure that it was one of the folks who bought pictures and videos from Harrietta," I said.

"Hmmm, huh. You probably right. That just goes to show you, there ain't no honor among thieves. Maybe she took somebody's money and didn't send them the right nasty pictures of whatever the hell it was they wanted. My Lord! Only demons would find a child sexy!" Muh'Dear sucked in a deep breath and began to rub circles on her chest. Suddenly, she gasped and covered her mouth. Then she gave me a pitiful look. "Good God! This must bring back all kinds of memories to you about that dog Boatwright and what he done to you when you was a young'un!" Muh'Dear shuffled across the room and joined me on the couch. She wrapped both arms around me and hugged me so tightly I could hardly breathe.

I squeezed her hand and offered her a tight smile. "I've pretty much forgotten all about the things Mr. Boatwright did to me," I said, and it was true. I could barely remember my ordeal. "Thank God it didn't get that far with Charlotte."

Muh'Dear sniffed and mopped sweat off her forehead with the tail of her blouse. "When you get that little devil home, I'll hold her while you whup her rump 'til it's mincemeat!"

"I don't think a whuppin' is what Charlotte needs right now," Lillimae said, entering the house, bless her heart. "She's scared and confused. She's been victimized, and the last thing she needs now is a whuppin' from the folks she thought would protect her."

"There won't be any more whuppings in this house," I stated firmly. "But I do want Charlotte to learn from this. And I want to make it clear to her that she can come to me and her daddy and talk to us about anything. I don't care if the Devil is threatening her; she can still come to us."

"The Devil *was* threatening her, Annette, and you wasn't listenin'," Lillimae pointed out.

"Well, from now on, I will be listening to my child," I vowed.

CHAPTER 65

The investigators had already interviewed Charlotte several times about Harrietta and Hollywood, and I wanted her to get through all that before she came home. Harrietta had already pleaded no contest, so there would be no trial.

We were lucky. That Hollywood fool had pleaded guilty to all of the charges against him, so there was not going to be a trial for him either. I didn't think that I could survive my daughter going through *one* trial, let alone two.

Despite my latest dilemma, I still found time to check in with Rhoda about her daughter. Yes, I had been lucky, but Rhoda had not. Jade was in a much deeper and darker hole than Charlotte. I called Rhoda the first chance I got, that Monday, a couple of hours before Pee Wee and I went to collect Charlotte from juvenile hall. "How is Jade doing?"

"As well as can be expected, I guess. She's still in county lockdown until her hearin'. She continues to deny packing the drugs, of course, but they all do that," Rhoda told me. "Otis is mad as hell. Daddy still feels that she got what she had coming, but he and my in-laws and my mother want to hire the best attorney that money can buy. You know what?" Rhoda paused and let out a dry laugh. "The girl just might beat this case."

"But how? If they found drugs in her possession, how do you think she can beat this?"

"I found out from the authorities that last month some baggage handlers in Jamaica got caught smugglin' drugs into the States in the luggage of unsuspectin' travelers," Rhoda told me.

"What?"

"There is a large gang of baggage handlers workin' together, mostly in Jamaica, Thailand, Malaysia, Colombia, and several other foreign countries. All they have to do is snoop around until they come across some unlocked baggage. Then they hide the drugs on their end and notify their cohorts in whatever city the unsuspecting traveler is going to give them all the necessary information. The cohorts intercept the baggage on their end, remove the drugs, and nobody knows."

"So Jade can claim that this is what happened to her?"

"She could, and they just might believe her." Rhoda sounded worried. "I just read a piece on the Internet about some girl travelin' from Australia to Bali with two kilos of heroin in her suitcase. They tossed her into jail immediately and hinted that she might be sentenced to death! Anyway, a cellmate had told her about those baggage handlers. The girl's family got a good lawyer, and he hired somebody to launch an investigation. Right away, two of the baggage handlers in Australia got caught red-handed on tape puttin' some of that shit in some other innocent travelers' luggage. Ironically, it was the same two who had put that heroin in that poor girl's suitcase. They confessed and Bali let that Australian girl off scot-free."

"Hmmm. So if Jade's lawyer is smart enough to talk a judge into believing that she was just another innocent traveler caught up in this baggage-handler smuggling shit, she could get off, too, huh?"

"Uh-huh." Rhoda sounded even more worried.

"Then you'll have done what you did for nothing. What if she beats this case and they turn her loose? What will you do then?" I asked.

"I'll cross that bridge when I get to it," Rhoda quipped. "Right now, at least Otis and I know where she is. Well, we can be happy to know that at least two criminals are goin' down for sure. No other mother will have to go through what you and I went through on account of Hollywood or Harrietta. Those snakes' heads have been cut off."

"True. But there are a lot of Hollywoods and Harriettas in this world," I said. "In cases like these, when you cut off a snake's head, two more grow in its place."

"And that's more food for the mongoose," Rhoda grunted, spitting out the words like she was spitting out mucus.

I was still experiencing headaches, and I was having a hard time getting to sleep at night, but I felt better than I'd felt in a long time. It was almost spring, my favorite time of the year. The snow was gone and a few trees had already begun to bloom. It was refreshing to watch the squirrels play hide-and-seek in my front and backyard. I even felt different. For the first time this year, I felt different in a positive way. I had even lost the weight that I had gained by eating all of that food Lillimae had put in my face.

Rhoda was doing so much better now too.

"Have you . . . have you talked to Jade? Have you been to visit her?" I asked. It had been a week since all the hell in our lives had broken loose.

"Not yet. I'm the last person she wants to see right now." Rhoda sighed. "Like I said, at least I know where she's at now, and what she's doin'. I've turned it over to God. Whatever mysterious thing He does to make things right again is fine with me. I think we've all learned from all this shit we've been through."

I agreed with Rhoda. What had happened to my daughter with Harrietta was bad, but it could have been a lot worse. Had I not received such a mind-blowing wake-up call, there was no telling what might have happened to my child down the road. And because of what Harrietta had done, I knew that I could *never* let my guard down again. Had I listened to Charlotte's vague, but frequent cries for help earlier, this was one mess that I could have avoided. But it had happened, and it had happened for a reason.

"Maybe Otis was right when he told me 'God don't make no mistakes,' " I said, talking more to myself than I was to Rhoda.

"What?"

"Oh, that was something your husband said to me a while back. He meant 'God don't like ugly.' "

"And it is so true. Both. God don't like ugly and God don't make no mistakes," Rhoda insisted. "Hey, wanna go out for a drink tonight?"

"Pee Wee is coming over in a little while. He's bringing the rest of his stuff," I said shyly. "It's time for him to come home. He and I and Charlotte have an appointment with a family counselor on Tuesday."

"I'm glad to hear that! It's just a damn shame that you had to go through so much mess just to end up right back where you started."

We both laughed.

"Lillimae's husband keeps calling and begging her to come home," I revealed. "I know she wants to go home, but now Muh'Dear wants her to stay up here and help with the cooking at the restaurant."

Rhoda laughed again.

"I wish she would stay, but I think it's time for her to be with the people who need her the most right now. God sent her up here to be with me, because at the time, I was the one who needed her the most."

"Well, girl — hold on. I have another call comin'," Rhoda told me.

It was five minutes before I heard her voice again. And when I did, I almost didn't recognize it. *"It was her!"* she squealed. "Jade wants me to come visit her. Oh, Annette, she was cryin' like a baby. She couldn't stop tellin' me how sorry she was for the way she behaved. She . . . she sounded so . . . so remorseful! She even wants me to bring her a Bible. Jade — *the biggest Devil in Richland!"*

I didn't know what to say. But I had to choose my words carefully, because the last thing Rhoda needed right now was for me to sound skeptical. "Oh, Rhoda, I am so happy to hear that!" I exclaimed, and I really was.

"But listen to this. She said she had planned to hide some drugs in her luggage, but her connect didn't come in time! Do you know what that means?" Rhoda didn't give me time to respond. "If she had put drugs in her luggage, and if they had searched her, she would have been arrested and detained anyway! And if it hadn't happened this time, it would have happened sooner or later anyway! She may have even got caught with a much larger stash, and that would have made it even worse for her. They just charged her for possession, not smuggling with the intent to distribute. So what I did was not such a bad thing after all! At least it shook her up enough for her to be sorry for doin' all the shit she did to me last year!"

Like I said, I didn't want to sound skeptical, even though I was. I decided to say something neutral. "I am so happy to hear that Jade has finally come around." It made my tongue tingle for me to speak those words, because I didn't know if they were true. "I'll let you go so you can do whatever you need to do now. I need to get off the phone anyway so I can go pick out a cute outfit for Charlotte to wear home from that place. We'll talk again as soon as we can."

"Annette, I am so happy that things worked out so well for Charlotte. I'm glad you told me that she was the one who sent that stuff to that reporter. And you don't have to worry about me ever tellin' anybody that. But who would have thought that a Morgan Freeman movie would be so important?"

"Speaking of movies, remember when we saw *The Usual Suspects* two or three years ago?"

"Kevin Spacey and Stephen Baldwin," Rhoda swooned. "How could I forget a movie with those two? Why do you ask?"

"Remember that line from the movie that went something like: *The Devil's greatest trick was convincing the world that he didn't exist."*

Rhoda's silence told me that she knew where I was going with this reference.

"Rhoda, I know you love your daughter, and you want the same thing for her that I want for Charlotte. And please don't get mad about what I'm going to say next. But I'm going to say it anyway because it needs to be said: No matter what Jade says to you, don't ever let your guard down again with her. She's got some issues that won't go away overnight. One of *her* greatest tricks was convincing me that she cared about me all those years." I blinked back a tear.

"I agree with you. My daughter was, and may still be, a devil. I don't believe that she's made a complete turnaround this fast. But the main thing is, this is a new beginning. I have to give her a chance."

"And I'm glad to hear that," I said. And I was.

After I hung up, I thought about everything that had happened to Rhoda and me and our children in the past twelve months. It was because she and I had supported one another so diligently that everything had been somewhat resolved . . . this time.

EPILOGUE

May 27, 2012

My first grandchild, a boy, was born ten minutes ago, three minutes after midnight. My daughter, Charlotte, had endured a long and rough delivery.

A few seconds after Dr. Morris cut the baby's umbilical cord, Charlotte rose up in her hospital bed and yelled, "Y'all better enjoy this baby, because I am never going through this kind of pain again!" At the grand old age of twenty-six, she still looked like a teenager.

Charlotte's handsome husband, Anthony Borden, one of the young attorneys at the law firm where they both had recently made partner, had almost fainted during her labor. He breathed a sigh of relief when it was over. I had a feeling that this was something he didn't want to go through again either.

Had my parents lived a few years longer,

they would have been here to celebrate this blessed event with me and Pee Wee. They died two weeks apart, four years ago. Three years earlier, Scary Mary passed. Not from old age, or one of her many alleged illnesses; she died in an automobile accident. A drunken driver, going in the wrong direction on the freeway, had hit her van head-on.

Now that there was finally a baby boy in our family, Pee Wee was grinning from ear to ear. I knew that he was going to spend the rest of his life spoiling this child like it was his.

Rhoda would too. She was in the delivery room with me, Pee Wee, and Anthony. She looked so tired and old. She no longer dyed her hair, so it was almost completely gray, like mine. Looking good, or "younger," like Rhoda and I had tried to do for so long didn't seem so important anymore.

We had our share of wrinkles and ailments associated with age, but we were all still in fairly good health and things were going well.

Rhoda and Otis were still together and had even renewed their vows on their fortieth wedding anniversary three years ago. She had finally ended her long affair with her husband's best friend, and as far as I knew, her husband had never found out about it.

My marriage had been restored, and even though Pee Wee and I still had a few ups and downs every now and then, our relationship was stronger than ever. Charlotte was a loving, intelligent young woman who enriched our lives in every way. The trauma of what she had endured when she was twelve at the hands of Harrietta Jameson and that pimping fool they called Hollywood had not affected her that much. At least not in a negative way. She never lost her spark or got moody the way some abused kids did. She didn't like to talk about that ugly episode too often. But when she did, she bragged about the fact that because of her, two monsters would be behind bars for a very long time. And she vowed that she would get a lot more of them off the streets. Charlotte's nightmare was the reason she had decided to become a lawyer.

One of the biggest mistakes I had made was not listening to my child's cry for help — in time — when she had repeatedly tried to tell me that something was not right about Harrietta.

Pee Wee and I retired early from our jobs a few months ago, but our new "job" would be looking after our grandson when Charlotte returned to work. The happiness and safety of my family continued to be the most important things in my life. Now more than ever.

It was moments like this, me seeing my grandchild for the first time, that made me feel so grateful to be alive. Even though this would probably be my only grandchild, I realized how fortunate I was. I felt so blessed that it was hard for me to contain myself. I wished that every woman could experience this kind of bliss. Even though I had a huge smile on my face, I also felt unbearably sad inside because I knew that one of the most important women in my life would never be a grandmother.

Rhoda.

Her lineage would end with her children. Her only son, who had moved from Alabama to Paris, France, was as gay as he could be. He had no interest in raising a child. Rhoda's daughter Jade would never have children either.

After Rhoda's family had hired a powerful team of lawyers and paid off enough people to get international drug smuggling charges against Jade dropped back in '98, she had stayed out of trouble for a few years. She even landed a job as a receptionist in the main office at the steel mill where her father worked. Everything seemed to be going all right for about six months. But since she continued to associate with her stripper friends and other unsavory characters, she couldn't keep her nose clean. Those same friends dragged her to hell with them. The man she was living with at the time had her selling drugs to some of her coworkers. And when somebody blew the whistle on her, not only did she get fired, but her daddy almost lost his job!

"Sometimes I find myself wishing that they had locked Jade up for a few years when she got arrested for smugglin' drugs from Jamaica into the States," Rhoda told me the day after Jade got fired. "I still think it would be better for everybody involved if that girl spent some serious time in jail."

Rhoda got her wish.

A week after she made that remark, Jade stabbed her married lover and his pregnant wife to death in front of two witnesses. To avoid the death penalty, Jade made a full confession and pleaded no contest to the charges against her. She was going to be old enough to be a great-great grandmother by the time she got out of prison, if she didn't die first. Case closed.

"Mama, why are you looking so sad all of a sudden?" my daughter asked, struggling to sit up straighter.

I blinked and shook my head to clear my thoughts. "Oh, uh, I was just wondering what you're going to name the baby," I answered. "My daddy would have been so proud to see his only great grandson."

"If Anthony doesn't mind, you can name him," Charlotte said, looking at her husband.

A smile crossed Anthony's face and he nodded. "Oh, I don't mind, as long as it's not Anthony. I'm the fourth male in my family named Anthony and it gets a little confusing at family events," he muttered with tears in his eyes as he turned to me. "Mamette, do you have a name in mind?" I loved the way my son-in-law had combined Mama with my name.

I didn't have to think long or hard on that. "What about Jerry?"

Pee Wee sniffed and blinked back a tear. "Nobody has called me by my real name since Charlotte was a baby," he mumbled. "After all I put you through, I'm surprised you'd want to do me that honor," he told me.

"Well, if it had been a girl, I would have suggested Annette," I chortled. "And I've put you through a lot, too, *Jerry Davis.*"

"Can I make a suggestion?" Rhoda asked.

Everybody looked at her. "If you name him Jerry, can we *not* call him Pee Wee too?"

We all laughed. Even Dr. Morris.

AUTHOR'S NOTE

This is the end of an amazing journey. I hope that if you've come this far, it was as much fun for you as it was for me.

From myself and the entire *God Don't Like Ugly* series cast: Thank you for joining us!

Good-bye and be blessed.

■ ■ ■ ■

A READING GROUP GUIDE
GUIDE
GOD DON'T MAKE
NO MISTAKES

MARY MONROE

■ ■ ■ ■

ABOUT THIS GUIDE
The suggested questions that follow are
included to enhance your group's reading
of this book.

DISCUSSION QUESTIONS

1. Annette and Pee Wee are separated, but they continue to have a sexual relationship. Do you think that this is a bad thing for any estranged couple to do?
2. Do you think that Lizzie is wrong to tell Annette about her pregnancy before she even tells Pee Wee?
3. When Jade accuses Bully of attempting to rape her, Rhoda believes her until Annette comes forward to report that she accidentally witnessed the incident. This causes a major rift between Jade and Rhoda. Should Annette NOT have told Rhoda what she saw?
4. Jade becomes irate at Rhoda when Rhoda confronts her about lying on Bully, and Jade initiates a violent confrontation between her and Rhoda. Do you think Rhoda is justified in ordering her own daughter to move out of her house?
5. Do you think that it is wrong for Rhoda

— or any mother — to use violence against a violent child, or do you think the use of violence is okay in a case of self-defense?

6. When Annette's half-white, half sister Lillimae comes for an extended visit, this causes a problem between Annette and her mother, Gussie Mae, who is still bitter about Annette's father leaving her for Lillimae's mother. Are you glad that Gussie Mae eventually accepts Lillimae?

7. Because of a medical condition in his past, Pee Wee is no longer able to father children, which is how he knows that he cannot be the father of Lizzie's baby. Do you think that he is wrong not to tell Annette about his condition until he is forced to do so?

8. Despite Jade's horrendous behavior, Rhoda wants to reconcile with her, but Jade is not interested. To get her away from the dangerous environment she is in now with pimps and drug dealers, Rhoda plans to plant drugs on Jade so she can get arrested. Is this going a little too far, or is it the only choice Rhoda has to "save" her child?

9. Harrietta Jameson is one of the worst kinds of child abusers because she does not fit the typical profile. She is a seemingly normal, likable woman with three

young daughters of her own. Were you shocked to find out about her involvement in child pornography?

10. Annette's daughter, Charlotte, is too afraid to expose Harrietta, so she sends the information anonymously to a reporter. Do you think this was a bold and clever thing for a twelve-year-old to do, or should she have told Annette first?

11. Annette knows firsthand how difficult it is for a victim of child sexual abuse to expose her abuser. As diligent as she is about protecting her daughter from predators, it happens anyway. Should Annette have investigated Charlotte's frequent complaints about Harrietta more thoroughly?

12. Annette tries to talk Rhoda out of setting up Jade to get arrested. But when Charlotte runs away and moves in with a pimp, Annette does not hesitate to set *her* up to get arrested. Do you think these two mothers crossed the line? Do you think that they could have come up with better plans to rescue their children?

13. Jade is remorseful and frightened — or so she claims to be when she calls Rhoda from jail and begs for a reconciliation. Rhoda is receptive, but Annette still has some doubts about Jade's sincerity. Jade

eventually commits a more serious crime and ends up in prison for a very long time. Were you surprised?

14. Now that the series is over, are you happy with the way it ended? If not, why? And how would you have ended it?

ABOUT THE AUTHOR

Mary Monroe is the third child of Alabama sharecroppers, and the first and only member of her family to finish high school. Mary never attended college or any writing classes. She spent the first part of her life in Alabama and Ohio, moved to Richmond, California in 1973, and has lived in Oakland since 1984. Her first novel, *The Upper Room,* was published in 1985 and was widely reviewed throughout the U.S. and in Great Britain. She is a recipient of the PEN/ Oakland Josephine Miles Award for her novel *God Don't Like Ugly.*

ABOUT THE AUTHOR